THE GIRL IN THE TRUNK

The Girl In The Trunk

A Novel By

Anthony DiFranco

Makamah Press
Northport, New York

Originally published by Tominy Publications

Library of Congress Control Number:
2001119164

ISBN: 0-9714427-0-3

Makamah Press
P.O. Box 697
Northport, New York, 11768

p-pix.com

First Edition

For Allyson, Elizabeth,
Dorothea, and William

Other Books By Anthony DiFranco:

The Streets Of Paradise

Ardent Spring

Back To The Present

Books and catalogue are available through Makamah Press at website **p-pix.com** or by mail from Makamah Press, P.O. Box 697, Northport, New York 11768.

- ONE -

They found the trunk on the sidewalk on the west side of Mosholu Parkway at a little past four in the morning on a Wednesday in late September.   It was an old, battered dormitory model with leather handles, and inside was the body of a delicately lovely young woman, fully dressed.   The credit cards in her handbag identified her as Elizabeth Albano of 1644 Rhinelander Avenue, in the Morris Park neighborhood of the West Bronx.   At 4:16, the sector patrolmen called in the duty detectives from the 52nd Precinct.   By 5:05, Anthony Rizzo from the Homicide Squad was on the scene.

Rizzo was a compact, wiry man in his mid-thirties with a reputation as a tough investigator who knew his stuff-- stubborn, methodical, cocky.   He took one look at the dead girl in the trunk, asked a few questions of the patrolmen, and then sent a man to get his buddy Mike Villanova out of bed and bring him over.

There was a glow in the eastern sky by the time Villanova arrived.   He was bigger and rangier than Rizzo, a little older, and quieter.   The cops knew him, but he wasn't a cop.   They knew him because he had done work for the Homicide Squad on and off for a number of years, and also because he wrote a crime column for the *Spectrum* that some of them liked to read.   He made the better part of his living as a private investigator.   Villanova happened to live in attic rooms only a few blocks off Mosholu, down Bainbridge Avenue, but that didn't seem a good reason to him, he told Rizzo, to be shouted out of bed to look at a trunk. What he didn't tell Rizzo was that he'd been wrapped in pleasant sleep with a woman who mattered to him when the pounding started on the door. Rizzo told him to calm down and go look in the trunk.

Mosholu Parkway was really a boulevard with a grassy median, flanked by pre-war apartment buildings of four or five storeys. Sycamores and overgrown sumacs blotted out the streetlights, and the trunk sat concealed in the gloom a little to one side of the double-door entry to 658. The lid hung open, and one of the patrolmen threw a nine-volt torch on the inside so Villanova could look. Villanova said later that it made all the difference, seeing it in the light that way, so that you could feel what a desolate thing night really was and how terrible it could make anything at all.

Inside the trunk was a slender young woman in a black or dark blue dress. She was on her side with her knees jackknifed against her chest and her arms folded around her shins. Her face was tilted upward so that the torchlight caught all its white beauty and filled her wide brown eyes with false luster. She had a fine nose, high cheekbones, a round chin, a delicate brow. Her rose-colored lipstick was slightly smudged, her long, dark, wavy hair disarrayed. She wore a plain silver bracelet, a college ring, black high-heeled pumps, and stockings. The only visible mark on her was a fine ligature burn on her neck. Like everything dead, she had a ghastly, inhuman look, but there was something perfect about her too, pale, smooth, and frozen, like the marble statues in churches. What Villanova looked for as he stared into the trunk was a bit of rescuing ordinariness, so he could get about the work to be done, or else tell Rizzo to leave him alone and let him go back to bed.

But he couldn't find it. He studied the dead girl's face, the faint crease in her brow that caught all her childlike frailty as well as the terror and surprise of her last moments. Something cold closed on his insides, something between dread and anger, and he walked away into the dark and stood with his back to the trunk and the cops and the lights. After a while, he came back and said to the cop with the torch, "Who took the handbag out? You?"

"I did," Rizzo said. That was by-the-book procedure when the crime was warm.

"What did you find in it?"

"Nothing much. Forty bucks in cash. A glass heart in a gift box, with a card, 'For Margarita.' Change, keys, make-up, the usual."

"Where was the bag?" Villanova said.

Rizzo pointed. "Behind her head, in the corner."

"And where's the guy that first opened the trunk?"

"That big guy over there with the precinct men."

"You talked with him?"

"Yeah. And the Super too. The trash cans are kept in the alley. The sidewalk was clean at eleven last night."

Villanova went over to the beefy guy standing beside the two uniformed cops. "You the one who opened the trunk?"

"No."

"Aren't you the one who called 911?"

"I just peeked under the lid, I didn't open it."

"You didn't move anything?"

"No."

"See anyone?"

"Nope."

Rizzo came over. "I already talked with him," he told Villanova. "He bartends down at the Web. Walks home three-thirty to four A.M., six nights a week. 654 Mosholu, second floor. We went up and checked with his wife, we got his boss on the phone."

Villanova turned away and walked down the sidewalk, and Rizzo walked after him. They stopped about fifteen yards away from the others and stood half-facing each other. To the east, the sky above the apartment houses was streaked with pink, and the dark froth at the southern end of the Parkway had sharpened into the outline of the Botanical Gardens. Villanova pulled a pack of Chesterfields from his shirt pocket and lit one with an old-fashioned nickel-chrome lighter. The flame illuminated the deep brown eyes and coal black brows that gave his face its striking quality. It was an appealing face, strong-featured, intelligent, expressive. Hope, appetite, outrage, grief, tolerance, fatigue, humor, disillusion, determination had all written on it. Rizzo's face, fairer and less regular in feature, a face not handsome but compelling in its own way, was cut to fewer and coarser facets: ambition, lust, obstinacy, pride, good humor. Rizzo was a married man, a sports buff, a sometime drinker and womanizer; he liked poker, nightlife, guns, and country-western music. Villanova liked jazz, tools, books, old cars, old movies; he was a widower, a traveler, a thinker, a loner. Both men liked women and liked each other. Both had grown up playing stickball, handball, and pick-up basketball, both could handle themselves in a fight. Each lived his own life, and a few times a year, in observance of a cycle neither had ever figured out, they put their heads together on a case. Villanova had to do some adapting for these ventures; Rizzo was a Juggernaut-style investigator with a savvy all his own and a legendary stamina: he could operate for days at a time on nothing but black coffee. But he was open to Villanova's more serendipitous style, too.

It was an old habit, in fact, a method, which required that Villanova see everything that Rizzo had seen at the scene of a crime and ask some of the same questions. Urgency was part of the method too, especially in a murder. Villanova, particularly, believed that the experience of a crime could still be entered hours after the victim had died. The breeze, the starlight, the quality of silence, the situation of things and people, the facial expression and posture of the victim, the mood of the time and place, all these survived for a little while before dissipating or being disturbed by the boys from the Crime Lab, and were vital to the way Villanova worked. Villanova also believed that the spirit left a corpse slowly, like warmth, and that there were things a detective could sense if he could get near soon enough.

Rizzo let Villanova think for a while, away from the others, and then he said, "Well, Buddy?"

Villanova looked at him uneasily. He was going to be shaken for a long time by the sight of that dead girl, but not for the reasons that Rizzo believed. Finally, he shrugged and said, "All right."

Rizzo glanced at his watch. "The duty men went over to the family at a little after five. They've had an hour and a half."

"Okay, then," Villanova said, "we might as well go." The Crime Lab van was making a U-turn down at the corner. Villanova looked back toward the trunk and said, "Couldn't we just close her eyes?"

"You know we can't, Buddy."

* * *

Rizzo had an unmarked car, a wreck of a four-door Plymouth that was past going out to bid. As they pulled away down Mosholu, Jay Stefanek and Tommy Layer from the Lab were already setting up the lights for the photographs and diagrams. "That's the end of it," Villanova said. He meant that the human life of Elizabeth Albano was finished...that whatever was on the sidewalk now was an object inside an object. Rizzo nodded.

The dawn put a blush on the tenement rows as they drove down Webster to Fordham Road, but to Villanova the area had a perpetual stripped and embarrassed look without the old El. The Shamrock, Joe D's, the Web, even the Flim-Flam looked sheepish and harmless in the morning light. They took Fordham Road past the campus, Villanova's *alma mater,* to Williamsbridge, then turned down Morris Park Avenue. It was a six or seven minute ride. The Italian bakeries weren't open yet, but one of the little markets was, and people were going in and out. "I've gotta get coffee for this," Rizzo said, and they stopped. The place was narrow and cramped, with a tiny counter way in the back and no proprietor in sight. There were customers ahead of them, and each helped himself and left money on the counter, calling out "I've got a *Post*, Angelo!" or "Pack of Marlboros, Angelo!" One guy crowed, "Hey, Angelo, the Mets died last night!", which brought from somewhere in the back: "Your *mother* died!" Then Angelo appeared, stocky and greying and dull-eyed, with a tray of buttered rolls and bagels wrapped in wax paper, and sold Rizzo and Villanova their coffees, which they gulped down in the two blocks before Rhinelander Avenue.

The street, like most in Morris Park, featured well-kept row houses and detached two-family's, with tiny flower gardens and solitary mimosa trees, a statue of the madonna here and there, and chain link fences to compartmentalize every driveway and square of turf. A precinct car sat in the driveway of number 1644. The house was red brick with a Spanish tile roof and vintage stained glass panels around the front door. Elizabeth Albano's father, a slender, handsome man wearing a white t-shirt, slacks, and jogging sneakers, let them in. His thick-browed, unshaven face looked strained and distraught.

Rizzo took over and sorted things out quickly. In the kitchen were the precinct detectives and the dead girl's two older brothers, big, well-made men. The women were in a back bedroom with the door ajar, the mother and a daughter-in-law, huddled on the edge of the bed, their faces red with crying and their eyes dazed. The father was trying to be in charge, and the sons kept trying to insulate him and show him that *they* could be in charge. "Go in the bedroom," they kept telling him, "go sit with Ma," and he kept ignoring them and trying to be helpful. The precinct guys had broken the news, gotten the two brothers and the sister-in-law down from the upstairs apartment, checked photographs, culled the dead girl's personal effects for leads, and arranged to take the brothers downtown to the morgue for a personal ID. Neither brother would go alone, and neither would let the father go. The precinct guys were eager to get out of that painful atmosphere, and as soon as Rizzo was done debriefing them, he let them take the two sons and go, while he and Villanova gave the dead girl's room and effects another going over, with the girl's father hovering.

When they were done, the father, Tom Albano, went with them into the front room to answer questions. He offered them a drink or a shot of whatever they wanted. They declined, and all three sat in the plush armchairs. Albano dropped his face in his hands for a few seconds, but then pulled himself up. He looked like a man who had learned, from a few agonizing events over five decades of life, how to steel himself.

"The first thing we have to assume in a case like this," Rizzo explained to the man, "is that your daughter was harmed by someone she knew. So you've got to do two things for us. You've got to help us reconstruct her movements up to the last time she was seen. And you've got to name for us any enemy or acquaintance or boyfriend who might have harmed her.

What we want to do is eliminate the chance that she just wandered into a dangerous situation, or was made a random victim."

"No," her father said, "that's one thing she wouldn't do. She was smart, she knew where she shouldn't go, what streets she shouldn't walk. She wanted to go away to school, but that's the reason we wouldn't let her, you know, go off somewhere where God-knows-what could happen to her. You read about kids getting raped in their dormitories, what have you. Drugs and sex and abortion, you name it. We sent her to Fordham, so she could live at home. All my kids went to school at home. The boys went to Manhattan College. Liz wanted to go to N.Y.U. downtown, but no, I wouldn't go for that. Ride the subway, at night and what have you? Forget it."

"Your daughter was a college student, Mr. Albano?"

"Graduate student. At Fordham. A Ph.D. student."

"What's her age, exactly?"

"Twenty-three. Twenty-four next February eleventh."

"She was wearing a dress and heels. Did she dress that way for school?"

"No, for work. At school the women wear pants. Though Liz was more of a dresser. We taught her, you know, to take pride, to be a lady."

"Where did she work, Mr. Albano?"

"At Mount Saint Mary's, up Bedford Park Boulevard. An English teacher. She just started, day after Labor Day."

Rizzo got busy with notepad and pen. "Did she go to work yesterday? What were her hours?"

"Seven-thirty in the morning, she leaves." Albano's voice wavered suddenly, and he struggled to maintain his composure. "About this time," he said quietly, glancing at his watch.

"And she went yesterday, same as always?"

Albano nodded.

Villanova watched and listened, and meanwhile mapped the room with his eyes. It was a fairly ample but crowded room intended to be formal. The walls were Federal blue, the drapes and carpeting a deeper shade. A walnut bookcase sported the Encyclopedia Britannica and the Britannica Junior, and the Book of the Year up to 1993. Oversized lamps stood on their own scimitar-base tables, and sconces studded the walls on either side of a false fireplace. A huge mahogany TV cabinet with sliding front panels took up almost a quarter of the room. Framed photos clustered on every surface, family portraits from years past. From many of them Elizabeth Albano's face stood out--she was a hauntingly beautiful and highly photogenic girl. There was a fineness about her, a grace and self-possession that separated her from the rest of her family, though it was also easy enough to see where her looks came from, as a number of the photos captured Tom Albano and his wife in their youth. Albano had a thin, dark, handsome face, and his wife was fair and round-faced and dimpled, with faintly Asian cheekbones and clear, artless eyes--a knockout. Together, they looked like street kids endowed with a vibrant and wholesome beauty. Elizabeth had her father's features and expressions, her mother's bone structure and complexion, a very happy combination.

Albano, talking quietly and unconsciously wringing his hands, explained that his daughter had begun high school teaching reluctantly, that she had been expecting an assistantship or something at Fordham which didn't come through, that she'd been struggling to handle the workload on top of preparing for exams. She had, to his knowledge, spent the previous day at Mount Saint Mary's and at Fordham, and had not come home for dinner, which was not unusual. She worked on her dissertation in the library in the evenings, sometimes went out afterward with friends and came in at one or one-thirty, long after her parents were asleep. Usually, she called home if she was going to be very late, but not always.

She was a wholesome girl, Albano stressed, a chaste girl, "a good girl"--it was when he used this phrase that Villanova could hear his despairing sense of loss, right under the surface. "All her life she loved to read," he said. "In grade school, she was nuts about the space program. She built models of Atlas rockets, lunar modules, what have you. And then she taught herself how to sew. She started making all her own clothes." A pride came into his voice as he enumerated his daughter's virtues: she got along well with people, helped her mother with housework, learned to cook, even painted her own room every year. As a high school student at Mount Saint Mary's, she was on the student government and wrote for the school paper. She never went through a rebel or boy-crazy stage. All through college she was an "A" student and a volunteer in various outreach programs. For the past two years she'd been tutoring ESL students one night a week at John F. Kennedy High School on Fordham Road, without pay. "Liz felt sorry for people who're up against it, she was always trying to help someone. But she never wanted any kind of praise." She was a good Catholic, Albano said, and never missed Sunday mass at Saint Clare's, where he himself was an usher. She still wore her Confirmation crucifix on a gold neck chain. Two of her high school classmates had gone into the Dominican novitiate at Sparkill, and Liz had even had a friend who was a priest, but she always wanted a home and a family.

"Was she wearing her crucifix yesterday?" Rizzo asked.

"Probably," Albano said.

"Would you recognize it if you saw it?"

"I'm the one who gave it to her."

"What night is her class at JFK?"

"Wednesday night--that's tonight." Albano's voice wavered again, and this time Villanova was sure he was going to lose it. But he held on. "I guess I better call them," he murmured. "I better call Mount Saint Mary's too."

"We'll do that if you want."

"No. It's my responsibility. I'll do it."

Rizzo and Villanova glanced at each other and nodded.

"JFK is a pretty rough school," Rizzo said. "Didn't it bother you that she went there?"

"You bet it bothered me. I made a real stink about it."

"And?"

"'I'm a bigger girl than you think,' Liz told me. 'I can take care of myself.'"

"What about friends? Did Liz have a girlfriend we could talk to, somebody at school maybe, or in the neighborhood?"

Albano shook his head. "That's one funny thing, she wasn't close with any girl. Her high school friends, they all got married or moved down to Manhattan to work. She lost touch with them."

"How about someone named Margarita? That ring a bell?"

"Margarita? No, never heard that name."

"What about boyfriends? Did Liz date?"

"She went with boys, sure. Three years in college, she went with this one boy, an Irish boy. Name's Tom, like me. Nice boy, an unusual boy. Built like a bull, likes to write poetry. He didn't graduate. His father died and he went back upstate. The family has a farm, or orchards or something. After him, Liz started dating again, you know, but nothing serious. Last year, not so much. Too busy, I guess, with the studies and all. She was always at school at night, always at the library."

"Nothing like a steady boyfriend, then? How about male friends? How about any man who seemed interested in her?"

"There was a guy at school, a professor.   He was definitely interested. Maybe there was even a little something starting between them. But then it turns out he's married. My daughter must have really frozen him out when she found out, because this guy got worked up enough to come over here to talk to me."

"When was all this?"

"About three weeks ago, he came to see me. Talking a mile a minute, asking questions...trying to feel me out, I guess. I couldn't tell if he was mad or scared. What did he think I was going to do, give him my blessing? I felt like pitching him out of the house." The muscles in Albano's jaw tightened; he let off wringing his hands for a moment and clutched one in the other, fist to palm. "But after a while I sized the guy up, I saw that he really had it bad for my daughter. So I said, 'Look, you got a wife, you care about her, right? You don't want to hurt her. What do you need this kind of heartache for?'" His brow furrowed and his eyes held Villanova's; there was a poignant blend of emotions in them, a stoical compassion mixed with repugnance. For an instant, Villanova sensed he was seeing Elizabeth Albano alive, in her father's expression.

"What's this professor's name?" Rizzo said.

"McVicar. Brian McVicar. An English professor."

"Ever hear from him again?"

"No. I didn't mention to Liz that he was here.   I figured the less said, the better."

"Could he be still in the picture?"

Albano shrugged. "From his end, maybe."

"What else? Any other men she might have been dating in the last month or so?"

Albano took a breath and let it out heavily. "There was an artist guy she went around with. A friend, not a boyfriend, I think. He only showed up here once, uninvited. A wise guy. Made fun of us, the furniture and everything. Here, look, he made fun of these pictures. That's me with Cardinal Cooke. And this is when they swore me in as Grand Knight, in '89. Gate of Heaven Lodge."

"Can you give us this artist's name and address?"

"His first name's Jack. All I know, he lives near Fordham, over on the other side of Fordham Road, with the Puerto Ricans."

"Would your wife know this guy's last name?"

"I don't think so. We only saw him the once. And Liz wouldn't talk about him. She was funny that way about her friends, private, you know?"

"Tell us what this guy looked like."

"Long hair, glasses, red face...ugly. Not big but solid, rough-looking. Late twenties, I'd say--Jeez, at his age I already had a wife and three kids."

"Where did Liz know him from? School?"

"I don't think so. Could be. Fordham's changed a lot. When I was a kid, I used to look through the fence and see these guys walking around in gowns, like the Middle Ages. It impressed me, you know?" He shrugged. "My wife and me, we never got to go to college. But I wanted my kids to have that." He went back to wringing his hands.

"How about a photo of your daughter. Got one that we can have, just a plain one, no big smile or anything?"

"No smile? Take this one here." Albano leaned across and retrieved a framed three-by-five from the end table. It showed Elizabeth sitting in the dappled shade of a willow, looking up at the camera with a serene, precociously sage expression. Albano tugged it out of the frame and handed it over.   Rizzo took it and passed it along to Villanova for safekeeping.

Rizzo asked a few more questions, and Albano, as he ran dry on hard information, grew more digressive, talking about changing times, the happiness and closeness of his family in the early years, his aspirations for his children-- decent, modest aspirations.   Villanova was glad that Rizzo didn't stop the man. He was very sorry for Tom Albano, and also knew it would be important to hear how he saw and thought. Above all he hated how these interrogations reduced a life to a paragraph of notes, and forced the victims themselves to do the reducing.   Albano was going to succor himself by declaiming for his daughter, and himself.   He explained that he'd worked his way up from a mason to a tile and terrazzo contractor, a member of the electricians' and carpenters' unions. He motioned toward the tilework on the kitchen floor, he again offered drinks, and stood and opened the mahogany TV cabinet to display the dry bar he had custom-built inside it: the design and the refinishing were first rate.

This time Villanova accepted a shot of bourbon.   He understood that Albano needed to be acknowledged as one in spirit with ordinary, physical men, like cops and other working stiffs. He was a plain guy with no illusions, and his decency, bred out of deprivation early in life, was sincere.

After a while, Rizzo went into the other room to talk to the dead girl's mother.   Villanova stayed with Tom Albano. He could see that the man was desperate to keep talking and not be alone with all that misery dammed up inside, so he asked him a few questions and let him rattle on about the Knights of Columbus, his business partner's paraplegic son, the guy next door who took all five of his sons into his lumber business and who stewed a year's supply of tomato sauce every fall in the back yard, his own sons' athletic prowess, his childhood, his drunken father, his broken home, his kind aunts and cousins who raised him, his suffering in the streets and in shape-outs and in the army, his youthful romanticism, his life of toil. When the sounds of crying started up in the back bedroom, Villanova asked Albano to show him around, and got a narrated tour of the basement machine shop, the weight room and heavy-bag, the renovations Albano and his sons had effected inside the house and out: the new plumbing, the new natural-gas fired furnace, the fresh-pointed brick and everlast windows on the facades, the aluminum-clad eaves, the glass-bricked basement windows, the electronic security system, the permanent and maintenance-free and shatter-proof, vermin-proof, rot-proof carapace he had fashioned for his family to live in and be at ease in. It took a while, but Villanova understood that Albano was making an incantation: family was all that mattered, and with a fortress to shelter it, a family was supposed to be safe from hurt. This was the dogma of his life, and his talk was a workingman's long and oblique and eloquent cry of outrage.

The last thing Villanova did was ask Tom Albano to leave him alone for a few minutes in his daughter's room. He stood there in the quiet and let his eyes roam over all the things the unsuspecting girl had thought she was coming back to: the folders of notes, the index cards, the piles of books and the proofmarked manuscript of her dissertation-in-progress; the half-knit sweater in a basket by her bed; the open copy of *The Sins of the Fathers: Hawthorne's Psychological Themes* on her nighttable, its margins heavily penned; the Claude Bolling tape in her portable deck; the unironed cotton blouses hanging on her closet door; the tray of perfumes, polishes, make-up, the jewelry case, the vinyl bag of hairbrushes, grooming items, ornaments; the stack of essays written by her students, partially graded, with a little note to herself on top: "Finish!"

Villanova flipped through some of her books. Many of them, including the one on her nighttable, were annotated in two hands, and bore the initials "B. M." inside the cover-- Brian McVicar. A critical text authored by McVicar himself, titled *The Dimmesdale Complex*, lay among the books on her desk. Its margins too were richly worked.

He paged through her dissertation, which, by its outline, was something like two-thirds complete. He read enough to get a grasp of its argument. The writing was competent, even good, and there were citations a-plenty. Up to the last couple of chapters, *The Dimmesdale Complex* was the heavily favored source; then the references to it virtually disappeared. That was no surprise, in light of what her father had said.

Lastly, he glanced through the student papers and read a few of the comments she'd penned on them: "Great sentence!" "Is this really the word you want?" "Much better than last time." "Describe more here, let me see what he looks like." The hand she wrote in was scarcely less childlike than her students'.

Little more of her was on display, and her few keepsakes were wholly plain: no trophies, concert tickets, cute photos, mugs, buttons, or trinkets; the one obvious treasure was a faded Sweet Sixteen birthday card from her father. There was a quiet innocence all through her room, bespeaking a simple acceptance of the world as given, with its duties, roles, and hopes. It was the same kind of innocence that had once stirred Villanova to love, the same kind that had seared his insides when it fell to the world's savagery. His young wife had been dead for many years now, the person responsible had walked his own anonymous path for many years, but the outrage still smoldered in Villanova's breast, a secret from all the rest of the world, including Rizzo. The sight of Elizabeth Albano's bedroom gave that fire a good stoking. Her room was full of the naive certainty that tomorrow follows today, that the world is worth exploring, that people get better at what they do.   It was full of the trust his own wife had left behind for him to see and touch, to fold away, seal up, and forget, just as Tom Albano would now have to fold away the life of his beautiful child.   Villanova felt himself starting to cook, and was sure that it had been a mistake to let Rizzo bring him into this case.

And just at that moment, Rizzo came into the room, and it was time to go.

* * *

They stopped at Angelo's market for breakfast specials, then pulled under the trees on Pelham Parkway to eat and talk.   The day had bloomed mild and overcast, and the commuter rush, mostly day students heading toward Fordham and Bronx Community College, was in full stride.   "Well, what do you think, Buddy?" Rizzo said as he unwrapped his "Hungry Man Special"--double-egg, cheese, sausage, and home fries shoveled into a hero bun.

"You first."   Villanova didn't like to put words to his feelings until he was sure they had finished stewing.

"No, you."

Villanova unwrapped his double-egg-over-easy-with-bacon and popped the lid off his coffee.   He took a swallow of the strong, hot brew.   "She sounds like a damn sweet girl, if you go by her father," he said.   "But even if you don't, she looks like your basic decent person: a good student, a hard worker, on good terms with everyone in the house, moving along on an academic track, a degree program, a fellowship, some part-time teaching, regular hours.   She was under a bit of strain, but no despondency, no romantic upheaval, no obsessions, a steady supply of attention, but she doesn't sound like one of those really pretty girls who get greedy or arrogant about it."   He pulled the photograph of Elizabeth from his shirt pocket and studied it. "I read her as a kind of outsider in her family, nice, like they are, and decent, but with one foot definitely out there in a larger world."

Rizzo nodded. "Good. So basically we've got a real nice girl...and the question is, how did this girl go off her nice safe track between her house and the college and Mount Saint Mary's and wind up in a coffin over on Mosholu Parkway?" He took a man-sized bite of his sandwich. "We've got to work backwards and forwards, soon as Pathology gives us the time-of-death...soon as we talk to the people who last saw her alive, at work or whatever. We can figure she got knocked off indoors someplace, because someone had to find a way to hide her body and dump it."

"Right," Villanova said. "If some street punk dragged her into an alley or something, there'd be no reason to hide her and dump her somewhere else. So it had to be someone who knew her and knew we'd be coming to look."

"Or else someone who had to hide her from someone else who lived there." Rizzo took a gulp of coffee; almost half of his enormous sandwich had already vanished. "Mosholu Parkway is only about four blocks from Mount Saint Mary's. I say we start by having the canvassing squad work Mosholu in both directions from 658." He looked at his watch. "It's time to make a few calls. The Crime Lab might have something ready, and we need to call Mount Saint Mary's, and we need an address on this English professor--he's our lead, right now. Too bad the girl's address book didn't turn up, but we'll have one of the boys contact all her teachers and work connections and any close friends we can come up with." He began listing items in his notepad as he spoke. "We'll run down her credit cards and see if we can find out who sold her that glass heart. And we'll have Gilman get the LUD sheets from the phone company and check out who's gotten a call from the Albano phone over the last few weeks. He can check out the faculty phones at Mount Saint Mary's too. --Hey, Buddy, you with me?"

Villanova had been staring at the photograph. The eyes of Elizabeth Albano, youthfully serene on the surface, full of somber wisdom underneath, stared back at him. "Yeah," he said. "I'm with you." He put the photo back in his pocket.

"There's phones up under the El stop at White Plains Road. Here, hold my coffee for me, will you, Buddy?"

Villanova took it. "Jesus, what is this, a 48 ounce cup?" He held his own cup between his knees so he could eat.

Rizzo bulled his way into the traffic and headed west on Pelham Parkway, steering with one hand and eating with the other. "What else did you get out of the girl's father?"

"Nothing much. He's in a lot worse pain than he looks. What about the mother?"

"She's a study. Wants to help, wants to communicate, but hasn't got many words. A little bitter underneath, I think. Didn't see the point of her daughter 'spending her life in school.' Wished she'd just settled down and got married like her brother. As if that would have saved her life."

Villanova nodded. "How about the girl's room? You get a fix on it?"

Rizzo shrugged. "Plenty of books. Neat as a pin."

"Right. That figures, in a way. Did you see how many books were initialed 'B. M.'?"

"Sure. What do you suppose that stands for--Bowel Movement?"

"She was halfway through her dissertation. The chapter drafts were on her desk, 'Dimmesdale and Hysteria.' That figures in a way, too."

"The room speaks to you, Buddy? What does it say?"

"Everything neat and tidy, like you say, meticulous, even." Villanova bit into his sandwich "And yet there's a funny kind of tension underneath it all. --*Shit!*"

"What happened?"

Egg yolk had spurted down the front of Villanova's bar striped Oxford. "Every goddam time I put on a good shirt!"

"You put on a good shirt for *this*?" Rizzo said through a mouthful of bread and cheese.

"Christ, you're the one that eats like a pig. How come *you* never get it?"

"What do you mean, I eat like a pig?" Rizzo took another huge bite of his sandwich, tossed the remnant over the back of the seat, and relieved Villanova of the coffee. The floor in the back was littered a foot deep in brown bags, styrofoam cups, stale danish, and empty apple juice bottles. "The way *you* eat, Buddy, you oughta buy shirts off the back of a truck. Like me." He punched the horn, beat the traffic signal at White Plains Road, and pulled over in the shadow of the El.

They got out and made the calls. Rizzo took his coffee with him and called the Crime Lab and the Homicide Squad. Villanova lit a cigarette and called Mount Saint Mary's and Fordham University. Villanova got back to the car first.

"She signed out at the high school at 11:30, the end of fourth period," he told Rizzo when he slid back behind the wheel. "Her usual time."

Rizzo nodded. "And Pathology figures time of death between noon and one o'clock."

"Cause?"

"Smothering. She was probably unconscious when it happened. Hair and Fiber came up with nothing, fingernails included. The guess is, her face was pressed into a mattress, or something soft was held over her nose and mouth."

"What about the ligature burn?"

"Only partial. They figure a cord, maybe...something that broke, like a shoelace."

"Or a chain. Any sign of her crucifix?"

Rizzo shook his head. "And no prints, either, not even from her handbag. Wiped. On the inside, just her own."

"Was she molested?"

"Nope. And we know she wasn't robbed." He took a long pull from his coffee cup. "Not robbed, not molested... but you know what?"

"What?"

"Pregnant. About eight weeks."

Villanova raised his eyebrows.

"You get an address on the professor, Buddy boy?"

"Yup. 2317 Decatur."

"That's only a couple of blocks from Mount Saint Mary's."

"That's about half way between Mount Saint Mary's and Mosholu Parkway."

Rizzo nodded and checked his watch. "It's 9:05. Is Professor Bowel Movement in his office yet, do you suppose?"

"Professor Bowel Movement is home in bed. He's scheduled to teach one class a day, 1:00 to 4:10 p.m."

Rizzo drained the coffee and flipped the cup into the back. "Let's go."

- TWO -

2317 Decatur Avenue was a solid, decently-kept, Thirties-period apartment house in the middle of a shabby-genteel block. It had a portico entry, nickel-plated front doors, and the remnant of an art deco lobby. At 9:15 a.m., Villanova and Rizzo buzzed the Super to let them through the inner door. They asked a few questions, too, and checked the names on the mailboxes before going up to 3-C and rapping on the door. The general idea was to give McVicar as little time to think as possible.

The professor had a game spirit; he opened his door only seconds after Rizzo had identified himself as a police officer and raised his I.D. toward the peephole.

McVicar was a tall, ruggedly handsome, well-built man with curly, greying hair, a disarming smile, and a stage actor's bearing. He wore jeans and a rugby shirt, deck shoes, steel-rimmed glasses, a wedding band. His breath smelled of liquor. The first couple of questions he took right there in the doorway, standing his ground and making a show of his ease. When Elizabeth Albano's name was mentioned, fright came into his eyes, but not precisely the kind of fright that Villanova had learned to recognize as mortal. The professor's wife, a slender brunette in a blue warm-up suit, had by this time appeared a few feet behind him, and McVicar, as if to reassert his poise, invited the two callers in.

The apartment was furnished densely and yet with a peculiar elegance. A mauve sectional formed a broken oval beneath the living room window. Around it radiated fine and understated bits of furniture--a delicate Windsor chair, an old oak writing desk, antique brass floor lamps--punctuated by offbeat art work: framed broadsheets, poetry reading programs, concert posters, literary maps. Every other surface was crowded with books, books by the hundreds and thousands, but the texture they produced was flat and hermetic rather than rich. The whole bohemian flavor of the room seemed studied.

"What exactly did you want to know about Elizabeth?" McVicar said in easy tones when the three men had sat on the sectional. A bottle of J & B and an empty rock glass perched atop a two-volume *Oxford English Dictionary* on the cocktail table in front of them. McVicar's wife, watchful, demure, considerably younger than her husband, stood behind the couch leaning over his shoulder. Her long, straight hair fell partly over one side of her face. She was attractive in a pale, cerebral way--just short of pretty.

"First, how well do you know the girl?"

"Quite well. I'm her doctoral mentor. Drink?"

"No thanks."

"You're Elizabeth's mentor?" Villanova said.

"That means I oversee her dissertation project," McVicar said, pouring himself a refill. "I'm her coach, sort of."

"I know what it means."

"How much time do you spend with her, usually?" Rizzo said.

"At this stage of the game, about an hour, maybe once a week."

"And when was the last time you saw her?"

McVicar arched his brows and smiled as Rizzo's notepad made its appearance. "Look," he remarked to his wife. "Porfiry Petrovich."

"What's that?" Rizzo said.

"Famous detective. Like Columbo."

"What we're doing here is serious," Rizzo said.

"You bet." McVicar toasted solemnly and took a swallow of his drink. "The last time I saw Elizabeth...let's see. Not this week, must have been last. Tuesday, I guess. That's our regular day."

"And what time would that be on Tuesdays?"

"Noon, or thereabouts."

Villanova felt Rizzo shoot him a glance, and saw McVicar take note of it. Noon or thereabouts on Tuesday was when Elizabeth Albano had died.

"Why didn't you see her this Tuesday?"

McVicar shrugged. "She didn't show up."

"Any idea why?"

"No. It isn't the first time. I really think, though, you ought to tell me what you're after."

Villanova said, "If you weren't with Elizabeth between twelve and one yesterday, where were you? Did you stay in your office?"

"Well, I don't usually meet with her in my office."

"Where do you meet?"

"It depends. We've met in a number of different places. Sometimes outside, sometimes we grab a bite off campus."

McVicar's wife, who'd been as still as a statue, flinched at that.

"Any reason you wouldn't want her around your office?"

"What do you mean by that?"

"Where were you supposed to meet yesterday?"

"The music room. Upstairs in the Campus Center."

Villanova glimpsed an odd weariness creep into Mrs. McVicar's eyes. "Is that a regular meeting place?" he said. "I mean, do other professors meet with students there too?"

McVicar frowned. "I wouldn't know."

"Anyone see you waiting there?"

"No. I hung around for ten, fifteen minutes, then I came home to have something to eat."

"Anyone see you go off the campus? Anyone see you come into this building?"

"Tell you what," McVicar said, resting his glass on his knee. His stage-ham cheer had dimmed considerably. "You tell me what you're after, and I'll keep answering your questions."

Rizzo returned cooly, "You verify that someone saw you here between twelve and one, and we won't have any more questions."

McVicar eyed him. He seemed to be playing with the idea of turning nasty. After a moment, he said flatly, "My wife saw me."

Everyone turned to Mrs. McVicar. "Is that right?" Rizzo said.

The woman studied her husband's eyes. Her whole affect was lethargic, almost torpid, but her gaze was steady and intelligent. "Yes," she said.

"You were here when he got home?"

"Yes."

McVicar smiled and took a swallow of scotch. "I get the feeling you're going to tell me this girl's run off or something."

"Is that the feeling you get?" Rizzo said.

"Well..."

"What I'm going to tell you is, the girl's dead."

McVicar's smile faded. There was a silence.

"Somebody did her for keeps," Rizzo snapped. "We think you know something about it."

Villanova watched McVicar's eyes. First they were scared. Then a kind of hurt came into them. After a few seconds, the usual sputterings of disbelief and dismay began.

Villanova scowled and blurted out, "Listen, McVicar, we know you were involved with the girl."

McVicar glared at him. "What does that mean? What's 'involved'?"

"We just had a chat with her father. Maybe you'd rather talk to us alone. Maybe you'd like to go with us into another room."

"I have nothing to talk to you about," McVicar said with withering contempt.

"Just come with us into the bedroom there. Or send your wife in there."

"I'm not being sent anywhere," Mrs. McVicar said. Her voice was as thick as all her movements, but there was a heat in it, a slow, reluctant heat. She drew herself up and looked down at her husband.

"What're you up to?" McVicar growled at Villanova.

"You don't want to hear this in front of your wife."

"You go to hell. You're a wise guy."

Villanova nodded. "The girl was pregnant."

McVicar stared but didn't respond. Villanova nodded again and glanced at Mrs. McVicar. Her eyes were full of pain and anger.

"This show's over," McVicar finally blustered. "End of interview." He rapped his glass down on the coffee table.

Mrs. McVicar made a choking sound. Then she began to cry. She turned her back to them.

Villanova felt an odd relief. "That's good," he said quietly in Mrs. McVicar's direction.

"Don't let these wise guys get to you," McVicar began to caution his wife, and then he had the wisdom to shut up.

The woman glanced back at him bitterly, then crossed the room into the bedroom and shut the door. McVicar got up and went after her. Villanova made to stop him, but Rizzo waved him off. They stood back and watched the McVicars shut themselves up in the other room.

"You're going to let them get their heads together," Villanova warned.

"Relax, Buddy. The guy's in the cookpot now." Rizzo made himself comfortable on the couch.

"The bastard makes me sick."

"Me too. But let him stew a minute and he'll come out and spill what he's got."

Villanova paced the room. "He was the girl's mentor," he said. "You know how much power over her that gave him? He might as well have forced himself on his own daughter."

Rizzo nodded. "Can I say something, Buddy?"

"Go ahead."

"You seem kinda worked up. At first I thought you were just doing the 'bad cop' routine."

"Yeah? And now?"

Rizzo shrugged. "What's wrong?"

"Nothing's wrong. I don't like that pompous sonofabitch, that's all." He stopped pacing and skimmed the bookshelves. There were dozens of books he knew, books full of mystery and power, books making war against the illusion, the lie, the dreamsleep of life. There was Melville, Whitman, Dostoevsky, Lawrence, Hesse, Mann, Hemingway, Miller, Dahlberg, Wolfe, Camus. Surrounding each were the works of the academic scavengers: the books of criticism, the literary biographies, the biographies of the biographers, the commentaries on the commentaries on the commentaries. The room was a museum of passionate ideas, choked by parasitic clamor, homogenized and stacked into a wall against life. McVicar himself had a book on the shelves, conspicuous by the number of copies--it was the same text Villanova had seen in Elizabeth Albano's bedroom. He gave it a closer look this time: a psychobiography of Hawthorne, a writer he himself much admired; chapters focusing on incest themes, homosexuality, latent perversion manifest in the man's work. He shoved the volume back into place.

"You don't like his books, either?" Rizzo said.

"The little shit. He's a spoiler, one of those academic voyeurs."

"What's it mean, 'Dimmesdale'?"

"That's a guy in another guy's book. He knocked up some married woman and then had a grand time feeling guilty while *she* took all the heat."

"And McVicar made money bullshitting about it? Good for him."

"The sleazy prick."

Rizzo shook his head. "Maybe you should cool it a little, Buddy."

"I'll cool it."

"Wonder how it's going for him in there."

"We'll know by his face when he comes out."

"The wife is a piece of ass."

"Is she?"

Rizzo wet his lips. "Someone ought to show *her* the game."

"Yeah? Maybe *you* should cool it."

The bedroom door opened and McVicar came out. "I want to talk," he said. His face had lost its color.

"Talk," Villanova said.

"Not to you, to him. You're a smart guy."

Villanova said, "Then I'll give you a tip, one smart guy to another. Using a lie for an alibi doesn't work unless you get your heads together *first*. If your wife wasn't really home around noon yesterday, we'll find out fast. If she has a job, if she has friends, an exercise class, a periodontist, we'll ask until we find someone who saw her, starting with Ramirez, your Super. No one's invisible. As for you, we know you had a class to teach at 1:00, so either you trotted home for a liquid lunch, or what you said before is bald-faced crap."

"My wife was here," McVicar said. "That part was true."

"Fine. Then it's time to play a little Post Office." Villanova gave a look to Rizzo. "Whose turn is it to be postman?"

"Mine!" Rizzo scrambled up and headed for the bedroom.

"Where's he going?" McVicar said.

"To get a story from your wife that we can match against yours."

The professor's face turned paler as the door shut behind Rizzo.

"Well, still feel like talking?"

McVicar gave things a quick thinking over. "Listen, I'll talk as much as you want so long as what I say is between me and you."

"There's no one else here."

McVicar searched Villanova's eyes, pleading for contact. Villanova softened a notch and let him have it. "Look, I don't give a damn how much you lie to your wife. Just tell me about noon yesterday."

"I was on campus. I waited for Elizabeth, like I said. When she didn't show, I went to the library to do some work."

"Anyone see you? You check anything in or out?"

"I was working up in the Archive, by myself."

"And nobody saw you? Isn't there a security guard at the main door?"

"There's a ledger you have to sign to use the Archive. A girl lets you in and out, a T.A."

"Then the girl saw you."

"Sure. I worked right up until it was time to go teach. Till almost one o'clock."

"That's easy enough to verify. Why the hell did you lie to us before?"

McVicar dropped his voice. "On account of my wife. She's...an intensely jealous woman."

"Jealous of what, your work?"

McVicar gave him a baleful look.

"Jesus, don't tell me you've got a thing going with the girl in the Archive?"

McVicar shrugged.

Villanova got a hollow feeling in his chest. "That's what you call 'working'?"

A smirk played on McVicar's lips, then faded. He slid his hands into his pockets.

"What's the girl's name?"

"Dolores. Dolores Loughlin. But be discreet. She's got a husband."

"Be discreet? How do you spend your lunch hour, fucking Mrs. Loughlin on the floor between the stacks?"

"That's not called for," McVicar said.

Villanova wanted a cigarette now, but pushed the thought out of his mind. "Where do you know the girl from? She one of your students?"

McVicar nodded.

"You're big on seducing your students, aren't you?"

McVicar's eyes narrowed. "What does that word mean, 'seduce'?"

Villanova flushed; even he hadn't had much use for the expression in a long time. He motioned toward the couch and said dryly, "Sit, Professor, tell me about Elizabeth Albano, tell me how you wound up sleeping with her and what went sour. Tell me exactly where you stood in her life as of yesterday morning."

McVicar eyed the J & B thirstily as he sat, and Villanova waved him a go-ahead. The man poured himself a healthy measure. With his first swallows, the color came back to his face. "I've known Elizabeth for two years," he said. "She was one of the brightest students I ever taught. That's a rare combination, you know, beauty and a mind like that. You can think whatever you want, but I always found that irresistible." He took another swallow. His body relaxed visibly; he crossed his legs, ankle over knee, and leaned forward slightly. "You know who was the brightest student to ever come through the program? Jeanne, my wife. That's right. We were both married at the time, too. I used to meet *her* in the music room, you see? That's why..."

"I really don't give a shit. Tell me about Elizabeth."

"The same kind of thing. She fell for me, and I went with it."

"Just like that, she fell for you?"

"Believe me, it's no novelty. She was one of the young ones, but you get these women, thirty, thirty-five, a little shut in, you know the kind, the first time they run into a certain caliber of mind, Christ, they get hot. It's like the biggest turn-on of their lives. They get shameless about it."

"What kind of crap is that? I had a good look at the family Elizabeth came from."

"No, you've got to understand the psychology of it," McVicar insisted. "There's a sheltered type, see, that's actually all worked up and bitter over it. They've read all this worldly, daring crap, but they haven't lived any of it, and then they step out of the provinces and meet sophisticated people and they get frantic with envy, they get into a kind of love-hate thing with worldliness. They want to know *nouvelle cuisine*, minimalist art, they want to hear witty talk, they want to fuck the professor, wife or no wife. And then on Sunday they go to church."

"Fascinating. How long were you and Elizabeth lovers?"

"About six months."

"She felt guilty about it, though, right? She started putting pressure on you to make a break with your wife, to put an end to the lying and sneaking."

"No way. We never talked about my wife. It's one of my rules."

"When was the last time you slept with her?"

"Almost two months ago. Near the end of July."

"You sure?"

"Positive. Just after summer session ended."

"The fun stopped as soon as she got pregnant, eh? That got her scared, and then she got mad, and then she started turning the heat up on you."

"Like I said, I didn't know anything about her being pregnant."

"No? But she was the one who broke off the affair, right? Why?"

McVicar tipped his glass this way and that, bringing the liquid right up to the brim. He said quietly, "She found out about the others."

"The others? How many others?"

"Only two. Dolores, she's new. The thing is, I had never tied myself into any of this monogamy crap with Elizabeth, but she imagined what suited her."

Villanova felt another dose of poison seeping through his innards. "I see. She thought she was your mistress, maybe even your sweetheart, and it turned out she was just a steady lay."

"Sweetheart? Mistress? Where do you get these words?"

"Don't smirk, you son of a bitch! What happened after she found out about your little chicken farm?"

"We had a blowout over it."

"You were ready to bail out anyway. Six months of fucking was good enough for you."

"No. The fact is, I tried to get her back."

"Yeah? Why? You had plenty of action."

McVicar took a long swallow of scotch. "Elizabeth was the one that mattered."

"I see. She mattered so much that you instantly gave up your other women."

"No...but I would have. I really think I would. Only she didn't give me the chance. She pulled a fast one. Right after our quarrel, she went to the department head and tried to get me removed from her dissertation committee. It was a 'not for cause' request, and it was denied, because I happen to be the expert on her area of research, and her project was too far along. But it sent me a pretty chilling message, so I sent her one back. I cut off her assistantship. Or let's say, I simply didn't speak up for it when that would have made the difference. I chair that particular committee at the college, you see. For T.A.'s, the third year of stipend is technically competitive. Most of the applications slide right through. Hers didn't. In fact, Dolores Loughlin got the appointment she should have had, the job in the Archive."

"That was a pretty nasty thing to do."

"I'm not proud of it. But it was within the rules. I mean the girl was trying to play this big, grown-up game. You don't play demimondaine and then go running back to Big-daddy Department Head when things get rough."

"Why punish Elizabeth if you wanted her back?"

"I had to protect myself. Remember, she was ambivalent as hell, and that's dangerous. Who knew what she might do next. Spill the beans to my wife? Start some kind of sexual harassment grievance at the college? Technically she had no grounds, she was an equal partner in the affair, but who knows? Her next recourse would have been to go over everyone's head and complain to the dean, and that guy's already got it in for me. I had to get her to mind her manners. Christ, we all rub shoulders with each other. We were all at the department kick-off party a few weeks back, Elizabeth, myself, the dean, the department head..."

"Did you speak to her?"

"Briefly. If she'd given me the chance, I'd have told her how much I wanted to put things right between us. Instead we wound up talking about her oral exams. They're scheduled for a week from today. I'm one of the examiners." He looked thoughtfully into his drink. "The fact is, if I'd wanted to I could have washed out her whole dissertation project, a year and a half of work. It was to her advantage to play things smart with me. But she was obnoxious that day, and a little tipsy too. And afterward, she avoided me even more than before." His eyes met Villanova's. "I got so frustrated I even went to her house. I saw her father..."

"Who shut you down real good."

"Yes. That he did."

"In fact, the poor bastard was under the delusion that his daughter hadn't known all along you had a wife. You're lucky he didn't know you'd knocked up his little girl to boot."

"Yeah, I'm a lucky guy, all right."

"You want to feel sorry for yourself? Go to hell."

McVicar's face colored. "Why pick on me? Look, I'm sorry the girl's dead. It's a shame. As a matter of fact, it's disgusting. But I'm not responsible for it just because I slept with her."

Villanova nodded.   "Now there's a word we both understand. 'Disgusting.'"

McVicar looked wounded.   He was about to reply when the bedroom door opened.   Rizzo came out and shut the door behind him.   His face told very little, except that he was done.   "Got a phone I can use?" he asked McVicar.

"In the study.   The end of the hall where you came in."

Rizzo left the room.   Villanova was nearly done too. He stood up.   "How much did you have to do with Elizabeth after that department party?"

"Practically nothing.   I saw her last week Tuesday for her regular directed reading.   The week before was a holiday."

"Did you quarrel with her?   Did you pour out your heart?"

"It was strictly business.   She was ice water."

"You ever see her with another guy?   A guy named Jack, a long-haired guy?"

"Yeah, I saw the guy.   Once.   She brought him to the department party."

"An artist?"

"*Claimed* to be an artist."

"From the college?"

"Hell no.   Some local character.   Nobody knew him."

"You get his last name?   Anybody get his last name?"

"A guy like that has no last name.   He's someone from the street, someone she picked up at the Web or the Killarney Rose.   Picturesque, in a theatrical way.   A bed partner.   Why don't you ask *him* if he knocked her up."

"Don't tell me what to ask.   How do you know he was a bed partner?"

"The whole point was for me to know that.   Look, there's something I don't think you get.   Elizabeth was a smart girl, but mixed up about who she really wanted to be.   When I went to her house that time and saw the straight little world she came out of, I threw her off balance. I mean, she'd always hidden that from me, she always went out of her way to strut her worldly shit for me. That's why she brought this guy Jack to the party, so I could see her new conquest. There was no other reason."

"Conquest? Can I ask you something? Did it ever cross your mind that maybe Elizabeth was a sweet girl whose head got turned by your bullshit *savoir faire*, who really fell for you and thought you were on the level, who tried to be what you wanted even after you made a fool of her, who got bullied and confused and then got killed?"

McVicar got that wounded look again. "You sound as if you're mad because it was *me* who got to sleep with her and not *you*."

Villanova's face grew hot. "Stand up," he said. His hands were balled into fists.

McVicar didn't move.

"You piece of shit!" Villanova turned away from him and went down the hall after Rizzo. He found him on the phone in a tiny office lined with books. He put his back to him and pretended to read more titles, taking deep, slow breaths. His eyes fell on a familiar book, and a knife-like pain tore through his heart. It was *Born in Paradise*, a girlhood treasure of his dead wife Ginny, a book she had loved like everything her spirit opened to, with a stubborn, uncritical loyalty. The last copy he'd seen had stood on a shelf in his Belle Haven home fifteen years back. He pulled the book from its place, held it, ran his hands over the binding: the same Literary Guild edition, the same faded blue cloth cover with the recessed lettering. He opened it: the same musty smell of a time and place long dead. His eyes grew moist, and he blinked the wet away. Born in Paradise--murdered, too, in paradise, and buried deep in the exotic groves, though not deep enough. Oh, he was in for it now, he knew, another round of Ginny's face in his dreams, Ginny's voice in other people's talk, her expressions in strangers' faces. Pieces of Ginny everywhere, her laugh, her words, her walk. Ginny, right here on McVicar's shelves, her favorite book inscribed with the bastard's initials. McVicar had been right about him, he'd struck home with his cruel comment. Elizabeth Albano was just the type of girl he'd have fallen for with all his heart; she was Ginny, one cynical, confused, vulnerable generation later.

He put the book back in place and composed himself; Rizzo was finishing up his conversation, and this was the one side of himself that Villanova never let his partner see.

Rizzo hung up the phone. "Guess what?" he said. "The guys in the squadroom got a call. Seems the 1010 news station put an item in the morning cycle about the girl in the trunk. A gypsy cabby heard it and called in from a coffee shop."

"He saw something?"

"Better. He dropped off a fare with a trunk on Mosholu Parkway. Picked him up on Third Avenue. A young guy, long hair, nervous."

"That's our man, the artist! Is the cabby coming in?"

"They lost him. He wouldn't give his name. Asked about a reward."

"Shit. Did they ask him where on Third Avenue he made the pick-up?"

"They did, but he clammed up. Scared...or else cagey."

"It could be worse. I say he'll call back."

"That's what he said too."

"Get the radio station, get them to insert any kind of reward. Just the word. Who's the reporter who pulled the story off the blotter?"

"Don't know. We can find out. How'd it go with Mister Professor?"

"Mister Professor's a dick. A first-class dick with an alibi." He told Rizzo about the Archive girl.

"The guy's a lady-killer, all right. You think he's more than that?"

"I think the man we want to find is the artist. What'd you get out of the wife?"

"She's a piece of work, all right," Rizzo said. "She's packing a bag."

"Seriously?"

"Looks serious. It's an awful big bag. She asked me to call her a car service. Maybe we oughta wait till they get here."

"We've got a hell of a lot to do. If this cabby doesn't call back, we're going to need McVicar and the girl's father to get together for a composite sketch. Our suspect doesn't seem to have a last name. And we've still got to check in at the Crime Lab and go over the Pathology report."

"How about we split things, Buddy? How about I wait here with the wife, and you take the professor to the precinct?"

"How about you give the wife a break, and I call the news station, and you go tell the professor to show up at the precinct, and then you take me home so I can grab the stuff I'm gonna need for this little campout?"

"And who starts canvassing Third Avenue?" Rizzo said. "And who waits in the squadroom for the callback? Who goes up to Mount Saint Mary's? Who runs down Liz Albano's connections?"

"Who gets paid to do all that shit?"

Rizzo went back down the hall, and Villanova made the call to the news station.

When he finished, Rizzo was waiting in the living room. The bedroom door was ajar, and a suitcase the size of a trunk lay open on the bed.   McVicar's wife, moving methodically, her hair draping her pallid face, was folding garments into it. The professor sat on the sectional cradling his rock glass in both hands, staring into the liquid. He didn't look up.

Rizzo gave the sign, and they let themselves out.

- THREE -

In Mike Villanova's mind, he'd lived a life in Three Acts with long and turbid interludes. Act One was a cozy childhood in a big, warm, energetic clan, with an endless succession of noisy gatherings and abundances of macaroni, ravioli, scallopini, chicken cacciatore, pasta con sarde, bresciola, sausage and peppers, calamari, scungili, rizzoto and veal, polenta, mannicotti, canneloni.... Act One was also the Catholic Church, a Redemptorist parish, School Sisters of Notre Dame, sung masses, incense, stained glass, Holy Week vigils, processions, midnight masses, an hermetic and yet all-encompassing world unified by ancient pagan mythology with a little spice of Thomist theology. It was a happy childhood.

The interlude was a steady and final apostasy with a peculiarly masculine Italian flavor, fractious, proud, solitary. By twenty-one, with a degree from Fordham University, he was a philosopher in a world without a God but with plenty of prophets: Nietzsche, Bergson, Schopenhauer, Freud, Jung, Fromm, Santayana, Marx, Spinoza, James, Whitehead, Veblen. He was a stoic, an idealist, a mystic, a wanderer, an outsider, a romantic. The war in Vietnam was part of this interlude. He arrived there at the finish of it, in time for one short, nasty battle. The worst of the horrors he saw was the top half of a child outside the muddy rim of a shellhole. Beyond that, the things that impressed him there impressed nobody else. He knew it wasn't the place itself that was being fought over, because the lowest reaches of hell couldn't have been hotter or more worthless. The *fight* was what it was about. What he saw was a stunning ritual, with the annihilation of beauty at its center...like a bullfight, except there was no symbolic bull, and the whole beautiful young audience was slain instead. That was the only way he could see an enterprise that turned human beings full of youth and courage into mutilated objects. It was the only way to understand an enterprise in which the greatest kindness you did your friends was to turn your eyes from the ghastly messes they had become. Some of the men he met in Viet Nam believed they had come there to die, but very few appreciated the difference between death and immolation. Villanova did. Death was only death, and it came with sorrow or anger. Murder was an obscenity that brought disgust to the senses of a normal man. But war couldn't be anything but a rite, and its proper emotion was awe.

So, awed, he flew home, Da Nang to Hawaii to San Francisco to JFK airport. Crossing the continent, the vastness of desert, the limitless plains, the verdure of farmland, the hills and peaks of the Alleghenies, the eastern forests, he intercepted the dusk at last over a tiny scab on the broad green back of the continent, the brownish excrescence of a desperately busy microbe colony. New York City. And he saw, for the first time, the frailty of this little crust, this mighty megalopolis that dwarfed Babylon and Babel and every monument built to appease or goad the Gods humankind dreamed up and murdered. He saw the pointlessness of all men's passions and ambitions, the futility of their struggle to separate good from bad, virtue from vice, victim from predator, saint from sinner. He saw the evanescence of all their history and conviction as plainly as the fog of his breath on the Plexiglas window, and once he saw it, he could never un-see it. The curtain came down, anti-climactically, on the Age of Innocence.

And then he re-met and fell in love with Virginia Romano, and the Age of Faith unfolded. Act Two. Ginny was the sweetest, gentlest, most loving girl he'd known at college, and pretty too. She played the guitar and sang with a lilting alto voice the ballads of Joan Baez, Judy Collins, and Buffy Ste. Marie, and she could play Beatles songs too, and harmonize. Her hair was long, straight, nearly black, parted in the middle in perfect line with her fine, straight nose. Her slender body seemed made for girlish frocks and bare feet, though the rakish angle of her eyebrows gave that sweet face of hers a permanent knowing and mischievous look. While he'd been in Viet Nam, she'd been in Haiti with the Peace Corps, teaching people how to breed rabbits for food, helping build tin-roofed huts, and taking her dawn baths in a cold stream. In antidote to that chill, their courtship was a yearlong afternoon in the sun, sometimes stoned, sometimes not, always tranquil, always immersed in the transcendental beauty of nature and suffused with a joyous hippie optimism. Ginny, opening to him like a blooming rose, was goodness incarnate, the happy flower of a close-knit, enlightened family and a recklessly optimistic decade. Ginny healed him.

If bliss entails a dazed kind of happiness, then their marriage was blissful. It was brief, idealistic, energetic, and, in hindsight, too hopeful for this hungry planet. They married in early spring and bought a handyman special in Belle Haven, Ginny's home town, on the north shore of Suffolk County, Long Island. He got a job on the staff of *Long Island Magazine*, and she began substitute teaching. He drew up elaborate plans for renovating the house, and the more notebooks he filled with drawings, the happier they got. They both wanted babies, and two months after the wedding, just as summer began, Ginny was pregnant--though he was the one who began to swell. Words poured out of his typewriter, his vision and voice expanded: the evanescent world now sustained eternal realities, the pathologic ooze was now a place where things could grow. The garden surrounding the house became the focus of his notebooks and his magnificent energy: he planted euonymous, lilac, holly, yew, juniper, peonies, forsythia, rhododendron, mountain laurel, hydrangea, azalea, and beds of daffodils, iris, and day lilies. He threw himself into grading, terracing, hedging, bordering, stonework. He built ponds, he moved fifty, a hundred cubic yards of dirt by wheelbarrow. Trees, even groves, became mobile elements in his vision. Misplaced saplings were re-transplanted, young dogwoods or white birches growing in the shade of the oaks were dug, balled, and moved, if only a few yards, to happier places in the scheme. He used a chain affixed to his car, an old, top-heavy Volkswagen bus, to drag the trees from their old pits to the new.

He endured teasing for his fanaticism, and didn't mind, because Ginny approved. Ginny was painting rooms, collecting furnishings, and doing most of the cooking on an outdoor hibachi because the stove was ancient and temperamental. She stripped and repainted a baby crib that had been in her family for thirty years, she refinished the old maple dressers from her room. She started writing songs, ballads based on folktales she collected and read, and she took to freehand embroidery on the beach after their evening swim in the Sound. Every night they watched the sun melt into the sea, each time a notch closer to the reach of Hazzard's Neck. Then they drove home and made love with the taste of brine still on their skin, and always took a long shower together afterward, a warm shower even though the Long Island nights were sultry. They lingered half an hour, an hour in each other's arms under that soothing cascade; as long as they didn't shut the water off, or even think of it, nothing could reach into the wholeness of their peace.

One drizzly evening they forewent the beach, and he finished digging up a young catalpa while Ginny worked on her embroidery inside. She was almost finished with the biggest and best of her creations, an Eden-like interpretation of his own garden, with every species of shrub and flower represented. She drove the Volkswagen to buy embroidery thread, and he asked her to hurry back with it so he could get the catalpa moved before dark. She liked the yellow-green of the catalpa leaves and took one with her to match against the thread. "Hurry," he reminded her, and she never came back. She was sideswiped into a tree on Route 25-A; the impact crushed out her life instantly. The driver responsible was never found.

And later, after his shock, his rage, and his mourning, in the quieter afterstage of grieving which darkened his life for half a decade, he understood why his bliss had been so intense and so preposterously full of plans and endeavour, and why the injunction "Hurry," one he never repeated to anyone again in his life, had been the true watchword of his time with Ginny. He understood that, in a mystical universe, what was to come informed reality as much as what had come before. What was to come, for him, was a long, passionate, fruitless search, in the name of justice, for a spectral culprit, the lost grail of his fading moral cosmos. More accurately, what was to come was a fifteen year Age of Solitude, at the end of which he would begin his far soberer Third Act, a worldly man somewhat learned in the art of crime and detection: Mike Villanova, the private investigator perpetually solving his first case. The natural laws of conservation of energy, compression and temperature, relativity and time had all been at work during that youthful marriage. As it turned out, his joy had lasted, beginning to end, five months.

* * *

It was late afternoon by the time Rizzo and Villanova had the composite sketch of Jack, together with the photo of Elizabeth, faxed out to the precincts and copied in quantity for the canvassing squad. Not many of the precinct men did door-to-door work with any gusto, but Homicide's canvassing squad, Rizzo's prize creation, was an elite team. Made up of two pairs of hand-picked, hand-trained men, the squad could cover a city block in an hour, or, under pressure, twice the ground working solo. Rizzo himself had made his reputation as a canvasser. As a junior grade detective, he'd used legwork to break a number of "impossible" cases, including a double murder covered heavily in the city's press. At 36, he was a first grade detective and number two man in the Bronx Homicide Squad, and his canvassers, Arcario, Dougherty, Torres, and Reinhart, had the *esprit* of a select team.

They were good, but even Rizzo and Villanova were surprised when Arcario phoned the squadroom with a lead at 7:40 Wednesday evening, after only two hours on the job. He was calling from the big ghetto west of Fordham Road known as the Wedge, practically in Homicide Squad's back yard. Rizzo and Villanova pushed aside the White Castle burgers they were eating, jumped into Rizzo's Plymouth, and sped up Third Avenue to the corner of 187th, where Arcario was waiting with an elderly Hispanic man, a slight, dignified, visibly nervous man.

"What's the deal?"

"This guy recognizes the photo."

"He's seen the girl here in the Wedge?"

"Says he's seen her every day."

Rizzo turned to the old man. "Where?"

The man gestured in a vaguely downtown direction.

"He doesn't speak English," Arcario said; both he and Villanova understood Spanish, but Arcario could speak it as well. He asked the old man in Spanish where he'd last seen the girl.

The man pointed downtown again.

"Get him in the car."

They all piled in and the old man navigated them down four blocks to 183rd and then over to Bathgate Avenue. This was the heart of the Wedge, once the boundary between the white and black sections, now a hodge-podge of immigrant poor, mostly Hispanics. The streets were littered, the stoops occupied, the tenements shabby with neglect. There were few shops and plenty of steel grates.

They got out where the old man indicated, in front of a bodega with two overhead storeys. Beside it was a vacant lot guarded by a high chain link fence. A little further up the block, half a dozen boys, playing street hockey in the last of the daylight, stopped their game to watch.

"Well?" Rizzo said.

The old man pointed into the lot.

All they could see was hardpan fringed by weeds, and a big mural covering the side wall of the bodega. The mural was eye-catching, a baroque street fantasy done in vivid hues: punks with boom boxes, mothers with baby carriages, girls playing double dutch, junkies, tradesmen, two fat cops, a pickpocket, an Infant of Prague, a pastel-toned '55 Chevy, a Krishna deity, a three-card-monte team, a naked Joan of Arc burning at the stake, a cleric brandishing a crucifix, a pair of Dobermans, a politicians' Last Supper, a gravedigger, alley cats, rats, pigeons, drunks, nuns, hookers, pimps, and johns. The tableau was vulgar, violent, erotic, mystical, and self-parodying all at once.

"What the hell is this?" Rizzo said.

The old man pointed. "*Mira--alli arriba.*"

"What's he's pointing at? Get a light up there. Arcario, use your flashlight."

"Look," Villanova said. "Look at Joan of Arc's face."

"Holy shit."

It was the face of Elizabeth Albano.

"Take the light off it," Villanova said, "it gives me the creeps." The beam seemed to kindle the flames beneath that beautiful victim.

Rizzo and Villanova went into the bodega. It was a far cry from Angelo's market; bullet-proof glass enclosed the cramped counter, and a sullen-eyed Akita stood watch over the shelves, held in check by a long chain. The guy at the cash register, a burly Puerto Rican of about forty, turned out to be the owner of the building. He looked plenty tough, but when he found out what they were after, he was helpful. Like everyone in the Wedge at this point, he'd heard about the dead girl in the trunk. He had teenage daughters himself, he told them. The mural was only about six months old. The guy who painted it was working off a debt. He still owed money. He lived in a basement apartment off an alley on Bathgate three blocks up toward Fordham Road. His name was Jack. He had long hair and glasses, and if they snagged the son-of-a-bitch, and if the son-of-a-bitch did whatever it was that had been done to that poor girl in the trunk, then he wanted to go along and help beat the shit out of him when they collared him.

They left Arcario behind to quiet the bodega owner, thanked the old man, took the car up Lorillard Place a few blocks, then looped down Bathgate to 186th. They parked and walked up the block and then halfway back again to the only alley that could lead to a basement apartment. Villanova went first and Rizzo followed, down three steps, under part of the building, past a closed steel door marked "Meter Room," past a big doorless room filled with trash cans and alley cats.

Villanova stopped to look. There must have been two dozen cats, all poised and watching. Villanova took another step and they exploded into flight, climbing the walls and vanishing into cracks and holes. "Jesus *Christ*."

"You're a cat-lover, right, Buddy?"

The last part of the alley was open to the sky. Four-storey tenements looked down on it from both sides. "There *is* an apartment," Villanova said. "There on the left."

"Lotta windows up there. Not easy to drag out a trunk on the sneak, even during the night."

"Maybe he didn't drag it. Maybe someone helped him."

"Maybe."

They checked the rest of the alley: three windows to the basement apartment, grates on the inside, blinds drawn behind them, no other exit. The alley ended in a high wooden fence flanked by brick walls. They went back to the door.

"You ready, Buddy?"

"I guess so. What're you carrying?"

"Just the .38. What about you?"

Villanova shrugged.

"Nothing? Gimme a break. You went home for shaving cream and toothpaste and you left your piece?"

"The guy's an artist, right? What's he gonna do, brain me with a canvas?"

"You never know."

They took their positions on either side of the door, and Rizzo gave it a few solid kicks. "Police!" he bawled out. "Open up!"

Nothing but dead silence.

"If he's in there, he's being sly," Rizzo said. "How about you stand watch while I go get a warrant?"

"Are you serious?" Villanova drew out his pick set and went to work on the lock.

"What the hell're you doing?"

"It's a knob lock, a piece of cake." Within a few seconds he'd released the lock and given the door a push. Daylight fell into a tiny kitchen, and a huge cockroach scuttled across the floor into the shadows.

"Police!" Rizzo roared through the crack. "Come on out!"

No reply.

Rizzo repeated the cry, and then Villanova pushed the door all the way open and stepped in.

"Are you nuts?"

"The roaches know when no one's home. Come on, let's get in while we have the chance."

"I can't even step in there, Buddy. It'll foul the case."

"You can't, but I can."

Rizzo started to protest, but Villanova went ahead. The kitchen had pots in the sink and a frying pan on the stove. The next room had a mattress on the floor, books, newspapers, and magazines heaped everywhere. The *Times Book Review* had its own stack, and so did the *Spectrum*. In the middle of the floor were half a dozen cardboard boxes, and a few more book stacks tied up with twine. There was clothing inside the boxes, neatly folded; someone was packing to leave. Villanova took a glance at the book titles: Rollo May, Lewis Thomas, Koestler, Jaspers, Edward Hall, R. D. Laing, Dubos, Jameson, Tillich, Levi-Strauss...pretty heady stuff. He checked the windows. The accordion grates were padlocked shut behind the blinds, with no key in sight. Whoever lived in this place lived in an underground cage. Any kind of fire meant a fricassee. A girl caught here with a killer would have only one chance: to scream and keep on screaming, until something got closed over her mouth.

The last room, the largest, was the studio. Villanova gave the ceiling chain a pull so he could see better. The canvases, most of them large, were leaning against the walls. They were a series, all women, all posed like *Hustler* centerfolds with those frozen smiles, those awkwardly splayed limbs. Many of them resembled Elizabeth Albano. But these temptresses were stripped of flesh as well as clothes. Most were skeletons below the neck, others putrefying corpses, others charred mummies. In the backgrounds of the paintings were vague images of barbed wire, freight cars, crematoria, all done in sensuous pastels. The blend of the grisly and the erotic was carried off with real technical mastery. Villanova wasn't sure what he was seeing--pornography, a comment on pornography, or some deeper metaphor of civilization's obscene core--but he could feel its power. It did something weird to his insides, made a vacuum of some kind that sucked everything down. He thought of the photos of Elizabeth he had seen in her family's living room. He felt queasy.

There was an easel near the window with a finished canvas on it. The image was the only one Villanova could bear to look at. It was a nude of Elizabeth Albano, almost photographically realistic. The youthful form was imbued with the blush of life, the face bore an ethereal expression something like the Joan of Arc's. The figure stood in an open coffin.

Villanova came back out to the alley and shut the door behind him.

"What've we got?" Rizzo said.

Villanova told him.

"I knew it, a pervert. By tonight this creep would have been long gone. See any signs of a struggle?"

"There wasn't even a... "

"Shh--wait!"

Someone was coming through the underpass from the street. The guy caught sight of them at the same time they did him. All Villanova saw was long hair and glasses, and a wooden crate under each of the guy's arms, and in less than a second the crates were flying at their faces and the guy was running. Villanova, ducking, took a glancing blow on the head and lost a few seconds sprinting after Rizzo, and then felt the pain start as he hit the sidewalk and saw the two men racing away, the artist's black hair flying behind him like an Indian's. He took off after them, caught Rizzo in half a block, pulled away and, with the throb in his head keeping beat to his strides, measured the distance between himself and that dancing Apache mane. Cigarettes or no cigarettes, unless the son-of-a-bitch was Jim Thorpe, he wasn't going to outrun an ex-cross-country man.

It took three more blocks, and when Villanova finally closed in, the Apache whirled around on him and threw such a barrage of kicks and punches that all he could do was tackle him and roll around on the sidewalk. Two guys working under the hood of a car just stood there and watched. Rizzo came wheezing up and gave the Apache a good kick in the back and then another in the side, and Villanova squirmed on top and threw his weight on the small of the guy's back. Rizzo stood on his neck. "Police, asshole!"

"Yeah, me too," the guy croaked.

"Fuck you, pal." They read him his rights and took him in.

* * *

Homicide Squad had half a floor in the "new" 48th precinct headquarters on Park Avenue, in the shadow of the elevated nightmare known as the Cross Bronx Expressway. The old building had had gothic gables and fleur-de-lis windows, wrought-iron railings, terrazzo floors, plaster walls, fifteen-foot ceilings, and sundry graceful vestiges of a forgotten era. The new one, shabby before the mortar was dry, had already been twice recompartmentalized to meet the growing volume of trade. A stump of the original Captain's

Boardroom comprised Homicide Squad's main workroom, and the rest of the former administrative suite had been mercilessly dissected into offices, interrogation rooms, a dormitory, file rooms, and store rooms. Tentacles of conduit roamed the walls, fluorescent fixtures dangled from cables, city-issue grey-green metal desks jammed every corner, grey-green file folders and legal forms spilled across every desk.

The Apache's name was Jack LeClerc. He was one quarter French and three-quarters mongrel, he claimed, a little of everything except Native American. He was thirty-one years old, scrounged his living from grants, freebies, and friends, and had a yellow sheet running back fifteen years.

They questioned him in a windowless room off the back corridor next to the lavatory. It was about the size of a walk-in closet, and every few minutes they had to raise their voices over the flushing of a toilet. Periodically Villanova rubbed the lump on his head, and Rizzo reminded him of his earlier cockiness with a wink. They kept Jack LeClerc's hands cuffed. Villanova smoked one Chesterfield after another and let Rizzo do most of the talking.

LeClerc was nasty, wary, and smart. His glossy, shoulder-length hair, his dark, reddish skin, his big features and thick, black-framed eyeglasses made such a strong impact that, as he turned his head this way and that, Villanova couldn't decide whether he was spectacularly ugly or exotically handsome. At first LeClerc wouldn't answer questions about Elizabeth Albano and insisted on a lawyer, but since they could comfortably stall his arraignment for a few hours, they ignored his demands. When they finally goaded him into talking, he coolly denied everything: knowing Elizabeth, knowing she'd been murdered, painting her likeness in a street mural, going to her house, being with her at a graduate school party; but after a few minutes, as if he'd been lying by reflex while he thought things over, he changed strategy suddenly and became contemptuously forthcoming.

"Sure I knew her. We met during the summer, over on the campus, down the Ramskellar. She was at my place every day."

"Doing what?" Rizzo said.

"Posing for me."

"You were her boyfriend?"

"I'm nobody's boyfriend."

"You and she were lovers, then."

LeClerc hesitated. "I slept with her, yeah. What of it?"

"When'd you see her last."

"Like I said, she was at my place every day."

"Including yesterday morning?"

"Including yesterday morning. She was at the door, she didn't come in."

"About what time?"

"Twelve-thirty or so."

"She had a gold chain and crucifix around her neck, right, pal?"

"I wouldn't know."

"You wouldn't, huh?" Rizzo stared hard at LeClerc. "Why didn't she come in? You quarreled with her, right?"

LeClerc shook his head.

"The people across the alley heard you," Rizzo improvised.

LeClerc shrugged. "*She* quarreled with *me*, is more like it."

"What about?"

"She wanted me to go somewhere with her, and I didn't want to. I was working. I don't stop working just because someone needs a favor."

A toilet flushed on the other side of the wall.

Villanova said, "Where'd she want you to go?"

"To see this spiritualist she dug up."

"A spiritualist?"

"A psychic. You know, read your palm, hocus pocus. She said the place was only a few blocks away."

"Are you serious? You telling me she was the type of girl who went to psychics?"

"All I know is, she showed up at my place yesterday morning, I told her I was busy, she tried to drag me on some shit-for-brains errand. We fought, right there in the doorway, she left. Hey, do you have to fill this place with smoke?"

Rizzo said, "She left, huh? At what time?"

"About a quarter to one."

"I don't suppose anyone saw her leave."

"I wouldn't know."

"Tell me, why'd you run when you saw us at your door?"

"I thought you were someone else. Someone I owe money to."

Villanova was keeping a close watch on LeClerc's eyes. They were remarkably cool, just as they'd been when he was obviously lying. The only suspects he'd ever encountered with eyes like that were sociopaths.

Rizzo said, "You told us you met Elizabeth during the summer, right? Exactly when?"

"Beginning of August."

"You put the girl's face on the side of a building. Guy we just talked to said you did the work six months ago. Now, how's that possible if you didn't meet the girl until August?"

LeClerc's eyebrows arched up a millimeter.

"Seems to me you don't have your story straight, pal."

LeClerc said, "I *met* Liz in August. I saw her plenty of times before I met her."

"Yeah? Just saw her on the street, huh?"

"In the Ramskellar. I hang out there."

"And you go around making a billboard feature out of anyone who catches your eye?"

"Why not? Some faces stick. My next mural, maybe *you'll* be the star."

Rizzo's face darkened. "And maybe you'll be holding your paintbrush up your ass, wise guy."

LeClerc shrugged.

Villanova said, "Why'd your girlfriend want to see a spiritualist?"

"She was sick. She had these bad headaches."

"How bad?"

"Bad. She stopped having sex with me. I told her, 'The nuns did a job on you, all right.'"

"You telling me a girl as intelligent as Elizabeth, a girl working on a Ph.D., wanted to see a spiritualist for a headache problem? You expect me to believe that?"

"People do weird things when they're sick."

"She was sick, all right," Rizzo snapped. "She was pregnant. You knew that, right? You found that out yesterday morning. That's what you fought about."

"She never told me anything about being pregnant."

"Gimme a break, LeClerc," Rizzo said. "If you're going to lie, put some effort into it. Look, the girl was murdered, you were the last one to see her, you quarreled with her, you've been arrested three times in the last two years for aggravated assault. You've got a history of losing your temper and beating people to pieces. Why don't you tell us what really happened? You were fucking this girl and you knocked her up and she fought with you over it and she got lippy and goaded you and you got rough with her. You got your hand over her mouth, and maybe you didn't mean to, but you stifled her a little too good. You panicked, you stuffed her in a trunk, you dumped her."

LeClerc stared at Rizzo and then laughed suddenly.

"You think it's funny?"

"*You're* funny. What if she *was* pregnant? Who strangles someone because they're pregnant? That's fixed easy enough. But now I understand why Liz stopped sleeping with me. Because *I* wasn't the one who knocked her up."

Rizzo's brows went up. "*That's* it, then. *That's* what you fought about. She'd made a sap out of you."

"Get serious. I told you, Liz and I fought because she wanted me to stop work on one of the best things I've ever done to go see a fucking psychic."

"Yeah? Where'd she get the idea of inviting *you* along to see this psychic? What made her show up at *your* dump?"

"How do I know? It was on the way. She told me she was scared to go by herself."

"Scared of what? Not scared to roam around the Wedge, but scared to go where?"

LeClerc was temporarily out of answers.

"You're telling us she left your place at a quarter to one?" Rizzo said. "One o'clock, *at the latest*, the girl was dead. Any idea how that happened?"

LeClerc's response was a contemptuous shrug.

"You say you want a lawyer? You're going to need three lawyers with a story like that."

There was a rap on the door. Gilman, one of the Homicide men, put his head in the door and beckoned to Rizzo. "Phone call. Wants *you*."

Rizzo frowned. "*Now*?"

"You bet. It's your cabby."

Rizzo hurried out. LeClerc and Villanova sat eyeing each other. Villanova felt an intense dislike for the guy, weighted with a visceral sort of dismay. LeClerc wasn't that much younger than he was, and his mind wasn't that wholly alien, yet every bleak and nasty sediment of the current age seemed to have settled in his gut.

"You know what your partner's problem is," LeClerc spoke up. "He's second-rate. I've been busted by better. Now a first-rate dick, he's got an instinct for the phenomenological approach. He comes into *your* universe, he doesn't expect you to be hiding someplace in his."

"I'll remember that," Villanova said.

"Seriously, this guy's too hung up on his own mythology. He hears 'sex,' 'pregnant,' and he can only come up with one scenario, some kind of vicious hysteria. I'll bet the sonofabitch is a Catholic."

"You're a theorist, all right. You give me a pain in the ass."

"Yeah? Why not go with it? Why not find out something?"

"Because you're full of shit. You play at nihilism, but your work is full of sacrificial emblems. Every goddam thing you put on canvas is about faith."

"It's about illusion. It's parody, my friend. But it's a Rorschach for a guy like you. I got you figured too. You're a retro man, just like your partner, only the romantic kind. You're one of those stuck-in-time guys. And *you* got a thing about women, too. I mean, they're just *people*, you know?"

"Swell, and what about you, LeClerc? You like women?"

"I'm capable of it. It hasn't happened much."

"No? You don't mind sleeping with them, though."

"I put my dick where it's happy."

A toilet flushed next door.

"So you're a big, bad user. What was Elizabeth Albano to you?"

"A trip. A study, a post-modern grotesque. 'Beauty Gets Fucked.' --Hey, there's a subject you could appreciate. The girl's father was the first one to fuck her, and the rest of us got in line."

"What are you talking about?"

"He fucked her head, man.   Miss Virgin Athlete Beauty Good Girl Saint Elizabeth.   Miss Pride-of-the-clan Graduate Student.   Daddy primed her good, and some slick professor came around the corner, took her down and fucked over the rest of her."

"You got something special against the professor?"

"Don't know the man.   Saw him once at a party. Watched him tank up on sherry, watched him and Liz go at one another over in a corner.   I guess I know now what they were arguing about."

"They argued?"

"Look the man up.   He'll tell you.   Mister Knock-em-up-and dump-em."

Villanova studied LeClerc's cold, arrogant eyes.   "Why complain?   The man set her up for you, didn't he?"

"What was left of her.   Don't think I don't know how I got her."

"And who'd *you* set her up for?"

"Go to hell.   The only one who fucked her straight was me."

"Yeah, straight onto a slab."

"You're not hearing me, man.   She got as good as she gave with me.   Better.   No post-modernist horseshit.   I taught her how to see.   *She* played a game or two, but only because she thought she was supposed to.   Too smart, too pretty, too worked up for her own good.   Too ripe.   Tell you one thing, the girl *knew* how to make love."

"That was the idea, wasn't it."

"Any woman can fuck.   Only a few can make love."

There was another rap on the door, and Gilman poked his head in.   "He wants you, Villanova.   I'll stick with this guy."

"What's up?"

"Lineup.   I'm working this end."

LeClerc said, "That your name--Villanova?"

"No, they just call me that." He told Gilman on his way out, "Watch him, he's a nasty one."

LeClerc called after him. "Yo, Villanova, you shouldn't smoke so much. It isn't healthy."

"Fuck you."

Villanova made his way down the corridor and found Rizzo at his desk with an open box of doughnuts and a huge plastic cup of coffee in front of him. "Hey, you sent out and you didn't get me a coffee?"

"Take it easy, Buddy. The cabby was calling from the Dunkin' Donuts, and he was good enough to bring something along."

"You got him to come in? Where is he?"

"Downstairs, in the john. He's a little nervous."

"How'd you persuade him?"

"The guy's got a conscience. He helped the killer heft the trunk last night, felt a little sick about it when he heard the radio."

"He didn't ask about the reward?"

"I didn't say he was Saint Francis of Assisi."

"Hey! You didn't leave me a Boston Creme?"

"There was only one. Here, have a jelly doughnut. You like those, right? There's coffee in the workroom."

"There's diesel fuel in the workroom. Shit."

"Here he comes. Don't say anything about LeClerc. I don't want to spook him."

One of the guys in uniform came through the maze of partitions escorting a swarthy, middle-aged man in jeans and an imitation-leather jacket. Rizzo introduced him as Hector Rodriquez, and Villanova shook the man's hand. It was cold. They offered him a chair, and Rodriquez sank down gratefully. He had a wide, flat face, thinning black hair, and a droopy moustache that made him look sad, or worried. His broad, stubby hands were trembling.

Rizzo said, "You want to go over what you told me in some detail this time? Tell the whole thing, for my partner's sake."

The cabby nodded. "It's okay to smoke in here?"

"Smoke away."

Rodriquez looked around for an ashtray.

"We use the floor."

Rodriquez shook out a Marlboro and lit up. "Well," he began, "last night I dropped off a fare at 184th and Third. I was just pulling away when this guy practically tackles the cab. I mean, he's running after me waving his arms."

"You saw his face when he got in?"

"Just a glimpse. It was dark."

"What time was it?"

"Around midnight."

"Then what?"

"He tells me to drive around the corner to pick up his luggage. I go down 185th toward Bathgate. He's got a trunk on the sidewalk there... "

"You remember what building it was in front of?"

"It was on the north side. The street's torn up there, some kinda construction. So I tell the guy, 'That thing's gotta go in back, it's too big for the seat. There's an extra charge for that.' He just shrugs, so I get out and the two of us pick it up and put it in the trunk of the cab."

"You see his face that time?"

"Yeah, I got a look."

"You remember it?"

"I think so."

"How old was he?"

"Around thirty."

"What was he wearing?"

"Jeans. High top sneakers, I think."

"Did he speak with any kind of accent?"

"Accent? No."

"How heavy was the trunk when you picked it up?"

"Plenty heavy. Without the handles, we couldn't'a managed it."

"You ever lift something that weighs a hundred pounds?"

"Me and my kid put the air conditioner in the window every year. That weighs sixty, seventy pounds. This was heavier."

"What then?"

"The guy tells me to drive over to Southern Boulevard. I cruise alongside the Botanical Gardens, and he tells me to keep going and turn up Mosholu Parkway."

"You didn't ask for an address?"

"No. A lotta time people go by sight, you know? A few blocks up Mosholu, he tells me to make a U-turn and let him out on the other side."

"You helped him heft the trunk again?"

"Yeah. We put it down on the sidewalk a little ways down from the corner."

"Corner of Bainbridge?"

"I think so."

"You saw his face again, then?"

"Not as good as before. It was dark, because of the trees. The darkest part of the block."

"See anyone else around?"

"No."

"How'd he pay you?"

"With a ten. I left him standing there on the sidewalk."

"You remember anything else he said? Did he talk to you in the cab?"

"Just once. I lit up and he said the smoke bothered him."

"What'd you do?"

The cabby gave a sickly smile. "I must've been nuts. I told him, 'Too bad.' I mean the windows were open. I already put myself out for this guy."

"What'd he say to that?"

"Nothing. He had his head half out the window. Jesus, he could of killed me."

Rizzo said, "We've got a guy in custody that we think is the guy you picked up. Do you think you could recognize this guy in a line-up?"

"I suppose so."

"Why don't we do that, then? That's all we need from you now is an I.D. You can handle that, right?"

Rodriquez nodded.

"They're probably ready downstairs. Are *you* ready?"

"Listen, this guy doesn't get to see me, right?"

"Right."

"Because I don't want that. I got kids of my own to worry about. I mean, I don't even give a damn any more about any reward."

"Don't worry, you're doing the right thing."

They took him down by the back stairway. They gave him a couple of minutes to get used to the little witness room, then signaled the line-up crew and brought the cabby to the one-way window.

The precinct detectives had done a good job. They'd found four guys in the building who were LeClerc's age and build, and two of them had long or longish hair. LeClerc was on the far right. He was, to Villanova's eye, relatively inconspicuous, and had had the savvy to chill his affect.

The cabby was wary about getting close to the window. "You sure he can't see through that glass?" They reassured him. He closed in and took a long look. His eyes went over all the faces several times, then back and forth between the two on either end. Finally his gaze settled on LeClerc.

"Well?"

"That guy on the end...without his glasses, maybe."

"The guy you picked up didn't wear glasses?"

"I don't remember any glasses."

Rizzo frowned. He buzzed the line-up crew and had LeClerc remove his glasses.

The cabby studied LeClerc some more. "Looks like him," he said.

"You sure?"

"No."

"Got to be sure. Take as long as you want."

Rodriquez took another long look. Villanova could feel Rizzo starting to climb out of his skin.

"It *looks* like him," Rodriquez said at last, "but I don't think it's him."

"No?" Rizzo said. "Look again. You want him to turn?"

The cabby frowned through the glass, then shook his head. He stepped back from the window and directed that worried face toward Rizzo and Villanova. "I'd like to help you guys, really. But I couldn't swear that's the guy I had in my cab last night."

"You don't have to swear it."

"I can't. Sorry."

Rizzo let out his breath. "You got nothing to apologize for. We're used to this. Don't worry, you can still help us. I'll take you upstairs to our artist, and we'll put together a little sketch. It only takes a few minutes. Then we'll take a ride and you can show us where you picked up that guy last night. And we'll want you to look at a trunk and make sure you recognize it."

"All right."

Rizzo turned a glum face to Villanova. "What do you think we should do with our friend LeClerc? Sit on him awhile?"

"We'll learn more if we let him take some line."

Rizzo nodded. "Take care of it for me, will you, Buddy, while I do this? Just make sure the bastard doesn't get seriously lost."

"No problem. You okay?" The color was off in Rizzo's face.

"Yeah, I'm all right. I just smelled blood, that's all. You know."

"Sure, I know."

Gilman and LeClerc were the only ones left in the line-up room by the time Villanova got around the corridor. He waved Gilman out and told LeClerc he was going home. If LeClerc was relieved, he didn't show it.

"One last thing," Villanova said. "Those crates you tried to bounce off my head before, what were you planning to do with them?"

"Put stuff in them," LeClerc said.

"Thinking of moving out of that place on Bathgate?"

"Maybe. Temporarily."

"Where to?"

LeClerc scrutinized him. "You going to stop me?"

"It depends. Tell me more."

"I leave Saturday morning. An artist's colony. I got a four week residency."

"Good for you. Which one?"

"MacDowell."

Villanova nodded. "Congratulations."

"You know MacDowell?"

"Sure. Not much trouble a person can get into up in Peterborough, even you. Just stay handy between now and Saturday, or we'll make life tough for you."

LeClerc was still studying him, his eyes close-set and opaque behind the lenses.

"By the way," Villanova said, "you always wear those glasses?"

"Can't see without 'em. Nada. Say, you're not the Villanova who writes for the *Spectrum*?"

"Probably not."

"Shit! I read your stuff."

"Come on, I'll get you to the outside. You want a ride? A precinct car'll drop you off." He steered LeClerc out of the room and down the corridor toward the duty desk.

LeClerc smirked. "Now it all makes sense. That stuff you wrote on Bensonhurst... the Goetz case, Howard Beach... you're a scream. You're like Kierkegaard and Emerson and Colin Wilson rolled into one. Shit, I was right. 'Sacrificial emblems'! What a riot."

"Yeah, well, keep laughing."

"Hey, no offense. You're a guy with ideas. We oughta have a talk some time, seriously."

Villanova walked up to the desk and told the duty man to get LeClerc a lift home.

"I don't need a ride," LeClerc said. "I'll get myself home."

"Suits me fine."

"What's eating *you*?"

"I don't know. Don't you think maybe you oughta stick around an extra day or two for your girlfriend's funeral? You know, a gesture. As if she meant something to you."

LeClerc looked uncertain.

"She's going into the ground, you know. Everything's over for her. This is the girl you spent a few months looking at in the Ramskellar, remember?"

For the first time LeClerc looked troubled.

"I mean the girl was good to you, wasn't she?"

"You're going to fuck it up on me, aren't you? MacDowell."

A ripple of disgust slid through Villanova's insides. He left LeClerc standing there.

Upstairs, he found Rizzo alone in his office, drinking his cold coffee. There was a fresh composite sketch on the desk in front of him. Villanova took a look. It was a slightly shaggier, slightly uglier version of the last one. "Where's the cabby?" he said

"Back in the john. He wasn't made for this stuff. What about LeClerc?"

"He's heading up to New Hampshire to paint."   He flopped into a chair and lit a cigarette.

"You tired, Buddy?"

"Dead." But it was disgust more than fatigue that had drained him. The investigation had so far failed to give him back the Elizabeth Albano he'd seen in her parents' home, the bit of archaic perfection he'd glimpsed in the trunk on Mosholu Parkway. The world had a way of deforming things in its own image; it was a nasty and stingy place.

"Still and all, we're in pretty good shape," Rizzo said. "The body in the trunk had to come from somewhere real close to where the cabby made the pickup. We'll know where in half an hour. After that, there's nothing between us and the guy with the long hair. We'll have him by morning."

Villanova nodded. Rizzo had his own way of feeling, his own system of rage, reaction, endurance. He had an instinct for channeling his emotions and playing the game to win. The only part of him a case like this could really mess with was his ego. The clock said 2:05 A.M., and he was sharp-eyed and flushed with energy, just hitting his stride.

"I mean, we've got the thing in hand now," Rizzo said. "We've got all the girl's movements down, from her house to Mount Saint Mary's to a broken appointment at the college to LeClerc's apartment. We know what she was planning to do when she left LeClerc's. Within the next quarter hour, she was dead. How much ground could she cover in a quarter hour? Everything's there."

"I don't need a pep talk, I need *coffee*."

"Okay, Buddy." Rizzo looked at his watch. "It's too late now for door-to-door, got to wait till morning. We'll have to stake out the vicinity of the building. Think you can stay awake?"

"Read my lips: *coffee!*"

"We'll stake out the whole damn street. By seven-thirty, I want to be shaking that block down. I want to catch that sonofabitch still in bed. Hey, didn't I tell you we're doing good? Twenty-four hours ago *you* were home in bed."

"Don't remind me."

"Aw, cheer up, Buddy." Rizzo put the lid on his coffee and closed up the box of doughnuts. "Tell you one thing that bothers me, though. That girl Elizabeth had class. What was she doing with losers like McVicar and LeClerc?"

"At least LeClerc's got testicles of his own," Villanova grumbled. "I'll take his brand of nastiness over McVicar's any day."

Rizzo smiled. "That's what I like about working with you. What's on your face has nothing to do with what comes out of your mouth. Jesus, where the hell's that cabby?"

Just as Rizzo spoke those words, Rodriquez came around the partition.

A light rain was falling when they got out to the car. They drove down the black sheen of Park Avenue, wipers slapping across the windshield, each man lost in his own thoughts.   Nothing moved anywhere, except one lone pedestrian on the unsheltered side of the street, barely visible against the dark barricade of the Penn Central tracks. Villanova caught a glimpse of him as they passed, his face closed, his body hunched against the rain, everything about him solitary, defiant, and miserable.   It was Jack LeClerc.

- FOUR -

The rain drummed on the roof of the Plymouth most of the night. They sat at the curb alongside a pile of garbage bags about fifty yards below the torn-up section of 185th where the cabby had picked up the trunk. Villanova smoked and thought, Rizzo talked, and the two of them picked away at the doughnuts until they were all gone.

Villanova had a liking for black, rainy nights. He liked the serenity and inertia of nighttime in general, but he particularly liked the rainstorms, snowfalls, deep freezes, and other cataclysms that periodically dampened the city's insanity and obscured the line between good people and bad. He liked being reminded that human beings are isolated with a violent and indifferent Nature, a truth easy to forget in a city blind to the cold light of the stars. He liked the eerie way his thoughts floated in the zone above analysis and judgment when he looked down a lamplit slum block like 185th Street in the rain.

That mood carried him halfway through the vigil. Then, suddenly, he felt immensely tired. He reminded himself that, with luck, the frantic part of this investigation would be over in a few hours. He reminded himself that Rizzo had probably gone without sleep a day longer than he had. His head began to ache.

Rizzo's conversation had grown thin and flat. Rizzo could rattle on at length about investigations he'd worked on, about the Mets, Knicks, Rangers, Jets, and sometimes about women. In the last case, especially when he was bored, he might slip into an extravagant style, as if he were hoping to tease himself awake. It had taken Villanova a while to understand that he wasn't boasting, that his bemused tone was sincere. Rizzo was a guy with a talent for the bizarre, and his romantic escapades were, for him, genuine marvels full of contradiction and wonder.

"How's that good-looking editor, that Mary Alice?" Rizzo asked somewhere along toward dawn. "You and she ever get together?"

"Hell no, we're just friends."

"That's all? You must be good and tight with that chick who lives downstairs from you, then. Ralphie's ex. What's-her-name, Helen."

"Tight enough, I guess."

"Is it true what they say about nurses?"

"What do they say about nurses?"

Rizzo laughed. "Hey, who you kidding? I was there at Ralphie's wake, remember?"

Villanova remembered, and his cheeks burned. He and Helen had done something grossly indiscreet in the parking lot of Grippi and Sons Funeral Home, and everyone had heard them. For *him* it was an indiscretion, anyway...for *her*, the kind of rash manifesto he still hadn't quite gotten used to.

"She's a dish, if you want my opinion," Rizzo said. "Especially in that uniform. And smart, too. Way too smart for a jerk like Ralphie. Now *there* was a mismatch."

"You said it. One of the great unsolved mysteries."

"I mean, I never noticed how much was going on in that head of hers, till I talked to her one time. She always

came off, you know, a little ditzy. But boy, I was wrong.
There's one serious woman. Serious as hell, underneath it all."
    "Yeah, well, she's got a hell of a serious job. Sick kids,
and all." It struck Villanova that the people with the grimmest
vocations were often the ditziest ones in their off hours. He
conjured Helen's face, the guileless, open quality of it, the
freckled nose, the innocuous blue eyes fringed by blondish
curls, and decided that the serious mode was the truer one and
the one he liked best, even if it scared him.
    Rizzo looked across the seat. "You guys shacked up
yet, or what? The word is, there was a broad in your bed when
we woke you up yesterday morning."
    Villanova reached for his cigarettes. "Forget me, pal,
what about you? What's new?"
    Rizzo smiled. "Me? Oh, not too much." He stretched
and yawned.   "There's this lady shrink, Daphne.   You
remember the Ferraro case? Well, the D.A. brought in this
new forensic psychologist."
    "And you hit on her?"
    "She had the eye for me, Buddy."
    "Yeah, you always say that."
    "Not always. Well, it's *true*. But this one here, she was
coy about it at first. You know, she's living with some guy,
another shrink. 'Does there *have* to be the kiss?' she says
when I got hold of her, in her office. As if it's embarrassing,
you know, to follow that old script. 'Well, we could skip step
one and two,' I told her. I don't mean to say she was easy. Far
from it. A classy woman, as a matter of fact. Soft-spoken,
does volunteer work in a woman's shelter, teaches part-time at
Pace. Likes to dress...hip, but expensive. And lots of
sensitivity, you know, the social conscience stuff. Thirty-five
years old, married once, father's a doctor. 'Does there *have* to
be the kiss?' she says, and two hours later she's giving it to me
in the car, up and down. Right here on this seat, I'm getting

her from behind, and her head's twisted down there by the armrest. She gets an earring looped around the door handle, would you believe it?"

"Ouch. Must have been a big earring."

"A regular hoop, some kinda Mexican thing. And I haven't even got her unsnagged before she's already started with the guilt, the boyfriend and the trust and all."

"Well, you stopped yourself to unsnag her, *that's* something."

"No, I finished first and then I unsnagged her. *She* was the one that didn't want to stop."

There was a time when Villanova had wondered whether meanness was the point of these stories. Now he knew that the animation that came into Rizzo's voice was not from glee, but from genuine amazement at the ways of some of the women he met, especially their sudden lusts.

"So I start seeing her once, twice a week. We go out to eat around Port Washington, Glen Cove, and have a great time, and then we go to her place. Coupla times she cooked for me."

"I thought she was living with a guy."

"She's got a little house in Bayside, and he's got a place down in Chelsea, and they take turns sleeping over, see? So I fit in on odd days, as long as she can get downtown before midnight or so. First thing she decides to do is break up with the guy, anyway, but I talk her out of *that*."

"She knows you're married, right?"

"Sure. But she gets a little starry-eyed, *you* know, on top of the usual complaints: the guy's divorce-scarred, he's committment-shy, and so on. But the main thing is the guilt. She doesn't like 'deceiving' him. Better to dump him, I suppose. Anyway, after a bit, the whining quiets down, and for a coupla months she's merrily banging away with me, she's buying negligees, garter belts, all this shit from Frederick's.

'Lace Whispers,' 'Garden of Paradise,' she knows all the names. 'Midnight Fantasy, this one's a favorite with transvestites,' she says. The woman testifies in sex-offense cases, she's an expert."

"Then what?"

"Then comes the problem with the dog. She's got this runty little dog named Max, a chihuahua or something, it's like a hundred years old, all shriveled up. I get sick to my stomach just to look at it, but she's nuts about it, she's had this mutt since junior high school. I mean, it's got a face like an ugly old man, and she kisses it on the lips. Every time I come in the house it snarls at me, like 'What're *you* here for?' And then one day she wants to let the dog into the yard to pee before we go into the bedroom, and she lets it out the back door, and I'm standing by the front window looking into the street, and I see the dog heading down the street. So I figure the dog must know what it's doing."

"Uh-oh."

"Right. Coupla minutes later, she's calling and calling 'Max!' out the back door, and then she goes out in the yard, and then she comes back in all upset and says she can't find him and the gate is open. 'Course it's *me* who didn't shut it right when I came in. One second later there's this screech of brakes."

"I don't want to hear this."

"Right. I'm thinking, 'road pizza.' We run outside, and it turns out the dog was never touched."

"Christ."

"Dead, but never touched. A clean miss, and the dog keeled over with a heart attack."

"You sonofabitch!"

"As God is my witness! And she's sobbing over this...this *rat* with big ears. Me, I'm standing there like a dope. And who do you think gets the job of schlepping the little stiff over to the vet? Eighty bucks for a cremation! But wait, there's more. After a while, she gets over the dog thing, see. Then one night we're banging away in her bed, and when I leave, she walks me out to my car and says, 'By the way, I'm getting married.' I'm a little stunned, but I play it cool. 'Congratulations. When?' I say. 'Next Saturday.'"

"Just like that?"

"Just like that."

"To the guy from Chelsea?"

"Right."

"Ahh--he felt the vibes, I'll bet."

"You got it. Guys sense when they're losing their hold. They get pressured into making a move."

"And when was all this?"

"Last week Monday."

"Okay. So?"

"So I bought her a wedding present. A set of earrings, big platinum hoops. I brought them over Friday night and we fucked each other silly. She tells me all about the wedding, how fancy it's going to be, all the little traditions, the gown and the flower girl and how the bridegroom isn't going to see her till eleven the next morning. I ask her to let me see the gown, and she takes it out of the closet, and I make a fuss over it and, just on a whim, I ask her to put it on for me. She makes me turn my back first, but I can see her perfect in the mirror. Then I turn around, and, let me tell you, I don't have to pretend my oohs and aahs. I mean, she was really something in that dress. Beautiful."

"Let me guess what happened next."

"Right. And before you know it, it's three in the morning. I wind up sleeping over for the first and last time."

"So you made love to this Daphne woman on her wedding day."

"That's the in and out of it. Crazy, isn't it? Once a woman says she loves you, she throws the rulebook out the window."

"She said she loved you?"

"Yeah, coupla times. You know, it's funny, when she put on that wedding dress and stood there looking at me..."

"Yeah?"

"I don't know. She got a look on her face."

"What kind of look?"

"Sad, sorta. Wistful." Rizzo shrugged.

"You going to see her again?"

"That's up to her, I guess." There was a pause, and then, to Villanova's surprise, a sigh. "You know what, Buddy? I'm gonna miss her. I miss her already."

Another pause.

"I think I blew it."

Villanova waited for Rizzo to take himself off the hook. After a moment he said, "That's some story."

"Isn't it?"

It wasn't the first tale of this type that Rizzo had told, though it stood out. Respectable women of his own generation were Rizzo's prey of choice, and, since most of them were married, impromptu lovemaking, fantastic deceptions, horrific near-misses had become the banalities of his campfire saga. But the Daphne story had a special poignancy. Rizzo's married lovers were always very game, full of appetite, and torn between shamelessness and guilt, and he didn't always come away unscathed himself. The awe he felt at their double natures seemed like an oblique acknowledgment of his own; a kind of dread came with it. A couple of times Rizzo had been in bed with a woman while she carried on a phone conversation with her husband, and, by reflex, he'd taken to phoning his own wife several times a day to "say hello." She was always where she was supposed to be.

Villanova had met Rizzo's wife only once, and that by mischance. She was attractive, and had the kind of old-fashioned grace he'd always appreciated. Rizzo cared about her, and none of his adventuring seemed to come from rage or spite. He liked to shrug and say he took orders from his testicles, but Villanova, giving him more credit, thought of his lust as more metaphysical than physical, a form of reckless curiosity. He was one of those grown men for whom the female secret stays as compelling as it is in boyhood, and sucks into itself all the profounder mysteries of existence. Rizzo had the religious thirst and energy of a poet, and the same kind of obsession with the transcendent. The more his profession drew him into the world of illusion and its vague traces, the more he craved contact with some eternal verity, and it made sense to Villanova that all his deeper energy should finally focus on something as symbolic as Woman. In the case of Daphne, he seemed to have made the splendid tumble into the personal. Villanova wondered how long it would take him to get over her.

"You're quiet, Buddy. Whatcha thinking?"

"Oh, I'm thinking about you and the chihuahua. I'm thinking, can this be the same guy who got his eyebrows singed saving an armload of pups?"

"It was kittens. *You* were doing the pups. That was a night, Jesus!"

"It sure was." It was the night of the pet store fire, when the hardware emporium over on Westchester Avenue had gone up, and the pet shop next door with it. He and Rizzo had picked up the call and got there before anyone, and made eight or ten runs scooping up the animals--the cute ones first, then the hamsters, gerbils, birds, rats, mice, and turtles in that order. The lizards and snakes came last, the fish got left behind in their tanks to poach.

"We coulda been heroes that night, Buddy, except some genius got the bright idea to dump all the animals in the precinct car."

"Where else was there to put 'em? How'd I know they were going to shit all over everything?"

"What do you *think* is going to happen when you put scared dogs and cats together? You cost the City of New York a few thousand bucks, there." The car, with shit in every crack, vent, and ashtray, had been retired. "And that's why I'm riding around in *this* piece of crap."

"You *like* this piece of crap."

"I like my mother-in-law's ass."

Villanova closed his eyes. He was very tired, and his head throbbed. The lump LeClerc had given him felt bigger than ever. He was cold, too. In fact, he was downright miserable. This was the black core of the hunt, the time of night shivers, the surreal time when stalker and prey alike measured themselves against the real enemy, the cold, empty universe. He wanted to sleep. He knew Rizzo wouldn't. It was all a fight now against the suction of chaos upon the thin text of artifacts, statements, motives, ends. Somewhere in one of these rooms facing the street, a man with a fresh murder on his soul lay dreaming. Or maybe LeClerc, McVicar, the girl in the trunk were a dream. In the dark, it took an effort to make the separation. Hunters hunting hunters, it was a nice joke-- the great caper, the almighty Sex Crime in the high church of philandery, with the white-robed choir of lechers, cads, panderers, sadists, and temple whores singing away. He just wanted to sleep.

But he didn't. At six o'clock the rain stopped and the sky turned a dirty red; at half-past, the street began to stir. At seven, Rizzo turned to him and said, "This is going to be a bitch without coffee."

"One of us could take a run down to the bodega."

"No, let's just do it."

Eyes burning, they stepped out into the haze of Thursday morning, and everything dream-like about the night vigil rose up and away with the mist. With copies of the sketch and photo in hand, they walked on stiff legs up toward the excavation. The orange-and-white barriers belonged to Con Ed, but someone must have hit a sewer pipe, because the whole pit stunk. That message wasn't lost on Villanova, who thought of the work he was about to do as a backwards form of prospecting.

They stuck to the north side and started with the tenement closest to the pit. The first hour of door-to-door was, for Villanova, a refresher course in slum canvassing: the frightened, hostile, damaged, brutish, sly, pathetic, and sometimes beautiful faces that materialized behind the chained, barred, triple-locked doors; the abundance of children and big dogs, the dusky light and bad odor of over-peopled places; the blind, deaf, amnesic denizens of each microscopic world, who truthfully didn't know the names of the people down the hall and had never set eyes on the ones who lived over their heads.

At 8:10, two tenements over, they had their first lead. Someone knew of a psychic in the next building who saw clients in her apartment. She was a healer, a highly regarded practitioner in the Hispanic community; word of mouth brought her patrons from all over, even from outside the Wedge.

At 8:20 they hit paydirt.

An old woman in a first-floor rear apartment recognized the composite drawing of the long-haired man. He lived two flights up directly over her apartment, he was a sullen, dangerous-looking character, he had a bad eye for women, and she had told her granddaughters many times to stay away from him. He lived with his mother, who was rarely seen outside the apartment, and who, the old woman believed, was a psychic.

There was more. On Tuesday night, while The Tonight Show was on the T.V., the old woman had heard a strange noise in the stairwell. She'd gone to her peep-hole, which overlooked the landing, and seen the long-haired man bumping what looked like a trunk down the stairs. He was struggling with the weight of it, trying not to make noise. The old woman pointed out the traces he'd left on the steps. Scrape marks were still visible on the lips of the treads.

Rizzo showed her the photograph of Elizabeth Albano. She'd never seen the girl.

The old woman was so eager to see the guy upstairs hauled away that she let them glance around her apartment to get a fix on the layout. The fire escape hung off the back bedroom.

They thanked her and went up. The stairwell ran box-fashion around a dumbwaiter shaft, so that every turn was a blind one. Each landing had one meager light. It was easy to see why Elizabeth Albano would have been afraid to come into this building.

Apartment 3-B faced the stairs, and while Rizzo rang the bell, Villanova was able to hunker down a few steps below the landing and check the slit of daylight under the door. No one answered. It was still pretty early. Rizzo gave the door a pounding. He kept one hand inside his jacket where his Police Special hung in a shoulder holster. Villanova watched the slit and saw a shadow approach the door. He signaled to Rizzo, who pounded on the door again and shouted "Police!" The shadow moved again, then froze. Rizzo drew his .38. Villanova crept up to the landing, positioned himself, and threw his 170 pounds into a kick alongside the knob. He didn't expect that to work the first time--several locks would have been the rule in this sort of place--but the jamb splintered and the door flew back against the wall with a crash. "Police!" Rizzo roared at the same time. A big grey tabby with its back up and its hair bristling spat at them and fled out of sight into the inner rooms. The odor of fresh paint rushed out at them. There wasn't anything else.

Nothing. Not a stick of furniture, not a trace of a wall hanging, a carpet, a curtain, a carton of trash. The place was stripped, scrubbed, and gleaming with new paint. "Shit!" Rizzo cried. "Do you believe this?"

Villanova had nothing to say. His pounding heart had just begun its plummet.

"Twenty-four goddam hours! It's a plot. Could *anybody* have got here faster than we did?"

A bitter taste seeped into Villanova's mouth. When it came to disappointment, he was always a little behind Rizzo.

"It shoulda been ours, Buddy. It shoulda been *ours!*"

Villanova walked around the rooms. Everything was clean, even the kitchen. The refrigerator was running, but empty and spotless. The cat crouched atop it, watching. It looked timid now. It was a young, fine-looking cat with big green eyes. "Maybe the guy's not through here yet. Maybe he's coming back for the cat."

"That's asking too much."

"Maybe we kicked in the wrong door."

"Stop dreaming, will ya, Buddy?"

"Maybe the place was like this when the girl showed up. We could be walking on the evidence."

"Forget it, the paint's still wet. Look at this, every goddam inch of floor's swept up. I'm telling you, this guy's *outta* here. It's a fucking conspiracy!"

There was a noise down below in the stairwell. "Hey!" a man's voice shouted up the stairs.

"He's coming up!" Villanova said.

"Relax, Buddy, my gut tells me that's the Super."

"*Hey!*" the man called again.

They spread out and waited for him, and Rizzo got out his badge and gun. The guy came flying up to the landing brandishing a baseball bat. He was a twig of a guy, a young Hispanic with a mop of curly hair.

"Chill out, pal, we're cops!" Rizzo barked at him as he came through the door. "Put the bat down!"

"What the hell's goin' on?"

"Put the fuckin' bat down! You the Super?"

"Yeah. Who busted the door? Jesus, that's a new lock! That's a twenty-four dollar lock!"

They told him what was up, and he quieted down. He'd taken them for punks breaking in to steal. "The sinks, the stove, the pipes, the sonsabitches'll steal anything!"

They showed him the sketch and the photo. Elizabeth's face meant nothing to him, but he knew the long-haired man. His name was Manny Cruz, and until a day ago he had lived in this apartment with his mother Julia.

"So where are they now?"

Rizzo was right. Cruz and his mother were gone, moved out, like most of the people in these tenements, in the middle of the night, owing rent, owing electric bills, and without forwarding addresses. Vamoosed in the wee hours of Wednesday morning with their shopping bags and cardboard boxes, leaving behind a few worthless bits of furniture and cookware. The Super and his brothers had finished stripping and repainting the apartment last night.

"What's the rush to clean up?" Rizzo said.

"I got a cousin just got married. They don't got a place yet, they're on their honeymoon. It's a surprise for them."

"What about this Manny Cruz? What do you know about him?"

"A creep. Walks funny, never looks you in the eye. Something wrong with him."

"Retarded?"

"No, a sicko. A creep, you know what I mean?"

"Did he have a job?"

"Who knows? Welfare, maybe. For two years, they paid the rent, that's all. Just this month they were short, first time."

"And the mother?"

"Did her business from the house. Nice woman, Mrs. Cruz. Very nice. Stayed in a lot. Sick, I think."

"When'd you see them last?"

"Mrs. Cruz, not for a while. The son, my wife saw on Monday night, going into the house with empty boxes. That's a tip-off, see? First thing Wednesday, I came up to collect. I shoulda waited that long. Poof, they were gone. The thing is, I figured Mrs. Cruz wouldn't do that. She's a nice woman, you know?" He shook his head.

"Who's the cat belong to?" Villanova said.

"That's Mrs. Cruz's cat."

"You mean this nice woman left her cat?"

The Super shrugged. "That's what they do when they take off quick like that. They don't leave stuff they can use, that's for sure."

"What *did* they leave?" Rizzo said. "Where's their stuff?"

"In the bin out front. The dumpster. But it's empty now. Pickup was yesterday afternoon."

"You threw their stuff in the Con Ed dumpster?"

"Sure. Those guys don't care."

"Shit, *that* makes things tough. You're a helluva eager-beaver. You want to be a millionaire, don't you."

"Hey, I got four kids. I got a lotta family to take care of. Listen, I run three buildings, they all make money."

"Great. You remember what kind of stuff you threw out?"

"It was just crap. Coupla beat up dressers, bed frames, a few dishes, like that. Whole buncha holy pictures and little statues of saints. If there was something good, I woulda kept it. One thing was a mattress, brand new. But I picked it up, it was wet underneath, it stunk of piss. I threw it out."

"Piss? You sure?"

"I put my hand right on it."

"The cat?"

"How's the cat gonna wet upside down? Anyway, the cat pees in the bathroom, under the sink. I had to put a box for him. That's just for today, though. I don't need any cat. He goes out."

Villanova said, "What do you mean 'out'?"

"Out in the street."

"That's no street cat."

The Super shrugged. "A cat's a cat."

Rizzo said, "What about any papers or books or letters? Did you save anything like that?"

The Super shook his head. "If it was worth anything, I woulda, believe me. Those people busted the door lock on me too."

"That right?" Rizzo said.

"Broke the key off in it. Maybe that's why they took off, who knows? Cost me twenty-four dollars. Now I got another busted lock." He made a wry face.

"What'd you do with the old one?"

"In the dumpster."

"You remember seeing anything like a gold chain when you were cleaning up? A gold chain with a little gold crucifix on it?"

The Super gave a shrug and a shake of his head. "Like I said, if there was something good, I woulda kept it."

"What room was the mattress in?"

"The little one."

"Show me where all the furniture was. Everything you can remember. Where were the beds?"

The Super complied. There were only two rooms besides the kitchen, and it was not hard to deduce how they'd been used. The larger room had held the woman's day bed and dresser and the table where she sat with clients. The tiny back bedroom was her son's, and there couldn't have been much more in it than a bed. Villanova stood in that room awhile and tried to get a feel of it. He tried to feel exactly what Elizabeth would have felt. He stood inside the freshly-painted closet. He opened the window blinds and looked through the bars of the grate at the nearby windows from which someone might have seen something. He studied the angles of the brick walls, and listened while Rizzo went on with the questioning in the other room. He took a look through the rusting fire escape into the maze of alleys below. There was something depressingly familiar about the sight.

He parted the slats of the blinds for a better view. What he saw shook him good.

He stood there a minute, his scalp tingling. He could hear Rizzo's voice rattling off the questions: "You see any damage before you fixed up? Any sign of a fight, bloodstains, damaged furniture, marks on the wall?" The Super's voice answered no. Villanova turned away from the window and faced the little room. A phantom image of Elizabeth Albano hovered in the open doorway. She looked at him with that little crease in her brow, those slightly parted lips, that expression of dread mixed with despair. Her eyes, full of pleading, stared right into his, and through them, as if she yearned to escape through that barred window behind him. She faded, and vanished.

He crossed into the other room. "You know any friends or relatives of these Cruz people?" Rizzo was asking the Super. "Was anyone in the building friendly with them?"

The Super shook his head.

"Any idea where they might have moved to? Any idea where they lived before they came here?"

Again the Super shook his head.

Rizzo told him to go about his business while they went over the place.

"Who's gonna pay for the busted door?" the Super said.

"Don't worry about that."

The Super left, and Villanova stood facing Rizzo in the larger room where Julia Cruz had read people's palms, auras, dreams, and hearts. They didn't talk for a minute. Villanova was glad that his own aura was invisible, that no one could see how dark his heart was. He felt a helpless rage at the room itself.

"Okay, Buddy," Rizzo spoke up at last. He drew a deep breath. "First, we get a forensic team in here and work the place over, and we get up a sketch of Julia Cruz. Then we get Gilman to work through our psycho files for the son, and we get a subpoena to hit the records in Bronx Psychiatric and Manhattan Psychiatric under the name Cruz. Hey, remember the old days, when we could get those records just for the asking?"

"Yeah, I remember," Villanova muttered.

Rizzo's eyes roamed the room. "Meanwhile, we'll scope out the Post Office, the phone company, Con Ed, Social Services, Unemployment. People don't move into a new place without tickling a computer somewhere. We've got a name and a description, we're in the driver's seat."

"You know how many Cruzes there are in New York?"

"Come on, Buddy, cheer up. What's the matter, you need some sleep? Soon's we get back to the squadroom, I'll have Gilman track down this phone exchange and check it against the LUD sheets for the Albano phone. And we'll get the canvassing squad to work on the real estate agents. We'll focus on the Wedge, then Morrisania, then Melrose and Mott Haven. Furnished rentals first--these people walked outa here with what they could carry. In fact, we'll set up a one-man stakeout right here, in case anyone comes a-calling. I say we nail our man in a day, two tops." He stopped to ponder, rubbing his chin and giving a pull to the skin of his throat. "Only one thing bothers me..."

"What's that?"

"No one saw the girl. We've got the psychic, we've got the guy with the long hair, we've got the trunk. What we don't have is something that says the girl was here, in this place, LUD sheets or no LUD sheets. We don't have something that proves the people in this place ever laid eyes on her."

"Oh, yes, we do," Villanova said quietly.

"And, Christ, I don't think I could take it if we went sideways again. I mean, what if some smart-ass defense lawyer wants to argue the the girl's body was stashed in the trunk *after* it was dumped on Mosholu Parkway."

"The girl was here. This is where she died."

Rizzo eyed him. "You know that, hah?"

"Yeah."

"You gonna tell me how?"

Villanova nodded. He led the way into the back room and yanked up the window blinds.

In the far corner of the alley below, cropped and framed by the walls of the neighboring buildings and the back ends of the Bathgate Avenue tenements, a piece of Jack LeClerc's street mural glowed in the morning light. The upcast eyes of Elizabeth Albano stared straight into Manny Cruz's window.

- FIVE -

4951 Bainbridge Avenue was not the peaceful old house it seemed. It was the last of the original clapboard homes on a street of middle-aged tenements, with a fenced patch of sooty ivy in front, a big detached garage and a scraggly vegetable garden in back, and the moribund look of an old homestead in which two aged pioneers wait out the final conquest of brick and mortar. Porches and all, it didn't seem much bigger than any other old house, and yet there were at least fifteen rooms under its gabled rooves, and six or seven noisy, combative, blood-related families living in them.

The Marinelli clan had lived in the Bronx since the days when most of the streets east of the Bronx River were still just lines on a map, since the days when there were fish worth eating in Van Cortland Lake, and enough of the old Mohican hunting grounds intact so that an ambitious hiker could stay mainly in the woods and finish the day with a swim all the way up at Tibbetts Brook. The house itself was of somewhat newer vintage: Marinelli, the patriarch, a Wall Street messenger through the stock market boom and crash, had had the good fortune to fall down an open elevator shaft in the brand new Majestic apartment house, survive a coma, and use his payoff to build a place of his own in '31 up in the sprawling new northern county. He'd filled the house with married sons--the eldest of whom had jobs for life as doormen at the Majestic and the Century--lived quietly with his wife in the garret, and died at 89. When his wife died two years later, the grasping siblings and squalling cousins in the rooms below had quickly put the garret to let, and a cousin by marriage, Anthony Rizzo, who was wise enough to live several neighborhoods away, had supplied a new friend and colleague as a tenant.

Villanova, once he was used to the place, dubbed it "the Topless Towers" after the splendid kinsmen's city built by the ancient Trojans. He liked the view from the garret windows, and imagined old man Marinelli standing there like grandsire Priam at the battlements of Troy, exhorting his fifty stalwart sons to hold back the besieging urban horde. He imagined the old man's loyal wife, with her "lank and all o'er-teemed loins," standing at his side. The house on Bainbridge Avenue brought out the finest of Villanova's irony. It was an eclectic monstrosity with a wholly decadent infrastructure: a Gothic heating system that worked on alternate days, Baroque wiring that blew fuses left and right, Rococo plumbing with almost no pressure--to take a shower, he had to balance on one leg and hold in a button on the faucet with his toe. The people who lived there, drinkers, grifters, pilferers, and professional malingerers on the municipal payroll, were basically decent to him, the outsider, and had even come to look up to him. They thought he was smart and pressed him into arbiting their squabbles, which ran to violence, police sirens, orders of protection, the works. From the start they couldn't agree who should collect his rent or how much it should be; *they* paid nothing but the tax bill, and brawled over that every year to boot. He didn't know for sure how he was cast in their epic, but was mindful that all the Trojan warriors worth their salt were doomed men. He only wanted to write his column, satisfy his clients, take his walks, read, watch movies on the VCR, and be left alone. His walks took him west to the Jerome Park reservoir and the cottage where Poe had written requiems for his dying wife; north to the Woodlawn Cemetery, or along the stream the Indians had called Mosholu up to Vault Hill where Washington's rear guard had burned campfires to trick the redcoats; east to the Bronx River, Agassiz Lake, and the glacier-scarred ridges of Bronx Park; south to the Zoo, the Rocking Stone, the University, and the tawdry bustle of Fordham Road. Among the consolations of these jaunts was the fresh conviction that, whatever the script, a wooden horse could never get through that rugged terrain.

There was, however, one other interloper living in the Topless Towers, and by astonishing coincidence her name was Helen. She was a spunky, down-to-earth, honey-haired woman of thirty-four, and Villanova, encouraged by Rizzo, had rashly gone to bed with her before considering her namesake's perilous status.

Helen, who worked as a pediatric nurse at Montefiore Hospital, was the wife of Marinelli's youngest son, Ralphie. Ralphie was a forty-five year old macho loudmouth who'd been living for years with a mistress a few blocks away, and who, true to family tradition, had been indicted for embezzlement, just a few weeks before Villanova had moved into the tribal homestead. Also true to tradition, Ralphie had come down with some conveniently debilitating illness soon after his arraignment, and had only recently stopped dropping in at the Topless Towers to bully Helen around. He was showing up on crutches for his court appearances, trying to avoid a jail term for siphoning off $12,000 of Transit Authority money. Villanova was suspicious of the crutches and glad about the jail term. He'd heard a great many nasty things about Ralphie, mitigated only by the claim that he was a Mama's boy who'd gone off the edge after his mother's death. A Marinelli cousin was doing the lawyering for Ralphie, and

Rizzo, out of similar clan loyalty, was showing his N.Y.P.D. face in court to help out.

Villanova was in the courtroom with him the day of Ralphie's sentencing. To his credit, Ralphie looked convincingly ill that morning. The judge offered to give him a break if he would return the twelve thousand. Ralphie said he'd like to, but the money was spent. "On what?" "A mausoleum, your honor." "A mausoleum? Don't you Marinellis ever quit conning?" "Not for myself, your honor. For my mother." Ralphie's lawyer smiled hopefully at the judge, but the judge just gaped at him. Then he shook his head and started cranking up to lay some real pen time on Ralphie. At that point Ralphie's lawyer got to his feet and interrupted. "You can't send my client to jail, your honor." "Why not?" "The man's really sick. He's only got a few months to live." Ralphie's jaw dropped: "What're you talking about?" "It's true," the lawyer insisted to the judge. "I've got an affidavit here from his doctor." "Yeah? Who's the doctor, another Marinelli?" "His name's Endicott!" the lawyer said proudly; "Subpoena him if you want. Here, read for yourself: *stomach cancer!*" Ralphie blanched, his eyes grew wide as half-dollars: "What the hell are you talking about!" he croaked out.   "Pipe down, you," the judge told him, and went on wrangling with the lawyer. Sentencing was postponed. As it turned out, six weeks later Ralphie was dead. No one had ever told him how sick he really was. They wanted to "spare him." That was the kind of family the Marinellis were.

Villanova might not have gotten involved with Helen if he'd seen the whole picture first.   She was bright, eager, attractive, good-hearted, and so frankly amorous that he felt there was almost no choice but to have sex with her. The first time was the day he met her, the day he'd startled her white-faced in the basement of the Topless Towers, where he'd gone to do his laundry. It was a dark, spooky place, a prowler's paradise lit by one little bulb, and she'd yelped and ducked behind an old, defunct freezer-chest when he came down the steps. He'd apologized, introduced himself, calmed her down. Two hours later, he'd had her life story, and two hours after that he'd had her, in her second floor rooms; she made enough noise at the finish to goad the woman in the flat below hers to turn up the TV--*Wheel of Fortune* at maximum volume. It took another few days before he tasted her cooking, and a month before he got used to it. He did all this carelessly, venturesomely, and even aggressively, because he thought that's how things were in the Topless Towers.

So he and Helen were lovers, and Ralphie stayed helpfully sick and absent until he died. At the wake, the whole clan turned up and the florists did a good trade. The mistress came too, a nice-looking, slightly over-groomed blonde. She paid her respects to everyone, including the widow, and then took a chair alone in the back, where Rizzo spent a good deal of time consoling her. Villanova was sitting beside Helen and could feel, every time her leg touched his, how violently she was trembling. He thought she must be desperately upset, but later she whispered in his ear that it was only desire, and that he was in imminent danger of having that nice suit of his ripped off. He believed her. She was the bluntest, straightforwardest, most candidly libidinous person he'd ever met, with the most ingenious sense of timing; after three months with her he'd learned to respect the uncanny way her body had of taking over the business of protest when it came to hypocrisy. She didn't want to be at that wake any more than he did, except maybe to make a statement. He took her outside to the parking lot for some air. She was definitely overheated. She pulled him into his car, jumped out of her panties, and straddled him on the front seat--*that* was her statement. And he, deluding himself that his heart was safely uninvolved, shrugged and went along with her, forgetting, until it was too late, how loud she was when she climaxed, how her wail roamed up the scale and blossomed into a feline cry before descending in a long, jagged moan. With the back of his head he could see all those black-suited Marinellis spilling like hornets out into the parking lot. But none of them did spill out. They only stared at him when he walked Helen back inside, and one of the very old women shook her head. The mistress and Rizzo were gone from the premises, and Ralphie was exactly where they'd left him.

This was not the way Villanova fell in love with anyone. It was the way he adapted to the convoluted and headlong and often tacky world of the Marinellis. It was the way he went forward in life, moving with the things around him that were real. It was the way he shucked the courtly habits of younger days and enjoyed the mind and senses he was endowed with. He'd been around plenty of women in plenty of ways, but was the last man in the world to let his dick lead the way to a relationship of value. So Helen was, for him, a spiritual frontier, because he truly liked and admired her. He enjoyed her sense of humor, her company, her way. He liked watching her sew and crochet things for the half-dozen children who lived in the Topless Towers, he liked helping her fix light switches and leaky faucets, he liked hearing the queer phrases like "fuckin' A," "holy moley," and "absotively posilutely" that punctuated her speech. He liked the way she could switch from a silly, almost dingbat mood to a sober, insightful one in the blink of an eye. He liked talking to her, taking walks, watching movies, eating Chinese food, and joining her in the hundred quirky activities her imagination led her to. He knew she was scarred--he'd seen the scars on her legs to prove it--and, to his surprise, he liked her even better for that. He was wary of wanting such a reckless woman for himself, and so he maintained the pretense that they each dated other people, and endured with superficial good humor her prying, her forwardness, and the awful food she sometimes cooked for him with great fanfare.   She was the best friend he'd ever had, and he was happy with her and even optimistic until he remembered the man she'd been married to, and the young, sweet, angelic wife he had loved so instinctively, so wholeheartedly, and so briefly so many years ago.

* * *

When Villanova left Manny Cruz's apartment after the failed stakeout, he had only a few small things to do at Homicide Squad before he could finally get back to the Topless Towers for some sleep.

First, he called his editor on the *Spectrum*, Sally Houk. There was just enough time to make the edition, and he sketched out the story and asked for space to run a police drawing of Manny Cruz and a cutline on the Albano murder.

"Are you kidding?" Sally said.

"Just a box," he said.   "Two inches, plus an inch of copy.   It could make the difference."

"First off, we're not a crime sheet.   Second, how much straight news copy do we run, a page?"   Sally's voice came through a telephone receiver like a machine gun.

"I need three lousy inches," he said.

"Third, priorities.   Our limit is one nasty per issue, and here's what we've got to pick from this week: an eleven year old gets raped and thrown off a rooftop.   An 84 year old survivor of Auschwitz gets bound, gagged, and beaten to death by punks in his apartment.   A woman strips her children and throws them one by one out a thirteenth storey window to save them from Satan.   Three other kids are found chained to beds in their apartment, covered in filth, sexually abused, never seen the outside their whole lives.   A sixty year old woman gets dragged under the car wheels by a drive-by purse-snatcher.   A pit bull chained in a marijuana patch mauls a two year old boy to death.   A thirteen year old boy ties an eleven year old to a cellar pipe and sets him on fire. A ten year old girl is force-fed birthday cake and suffocates. Shall I go on?"

"No."

"You think the readers want chunks of quivering flesh from the arena? You're right, Savages versus Innocents is the thing in this city. But your savage is too old-fashioned, and your innocent isn't innocent enough."

"You mean she isn't ten years old."

"It isn't pretty, but that's how it is."

"You're wrong. It doesn't work if you just keep pushing the 'Ghastly' button. No one feels a goddamn thing anymore."

"So, you have theories? You've got a column, go to town. Get your copy faxed in by two o'clock, and we'll pull your Central Park piece."

"No. I can't do that."

"Then my only advice to you is to call the *News*."

He did call the *News*, and got an assistant news editor. The man blew him off. "If the girl was raped, maybe. If it was a racial thing, maybe. You've got nothing there, pal. Listen, we have our own people to cover this stuff. Believe it or not, we know what we're doing." That was that.

The next phone call Villanova had to make was to Tom Albano. He kept the conversation brief by pretending to be in a rush, and fielded Albano's questions about the investigation without opening any further wounds. His main purpose, camouflaged by a half dozen other questions, was to get the name of the family doctor. Albano, ever helpful, went to the trouble of looking up the phone number for him in his personal address book. Dr. Parisi had treated the family for two decades, he said, though no one had been ill enough to need him for years. He was a personal friend of Albano's, a fellow member of the Knights of Columbus.

Villanova's last call was to Parisi's office.   The receptionist, soft-spoken and politely formal, was helpful once she learned he was involved in the police investigation of the Albano murder.   She pulled Elizabeth's card, sighing and fretting about that poor girl's tragedy, and rattled off the date of her last visit: Thursday the tenth, only two weeks ago.

Villanova took a precinct car over to Parisi's place of business on Pelham Parkway.   The receptionist, a slight, sixty-ish woman with a sweet smile, showed him into the doctor's musty little office to wait.   He remained on his feet; the smell of doctors' offices made him uneasy.   Parisi came in a few minutes later.   He was a very short man in his late sixties, white-haired and silver-browed, slightly stooped, with brown age spots on his bare crown and strong-looking brown hands.   His eyes, behind thick, wire-rimmed glasses, were heavy-lidded, intelligent, and kind.   He wore a jacket and tie under his frock.   "How can I help you, Mr. Villanova?" he said.

Villanova told him.

If Parisi felt some special sorrow over Elizabeth's lost life, it was subsumed under the philosophical tone and resigned affect of an aged physician.   After all the horrors of disease and accident, there didn't seem to be any outrage left in those tired old eyes.   He agreed to answer Villanova's questions as best he could.

"Why did Liz come to see you two weeks back?"

"She had an acute, persistent headache.   She'd been suffering intermittenty for several weeks before she came."

"Migraine?"

"No, it didn't fit the symptomology of migraine.   I did the usual tests to eliminate neurological, allergic, infectious causes and so on.   My diagnosis was what you would have expected."

"Which is?"

"Stress induced. Ph.D. examinations, a new teaching job, an unfinished dissertation...even a yogi could have crippling headaches under that load. I gave her a sample bottle of aminotryl, a pretty powerful drug. That seemed prudent enough for a situational complaint like this one. I felt Liz would have the good sense to use it the right way."

"What are the drug's side effects?"

"Oh, there's a range of mild to moderate effects, but none that would affect behavior or mood. I didn't write her a prescription. She had just enough tablets to see her through the oral exams. Twenty-one tablets, one a day. She was supposed to make another appointment after three weeks."

"Tell me, doc, you don't see obstetrical patients, do you?"

"Just long enough to give referrals."

"Could the early stages of pregnancy cause headaches like Liz had?"

"It's possible."

"Did Liz bring up the subject with you?"

"*I* brought it up. You don't hand over something like aminotryl if there's a chance the patient is pregnant."

"Then Liz told you she *wasn't* pregnant?"

"Right." Parisi gazed levelly at Villanova. "You telling me she was?"

Villanova nodded. "Eight weeks."

Parisi pursed his lips. "If she hadn't been so certain, I'd have done the standard test, just to be sure. I mean, if only to cover all bases on the headache diagnosis." He shook his head. "I can't imagine her lying to me. I've known her all her life."

Villanova felt bad for him. "Maybe she didn't know, or wasn't sure."

"She had to know. She had to miss at least one period. In today's world, that's followed by a trip to the drugstore for a pregnancy test kit."

"Well, you can see why she'd want to keep it from you. You being a pal of her father and all."

"Sure I can see it. You've met Tom Albano, I take it." His brow furrowed. "The poor kid." He sighed and sat down behind his desk, ignoring the awful squeal made by his swivel chair. He rested his chin in his thick, brown hands. "I guess there's no mystery at all now about the nature of her headaches. *That* degree of stress, on top of her other worries..."

Villanova nodded. There was no mystery, either, to Elizabeth's interest in a spiritual healer.

"In fact, now I can understand why she seemed so strained that day, why she said a couple of the things she did. I'd just finished examining her and was chatting with her about her dissertation. I said, 'You're your father's daughter, all right.' She looked at me oddly. 'What do you mean?' she said. 'I mean the hard work, the sense of responsibility. You're just like him.' 'Yes, he thinks so too,' she said. It sounded ironic. I didn't get it, so I started to rattle on like an old fool: 'If you knew the kinds of things your father and I went through when we were your age, the ethnic prejudices, the hardships,' etc., etc. 'And the women had it even worse... you're lucky to be young now, in this time, to enjoy the freedom,' etc. She just gave me a funny smile. 'You're not going to give me a chance to feel sorry for myself, are you?' she said. I laughed it off. I thought I was cheering her up."

There was a silence. Parisi studied the cluttered desk in front of him. Those heavy-lidded eyes seemed to want to close. "I knew the girl since she was a child," he said. "She was the soul of beauty. I don't use a phrase like that lightly. If you believe in such a thing as grace, she glowed with it.

Vibrant. Sweet. Sensitive. Instinctively generous. Wholesome inside and out, not a trace of narcissism. As a child, she was the only perfect thing I ever laid eyes on. I've still got her, up here," he tapped his forehead, "up in this junkyard I call a mind. My fossilhouse of treasures." He didn't look up or seem to expect any response. "Her father's the one I really feel sorry for. You know, when you get old, you accept after a point that you have to lose everything...your health, your pleasures, your wife and friends, your work, your wits. But still you get taken by surprise. You find there's no end to what you've got to give up. Your children. Your hopes. Your most private memories."

Villanova waited through another long silence. It struck him that every man who came anywhere near Elizabeth Albano wound up seeing in her exactly what he needed to see, himself included. Parisi's eyes remained fixed on the desktop. He looked suddenly very old and very frail. After a minute, Villanova thanked him and started to take his leave. Parisi stood up and detained him with a touch on his arm. He looked Villanova in the eye, and seemed half-ashamed for what he was about to say. "You going to catch this guy?"

That was a question Villanova hated and usually wouldn't answer. He looked back into those world-weary eyes. "We're going to catch him and put his ass in a sling," he said.

* * *

Villanova made a brief stop at the stakeout in the Cruz apartment, returned the car to the precinct, checked in at Homicide, and found the Crime Lab report on Rizzo's desk. He flipped through it and pulled out the inventory and the chem-screen profile. A vial of aminotryl tablets was listed on the inventory. 21 tablets. She'd carried the pills with her but hadn't taken any.

He glanced at the pre-autopsy photos, then skimmed the narrative section of the report. According to one of the notations, the panties the girl was wearing were urine soaked. That detail was typical of a strangulation murder. He glanced again at the photos. In a sex-crime case, the corpse was photographed in several stages of undress for forensic eventualities. Elizabeth Albano had been wearing a black garter belt and stockings under her dress, and black lace panties and bra. Villanova didn't even have the chance to ponder that before a whistle cut into his thoughts. It was Gilman, grinning at him from the corridor. "That's some murder victim you guys got there," Gilman said.

Villanova shut the folder and put it under his arm. "Where's the report on the trunk?"

"Not here yet. But the news is bad so far. No clean prints. Looks wiped."

"Shit. Did you come up with anything for us in the psycho files?"

"Not a thing."

"You try everything? Paraphiliacs, peepers..."

"I tried the works. Overheated the fucking computer."

"Where's Rizzo?"

"Popping his cork over at the D.A.'s."

"The D.A.? What happened? Oh, Christ--he didn't get the subpoena?"

"Uh-uh. 'Request too broad, I.D. circumstantial'."

"Too broad? Who the hell was on the bench?"

"Tatum. The word was, no evidence of deviancy, no priors on Cruz, no probable cause for a sweep of psycho records county-wide."

"Are you shitting me?"

"Them's the facts. And Tatum's the man until Judge Milstein gets back into the rotation next Monday."

Villanova felt the heat rising under his collar.   "What the hell is wrong with this city?   If you don't get murdered the same day you win the lottery, you're wasting everyone's time?"

"You shoulda seen Rizzo.   *He* was doing a dance."

"Are those stiffs in the D.A.'s office doing some squawking for him, at least?"

"Forget it.   Bev Cohn's the A.D.A. on the case.   She's useless."

"Assholes!"   Villanova shook his head.   "What did Rizzo say about this report?"

"Said for you to take it home and give it a read.   Said, 'Tell that boy to get some sleep.'"

"What about *him*?"

"Oh, don't worry about him.   Rizzo ain't human."

"Who's checking out the girl's connections?"

"Reinhart covered Fordham and Mount Saint Mary's this morning."

"Any leads?"

"Nothing warm yet.   Lot of prissy, brainy types.   The men liked the girl, the women pretended to.   The nuns at Mount Saint Mary's didn't want to hear anything about boyfriends, but people at Fordham had their eyes open."

"And who's covering JFK?"

"Rizzo's got it.   Relax, go home, it's under control." Gilman nodded toward Rizzo's desk, where a cardboard carton, flaps interlocked, sat on the blotter.   "That box belong to you?"

"Yeah.   It's from the Cruz stakeout."

"What's in it?"

Villanova set the lab folder on top of the carton and hefted it against his chest.   "A cat."   He headed for the outside.

* * *

The D train left him on Bedford Park Boulevard at the Grand Concourse, a three block walk from home.   The day was still overcast and grey, giving the lights along the Concourse a somber intensity.   A damp breeze rippled the silver undersides of the sidewalk trees; the first sweaters and jackets of the season appeared among the pedestrians.

Within minutes, Villanova was climbing the front steps of the Topless Towers. There was no one on the porch. The inside stairway was dark as night. The door to the basement, where he and Joey Marinelli had been building a model train layout for the past few months, was closed. He could hear the televisions droning from a couple of the first floor apartments: *Walkabout*; some game show. He started up the stairs.

"*Freeze!*" a woman's voice commanded.

He froze.

"*Freeze!*" the voice barked again, and then there was a groan and another cry of "*Freeze*, you idiot!"

He relaxed and muttered a curse. It was only Tina Marinelli, watching *The Price is Right* and bullying the amateurs on her TV screen. Tina wasn't the first woman he'd met who knew the retail price of everything in the world, but she was the first who had actually come home from a President's Day Sellathon with the single ninety-nine cent VCR that several hundred other fanatics thought they had a shot at. She was a drill sergeant among the shock troops of the Clearance Wars...and the *other* women of the Topless Towers sneered at her delicacy.

He kept climbing. The second floor landing was quiet, which meant that Sal and Roseann Marinelli were sleeping off their nightly drunk, and Helen was either out or working a double shift at the hospital.

As he neared his own landing, though, Villanova heard the rhythmic squeak of bedsprings. He hesitated and listened. Some hearty ram was battering away at a stalwart clip. Too weary for bafflement, he kept going, turned the knob, and pushed the door open. Helen was inside bouncing up and down on a miniature trampoline.   She was barefoot and wearing a slip and bra.   "What the hell?" he said, but she held up an index finger and continued her count out loud: "291, 292...."   She looked very good in her underthings; even fully clothed she was such a frankly *physical* creature.   He stood appreciating the shapely legs, the perfect, pear-shaped bottom, the white neck and shoulders, the beautiful, pale, lightly freckled ·contour of flesh below her throat.   She was a lovely woman, and he had no idea why she stubbornly envied women with more exaggerrated charms.   "...298, 299, THREE HUNDRED!"   She stopped, tottered over to the bed, and collapsed.

He shook his head.   "A new hobby?"

"Aerobics!" she panted, pointing to her heart.

"What happened to jogging?"

"No good. Joints."   She pointed to her knee and her elbow. "Neck." She pointed. "Tits." She corrected herself: "Bosom."

"Say tits if you want to."   He could see she was in one of her silly moods.

"No, no, bosom, great word."   She took a series of deep, rapid breaths.   "Terrific gadget, this thing.   No cartilege damage, see? No bone stress. Guess how much I paid, down in B and D's?"

"I don't know."   The contraption looked like an extra thick, extra tiny mattress.   "Thirty-nine ninety-five?"

"Freeze!"

"Make fun of Tina, right, but I notice you decided not to do your bouncing over her head."

"No, no, I just needed the higher ceiling up here.   I'd brain myself down in my place."   The garret was very high in the center, with four radiating gables, one for a sleeping alcove, one for a galley, one for a sofa and TV, one for a john. "Anyway, I didn't want to miss you before I go to work.   I've got stuff to show you. C'mere, look." She got up and headed for his dresser. "I want you to see where I hid the Christmas stuffies I made for the kids. You know, in case anything happens to me in the next three months."

"Nothing's going to happen to you. Don't be so damned superstitious."

"I'm not. Look, I put them in here, with your socks." She pulled open one of the drawers. "The kids don't come snooping up here, do they?"

"I hope to hell not. Jesus, how many did you make?" The drawer was crammed with gingham creatures in rich shades of blue, green, and red.

"Three for each kid. One elephant, one camel, and one kangaroo."

"This the kangaroo here? Not bad."

"No, that's the camel. Can't you tell, for God's sake? Hey, what you got in the box, sweetie?"

"A cat." He set the carton on the floor.

"A cat?" She gave him a doubtful look. She was neutral about cats, crazy about dogs. "Let's see it. Take it out."

He removed the folder and laid it on the dresser, opened the box, and very gently lifted the cat out onto the floor.

"A tabby! Where'd you get her?"

"Someone dumped her. She's been a little traumatized, I think. I had to bribe her to get her used to me."

But now the cat seemed self-possessed enough. She took a look at Helen with those big green eyes, then walked a hesitant circle, giving the room a careful scrutiny. Then, disregarding Helen's overtures, she made a dignified retreat under the sofa.

"Ignore her for a while," Helen said. "That's what you do with cats."

"Fine. All *I'm* really interested in right now is some shut-eye."

"Wait, wait, there's something else I've got to show you first. Come on over here. Come on, sweetie." She tugged him back toward the dresser. "Guess what came in yesterday's mail?"

"I give up."

"The ants!"

"The ants?"

"You know, for Danielle's ant farm. See, they're in this little container right here." She picked up a red and white box the size of a cigarette pack. "There's a queen and everything. Here's the instructions."

"They send ants in the mail?"

"I guess they do. I waited for you because it says here these ants *bite*. You're supposed to put the container in the fridge for a minute before you open it so they don't get too rambunctious. Then you use these tweezers, see, and you take 'em out one at a time and pop 'em into the farm through the little hatch."

"One at a time? Listen, you think we could just let 'em stay in the container awhile? I'm really dead, babe."

Her eyes softened as she copped to how fatigued he really was. "Aw, sweetie. Another case?" She came over and took his face soothingly in her hands. "Look at those eyes, like little red dots. Poor baby. Come on, let me make you a snack first, you'll sleep better. Sit, I'll scramble some eggs. You can tell me all about it."

"No eggs, sweetheart."

"French toast, then. You ever have my French toast?"

He protested, but she pulled him toward the table and made him sit, and seconds later she was rummaging around in the fridge. He watched her stoop to hunt the frying pan out of the clutter under the sink, her movements quick and graceful, her curls dancing around and over her face. With that smooth, lithe body of hers, she looked even younger than she was, strong, undamaged, ripe. Her slip rode up over her strong white thighs. Now he wasn't sleepy anymore. He got up and grabbed her from behind, and turned her into him for a hug.

"It's about time," she pouted. She laid her warm forehead into the hollow of his shoulder. They clung to each other for a good minute, just rocking slowly and kissing deeply. He trailed his lips down under her chin to the hollow of her neck, her favorite spot, and she shivered and drew his hips tight against hers, and then he reached behind her and unclasped the bra, and her breasts tumbled free, and he took a nipple in his mouth and heard her sigh with pleasure. And then their clothes were dropping to the floor, and she was on her knees in front of him and he was alive inside her warm, sweet mouth, caressing her shoulders and stroking her silky hair. And then they were on the bed, she atop him, her body white as milk in the soft daylight, and he wanted her to come first, because she didn't always, and he wanted it, and he met her thrust for thrust, and lifted his head and caught one of those bobbing breasts in his mouth, and drew the hard nipple in, and then he felt her tensing, and then she was thrashing against him, and the cry broke from her lips, and she let it go and it filled the room and broke apart and escaped in tatters through the open window, and he loved the sound of it and didn't care that everybody in the building heard it too.

And then, as if dazed, she was pulling herself off him, and she turned over on her knees and put her head down on the sheet so he could enter her from behind, the way he liked, and he thrust into her, and wrapped his hands around that perfect white bottom with all the fervor in him, and just before he came she reached between her legs to finger herself, and as he exploded into her with a series of quick, sharp cries, she let go again, softly, with a slow, plaintive, almost mournful moan. "Sweetie," she sighed, keeping him inside her as she settled down to the mattress. "My sweetheart."

The cat sat watching them indifferently.

* * *

While they ate, he told her about the case. He told her about the trunk, the strangled girl, the family of decent folks on Rhinelander Avenue, the missing crucifix on the gold chain. He told her about the philandering English professor and his pretty wife, the nervous cabby, the savage artist, the mural on Bathgate Avenue. While he talked, he ate French Toast that was singed on the outside and raw and eggy on the inside; "Is it good?" Helen asked him a couple of times, and he said, "Sure." He told her about the apartment on 185th Street, the vanished psychic, the long-haired son who'd been seen dragging a trunk down the steps, the abandoned tabby. He told her about the pregnancy, the headaches, the doctor, the pills, the photos in the Crime Lab report on the dresser.

"Can I see them?"

"Better wait till after breakfast."

"So what're you doing to track this creep down?"

He mentioned the computer scans, the stakeout, the canvassing squad and the real estate brokers.

She nodded, her face puckered in thought. It was a round, finely-boned, honestly attractive face that could not be enhanced by any kind of make-up, though Helen stubbornly envied her dark-skinned, full-lipped, sloe-eyed women friends. "Maybe I can do something to help," she said. The last of the girlish frivolity had gone from her manner; she was in her serious mode, the mode she took to work with her.

"Like what?"

"Saint Barnabas is over on 184th Street, and I've got plenty of pals working the wards. Some of the Hispanic girls use psychics all the time. Maybe we could try to tap into the network. There's gotta be one or two psychics on every block in that section of the Wedge, and they all know each other. The clients go from one to the other, you know? *Someone* should know something about where these Cruz people went to."

He nodded. Helen knew her way around ouija boards, tarot cards, and tea leaves nearly as well as she did stethoscopes and oxygen tents. She read Maslow and Rogers in bed every night and played Solitaire first thing every morning, hand after hand until she won safe-conduct into her day. He said, "That *would* be a help, babe. But a bigger help might be to get one of your friends at Jacobi to do some snooping in the Records room. You've got a psychiatric ward there, right? Any kind of treatment record might give us a lead."

"Very hard to do since computer security got upgraded. Anyway, if you want psychiatric records, you're better off hitting Bronx Psychiatric."

"Well, you've got friends there too, right?"

"No good. Everything's coded there now too. You'd have to be Einstein to beat all the security loops. Why not just get hold of the records you want up front?"

"We tried that. No probable cause for a subpoena. Technically, outside the Homicide Squad, we don't even have a sex crime yet."

"Are you kidding?"

"I wish I was. The girl wasn't molested, as far as we can tell. For the *record*, motive is still a question mark until we get our hands on this Manny Cruz guy and shake some shit out of him. Till then, thanks to the rulebook, we're stuck."

Helen stared at him. "You know what?" she said. "That really sucks." She looked down at her plate. She didn't say anything for a while. Villanova knew some of what she was feeling. She'd been sexually abused by her father, a drunk, when she was a kid. She'd had a long experience with the flat, plain surface of rich, demonic crimes. She was walking around with the uncomplicated mug of a California townie, but she trusted the innocence of nothing, despised all secrets, disdained privacy with a passion, and said exactly what she felt, especially when it came to giving nasty things their proper name. The Albano case was the kind that made her tremble with disgust. The murdered girl had the kind of dark, rich beauty Helen had always envied. She had the cheekbones, the lashes, the thick, dark hair, the full lips, the long neck...all the endowments that were supposed to bring the world's love; instead they'd brought the world's rage. If anyone knew that flip-flop of love and rage, it was Helen. She knew the degradation of victimization, she knew all the horror and shame of crimes intensely personal, endured alone and out of the world's sight. If anyone could feel a kinship with Elizabeth Albano, Helen was the one.

Finally she looked up and said quietly, "Do you know why I do the work I do?"

"I think so."

"It's because this world is full of kids that nobody cares about. It's full of kids who're full of pain, and their parents are so scared that they wind up telling them a bunch of lies. I don't. The truth is never as scary as a lie."

He nodded.

"I've seen things that were done to kids that would make you sick to your stomach. Things that couldn't have happened if someone was willing to call a spade a spade."

He nodded again. There was a long silence. Helen seemed to be fighting off a dark mood. Finally she brushed her hair away from her eyes and said, "I've gotta leave for work soon. Wanna do the ants before I go?"

"Okay, babe."

"You think the cat would like the leftover batter?"

"Why not?"

He set the bowl on the floor; the tabby ignored it. Helen cleared the table and fetched the plastic ant farm and the container of "100 Live Ants!"

"Someone actually counts 'em?"

She shrugged.

They popped the container in the fridge for a minute, then opened it up. The first few ants he went for with the tweezers were awfully quick. He maimed one trying to nab it, and Helen groaned in sympathetic pain. "Back in the fridge," he decreed.

The container went in and out of the fridge four times, and the number of whole ants went down to 95. He began to get an uneasy feeling in his stomach.

The last resort was the freezer.

"They're dying in there, it's too cold!" Helen protested.

"Relax, let 'em soak up a good dose of that chill."

"That's long enough. *Please*, they're gonna..."

"*Ouch! Bastard!*" He swatted. "Where'd that guy come from? Jesus, these things *bite!*"

"Hurry! Take 'em out!" she begged.

He pulled the container out of the freezer. It rattled. "Uh-oh." He shook it over the hatch, and ninety-four miniature raisins fell in a heap inside the ant farm.

"I knew it," she moaned. "They're dead."

He stared at his handiwork, shaken. The insect world was such a goddamned nightmare from top to bottom.

"Wait!" The heap had begun to stir.

"There they go!" he said. "See, they made it!" Half a minute later the ant farm was seething with activity.

Helen snapped the hatch shut. Her face was flushed with relief.

He was relieved too, though he hid it from her--she was so ready to see fateful metaphors in everything. He stood and stretched extravagantly; he was weary again, ponderously so.

"Don't you want to watch?" she said.

"Watch what?"

"Watch 'em do their thing. You know, tunnels."

"I want to sleep," he said. He headed for the bed. "Are those guys gonna stay put in there?"

"I guess. What's on for tonight, sweetie? You meeting me?"

"Sure thing. The Shamrock, for eats. Around seven."

"Should I wait?"

"Not too long. If I get stuck, I'll ring Donny at the bar." He made a feeble effort at straightening the bedcovers before sliding under.

"You wanna get tucked in, sweetie?"

"Sure."

That was one of Helen's literal phrases; her monstrous childhood had made her ritualistic about the security of sleep, and he was used to indulging her. She drew the blinds in the alcove, tucked the covers up around him, smoothed down his hair, kissed his cheek. Then she sat at the table with the Crime Lab report and began to read, and he glimpsed her once or twice through half-shut eyes, sunk in grim concentration over typescript and photos, and then he was gone into grateful slumber.

And he dreamed.

He dreamed he was walking down Third Avenue deep in the Wedge. The weather was dim and drizzly. A cab pulled to the curb and a young woman got out. It was Elizabeth Albano. As she walked toward him, he could see in the the stunning sensuality of all her movements what a beauty she truly was. 'I've been looking for you,' he accosted her. And that was true, he'd been searching for her for so many years that he couldn't remember anything else about his life. He looked into her eyes, and seemed for the first time to recognize her. His heart rose in a sudden surge of joy, tears of relief came to his eyes. 'I've been looking all *over* for you,' he said. 'You said you'd be right back.' 'I know,' she answered. Clearly she'd been very occupied; for her, all those years had been the equal of an hour. She looked around furtively, signaling him to be cool. 'Hold this for me,' she said, handing him a bright red apple--where had it come from? 'I'll be out in *one* minute, I promise.' Her eyes confirmed that he would never have to wait again. She side-stepped him and headed for the entrance to a building. She was wearing a nurse's uniform. The building was a hospital, and there was a watchman under the canopy.

He waited, holding the apple. He was very happy now. It was the end of a long, long time of loneliness. He spoke to the watchman. 'That's my wife,' he said. A minute went by. She didn't come out. The watchman turned his back, and he slipped by him into the hospital. This was against the rules. A civilian had no right to be inside. The penalty could be death. He didn't care. He went through the lobby. It was vast--the building hadn't seemed so large from the outside. There were dozens of people, so busy about their work that he was barely noticed. He kept going. There were throngs of people, hundreds. There were sidewalks and vehicle lanes, cobblestones and power lines. The lobby was huge as a city. There were streetcars and an overcast sky. The buildings, the streets, even the people, were grey and vaguely Oriental. No one would speak to him. He was a foreigner without status; no one would help him. The apple made him conspicuous; he thrust it deep into his pocket and tried to conceal the bulge. He kept walking. The others plodded about their business, faces down, drones in some vast joyless hive, a soulless empire as big as the world, from which there was now no way out. It was the empire of Death, he realized with a terrible despair.

And she was there somewhere too. And in front of him stretched an eternity of searching. Alone.

'Look!' someone cried accusingly. 'Look!' He tried to melt into the crowd.

"Look!" It was Helen's voice. "Wake up!"

He opened his eyes. She was standing beside the bed in her nurse's whites, her skirt hiked up above her waist. Her panties stared him in the face. "Look, sweetie!" she said.

"Babe, have a heart."

"No, no, just look."

He registered a blurry take of tawny skin and a white, lace-trimmed vee. "What?"

"Come on, sweetie. Wake up. Not a sex crime? Who took the girl's panties off, then, huh? The Medical Examiner?"

"What're you talking about?" He opened his eyes full and lifted his head. She was holding the Crime Lab photos toward him with one hand and clutching the hem of her skirt with the other.

"Look at me. See anything wrong?"

What he saw looked right enough, but she wasn't asking for any jokes. He said, "Just tell me, babe."

"My panties. They're on wrong."

"They are?"

"See the label?"

"No."

"Here. See where this little strip is? Well it doesn't belong there. It belongs on top. Panties have three openings, see? With these little skimpy ones, it's hard to tell which opening is the waist. Even if you know where the label should go, you still get it wrong sometimes. You get the waistband around your thigh, and the crotch winds up over here on the side."

"You saying you can put your panties on wrong and not know it?"

"No. You know it because they don't *feel* right. But they *look* right. Like in this photograph here."

He sat up.

"This photo was taken *before* the M. E. undressed the girl, right? Well then the girl didn't put her own panties on. Someone else did." She let her skirt down.

He took the photo and looked at it.

"See the lace pattern? That vee isn't the crotch." She slipped her panties off, demonstrated, and pulled them on right.

He got out of bed. Helen nodded encouragingly. He picked up the Lab Report, flipped to the narrative section, and re-read. Now, *now* it clicked. The panties were urine soaked...and so was the underside of Manny Cruz's mattress. The killer had suffocated his victim on his bed, maybe face down, maybe with a pillow. He'd taken her panties off, and then put them back on before stashing her and turning the mattress over. That definitely threw the case onto psycho turf. It meant they could get their court order.

He threw the report on the table and went for the phone. Helen headed for the door. "Where the hell you going?" he said.

"To work, sweetie. I'm late."

"Jesus, gloat for half a minute, won't you?"

"Over what?" she said soberly, and she left.

Within two minutes, he had Rizzo on one of the A.D.A. extensions.

Half an hour later they had a subpoena for a records search under the name Cruz at Bronx Psychiatric and Jacobi.

And an hour after that, partly to their own surprise, they had a fix on Manny Cruz's whereabouts.

- SIX -

Bronx Municipal Hospital was located on the edge of the Morris Park neighborhood, in the angle of the Pelham Parkway and Hutchinson River Parkway juncture. The hospital buildings stood on one side of Morris Park Avenue, Albert Einstein College of Medicine on the other. Across Eastchester Road and the Conrail tracks, Bronx Psychiatric Center squatted over the polluted mouth of Westchester Creek. To the west, tree-lined residential streets like Tenbrook and Narragansett and Yates housed many of the complex's nurses and interns. One of these streets, Rhinelander Avenue, abutted the grounds of Jacobi Hospital about eight blocks east of the Albano household, almost directly in line with the morgue. In the old days before the M.E.'s function was centralized downtown, Elizabeth's refrigerated body, its violation completed in one of Jacobi's autopsy rooms, would have awaited pickup there by Grippi and Sons undertakers. Now it was on its way up First Avenue in a Grippi hearse.

Four floors above the morgue, Julia Cruz of 691 East 185th Street, lay reading magazines in a bed in the surgery ward.

Before heading up to the ward, Rizzo and Villanova did as much fast checking downstairs as they could. Mrs. Cruz had been admitted to Jacobi two days earlier, at 2:35 on Tuesday afternoon; that was the item that had raised the flag in their computer search. She'd had one would-be visitor so far, a longhaired young man who'd been turned away on Wednesday afternoon because the patient was undergoing CAT-scans. Mrs. Cruz's case was serious: she'd had an angiogram earlier in the day, and was on a priority basis for brain surgery. The doctor they spoke to, Salzman by name, was involved in the case in an accessory role. Capogrosso, the neurosurgeon who headed the O.R. team, was off the ward.

"What've we got here?" Rizzo put it bluntly to Salzman. "This woman's tied up in a murder case. Did someone brain her?"

"Nothing like that. She's got a tumor, an acoustic neurinoma. That's why I was called in. I'm the ENT man."

"ENT?"

"Ear-Nose-Throat. When the surgical team goes in, they'll need me to excavate the ear canal. That's my territory. All the rest, Capogrosso does himself."

"A brain tumor's not something that comes on quick, right? Maybe someone roughed her up, aggravated it?"

"It doesn't work that way."

"So how come just *now* her tumor acts up?"

"It isn't just now. She was here for neurosurgery two years back. Capogrosso did that one too. The computer must've told you that, right?"

"Wrong."

"Well, *that's* how it works. Tumors grow back. This woman's had symptoms for months. She put off coming here until she couldn't stand it any more."

"Couldn't stand what? Pain?"

Salzman shrugged. "The man you really want to talk to is Capogrosso."

"Okay, get him."

Salzman looked at his watch. "He'll be back on the ward in forty-five minutes. I could beep him, but the guy doesn't get much chance to sleep."

"Let him sleep," Villanova said. "Is Mrs. Cruz awake? Can she talk?"

"I guess so. They haven't moved her up to Sic-U yet."

"Sick-you?"

"Surgical I.C.U. Right now she's on the fourth floor."

They arranged to have a plainclothesman posted in the lobby, alerted the main desk and hospital security to keep watch for Manny Cruz, and took the elevator up to the fourth floor. It was only when he stepped off the elevator on the fourth floor that Villanova remembered the hospital dream held been having just an hour earlier.

Julia Cruz's room gave a view across the Eastchester Road rooftops to the busy interchange of the Hutch. The second bed in the room was empty. Mrs. Cruz didn't look at all like what Villanova had expected. She was petite and delicate-featured, with wavy, dark brown hair, a high, expressive brow, and warm eyes the hue of a dusky absinthe. She was tiny and perfectly made, and her eyes, though puffy and ringed by many fine lines, had the deep, serene focus of a child. The record gave her age as 51.

She was awake and affable, and nothing in her face changed when they told her they were detectives working on an investigation. She agreed to answer as many questions as they cared to put. Her voice, slightly nasal and with a trace of a Hispanic accent, was as small, inoffensive, and soothing as her presence.

Rizzo stood close to the bedside with his back to the window, while Villanova remained at the foot. "Mrs. Cruz, you make your living as a psychic, don't you?" Rizzo said.

"A spiritual advisor," she corrected.

"And your son Manny lives with you, Mrs. Cruz?"

"Yes.   Please call me Julia." She pronounced it 'Hoolia.'

"Julia, do you know where Manny is right now?"

"No. But he'll be here soon. He'll come this afternoon to see me."

"He told you this?"

"No, but I'm sure he'll come."

"When did you talk to him last, Julia?"

"Tuesday. The day I came here."

"Did you know that Manny moved out of your apartment during the night on Tuesday?"

Her eyebrows went up. "No. He told me he would, but I didn't believe him. He's said it before, many times. Whenever we argue."

"You argued?

She nodded. "We argue a lot lately, Manny and I."

"He left in an awful hurry. He even left the cat behind."

Her brow furrowed. "Mirabel? Where is she?"

"She's okay," Villanova said. "I've got her."

Julia took him in with those deep-focused eyes.

Rizzo said, "Do you have any idea where Manny went, where he slept the last two nights?"

She shook her head. "He's a strong boy, he could sleep anywhere. On the street, even. That's what I'm afraid of. Manny has nowhere to go, no job, no friends, no money."

"Julia... " Rizzo leaned forward and rested his hand on the bed. "Why did Manny move out? Why did you argue? Is he in trouble?"

Julia gave a resigned shrug. "We're both in trouble. Manny has no way to live, no home...and me..." she indicated with one small gesture herself, the bed, the hospital room, "I'm sick and I don't think I'm going to get better."

Villanova didn't like to hear people talk that way; it frightened him unreasonably. Julia turned a comforting gaze on him. "It's all right for me to say it," she said. "It's true."

"Why did you argue with Manny on Tuesday?" Rizzo repeated.

"He didn't want to take me to the hospital." She shrugged. "It's complicated. He doesn't want me to die. He was in an awful mood Tuesday, and I understand, I pity him. I'm sick, and so he's full of dread. On Monday also, we fought. About other things, and yet it was the same thing, his fear of losing me." She looked from Rizzo to Villanova and back. "Has Manny done something bad?"

Rizzo answered in a flat, unappeasing tone: "We don't know. Suppose you tell us what you can remember."

She hesitated, then looked toward the window as if to collect her thoughts. "On Monday," she began, "I was feeling very sick. For two, three weeks, I wasn't feeling well, but now it was worse. Then in the afternoon, I started to hear the ringing in my ear, and I knew what it meant. It was just like last time, the dizziness, the pain, right here in the back of my head. I knew I had to go see Dr. Capogrosso. Manny was hanging around the apartment, and I scolded him, I told him to go find work. I was afraid to tell him what was really wrong. See, *I* was the one that started it."

"So you argued."

"Yes. And all the while I didn't tell him that the tumor was growing again. I yelled at him that we had no money, we were behind in the rent, already the telephone was shut off. There was no food, even for the cat..."

"The phone was shut off? When did that happen?"

"About two weeks ago. Because the bill wasn't paid. I told Manny we would have to run away in the night just like before, and it was his fault, because he quit a good job."

"What job would that be, and when did he quit it?"

"The custodian job that he had for two years. In the school. And he just switched to nights, for higher pay. Then all of a sudden, no warning, he quit."

"What school was that, Julia?"

"The high school, over on Fordham Road."

"John F. Kennedy?"

"That's it."

Rizzo's eyes met Villanova's, and Villanova felt the start of a rush.

"And when exactly did he quit?" Rizzo said.

"Last week. He never liked the job. He didn't like the kids, they mocked him. 'Animals,' he called them. But night work should have been better for him, then, am I right?" She looked to Villanova for confirmation. "No, he just quit and he waited three days before he even told me, and then not even a reason. And after that, we had nothing but trouble. A man with no money in his pocket, *he* is like an animal. He gets a look in his eye, he walks different." A look of fear flitted across her face. "And Manny, right away he was getting nasty with me, blaming me. And my customers too, he was making them nervous, always hanging around the apartment. People want a safe place when they come for advice. Their troubles are private. So for two weeks the money I took in was less than half. And with no phone, even less. Then the tumor again, and I even had to turn customers away because of not feeling well. So I was scared, for myself and for him, that without me, he can't live, can't take care of himself. A man twenty-six years old. This is why I fought with him, to make him blame himself for his troubles, to make him stand up for himself."

"And what did he say?"

She shook her head. "He got angry, he screamed at me, he told me he'll find a new place to live, without me. He told me how he hates the apartment anyway, hates his pigeon-coop of a room, hates me. He's ashamed of his life, he said, he has nothing fine, he can never even let a woman see the hole he lives in."

"And you?"

"'A woman?' I told him, 'When did a woman ever look at you, a boy with no job?'"

Villanova flinched. Talk like that never did any male any good.

Julia turned her gaze on him again. Her eyes were suddenly wet with tears, and their greenish hue was striking. "Yes," she said, "it was a mistake, being cruel that way. But I thought it would do him good, you see? Make him do something for himself. If I were a man, I would know how to talk to him."

"How did he react?" Rizzo said.

"He called me 'Bitch!' and slammed out the door."

"Then what?"

She shrugged. "I came here. I took the bus on Fordham Road."

"You saw Dr. Capogrosso?"

"Yes. Monday afternoon. And Dr. Capogrosso was very worried, after the examination, I could see it. He wanted to admit me right away. He made some telephone calls, he yelled at someone on the phone, and then he told me, 'Come to Admitting in the morning, first thing.' He gave me ten dollars to take a taxi home. I didn't use it, though, I took the bus."

"He gave you a ten dollar bill?"

"Yes, a ten dollar bill."

Rizzo took out his pad and made a notation. That flat, almost cool manner of his hadn't softened in spite of all Julia's openness. It was as if her odd candor itself had triggered some skeptical reflex. "And was Manny there when you got home?" he said.

"No. He came in at night. He wouldn't talk at first. Then he said he was looking for a new job. He said as soon as he got one, he would borrow money and move out. He had boxes from the bodega. He said he was going to pack his things."

"Did he?"

"He started, next morning. I got dressed, I woke him. I told him I was sick, I had to go into the hospital." Again her eyes filled with tears, and she turned her miserable gaze on Villanova. "The fright on his face! And then the anger! You don't understand. He needs me like a baby, my Manny. It's not his fault, he's not right in his head." She gestured toward her own head.

"How not right?" Rizzo said.

"He can't leave me, even for a day, and for that he hates me."

Rizzo nodded without expression. "Has he ever tried to hurt you physically?"

"Once," she said quietly. "The first time I had to come here, two years ago, he tried to stop me. He threw me against the wall."

"You got hurt?"

She nodded, and pressed one of her hands to her side. "My ribs were bruised. The pain was there for months."

There was a clatter in the corridor, and the rhythmic squeak of casters. "And that was the only time he put hands on you?" Rizzo said.

"After that he didn't dare. But many times I think the wish was there."

"Has Manny ever been in trouble with the law?"

"No," she said. "He stays away from people if he can."

The squeaking stopped; an aide with a meal cart had halted outside the open door. Rizzo fell silent briefly, and Villanova was relieved for Julia's sake. The aide, a young, heavy-set black woman, brought in Julia's tray, smiled and nodded as she set it on the moveable stand, and departed without a word. Everything on the tray was liquid: soup, juice, and jello. Villanova, hungry as he was, was glad not to have to eat it.

"What does Manny do when he's home, Julia?" Rizzo said as soon as the aide had moved on.

"Daydreams. Reads his comic books."

"What kind of comic books?"

"Ugly things. *The Punisher, Doc Savage.* He won't let me touch them. He gets angry if I come into his room, even to clean."

"Do you think Manny *did* borrow money and move in somewhere else?"

"No, Manny's way is to roam the streets for a day and then come home without a word."

"What happened after you told him about the hospital this time?"

"I waited till he was quiet again, then I asked him not to let me go there alone. I begged until he said yes. We went to Fordham Road to get the bus. We waited and waited, and the bus never came. Manny wouldn't talk to me. He just cursed to himself and looked to where the bus comes around the curve at Webster Avenue. Ten times he looked at his watch. Finally he gave up. He said he had to go look for a job before the day was gone. He asked for money, and I gave him the money Dr. Capogrosso gave me."

"The ten dollar bill?"

"Yes."

"What time did the bus finally come?"

"About twelve-thirty. I got on by myself."

Rizzo flipped a page in his notepad and jotted the time. Villanova's eyes drifted to the window, to the endless stream of cars sliding round the loops of the interchange under that low, grey sky. The net of culpability was closing fast around the suspect now. Manny Cruz could easily have been back in his apartment by twelve-forty. He would have been alone, agitated, and primed for a nasty piece of business when Elizabeth Albano came knocking. Once he got his hands on her, it wouldn't have taken much for him to overpower and smother the life out of her. Yet the atmosphere in this room at this moment was eerily tranquil, and Villanova's rage at Manny was, for the first time, diffracted. It was the way Julia Cruz spoke, he realized. It was her soothing voice, her slow, delicate gestures, punctuated by moments of intense personal connection. It was her presence itself, so peculiarly linked with everything, his own mood included. He put his back to the window and took a good look at her. Her gaze had anticipated his. All the while she'd been answering Rizzo's questions, she'd been mainly holding Villanova's eyes. There was a fathomless patience in her face, a guileless and yet seductive solace. Those absinthe-eyes of hers filled him with a sense of incredible peace. He wished Rizzo would go gentler with her.

"And you haven't seen Manny since?" Rizzo said.

An odd look of sorrow came into Julia's eyes. "I *did* see him," she said. "I went back home, and he was there."

"You went back home? You said you got on the bus."

"I did. It was so slow, going up Fordham Road. I was upset about Manny, and I was thinking, thinking. I went all the way to the hospital, and I got off and stood on the sidewalk for a long time. I knew Dr. Capogrosso would be angry, but I had a *feeling* that I should go home again and talk with Manny. You know, a *sense*. When these feelings come, I always listen. So I turned around and went back home on the bus."

"Do you remember the time? Did you see anyone you know?"

"I only saw Maria Iglesias sitting on the stoop across the street. She called to me, but I just waved, because I owe her cousin money. She's a relative with the Super, a real busybody."

"You didn't talk with her?"

"No. She can talk all day, Maria. About her family in Puerto Rico, her niece's wedding, the bride-dress, the flowers... With the son I have, do I want to hear about a wedding? I went upstairs."

"About what time was that?"

"About one o'clock."

And was Manny there when you went up?"

She nodded. "The key wouldn't go in the lock. I knocked, and after a while he slid the bolt and opened. He was very angry, very upset. He wouldn't even put his eyes on me. He went to his room. I think he was packing his clothes."

"What happened to looking for a job?"

"I don't know. I didn't ask. I was so dizzy that I had to go lie on my bed. I kept my eyes closed, not to sleep but, you know, to dream. And what I dreamed of was Death. I knew what it meant. I opened my eyes and called to Manny. I got up and knocked on his door. When he opened, I told him that I wasn't going to live much longer."

Villanova stiffened. He said, "Did Dr. Capogrosso tell you that?"

"No. But that isn't Dr. Capogrosso's way."

Rizzo said, "And what did Manny do when you told him?"

"Nothing. He wouldn't look at my face. I asked him again to take me to the hospital, and he just closed his door to me." She shrugged sadly. "So I went by myself. Here I am."

Rizzo nodded. "What time did you last see Manny on Tuesday?"

"About one-thirty."

"Tell me something, Julia," Rizzo said, and his eyes narrowed a degree. "Does Manny own a trunk? You know, for clothes?"

"A trunk?" She shook her head.

"Could he have got a trunk somewhere and kept it where you wouldn't see it? In his room... under the bed, maybe? Think for a minute, now, be sure."

She closed her eyes for a few seconds, then opened them and shook her head. "The bed is too low. His room is very small. Nothing is big enough to hide a trunk."

"You're positive? It's very important."

She sighed. "What has my son done?" Her words were directed at Rizzo, but her eyes were on Villanova.

Villanova didn't have the heart to be coy any longer. He reached inside his jacket and withdrew the photo of Elizabeth Albano. "Have you ever seen this girl?" he said, holding it toward her.

Julia took the photo. Her eyes took in the likeness. Her brows gathered, and something like apprehension passed across her face. "Such a beauty," she murmured. She shook her head slowly. "No," she said, "I don't think I ever saw her." But her gaze seemed uneasy as she handed the photo back. "Has something happened to her?"

"The girl's been murdered. "Her body was found in a trunk on the sidewalk."

Julia winced, and nodded. Sadness welled up in her eyes. She seemed to sink deeper into the bed. She said nothing.

Rizzo said, "The dead girl's father gave us this picture. Maybe you could help us out the same way. Do you have a picture of your son?"

"A picture? Not like this one. Just an old one... She leaned across the bed, opened the nightstand drawer, and removed a worn, black vinyl handbag. From inside she withdrew a walletsized snapshot in a clear plastic sheath, and handed it over.

They took a look. The snapshot showed a pretty, fine-featured young woman in a lacy shawl, with a dark-haired boy of two or three on her lap. The child, squat and homely, clung to his mother's shawl with a sulky frown, but the woman gazed down at him with radiant and tender love. It was a beautiful photograph, worth treasuring.

"This is you and Manny?" Rizzo said.

She nodded. "When we lived in Puerto Rico. --You're not going to take it from me?"

He gave it another look, shook his head, and handed it back.

The corridor door opened then, and someone motioned to Rizzo. It was Dr. Salzman. Rizzo excused himself and went out, and Villanova stood at Julia Cruz's bedside. She took a long, wistful look at the snapshot before returning it to her handbag and settling back onto the pillow again, turning that troubled gaze of hers to the square of grey sky framed by the window. Villanova felt a deep compassion for her. It had nothing to do with her belief that the end of her life was near. It had more to do with the obscene corner her fate had backed her into. It had to do with her struggle for dignity, and her willingness to be helpful, without even knowing how much she had to lose. He liked Julia Cruz very much and didn't want to see her hurt.

She said, still looking out the window, "You're a kind man, Mr. Villanova."

"How do you know I'm kind?"

"I know. I trust you. I want to help you."

"Even though we're after your son?"

"Yes. It may be that he's done nothing."

"It may be. Have you told us everything you can?"

"For now."

"For now?"

"My memory is not so good right now. But if I
remember more, I'll tell you. I promise." She turned to look
at him. Her eyes were the wisest, most sensitive he'd ever seen.
She reached a hand toward him, and he took it, as if to seal a
pact. It was tiny and warm, like a child's.

The corridor door opened again, and Rizzo beckoned
him. Salzman was nowhere in sight. Villanova nodded to
Julia Cruz and left the room.

"What is it?" he said. "Manny show up?"

"It's Capogrosso, Buddy. He's downstairs."

They had a minute to share notes while they waited for
the elevator. "This lady on the square?" Rizzo asked.

"Ninety-five percent."

"Yeah, well, that's *nearly* good enough."

"It's twice what we could have asked for. She's in a
tough spot."

"What about the hocus-pocus stuff? That an act?"

"I don't think so. Jesus, she did as good a take on us
as we did on her, and *we* were asking the questions. I mean,
she read *my* mind two or three times."

"Yeah?" Rizzo gave Villanova a look. "You like her,
don't you, Buddy? Tell you one thing, on the square or not,
I'd hate like hell if *my* mother could see my thoughts."

"If she's any good at it at all, she'll be right about
Manny showing up here."

"She's *too* good. She gave us almost what we needed,
three times over. Jesus, she had me going, there. For a
minute I thought she was going to recognize the photo and
hand us our case."

"She gave us JFK, and that's nearly as good. It's our
crossover."

"Let's hope. If we get motive into this picture, we're in
business." The elevator arrived, and they stepped in. "Soon's

we get done with Capogrosso, over we go.   We'll check out
Julia's story on the disconnected phone too, but I'll bet you a
dinner at the Shamrock her exchange isn't gonna show up on
the Albano LUD sheets.   What we really need is for Manny
Cruz to take a serious shit when we nail him, or else cross up
his mother and lie himself into a hole."   He smirked.   "Some
cozy little household, huh?   If the girl was dead by one
o'clock, that means the mother practically walked in on the
murder.   The body had to be stashed somewhere, under a bed
or something.   And our psychic claims she didn't notice a
thing."

"She dreamed about Death, didn't she?" Villanova said.
"Don't count her out yet, she's going to help us.   She needs a
little working on...a little time."

"A little time is right, Buddy, if your medium's as sick
as she says."

"Let's just hope she's not."

"We'll know soon enough."

They exited into the lobby and headed for the main
desk.   The waiting area was vast, and there were plenty of
people sitting on the vinyl couches.   A burly, bored-looking
man in a bad-fitting grey suit lounged a few yards to one side
of the desk.   "Jesus," Villanova said, "whoever's been training
these new dicks for plainclothes isn't doing his job.   That guy's
got 'cop' written all over him."

"That's no cop.   That's Capogrosso."

"You serious?   Christ, he looks like a wrestler.   Where's
the guy from Homicide?"

Rizzo scanned the lobby.   "Not here.   Something's
fouled up."   He took another look around.   "Start in with
Capogrosso.   I'll catch you up.   I don't want this place without
a man in it."   He veered off toward the desk while Villanova
headed for the surgeon.

"You Dr. Capogrosso?" Villanova said.

"Right."

"I'm Mike Villanova. Can we talk a little? Out on the steps, maybe?" He needed a smoke badly.

"Let's just plop down in the corner there. Got to get off my feet. Spent the morning in the O.R." Capogrosso must have been six and a half feet tall and two hundred fifty pounds. His head was massive, his hands big and powerful, his back stooped under his bulk. He led Villanova to the far end of the lobby, where there were few people and a great many "No Smoking" signs. They settled in on one of the couches, and Villanova sketched in the situation and asked for whatever details of Julia Cruz's condition might bear on the investigation. Capogrosso listened quietly, his clear blue-grey eyes on Villanova's, until it was his turn to speak.

"The woman's got what we call an acoustic tumor," he explained. "They're a common enough type, but where they are and how fast they grow makes all the difference. In this case, we've got a bad situation."

"How so?"

"I operated on Julia Cruz a little over two years ago. It was one of the more difficult operations I've done. Fourteen hours in the O.R. We went in uncertain of what we were dealing with...meningioma, sarcoma, angioblastoma? In fact, based on the angiograms, we were hoping for an AVM, an arteriovenous malformation. It's a sort of birth defect, the kind of thing she could have had for decades without knowing, until it ruptured. Well, it wasn't that. When we opened her, we found a neurinoma, a particularly nasty one."

"A cancer?"

"No. A Schwannoma, a non-malignant growth. It's the kind that doesn't grow back if you get it out clean. But this one was a monster. It was in the worst possible place, the posterior fossa. Do you know anything about brain surgery, Mr. Villanova?"

"No."

"Well, a brain stem tumor is a neurosurgeon's nightmare. Juila's tumor had probably been growing slowly for two decades. It started on the eighth nerve and wrapped itself around everything, the brain stem, the basilar artery, blood vessels, nerves. It finally choked off the drainage of cerebrospinal fluid, and her brain began to swell. By the time she came to us the first time, she had double vision, headaches, hallucinations, memory loss. A little longer, a little more swelling, and her brain stem would have shifted under the pressure. She would have died. Just like that."

Villanova gritted his teeth. "Pretty grim stuff. And now we're dealing with the same scenario?"

Capogrosso nodded.

"The tumor grew back?"

"It grew back. And like most of them, it grew back bigger in two years than it had in twenty."

"Then she's as sick as she thinks she is."

"Oh, she's plenty sick."

Villanova shook his head. "She came to you on Monday afternoon with the same kind of symptoms? Memory loss, double vision, the works?"

"Yes. I gave her something for the pain, and started her right away on steroids to reduce the swelling. That's why I had to get her admitted fast, you see. Steroids knock down the immune system. Not to mention exacerbating the memory problem and making the patient generally a little weird."

"And Tuesday afternoon you saw her again?"

"Just to settle her in. And on Wednesday I gave her the pre-CAT-scan briefing."

"Did she mention any kind of trouble at home?"

"Not a word. Believe me, she had other things on her mind."

"What's the prognosis, doc? I guess the idea is to go in again and try to get all of the tumor this time?"

"That's the idea, yes, but..."

"But?"

"Second operations of this kind are a shaky business in neurosurgery. Plenty of surgeons won't even take the chance. Scar tissue changes the whole brain topography, you see. The colors are all wrong, the nerves are in the wrong place, vital formations are distorted. Major arteries can turn up anywhere. The first time in, there are a hundred perils, but at least there's a roadmap. The second time...well, chances of damaging or killing the patient on the table are very good. We lost one here just that way last week, a bleeder. Not me, one of my colleagues. Nicked an artery, couldn't find it. Big Red, we call it. Looks like the goddam Red Sea in the operating microscope. Not his fault, the poor bastard, just bad luck."

Villanova blew out his breath. "That's some tough racket you're in. And what if you don't operate?"

"In a case like Julia's? The patient dies. Matter of weeks, maybe less. But I've already committed to going in on Julia. I think I owe her that."

Villanova nodded. "The way things have shaped up, Doc, this woman is our only lead in a murder case, and maybe our only witness. We think she knows something she hasn't said yet."

Capogrosso smiled wryly. "In that case, you've got almost as much trouble as me. If I go in and lose her under anesthesia, or find the basilar artery the hard way, you're through, and I'm sitting where my colleague was sitting last week. My advice is, if you need Julia Cruz to say something, you'd better do it before it's her turn in the O.R."

"When will that be?"

"Right after the weekend...unless she worsens and goes on emergency status. Then she gets the first open slot."

"I'd appreciate being notified in either case."

"Sure. I wish I could paint you a nicer picture. You've got to understand, an acoustic neurinoma sticks like cement to every nerve and artery. You can't use a laser scalpel on a second try, because you'll burn a hole through an artery before you even see it. So you've got to go with the Cavitron and fight for every millimeter. That's why it takes ten, twelve hours."

Villanova nodded. "Does Julia know all this?" He saw Rizzo heading over.

"Not in so many words. But she knows. She's incredibly intuitive."

"She makes her living at it."

"I know. Between you and me, she's not the first tumor patient I've treated who had psychic powers..."

Villanova was just about to introduce Rizzo to Capogrosso. His mouth was open, and he was hesitating because he hated like hell to divert the conversation after Capogrosso's last intriguing comment. And just in that moment, he saw a long-haired young man cross the far end of the lobby from the street doors and press the elevator button. He jumped up and gave Rizzo a poke, and the two of them gaped as Manny Cruz entered the elevator, turned, and looked back at them from behind the closing door.

"That's our man!"

"Shit! Where's the stairs, Doc, quick!"

Capogrosso pointed.

"Call security, cover the elevators!" Rizzo barked, and they ran.

They flew up the stairwell. *It was over now*, that was Villanova's only thought as he sprinted behind Rizzo. They'd raced elevators before--three flights was always a dead heat at the worst. Seconds later, they broke out onto the fourth floor, slalomed around a couple of gurneys, and skidded up to the elevator bank just as the call for hospital security came over the P.A.

"Fuck! He's wise!" Villanova panted, pointing to the illuminated register. The elevator was on its way down again.

"Go get him, Buddy! You hit the lobby, I'll take the floors!" Rizzo put his hand on the grip of his .38.

They took the stairs again, Rizzo breaking off through the landing doors to scan the corridors while Villanova made like the express. When he hit the lobby, he stepped into pandemonium. The people who'd been on the couches were on their feet, guys in frocks were heading down the corridor on the run, and a roiling knot of people completely blocked the elevators. Villanova got himself over there and shoved his way through.

One elevator door was open, and two men were sprawled on the elevator floor. The one on top was Manny Cruz. His face was scarlet, his eyes bulging, his whole body straining for escape. The second man, lying on his back, had Manny locked in a crushing embrace. That man's face was hidden, but his huge arms and hands were unmistakeable. It was Capogrosso.

Rizzo came pushing his way through. He stood there, puffing, and took in the sight. "Nice work," he said to Capogrosso.

"Don't encourage me," the wry voice of the big man rumbled up.

A security guard shoved in behind Rizzo, then another. Rizzo nodded. A half-smile formed on his lips, though his eyes were mirthless.

"Cuff the sonofabitch," he said.

- SEVEN -

The interrogation room they used for Manny Cruz was right across the corridor from the one they had used for Jack LeClerc. They sat him down at the table and read him his rights, glossing his right to prompt arraignment, and with it, counsel.

"This is bullshit. I didn't do nothin'," Manny said. He was a little shorter than LeClerc, but beefier and plenty strong.

"Tell us about it. We'll listen," Rizzo said back.

"What you got behind that mirror, man?" Manny jabbed a finger toward the one-way glass on the wall. He was clumsy in movement, beetle-browed, bad-smelling, full of menace.

"Nothing that matters to you. Shall we get started?" Rizzo took out his notepad and closed in. He did a good imitation of routine, but certain special precautions had already been taken. Two phone calls had gone out from his office, the first one to the D.A.'s office. A psychologist was on his way over to the Homicide Squad, partly to advise on the handling of the interrogation, partly as a failsafe against a sudden incompetence or insanity plea down the road. The second call had gone to the home of Hector Rodriguez, the gypsy cabby who'd claimed he could I.D. the fare with the trunk. Rodriguez wasn't home, but a call for him went out on the police radio.

"How about telling us everything you can remember from Monday afternoon on?" Rizzo said. He stood to Manny's right, and Villanova sat across the table with his back to the mirror. "Start with what went on between you and your mother."

"My mother? You guys talked to her? You got no right!"

"Why not?" Villanova cut in angrily. "Does she know something we're not supposed to know?"

"You got to let me see her."

"Forget it, pal, you're in big trouble. Come on, you know why you're here. What did you do, Manny? Did you do something to a girl?"

"I didn't do nothin' to no girl. My mother..."

"Fuck your mother!" Villanova cut him off. "Tell us what you did to the girl!"

Manny seemed startled. He glared at Villanova, and Villanova glared right back. He didn't like the bastard. He didn't like his flat, surly voice, his matted black hair, his filthy sweatshirt and jeans.

Rizzo said, "Come on, Manny, let's do it. Start anywhere. You and your mother had an argument on Monday, right? What about?"

Manny nodded sullenly, still glaring at Villanova. "She gave me shit about not working. It's all bull. For two fucking years I worked that job, until I had to quit."

"Why'd you have to quit?"

"Because I had to, man. Because the job sucked."

"What'd you do Monday afternoon?"

"Went looking for work. Up Fordham Road. The bagel place. The furniture place."

Rizzo jotted in his notepad. "You get hired? Anyone take your name?"

"You kidding? Those people look at me, they think I'm gonna steal. They think I'm gonna hurt somebody."

"You wouldn't hurt anybody, would you, Manny?"

Manny's answer was a scowl.

"*Do* you steal?" Villanova put in.

"Sure. Because they want me to. Because I'm ugly."

"You think you're ugly, Manny?"

"No, I'm a fucking movie star. You want to see ugly, man? Keep looking over here, have a good time."

Villanova took out his cigarettes and lit one, taking care to blow the smoke in Manny's direction. Ugly was the right word, and it was easy to see why people were afraid of the guy. He sat hunched and tense, his wary eyes scanning the room; they were like wolf eyes, narrow and wide-set on his swarthy face, with an opaque, ruthless quality. Villanova felt caged with a brute, a monstrous exaggeration of the little boy he'd seen in Julia's snapshot.

"Tell us about Tuesday, the day your mother went to the hospital," Rizzo said. "What time did you take her to the bus stop?"

"I don't know. Lunchtime."

"Doesn't that watch you're wearing keep time?"

"It was around twelve-thirty, man."

"Why didn't you wait with her till she got on?"

"I went looking for work again. Down to John F. Kennedy. I got my old job back."

Rizzo's notepad went down, and he exchanged a look with Villanova. "You what?"

"Got my job back. At JFK. I went in and looked for Windy, the day captain. He was the one that told me I could come back if I want to. I figured, one o'clock, he'd be there, but he was still out at lunch. I waited in the receiving room."

"Anyone see you? There's a thousand people in that building, right?"

Manny shook his head.   I went in through the custodians' locker room. We don't see nobody that way."

"How long did you wait for this Windy guy?"

"Till one-fifteen. I read a comic book awhile, *Doctor Strange.*"

"You sure it was one-fifteen?"

"Sure. I had my eye on the time-clock."

Villanova said, "You like comic books, don't you, Manny. Women get hurt in comic books, right? You like to see women get hurt?"

"They don't always get hurt."

"No?"

"No. Sometimes someone saves them."

"Who saves them? You?"

Manny glared, and Villanova glared back. He lit another cigarette, but left the first one smoldering on the floor. The little room was already full of smoke, but Manny hadn't so much as flinched, though his eyes were watering. Those brute eyes of his had only two expressions, one predatory and merciless, the other shifty and treacherous. His hands were on the table, broad and stubby, with thick veins snaking under the skin. Villanova imagined those clumsy hands on Elizabeth Albano's neck.

"Hey, tell this guy to quit looking at me," Manny said to Rizzo.

"You told him to look, didn't you?"

"Well, I don't like the way he looks."

Villanova blew more smoke Manny's way.

"What happened when Windy showed up at JFK?" Rizzo said.

"He told me they still needed a guy on the second shift. I could start right away, four to twelve. So I was back in."

"Even though the job sucked?   That's what you told me."

"It does, man.   Cleaning toilets.   Try it and find out."

"It's not so bad," Villanova put in.   "There's girls to look at, right?"

"There's nobody to look at."

"There's teachers, right?   Women in dresses and high heels.   That's the stuff you like, right, Manny?"

"I don't like nothing."

"Come on, you like pictures of women, right?   You must love those bookstores down in Times Square.   I bet you like those peep booths too, am I right, Manny?"

"Not me, man.   No way."

"Come on, don't kid us.   I bet you live in those booths, Manny."

"Those places are fucked, man.   They know you're looking."

"So what?   So what if they know you're looking?"

"No way."   Manny shook his head.

Rizzo said, "Why'd you move out of your apartment, Manny?"

"'Cause Windy said okay by him if I move my stuff into the receiving room.   You know, sleep there a few days."

"But why'd you want to move?   Why all of a sudden like that?"

"Like I told you.   'Cause my mother bitched me out."

"Your mother's sick, you know," Villanova snapped, an unreasoning hate rising in him.   "She's goddam sick, and you know what?   Something you did made her sicker."

"You shut your face, man.   Don't blame me for that."

"Why not?   Why shouldn't I blame you?"

"Don't fucking blame me!" Manny exploded, and for a second he seemed about to rise up out of the chair.   "I get blamed for everything!   My sister dies, I get blamed!   My old man splits, I get blamed! Everything, just because I'm ugly! You want to blame me for my mother too? Fuck you!"

"What're you talking about? When did your sister die?"

Something wounded and vicious gathered in Manny's eyes. "You know what? I wish I *did* kill her. I wish I did!"

"What happened to your sister? What's this about?" Rizzo said.

"In her crib. Back in Puerto Rico. My mother blamed me," he said bitterly.

"Why you?"

"She left us alone in the house. The blanket got around her face. How's that my fault?"

Villanova caught Rizzo's eye, and saw there the same disgust he was feeling. "Your mother blamed you?"

"She won't say it straight out. But she did. I know what I know."

"Then you better start talking, you creep sonofabitch. Your mother's in the hospital dying, and you're wasting time."

"Nobody's dying!" Manny shouted. "You got no right to keep me here! I want to see my mother!"

"She's dying, you stupid bastard, and you're *never* gonna see her!" Villanova shouted back.

Manny's eyes turned to slits. "You big shots think you got me boxed in here? You think I can't get out of this little pisshole?" He sneered. "You don't know me. I can get in or out of anything. You watch me, I'm like a fucking cat."

"You're like a *rat*," Villanova shot back. "What did you do to the girl? You took her panties off, didn't you? What'd you want to see? Didn't you ever see what a girl looks like before? Didn't your mother ever show you?"

Manny's eyes glowed crimson. Villanova had been the object of murderous looks before, but never one as savage as this one. Manny looked about to leap across the table, and

Villanova wished he would. He wanted to meet that ugly face with his fist, he wanted to pound it to paste. Rizzo caught his eye--his face must've been a shade of purple. His heart was pounding and the sore spot on his head was throbbing again. He eased back in the chair and took a pull on the Chesterfield. The smoke was so bad his own eyes were starting to burn.

There was a knock at the door, and Rizzo, looking relieved, waved him over. Villanova dropped his cigarette to the floor and went see who it was. On the way, he glimpsed his face in the mirror. The thick brows seemed thicker, the jaw taut with anger, the eyes an unapproachable black. He averted his glance.

Out in the corridor, he found Gilman waiting. "How's it going in there?" he asked.

"The air's a hell of a lot better out here."

"We got the cabby. He's on his way."

"Good work. What about the shrink?"

Gilman motioned with his head toward the adjoining cubicle. "Inside."

Villanova went over, gave a rap, and entered. The room was dark except for the light coming through the one-way mirror. There was a woman at the glass, thirty-ish, attractive, dressed in an ivory linen blouse and a billowy blue skirt. She turned for a glance as he came in.

"Who're you?" Villanova said.

"From the D.A.'s office. I'm new."

"You been in here all along?"

"Sure. Jesus, this guy here's a study. Listen, when you two are done in there, I'd like to get in and ask my own questions. That okay?"

Villanova stared. Big platinum hoops dangled from her ears.

"What's wrong?"

"Nothing.... The D.A. told you to do an interview?"

"No formal work-up or anything. Bev Cohn just told me to help you guys play it smart."

He shrugged. "Then stay put for now. We've got a witness coming in any minute."

"Can I smoke?"

"No dice. The guy might catch the glow through the mirror."

She nodded and turned back to the glass. Villanova stood behind her and watched over her shoulder. The big fluorescent ceiling fixture of the interrogation room threw a stark, almost surreal light on the two men below. The eerieness of the scene was heightened by the closeness of their voices through the speaker. Rizzo was still working on Tuesday afternoon, pressing his questions on Manny as fast as he could get the answers. Manny claimed he'd gone right home from JFK, and his mother had come in a few minutes later while he was packing his stuff.

"She surprised you, then, showing up like that?" Rizzo said. "Why'd she come back from the hospital?"

"Who knows? We didn't talk."

Rizzo drew closer, crowding Manny without exposing his own front. "You didn't feel like bragging to her about getting your job back? Or maybe you were too upset to talk? Maybe something happened before she got home?"

"Nothing happened. Why don't you back off, man? Lemme breathe." Manny gave up an inch of space, and Rizzo took it as artfully as a bullfighter.

"Maybe something happened that you had to hide?"

"I told you, man, nothing happened. She laid down a few minutes, then she went to the hospital. I stayed in my room. Quarter to four, I went to work."

"You punched in?"

"In and out. Four to twelve. Then, back home."

Villanova whispered to the shrink, "What do you think?"

"Evasive, cagey. Not delusional. Shhh."

He shoved his hands in his pockets and closed his fingers around the familiar shape of his cigarette lighter. The shrink's perfume started to get into his nose, nice, subtle stuff, gardenia scented. She wore her hair in a French knot and had a very long, very suntanned neck, girdled by a strand of baby pearls. Rizzo was right, she was the picture of class. He wondered how she felt, secretly watching her ex-lover at work. She was all eyes, that was obvious enough. Himself, he never felt good about standing in the dark only a few feet from people who couldn't see him. Something queer always happened to his head; he began to feel a little separated from his own body, from reality itself. It was happening now, as he watched the performance of the two mannekins in the parallel cubicle, as he pondered the secret of the woman standing in front of him, and his own secret knowledge of it. He held onto his lighter and tried focusing on Manny Cruz's words, on the distorting mirror the lying bastard was holding up to the truth. But other thoughts pushed into his head. Elizabeth Albano's beautiful face in LeClerc's gruesome holocaust portraits. Her ethereal image staring into Manny's bedroom window. The sight of Manny from the old woman's peephole, dragging that little coffin down the stairs. The image of Rizzo's lover in her bedroom mirror, pulling on her double-duty wedding dress. Twin worlds everywhere, dark and light, hidden and revealed, illusory and real, false and true. Translucent secrets, all separated from each other by the flimsiest, most fragile of membranes.

Rizzo said, "You slept alone in the apartment Tuesday night?"

"Tuesday night I took my stuff over to JFK. I slept there."

"How'd you get your stuff over there? The school's, what, five blocks up. You take a cab?"

"No. I carried it. Three trips. The extra junk, I put in a crate and threw out."

"You lugged all that shit? Why not just take a cab, Manny?"

"I had no money."

"No? Your mother went into the hospital and didn't leave you a dime?"

Manny hesitated. Villanova whispered to the shrink, "Watch this. We know he had a ten-spot on him."

"Well?" Rizzo said.

Manny said, "She gave me money, yeah. Ten bucks. I used it to eat. Up the White Castle."

Villanova snorted. Manny was good. The White Castle on Fordham Road was one place where no one had a face.

With one quick sweep, Rizzo whisked Elizabeth Albano's photo from his pocket to the tabletop. "Take a look here. You know this girl from somewhere?"

Manny was caught off-guard. He looked at the picture by reflex, then pulled his eyes away. He shook his head.

"Come on, damn it, look at it! Don't play dumb!"

Manny glanced at the photo. His eyes seemed full of dread. Again he shook his head. "No way."

"No way? You mean this isn't your kind of girl? What's wrong, too pretty, too much class? Doesn't it piss you off, a girl like this that you can't touch?"

Manny muttered, "I don't need to touch *nobody*."

"Sure. You just keep looking at her, Manny. It's okay, she doesn't know you're looking."

Manny mumbled a curse and turned away from the photo.

Rizzo came around his other side and leaned in closer. "Tell me, Manny, you ever have any other jobs, before JFK?"

"Sure. Plenty."

"Did you graduate high school, Manny?"

"Tenth grade." Hey, man, you want this chair, or what? I'll give it to you."

"What about your father? Ever see him?"

"He's in jail in Puerto Rico."

"Why's he in jail?"

"Why? Because that's where *she* wants him. Somewhere he can't get out. She always gets what she wants."

"Your mother? What's she got against your father?"

Manny scowled. "He looks like me."

"Yeah? You hate your mother, Manny? You wish you could hurt her?"

Manny's eyes narrowed, but he made no answer.

"Do you have a girlfriend, Manny?"

"No."

"Did you ever have one?"

"Sure."

"You sure? You sure you like girls, Manny?"

Manny frowned. "What you talking about, man?"

"Tell the truth, have you ever been with a girl?"

"Sure I been with a girl."

"I don't mean a whore. I mean a girl that you don't pay money."

Manny reddened, and a venomous look flooded into his eyes. Rizzo had moved himself just out of lunging range.

The shrink cleared her throat. Villanova gave her a look, and was surprised to see that she seemed a little uneasy herself. Her eyes, faintly distracted, were locked onto Rizzo. "Seen enough yet?" he whispered.

She recovered, and shrugged. "Schizotypal personality disorder, a textbook case," she whispered. "Elements of paranoid-antisocial, too, but I don't think that's the key."

"Schizotypal? We talking psychotic here?"

"Not psychotic. Well able to separate reality from fantasy. Able to tell right from wrong, to conceal wrongful acts, to dissemble intentions, to lie...." She paused thoughtfully over those last phrases. "But extremely alienated from the world, a total social isolate."

"Run it through for me. In a nutshell."

"Sorry, I don't do quickies. A diagnosis takes patience, commitment. It's a delicate thing, a piece of art."

"I don't need a masterpiece, just a sketch. Listen, we're in a race with a brain tumor here. Give me anything, just an outline."

She turned to appraise him. Her eyes were a rich hazel color, intelligent and confident. When they probed his, he sensed a peculiar wariness in them; she'd surmised that he and Rizzo were buddies, and had begun to wonder how much he knew about her. He gazed back as evenly as he could; he didn't give a shit what she did in her spare time, and regretted being stuck with anybody's secrets.

Satisfied with that, she nodded and turned back to the glass. "A schizotypal," she whispered, "drifts in and out of jobs, avoids people and face-to-face interaction, doesn't like to be touched. Often has terrific ambivalence about his mother-- you know, dependency and rage. He's hanging onto his identity by a thread...." She trailed off.

"Go on."

She pondered. "Spooky affect, plenty of auto-stimulation and fantasy. Superstitiousness, metaphoric thinking, a tendency to obsess over religious images or symbolic artwork..."

"What kind of artwork?"

"Like the comic book he mentioned. You ever see those things? Sadism, erotica, the occult, all blended together. Very violent stuff. That's why, if there's a sex crime involved, you can almost count on the victim being unconscious before her violation, or even dead. The schizotypal wants a marble statue, see, not a live woman. He wants an icon to deface. The more his victim moves and struggles, the more rage and brute force she provokes. The schizotypal prefers to steal sex than be given it. To him, being loved is equivalent to being destroyed. Both tap into the same anger. He's a person who feels his inner self is vulnerable all the time."

"Vulnerable in what way?" Villanova said.

"The way we're all vulnerable when someone sees inside us." She glanced back at him. "Only magnified a hundred times. With this disorder, loving or being loved are both felt as lethal threats to the self, acts of great violence."

Violence was what he wanted to hear about, but now Rizzo was working over Manny's account of Tuesday evening, and closing in on crucial ground. Villanova signaled the shrink to hold off a moment.

"Do you own a trunk?" Rizzo said.

"No."

"No? Someone saw you dragging a trunk down from your apartment on Tuesday night."

"No one saw me drag no trunk."

"A woman downstairs saw you. How about it?"

"What woman? The old lady downstairs? She's crazy, man. I dragged a crate of junk down and threw it out in the bin. That old lady, she hates my guts. For nothing, too. I told you, I get blamed for everything."

"She's making it up, then, right?"

"She's blind, the old bitch. Ask anyone. She can't see shit."

"What about you, how good can you see?"

"Plenty good. 20-20."

Rizzo scooped the photo off the tabletop and pushed it in Manny's face. "And you're telling me you never saw this girl? You never even saw a picture of her?"

"Uh-uh."

"You lying piece of shit!   She's staring in your bedroom window, big as life! Don't keep shaking your head, you sick sonofabitch! Take a look at your dream girl. She's a real pretty girl, isn't she? Don't you think she's pretty?"

Manny didn't answer. He seemed to have pulled inside himself.

"You gonna tell me what you did to this girl, Manny?"

No response beyond a glower.

Rizzo leaned over him, his face only inches from Manny's. "You know what? You disgust me, you fucking creep!"

This time Manny's look of resentment seemed to come from somewhere so distant, so far away in the depths of him that it wasn't him at all.

"There," the shrink said, "that's typical.   See that removal? That's the schizotypal's only protection."

"What would make him get violent rather than hide that way?"

"The violence happens when something threatening invades that inner privacy...when something breaches the veil between real and fantasy life. Remember, the schizotypal is always in danger from the gaze of others. I know of one patient who'd been having masturbation fantasies about a certain woman he'd never spoken to. He got himself off in a public restroom one day, came out and ran into the very woman by coincidence, and felt that she was looking right through him into his secret. He attacked and raped her. You see, anything's possible under pressure, even environmental pressure, if it's extreme enough."

"Like a mother who's in danger of dying?"

"Absolutely. In fact, a pathenogenic mother is part of the classic pattern. You know, a smothering, over-protective mother, or one who doesn't let the child separate its identity. Think of it this way. Remember when you were little, and there was nothing about yourself that you could hide from your mother? And then you learned to lie, and you established a self that belonged to no one but you? Well, the schizotypal never accomplishes that. He can lie, but he never develops a self that's secure enough to link with others in relationships. That's why he's solitary, that's why he goes into a rage when he's looked at too closely. He feels that his self is always completely exposed, first to his mother and then to any one else who looks close. He feels literally made of glass, so that anyone can see through him at any time and break him to pieces."

Villanova nodded. It was beautifully coherent. He understood now why she'd been put off about hurrying her diagnosis. "Then this guy Cruz shouldn't be that tough to crack," he said.

"Right, but you want to be very careful about that. He's not going to crack like stone, he's going to splinter like glass. You'll wind up with an incompetency situation and no trial. I mean, that's why I was brought in, right, to make sure you guys don't screw things up by accident? Well, my advice to you is to let your partner handle the cracking. He's doing fine, he doesn't bore right into this guy the way you do. He moves in and out. He doesn't make it so *personal*."

"Oh, he's good at what he does," Villanova said, nodding.

"He's damned good."

Villanova had to smile. She was damned good, too. She was far better in life than in Rizzo's recollection. He said,

"In your view, then, right now we've got a competent and legally sane suspect in our hands? You're sure of that?"

"I'm sure, unless there's more than I've seen here. That's why I want to do some talking."

"Okay, in a bit. Keep watching."

There were two brisk knocks on the door then, and Gilman pushed in. "Rodriguez is here," he said.

"Good timing. Send him in."

"And here..." he handed over a thin sheaf of faxes. "We got the LUD sheets from the phone company. Rizzo'll want to see these."

"Great." Villanova folded the pages into his hip pocket as Gilman backed out. Seconds later the cabby came in, his face as sad and worried as ever.

"You got here fast," Villanova said

Rodriguez shrugged. "I'm glad to get it over with. I haven't had any sleep, not for two days."

"Join the club."

"What do I do? Same as last time?"

"Right. Just take your time and have a good look."

Rodriguez got up to the mirror next to the shrink. Villanova stood behind them. After a half-minute, the cabby nodded.

"It's him?" Villanova said.

"I'm pretty sure this time."

"Watch for a while." Rizzo had started the questioning from the top again, Round Two. By Round Four or Five, even a good liar like Manny Cruz would be screwing up a detail or two. That's what lawyers were for.

The cabby nodded again. "That sounds like his voice, too."

"You can swear to that in court?"

"Court?"

"Maybe it won't come to that. But we've got to know we can count on you."

Rodriguez's shoulders slumped noticeably. He did a little fumbling, and all of a sudden he had a cigarette in his mouth and was striking a match.

"Jesus, douse it!" Villanova hissed.

"What?"

Villanova knocked the match from his hands.

But it was too late. Manny had stopped speaking in mid-sentence. He was staring at the mirror, that beetle brow of his frowning.

"Can he see us?" Rodriguez whispered.

"No." But Villanova's heart had begun to race.

Manny's eyes seethed with hatred. His face colored.

"Jesus, he's looking right at me!" the cabby said. He took a step back and almost fell over Villanova's feet.

"Don't move! If it's a reflection..."

"Oh my God," the shrink said, "my earrings?" She cupped her hands over her ears.

Manny reared up like a vengeful demon. With a snarl, he snatched one of the wooden chairs and flung it across the table at the mirror. Villanova dove to the side, dragging the shrink with him. The chair came through the glass with a terrific crash and struck the cabby in the chest. "*Fuckers!*" Manny screamed.

"Down!" Villanova hissed to the cabby. Rodriguez stood there frozen.

"Spying on me! You fuckers are spying on me!"

"Down!" Villanova scrambled up and pulled the cabby out of the line of sight. Through the jagged opening, he glimpsed Gilman charging into the interrogation room, and Rizzo trying to wrestle Manny back into his seat. "Sit down!" Rizzo's voice bellowed.

"You fuckers got no right!"

"Sit!"

"Spies! Bastards!"

"Sit, motherfucker!"

Villanova stood at the opening and watched. The two cops had Manny from either side, his arms screwed behind his back. His face was twisted with rage, his body heaving. His wolf eyes darted this way and that, looking for escape, an ally, a weapon. They finally found Villanova's face, and locked there with an expression of withering hatred. Villanova tensed.

But Manny was pinned. The rage peaked. The wolf look receded. Slowly, he relaxed. "You got no right," he panted. He sagged down into his seat.

Rizzo and Gilman cuffed him to the chair.

Inside the witness room, it looked as if a dozen windows had shattered onto the floor. In spite of himself, Villanova was impressed. There was something damned persuasive about violence. He'd never seen a game busted up so fast.

He slipped the shrink and the cabby out into the corridor. Both looked pretty pale. "You okay?" he asked the woman.

She nodded.

"What about you, pal? The chair hurt you?"

The cabby shook his head. He had a cut on his hand. Blood was dripping to the floor. "That guy saw me," he said weakly.

"Let's have a look at the hand," Villanova said.

"He was staring me right in the face!"

"Forget him, he's through."

"What'm I doing here? I'm outta my goddam mind!"

"You're fine. Come on, let's see the cut." He was surprised at how cold the man's hand was when he took it.

The cut looked clean and not too deep. Pressure on the wrist damped nearly all the flow of blood.

Gilman came out, and Villanova said to him, "Take care of Mr. Rodriguez here, will you? He got sliced a little."

"Sure. Christ, you ever see the likes of that? An animal!" He took the cabby by the elbow and steered him to the stairwell.

Villanova turned to the woman. "You sure you're okay?"

"It's no big deal." The color started coming back to her face.

"Did Cruz spot you too?"

"I don't think so."

"Listen, you had a pretty rough start here. This guy needs a keeper, not a shrink. Maybe you want to leave this one alone? Bev Cohn can send someone else down."

It was as if he had pushed a button. She drew herself up and gave him a cold look. "Bev sent *me* down. Broken glass doesn't bother me any more than it does you."

"Well, it bothers the hell out of me."

She didn't smile. "How about letting me inside so I can do my job?"

He nodded. "Just hang out in the stairwell another minute till I clear it."

He waited till she was out of view, then opened the door of the interrogation room and signaled Rizzo to come to the doorway. Manny, scowling, watched from his seat.

"Did we do something stupid?" Rizzo whispered.

"Not too stupid. That Manny's a pretty eloquent bastard after all."

"Anyone hurt?"

"The cabby took a cut. The shrink's a little shook up, but won't let on."

"The cabby saw, though, right? What's the magic word?"

"A healthy baby boy, Papa."

Rizzo smiled.

"The shrink's in the stairwell. Wants in to see Cruz."

"So?"

"So get ready."

"For what?"

Now Villanova smiled.

"What's with you? We gonna work this character, or what?"

"Listen," Villanova said. "You work him. I'm gonna take a run over to JFK. Maybe I can catch this guy Windy before he punches out for the day."

"Good thinking, Buddy. We could use a little squeeze, because I got a bad feeling this creep in here isn't going to shit for us on his own. Just make sure to pin down the times real good, write everything down. This sonofabitch tells a tight story. Except for fifteen minutes, everything matches with the time frame his mother gave us. And you know which fifteen minutes I'm talking about."

"Relax. I'll be back in an hour, notes and all."

Rizzo held him by the wrist. "This is our crossover, Buddy. If motive comes into the picture, here's the place. To nail this guy's ass, we gotta prove where he was and where he wasn't between a quarter to one and one o'clock on Tuesday."

"I hear you, pal."

"And listen, if you find Manny's personal goods, be careful not to queer any of the evidence."

"Yo!" Manny called. "You fuckers talking about me?" He tried to stand up.

Rizzo went back in and shoved him down.

The shrink came out of the stairwell then, and put her hands on her hips. Villanova waved her into the interrogation room.

Rizzo and Manny looked equally surprised at first sight of her. Rizzo kept on staring, and Manny turned away, which was good because for a few seconds Rizzo looked a little shaky. The shrink gazed right back at him, and something very personal and almost tender flashed between them.

Finally Rizzo cleared his throat to speak, but the shrink got her words out first. "Jesus," she said, "how can you guys stand the smoke in here?"

Villanova pulled the door shut and headed back through the Squadroom.

The big room was vacant except for a uniformed cop on one of phones, and a somber-faced woman waiting at Gilman's desk. Villanova was almost past her before he recognized her. He turned back. "Mrs. Albano?"

Recognition came to her eyes as well. She nodded to him. She looked a little wobbly; her collar was askew, the colors of her blouse and slacks clashed under the fluorescent lights. "I came to talk to your partner," she said.

"He's tied up right now. Maybe I can help you." He scanned the corridor behind her. "Your husband here?"

"I came alone."

"What is it, Mrs. Albano?"

"I found something." She opened her handbag. "It was with Liz's knitting, under the yarn."

She handed Villanova a posted letter. It was addressed to Liz Albano; there was no return address on the envelope, but the postmark read "Tannersville, N.Y. / August 25."

Inside was a single sheet penned in a cramped hand:

Liz!

No, I'm not still sore at you. Want to know the truth? Your letter was the best thing to happen to me in a year. I mean it. I figured you'd given up thinking about me.

How am I? Okay, I guess. Working my butt off, basically. I wake up, and I think about what I'm working on, then I go cut wood for 3 or 4 hours (which I load in the pick-up and sell) and then in the hot part of the day I do my writing out on the porch (no air-conditioning in this dump. No cable tv, no vcr, no non-stop New York hype). People here think I'm nuts for taking the phone out. Yes, I do have plumbing, and a great old clawfoot tub. When I need a break, I camp in the woods for a few days, no thinking allowed.

I'm glad you're thinking about dropping out of grad school. It's bullshit, Liz. And don't take that dumb high school job, either. Come up here. You can take a dumb high school job here, if you want.

Seriously, I still love you, I still want everything I always talked about, you, a bunch of kids, our own world. I'm calmer now, not like I was back when we were fighting over this.

*Listen, Liz, I'm poor but I do own this chunk
of land, and it's beautiful.   We could make
anything we want of it.   Say yes.*

Love,
Tom

*P.S.   Christ, I hope you're not playing with
me.   Because then I really would be pissed.
By the way, why can't I phone you?   What's
with the secrecy?*

Villanova looked up at Mrs. Albano.   "What's Tom's
last name?" he said.

"Reilly."

"And what about an address?   Do you know if Liz
answered this letter?"

She pointed to the envelope.   "That's where she's
gone."

"What?"

"That's where she's gone.   He came with his truck and
got her.   That's why she hasn't come home."

He looked into the woman's dazed eyes.   "Mrs.
Albano, where's your husband?"

"Talking with the people over at Grippi's.   The funeral
home."

"Did you show him this letter?"

She nodded.   "It's all a mistake, you see.   She's up
there, with him."

"Mrs. Albano, listen," he said softly.   "Your daughter's
dead."

She tilted her head slightly to one side.

"Do you understand what I'm saying?"

Her eyes cleared. She took him in. Her gaze moved around the room, over the cluttered desks, the flimsy partitions, the littered floor. An anger sharpened in her face. The pretty woman that she actually was emerged.

"Why don't you let me arrange for someone to take you home. I'll see that my partner gets this letter."

"You know, she *should* have gone with him, two years back," she said. "When she graduated. It's all his fault."

"Whose?"

"The one who talked her into more school. That dean." She was rocking almost imperceptibly from foot to foot, swaying. She took the letter and envelope from his hand. "Just don't tell my husband."

"Don't tell him what?"

"About Liz being pregnant. It's better if he doesn't know." Her red-knuckled hands pushed the letter back into her handbag.

"How did *you* know?"

"I'm her mother."

"Did Liz talk to you about it?"

Irony came into her eyes. "Talk to me? I'm no one to talk to. The last time was when she was twelve. And already she was more than I was." She sank down onto one of the grey-green folding chairs facing Gilman's desk. "I'm no one that matters. That's why no one hears anything I say."

Villanova glanced uneasily at the Squadroom clock.

"Go, go on with your work. I'll wait for the other one, your partner. He understands."

Villanova couldn't delay any longer--and he couldn't bear the thought of leaving her where her path might cross Manny Cruz's. He caught sight of Gilman coming down the corridor, signaled to him broadly, and got a nod of reassurance in return.

He left the woman sitting with her ankles crossed and her handbag hugged tight against her midsection.

- EIGHT -

John F. Kennedy High School sat grandiosely on Fordham Road with its face toward the university and its grimy back to the ghetto it served. By the time Villanova arrived there, less than an hour after dismissal time on Thursday afternoon, chains and padlocks already sealed the entrances, and the last of the students had vanished.

He searched down the side street and found the receiving bay, which, because of the slope of the street, led into the building's sub-storey. He checked out the custodians' locker room first. It was a cockroach heaven, full of wet and rust, with strings of matted asbestos dripping from the overhead pipes, and a putrid smell in the air. An old formica cafeteria table, a wooden bench, and a half-dozen *Cheri* centerfolds made up all the furnishings. He found the time-clock and the rack of cards with little trouble. Manny's time card was in place with the others. His full name, Manuel Jesus Cruz, was written in pen at the top, along with a Social Security number. The card had been punched in and out, four to twelve, on Tuesday and Wednesday, just as Manny had said.

"What're you looking for?" a voice snapped, and Villanova jumped.

He turned to see a very large, very fat man standing in the doorway, garbed in custodian's greens. "Jesus," he said, "how'd you come up on me so quiet like that?"

"A big man don't have to make a big noise. What're you messing with those cards for?"

"I'm looking for a guy named Windy."

"That's me, Mister. What's your business?" The man was about fifty, with a bulldog face and a short-breathed, gravelly voice.

Villanova identified himself and told him where Manny Cruz was and why.

"Christ," Windy said. "Christ. That kid's in trouble."

"He says he was here on Tuesday afternoon asking for a job. Says he was waiting here till you got back from lunch. That so?"

"Yeah, that's so. Sorta. He was messing around in the receiving room when I come back from lunch. It was me that asked if he wanted his job back."

"*You* asked?"

"Right. I figured he either come back to steal something or to get back on the payroll. I told him, 'You wanta work late shift again? We need somebody.' He asked could he hole up in the back room a few days, and I said sure, if he took the shift."

"Good. You remember what time that was?"

"Just after lunch, usual time. Around one-thirty, give or take a half hour."

"Shit, don't you punch out for lunch?"

"Hell no. We got a union here, Mister. I.U.O.E. doesn't take any crap from anyone."

"That's swell for I.U.O.E. Where'd you eat on Tuesday?"

"Burger King. Arby's. The White Castle. Take a look at me, Mister. I eat all day long."

He was a three-hundred pounder, easy, and his voice whistled out of him like wind through the cracks of an old house. Villanova had to fight down a panic at the way he blocked the doorway. "Who'd you eat with. Maybe someone *else* looked at the time..."

"I ate alone. You don't get it. The only time anyone pays attention to here is quitting time." He checked his watch. "That's why I come down here now, to punch out."

Villanova shook his head in frustration.   He sank down on the bench, and lit a cigarette.

"Hey, don't get all bothered about it, Mister, that's how this place is run." Windy pulled out a pack of Camels Filters, shook one out and lit it. He finally cleared the doorway and joined Villanova at the table.

Villanova felt the bench take his weight.   "Listen, Windy, I got a serious situation here. You want to help, or not?"

Windy shrugged. "I guess I do."

"You were Manny's boss for two years. Did he ever cause trouble?"

"Nope. Did his work, didn't talk to nobody. Gave a few of the girls the willies, but we're used to that. In the old days, he'd of been out of here fast, but not these days."

"You been here a long time, Windy?"

"Twenty-seven years. I make more money than the teachers.   Shit, I make more money than the fucking principal. You know who's the highest paid guy in this place? Me. Ninety-six thousand bucks last year, with overtime."

"That's a hell of a lot of money."

"Used to be fun, too. Never hard work. All Irish guys when I came here, scamps. And the girls used to be fun to look at. Skirts, stockings. High hopes, this place had in the beginning. No more. Nothing to believe in, everyone just out for the buck--the teachers, the kids, everyone. Even the girls, tough as nails. Knives in the pocketbook, crack vials. All we hire now to work the mops is Nicaraguans, Haitians. We hire on temp now, coolie wages, that's why we can't keep 'em.

Manny, he's got a creepy look, but he cleaned the toilets for two years, steady."

"Why'd he quit?"

"Don't know. All that time, no trouble, then he goes on nights, two weeks, boom, he quits. *Less* than two weeks. The Thursday, he only showed up to clean out his locker."

"Something happened on Wednesday night, maybe?"

"Maybe. He looked a little scared the next day... spooked, like. And then a week later he's back, and he takes his job back, and he still doesn't say nothing."

"Still look scared?"

"Sort of. Different, though."

"Is one of these lockers his?"

"No more. He's got his stuff in the electrical closet."

"Want to show me? I don't have to touch anything, just put my eyes on it."

Windy shrugged, took a last pull on his cigarette, and doused the butt in one of the mold-spotted styrofoam cups on the table. He heaved himself to his feet.

Villanova followed him into the receiving room. The place was dim, especially near the back wall where metal storage racks were crammed with dust-covered equipment and crates. Windy had a little trouble negotiating the random aisles among the clutter of maintenance equipment and student desks, but he worked his way through and pushed open a metal door marked "High Voltage--Keep Out." He flicked on a light switch and led the way inside.

The room was tiny, bare, warm, and airless. The walls were covered with conduit, circuit-breaker boxes, banks of meters. In one corner there were half a dozen cardboard cartons stuffed with clothes, and a makeshift bed: a layer of clothing and a blanket on a sheet of rough plywood. Villanova drew nearer and observed what he could: a pair of high top sneakers, placed neatly, toe-in, against the wall, with a toothbrush standing in one and a hairpick in the other.   A liter-size bottle of Root Beer, about a third full.   On the bed, scattered comic books: *Wolverine, Doctor Strange, Deathlok, Silver Storm, Dr. Fate.*   There was nothing else resembling personal effects.   Clothing stuffed into a pillowcase served as a pillow.   Villanova nudged it over.   There was no sign of a lipstick smudge on either side.

Villanova stood awhile and took in the feel of the place.   This rat-hole was about as much of Manny's life as he was going to get close to.   The heat of the room brought sweat to his scalp.   He could hear, or thought he could, a faint hum of electricity.   After a minute, the profound hopelessness of the scene before him seeped into him, and with it came the feeling he hated most, an empty, weak sensation in his groin.   He wanted to get out.   Once again Windy's bulk blocked the doorway.   Villanova asked, "Did Manny sleep in here with the light on?"

"Search me."

He guessed he did.   He hoped he did.   In the dark, the place was a coffin.   He turned to Windy.   "I need to phone in for a warrant."   The goods would have to be worked over by the Crime Lab.

"You're going to have to do it from the Office, then," Windy said.   "I don't want the responsibility."   He turned and led the way back into the maze in the receiving room.

"I'll want to talk to the principal, too.   He in?"

"You kidding?   Ten minutes after dismissal, Newmark's outa here like a shot.   The secretaries'll take care of you.   You coming?"

"Hold on a second."   Villanova's eye had picked something out of the gloom.   Near the back of one of the shelves, surrounded by a thicket of theater lights on black tripods and ropes of electric wire, was an old trunk.   "What's this?"

"The trunk? Oh, there's a few of them in there, been there for years. That's the old P.A. system from the theater, packed away."

Villanova was excited now. He pushed some of the lights out of the way and took a better look. "A few? I see two trunks, looks like."

"Two? Should be more. They're leftovers from the old summer Band clinics, unclaimed. We tossed the kids' crap out of 'em and packed 'em with speakers and mikes. Long time back." He came up close behind Villanova to take a look; his rapid, shallow breathing warmed Villanova's neck. "Hey, looks like speaker cable crammed back there."

"Sure does!" Villanova was smiling broadly now. "Looks like one of those trunks got dumped, Windy."

"Sonsofbitches!"

"Tell you what. I can find my way to the Office by myself. How about sitting here and making sure nothing gets touched until the boys from the Crime Lab get here?"

Windy shrugged. "Overtime's overtime. At forty-six dollars an hour, I'll sit anywhere you like."

* * *

A few minutes later, Villanova was on the line with Homicide Squad. It took only another minute for Rizzo to be brought to the phone. Villanova told him what he'd found.

"Trunks too? Nice work, Buddy, that's gonna help." The optimism in Rizzo's voice was good to hear. "I'll hit Tatum for a subpoena, and we'll haul the works in. What do you think, we gonna find anything in Manny's personal shit?"

"Can't say. I'd love it if a crucifix on a gold chain turned up, but I wouldn't bet my bank account on it."

"Me neither. What's the word on the alibi, Buddy?"

"The alibi stands. Windy's just an ordinary working stiff with an ordinary memory."

"Shit. And this fucker's stuck on his story like a clam."

"And it all checks out, except Windy says he asked Manny about his job, and not vice versa."

"Yeah? Sounds like Manny went over there looking for a trunk, not a job."

"Sounds like."

"And meanwhile we're running cold in every other direction. Reinhart came up with no leads, and Gilman couldn't find any credit record for that glass heart in the girl's handbag. The Lab report has it down as quality stuff, crystal."

"What about Mrs. Albano? Did she show you that letter she found?"

"Yeah. Gilman's on the wire now with the Sullivan County police. The Registrar at Fordham had no upstate address. If we can locate Reilly, I'd like to get hold of whatever letters the girl sent him. Hear what he has to say, too. You never know."

"Sad case, that Mrs. Albano. Did you get her home?"

"She wouldn't take a ride with one of us. Didn't want her husband to know anything. Gilman put her in a cab. And by the way, Buddy, Gilman says he handed you the LUD sheets. Says he ran all the numbers for us and everything."

"Christ, I forgot. Hold on, they're right here." He drew the folded pages from his pocket and opened them up. Gilman had labeled the Outgoing Calls printouts neatly by source: the Albano phone, the McVicar phone, the Cruz phone, the JFK Office phones.... Villanova scanned them for notations, sheet by sheet.

"So what've we got?"

"Looks like nothing.... Nothing...nothing... Wait a sec, what's this?" On the final sheet, Gilman had circled two numbers and identified them in pen. "Hey, listen to this. Two calls went out from the faculty phone at Mount Saint Mary's on Tuesday morning, 11:26 and 11:27. The first one went to the Fordham Graduate English Department. The other went to McVicar's home phone."

"My, my, my," Rizzo said. "Sounds like Elizabeth Albano called Mister Professor just before she left work for her appointment with him. Now why would she do that?"

"That's easy. To confirm or cancel."

"Hmm. McVicar told us he waited for her to show, and she didn't. That *might* be the truth..."

"Except why didn't the creep mention to us about getting a phone call? The man's a liar. How come we haven't checked out his story yet?"

"Slow down, Buddy. The man's a liar, we knew that already, but so what? Everybody lies when they're scared, innocent or guilty."

"Maybe he knew Elizabeth wasn't coming Tuesday morning, or maybe they changed the meeting place. Maybe he *didn't* go to the Archive from twelve to one..."

"Yeah, yeah, but what's it matter? Come on, Buddy, McVicar's a side-show here. Manny's sitting in the main ring with an alibi we can't crack. And once he's arraigned and the lawyers get into the act, we're through squeezing him."

"All right, so squeeze him now. Get your shrink friend to do her thing. She's eager, right?"

"We tried. Squeezing that guy is like squeezing cement. The thing we've got to break up is his alibi. We're missing something."

"I know it. Why don't we piece the puzzle together and have a look?"

"Good idea. You start."

Villanova put his back to the door and lit a cigarette; he was shut up in Newmark's office, seated at his desk, and right outside there were three hulking, sullen, overworked secretaries and a host of "No Smoking" signs.   "I'll do Elizabeth first. You ready?"

"Shoot."

"She leaves her house 7:30 Tuesday morning, goes to teach at Mount Saint Mary's, phones McVicar at 11:27, signs out at 11:30. Her noon appointment with McVicar isn't kept... according to McVicar. By 12:30 she's at Jack LeClerc's apartment over on Bathgate Avenue, trying to persuade him to go with her to see a psychic in the neighborhood. At 12:45 she leaves LeClerc. By 1:00 she's dead."

"Check," Rizzo said. "And Julia Cruz's apartment is two blocks from LeClerc's. A five minute proposition."

"Assuming Elizabeth knew exactly how to find it."

"Check."

"Now, what else do we know?" Villanova took a deep drag on his cigarette. "We know the girl's pregnant, but the two guys who could have made her pregnant claim they don't know it. We know she's facing exams, she's under terrific stress, she writes to an old boyfriend...that had to be before she knew she was pregnant. Couple of weeks later she goes to the family doctor with a headache problem, but doesn't take the drugs he prescribes. Somehow she hears about a psychic who cures headaches..."

"Hold it," Rizzo said. "How does she hear?"

"I don't know. Okay, let's think for a second. The network is mainly Hispanic. Maybe she hears from one of the teachers at JFK."

"Good."

"Or from one of the students in the ESL class."

"Even better. You catch what you're saying, Buddy?"

"Yup. We'll get a roster from the principal, soon as we track the sonofabitch down. Or maybe I can shake one out of these harpies in the Main Office. With luck we'll be able to show that Elizabeth was on her way to a *certain* psychic's apartment. That way there's no slack in the chain."

"Good. Buddy, we've got an awfully nice circum-stantial case here, but we had that already."

"Let's just keep working it through. Let's do Julia and Manny. You got your notes there?" Villanova heard the riffling of paper through the receiver. He searched around for a place to flick his ashes, and couldn't come up with anything better than the wastebasket. Newmark was one tidy bastard; his desk was spotless and precisely organized. His whole office was a showpiece of meticulous order.

Rizzo said, "According to Julia, she was sick on Monday afternoon, fought with Manny, got sicker, and headed over to Jacobi to see Capogrosso. She came home, went to bed, saw Manny come in later with empty cartons. Tuesday morning, she says, Manny left her at the bus stop around 12:30, after she handed him a sawbuck. She got on the bus, turned around and came home again, waved to someone named Maria Iglesias on the street, got back to the apartment a little after 1:00. Manny was packing his boxes, she says. By 1:30 or so, she'd left again for the hospital."

"Good so far. She's got Manny in the apartment right around the time of death. Now, do Manny."

"Manny says he left his mother at the bus stop around *12:45*. That's fifteen minutes later than Julia's guess. His version is a little behind on the clock all the way through."

"By Julia's version, he could have killed the girl, holed up in his room till his mother left the apartment, and still got over to talk to Windy by 1:45."

"And by his own story, he didn't have enough time to kill the girl, and he didn't even get back to the apartment until half an hour or so after time of death."

"That puts a lot of weight on the M.E.'s estimated time of death. Forensically speaking, it seems like a pretty narrow calculation..."

"I told him the same thing, Buddy. He's sticking to it."

"Good for him. So if we knew exactly what time Manny left Julia at the bus stop, we could bust his story..."

"But we don't. Even if we knew for sure what time she got on the bus the *second* time, we could work back from there, but we don't know that either."

"We don't? She was on her way to Admitting at Jacobi, right? Did we check what time they clocked her in?"

"Their record says 2:35. She had to wait her turn, though. There's no way to be sure how long she sat there. And then there's also the bus ride itself. I just had Arcario ride the bus back and forth from Bathgate Avenue to Jacobi a few times, and he clocked times from six minutes all the way up to nineteen. So Julia *might* have left the apartment at two o'clock, like Manny said."

"Great," Villanova muttered.

"Of course, if the M.E. wants to fudge a little...."

"What's the point? The puzzle has to fit together right for *us*." He pondered, dragging on his Chesterfield. The pieces did interlock, but they still allowed Manny's alibi to slip through. That meant that some element was out of place. Where? He took the pieces apart one by one, turning them this way and that.

"You there, Buddy?

"I'm here. Tell me something. What's our biggest problem?"

"Our biggest problem is that no one saw Elizabeth and Manny Cruz anywhere near each other at the time of her death, even if we can find some connection at JFK. We can't prove that she died in the Cruz apartment, and we can't even prove that she ever went there, even after three canvasses of the building. We can prove that Manny dumped a trunk, but we can't prove what was in it when he dumped it."

"And tell me something else. LeClerc was the last one to see Elizabeth alive, right? What do you think happened in those fifteen minutes after she left his place?"

"The same thing you think. I think she went straight to Julia's apartment, and I think Manny got there first. It's like Red Riding Hood and the wolf, only the *grandma* walked in right after the little *girl* got eaten."

"Good.   Red Riding Hood is good.   Think for a second, think about how cramped all the timing is around one o'clock...and think about how easily Manny answered all our questions about time. Doesn't that strike you odd? Doesn't it strike you odd that Elizabeth had just enough time to get to Julia's apartment, and Manny had just enough time to get there before her? It's as if he knew she was coming, just like the wolf."

"I get you. Go on."

"What was it LeClerc said? He said the psychic's place was nearby, right? And Elizabeth was scared to go there by herself. Why? Not because the *neighborhood* frightened her. Because something else frightened her."

"Good, Buddy. Lay it out."

"There it is. The girl must've had an *appointment* with Julia Cruz, and Manny somehow knew about it.   Elizabeth knew exactly where Julia's place was and what it looked like because *she'd been there before*, and she'd seen Manny there. That's why Manny had such a good fix on the time when we questioned him. I bet his whole morning on Tuesday was built around the clock."

"It's good, Buddy!   Elizabeth *would've* had an appointment, and she couldn't've made it by telephone if Julia's phone was out of service.   And she was carrying enough money with her to cover a fee...forty bucks, wasn't it?"

"Right. And like you say, Julia showed up at the apartment minutes after the murder. Maybe that was coincidence, maybe intuition...or maybe it was something else. Maybe it was sudden recall of an appointment with Eliabeth Albano."

"Excellent! Except for one thing. Why would a woman in serious pain turn away from a hospital to keep an appointment with a stranger?"

"I don't know. But my gut tells me there's going to be a good reason."

There was silence on the other end.

"Well? Talk to me."

"What can I say, Buddy? If your idea's on the money, your psychic's holding back on us big time. The woman said she never laid eyes on that girl."

"That's what the woman said."

"And then she sits there putting on an act like she wants to help us. Didn't I tell you she was a little too good?"

"She does want to help us." Villanova believed this; a woman as ill as Julia didn't have to tell any part of the truth at all. "Think about it: couldn't Manny be the one who's a little too good? He could've been home alone on Monday when Julia went to see Capogrosso. Elizabeth could've showed up looking for Julia, and Manny could've told her to come back the next day. Maybe he just never mentioned it to his mother. Maybe he thought it over and got cagey about it. Or maybe his chance just fell in his lap on Tuesday when Julia had to go to the hospital, and he took it."

"Maybe," Rizzo said. "Maybe I'm going to go back inside and squeeze the juice out of that miserable turd. And maybe you oughta get back over to Jacobi and start turning the screws on our little clairvoyant."

"My thinking too. Except that in her case we're in no position to turn any screws."

"Then charm her. She likes you, right? I'll send a guy in uniform to relieve you at JFK. We want a solid chain of custody on Manny's goods till we get a subpoena. Then off you go to Jacobi."

"What about McVicar? I'm a block away from Fordham."

"Fuck McVicar. First things first."

"Listen, I can see the goddam library from the window."

"Jesus Christ, Buddy, where's the logic? Shit, do it my way just this once, won't you?"

* * *

The Fordham library was an abbey-like building of greystone and stained glass, with polished hardwood, wrought iron, and a third of a million volumes on "open stacks" in its many odd-shaped interior rooms. Villanova had shelved books there for minimum wage as an undergraduate, and still had a real affection for the place, especially for the musty Humanities wing with its castle-like appointments, its spiral staircases, its monochrome prints of Siegfried's journeys.

The Archive was located in the narrow, vaulted rooms above the Philosophy stacks, accessible by a single metal stairway. The hours were posted on the doorframe: noon to 4:30 Tuesday through Friday, 9:00 to 6:00 on Saturday, closed on Sunday and Monday.

Villanova found the T.A. sitting where she was supposed to, at a desk just inside the Archive's heavy wooden door. "We're closing in five minutes," she greeted him, barely looking up from the book she was reading. It was a big, thick book, and she was a small, cute woman, with dark hair in a pixie cut, and wide brown eyes behind delicate and very round steel-rim glasses. The door to the university's precious cache of original documents stood ajar behind her. The reading room itself held only a half dozen untenanted carrels.

Villanova identified himself and asked if he might have a look at the registry, which was open on the desk facing him.   The young woman assented with a shrug, and kept reading.

No more than a handful of people a day had signed the registry. Villanova found McVicar's signature twice under Tuesday's date, 12:00 in and 1:00 out. A few other signatures followed, and then McVicar's appeared again at 4:10 and 4:30. "That's funny," he said to the T.A.

"What's funny?"

"Look here, this one person signed in here twice in one day.   And the second time was only twenty minutes before closing time. Isn't that strange?"

"I suppose."

"Do you remember seeing this Brian Mcvicar here on Tuesday?"

She nodded, glancing up.   Her eyes were cool; he realized she was only pretending to be absorbed in her reading.

He flipped backwards through the registry.   Most names appeared in strings of days.   McVicar's name was nowhere to be seen. Villanova looked back through an entire month, and then another.   The signature he encountered with increasing frequency was Elizabeth Albano's; back in July she'd been in the Archive for hours every day.

"Tell me, why would a guy who never comes here show up twice in one day?"

She frowned.   "People get hot on their research some-times."

"They get hot?   Your name's Dolores Loughlin, isn't it? You're involved with this guy McVicar aren't you?"

She stood up; she wasn't nearly as petite a woman as she looked. "What does that word mean, 'involved'?" she said. She lifted her chin abruptly and announced over Villanova's shoulder, "Closing!" A sigh rose up from one of the carrels, followed by the shuffling of papers.   Villanova caught a movement, and noticed for the first time the convex mirror high on the wall behind the carrels. He flushed--he'd been clumsy. Moments later, an elderly man in a worn brown suit pulled himself to his feet and came forward from the carrel with a cardboard storage carton in his arms. His myopic eyes passed over Villanova's with a trace of puzzlement. Villanova nodded at him and stood clear as he slid the carton onto Dolores' desk.

Dolores performed the check-in procedure with an excess of precision. She opened the carton, straightened the already straight folders as if to warrant that all were present, watched while the elderly man put his signature to the filecard taped inside the lid, then resealed the box. She inspected his yellow pad of notes, took his signature in the registry, reached beneath her desk and handed over an attache case, smiling politely and with great self-possession as he thanked her and departed.

"I apologize," Villanova said as the man's footfalls receded down the metal stairway. "I didn't know anyone was here."

"You don't need to apologize," Dolores returned cooly, "I'm not ashamed of my friendship with Brian."

"Did he come here Tuesday to see you or to do work?"

"Both."

"He checked out one of these cartons?"

"That's right.   The Robinson file.   Hawthorne materials." She spoke in a firm contralto; on her feet, with her little lipsticked mouth set and her surprisingly large breasts thrust against her white cotton blouse, she looked anything but fragile.

"Could I see this Robinson file?"

She shook her head. "There's six cartons in the file. You're only allowed one at a time, and I've got to get to a class. Besides, you have to be a doctoral student to even touch these cartons."

"I'm an alumnus."

"Then you have to get a visitor card from the dean."

"You're pretty serious about security here."

"That's my job, and I do it. Nothing's going to get lost from here as long as I'm getting paid to watch it." She hefted the carton and carried it back into the Archive.

Villanova followed her in among the ranks of metal storage racks. "Say," she said, "you're a pretty pushy guy."

"That's *my* job. Look, I'm in a hurry to get out of here too. Just point out the Robinson file to me, and I'll be on my way."

She stood there eyeing him. The air in the room was thick, the silence impermeable. She turned and slid the carton into place on a shelf, and he saw how solidly she was actually built, how well she filled her jeans. So this was the place, he thought. She and McVicar, here, with the diaries and epistles of the magi to muffle their noises. She eyed him again, and this time he wasn't fooled by the vulnerable look her glasses gave her. "Right on the floor there," she said.

He raised his brows.

"Right in the corner."

He turned. The Robinson file occupied the lowest shelf in the first row, six nearly-new cartons. He stooped and lifted the lid of the third carton just long enough to glimpse Elizabeth Albano's multiple signatures...and then a hand descended on his shoulder. "No touching, that was the deal," Dolores said.

He stood and let her usher him out. She pulled the heavy Archive door shut behind them and turned a key in its lock. He watched as she gathered her things.   "Did you know Liz Albano?" he said.

"We all knew her."

"Then I guess you all know what happened to her."

She nodded, and those bold eyes of hers narrowed and hardened a degree. "What happened to Liz is too bad.   But I'm still not sorry I took Brian away from her."

"You took Brian away from her?"

"Sure. It had to happen. He likes pretty women. But the smarter they are, the better he likes them."

"Is that how you see it?"

"That's how it is." For the first time her gaze met his candidly. "Look, Elizabeth was the type that something bad *has* to happen to. She was in the wrong place, and she was unhappy as hell about it underneath. I can vouch for that, I saw her face almost every day."

"What do you mean, 'the wrong place'?"

"I mean here at Fordham. She had blue collar written all over her. Her father's some kind of bricklayer. When one of those girls gets ambitious, she winds up in no-man's land. I've seen it. No understanding at home, no real friends here either. No old-fashioned prospects to fall back on, nothing ahead but an academic career that she doesn't really want. She winds up alone and full of guilt."

"She had nothing to feel guilty for," Villanova retorted peevishly.

"Sure she did. For her ambition. For rejecting her past. It's the kind of thing men don't understand. Girls like Liz get self-destructive, they have accidents. Smart as they are, they wind up hurt or dead, or knocked-up at the least."

"Who said she was knocked-up?"

"Nobody said it. Was she?"

He looked at her with real annoyance. She was a whip, all right, she was going to show him what the word "pushy" meant.   "What does *your* father do, psychoanalytic research?" he said.

"My mother does psychoanalytic research.   My father does physics."

He nodded sourly.   "And what about your husband? Is he in the brain trust too?"

That dropped the tilt of her chin.   "He teaches junior high school.   What of it?"

"Nothing.   But for my money, you're way off base.   I hear Elizabeth Albano was a girl with real class..."

"Class?"   She smiled.   "After she got dumped, she wound up with some low-life artist.   *That* crook'll give her class, all right."

"What do you mean, 'crook'?   You know the guy?"

"I saw him at a party.   While she was across the room talking to Brian, he was lifting something from her handbag. Right in front of me."

"That so?   What did he take?"

"Why don't you ask *him*?   That's your job, isn't it?" She shut the registry and locked it in the desk drawer.   "Come on, time to clear out."

He did his best to keep his tone even.   "Can I tell you something, Dolores?   Maybe your friend Brian's telling the truth, and maybe he's not.   Maybe you're covering for him, and maybe you're not.   But Liz Albano deserved better than Brian McVicar, even if you don't think you do."

Her chin angled upward again.   "You don't get it," she said.

"No?"

"No you don't.   The man's brilliant."

"Is he?"

"Read his work."

He sighed and shook his head.

"On second thought, it would be wasted on you." She scooped up her books and brandished yet another key. "Look, I'm locking up here. You can stay in, or out."

* * *

LeClerc's basement apartment on Bathgate Avenue was only a few minutes out of the way, and Villanova took another minute for one more visit to the big mural on the bodega wall. He was surprised to find an inexpensive wreath leaning against the chain-link fence, and a few mums threaded through the links.

The mural looked different in the afternoon light: less surreal and yet somehow more intense, more byzantine and exotic. Villanova put his face to the fence, and this time he kept his focus away from the nude Joan of Arc and examined the other figures, the street thugs, the apostles, the divinities... The cleric drew his eye; he was the only figure who looked directly at the street-level viewer. His back was turned, but he watched nervously over his shoulder; that was because, in counterpoint to the crucifix in his right hand, he held a burning taper in the left: he was the executioner. The embers from his torch rained onto the cowl-garbed head of the grave-digger--or was that a grave-*robber*? The oblong pit was full of bones, and the cleric's morbid smirk, half-shadowed by the cowl, reminded Villanova in some strange way of McVicar as he sat drinking scotch in his book-filled ossuary...

A sudden snarl sent his blood rushing. The bodega owner had come outside with his Akita, and the big dog was lunging against the chain at Villanova and dripping saliva.

"Hey, that dog okay?"

"That dog'll tear your throat out."

"Well, keep him away from me."

"You're standing where he shits."

Villanova backed away and let the burly man and his dog have the strip of weeds along the fence. He checked the bottoms of his shoes.

"Don't worry, it's lucky to step in it. Hey, you're the cop that was here yesterday, ain't you? You talk to that artist creep yet?"

"Sure we talked to him."

"That motherfucker. He ruined my dog for me. Did something to him, now the dog's scared of him, won't go near him. Wouldn't go outside the whole time he was painting the wall."

"*This* dog? What'd the guy do?"

"I don't know. But once a guard dog's spooked like that, the heart goes out of him, he's finished. Crazy motherfucker. Did a good job on the wall, though." He glanced up at the mural. "It's good for business. People like to look at the girl."

"You recognize any of those faces up there?"

"Sure. The guy put *himself* up there. See the baby in the carriage?"

Sure enough, it *was* LeClerc, transformed into some kind of grinning gargoyle, a leering spectator to the pageant.

"Anyone else?"

"Nah. Just me. See the pickpocket? That's me."

It was true, and the man seemed genuinely flattered. "You don't mind being a pickpocket?"

"Hell no. I coulda been Judas. I coulda been the pimp. *That* would be an insult...I think." The dog began taking a crap at the man's feet.

"That's a good way to look at it, I guess. Who put these flowers along the fence here?

"Don't know. People say that girl up there's the girl who got killed the other day. They say that's her face."

"Yeah? Who started that story?"

"Don't know. But there's a lot of pissed off people around here. *Real* pissed off. We all got daughters, sisters...." He looked at Villanova. "You know what? You better catch that sonofabitch before we do."

* * *

Villanova knew as soon as he turned into the alley that LeClerc was home. Most of the cats were out of sight, rock music blared up the narrow walkway, and there were a couple of urchins hunkered down outside LeClerc's window, peering over the sill. "Hey!" Villanova called, and the startled boys leapt into flight, scaling the board fence and vanishing into the next alley as completely as the cats had the day before.

LeClerc's open door exhaled a stink of paint thinner along with over-pumped *Guns N' Roses*. Villanova went inside.

LeClerc, working at his easel in the big back room, gave no reaction at the sight of him except a roll of his eyes. "Don't you knock?" he said, but without pugnacity. He wore paint-spotted jeans and a t-shirt, and was hard at work, jabbing alternately at palette and canvas with what looked like a knife. Something about his face looked different, and Villanova was so busy trying to figure out what it was that he didn't notice the girl standing near the window till she made a move to cover herself. She was naked and dark-skinned and she looked about fifteen, and Villanova realized that LeClerc was scowling at her as she unfolded her arms and did her best to put a blank expression on her face and slouch against the wall just the way she'd been.

"You come here to gawk, or what?" LeClerc said in Villanova's direction; he was smirking now, and his mood actually seemed upbeat. "Welcome to the Jungle" pumped out of the Sanyo box, distorted through the little speakers.

"Hey--where's your glasses?" Villanova said.   "I thought you needed them to see?"

"Ever hear of contacts, pal?"

Villanova snorted. "Let's have a word," he muttered. "Let the girl cover herself so we can talk."

"Talk if you want to, it won't bother Anna."

Villanova looked around the room. There were a few cartons in the corner, but the big portraits of Liz Albano that had been leaning against the wall were gone. "...Welcome to the jungle/ We take it day by day/ If you want it you're gonna bleed/ But it's the price you pay..." screeched out of the little Sanyo. Villanova turned down the volume. "I've got one question. What'd you take from Liz Albano's handbag? Give me a straight answer, let's not waste time."

"What the hell are you talking about?"

"At a party three weeks back."

LeClerc laughed. "Three weeks back?"

"No stall, LeClerc, just give me an answer."

LeClerc chuckled again, his eyes full of mischief. His good humor seemed high-pitched and unnatural; he was either coked up or manic. "What I took was my housekey. That okay with you?" He scraped a clot of crimson paint off the palette, dragged it in a long arc onto the canvas. "Liz wasn't sleeping with me. She wouldn't pose for me any more. Why should she have a key?"

"Why not just ask her for it back?"

"What for, when it was easier to lift it? Anyway, I didn't trust her. She changed her mind about the paintings I did of her, didn't like them, didn't want anyone to see them. Why should I let her walk around with a key?"

Villanova raised his brows. "She didn't want the paintings seen? How come, all of a sudden? Maybe you hadn't let her see them herself? Maybe she stole a peek and got upset? Is that why she wouldn't pose anymore? Is that what she fought with you about when she showed up here on Tuesday?"

LeClerc, with mockery in his eyes, silently carried another bloody gob to the canvas.

"Where'd all the portraits go to?" Villanova said. "What happened to the one that was on the easel, the one with the coffin?"

This time LeClerc's brows went up. He turned his smirking face toward Villanova. "You've been in here before. That's against the law, pal. You know what? I could have you busted for breaking and entering."

"Where's the portrait with the coffin, you bastard?"

"You liked that one? I'll bet you did. Here, take a look at *this* masterpiece."

Villanova drew closer. The canvas looked like a raw wound. Near the top was a face resembling Anna's, and after that, blood, one great, gory cascade dripping into what was left of an open coffin. Villanova recoiled in spite of himself. "You covered it over, you sonofabitch."

"I do it all the time. It's called thrift." LeClerc scratched at something on his cheek and left a bloody streak.

Villanova peered into his eyes, trying to penetrate their manic sheen and discern just how crazy the guy was. All he got back was scorn. "You going to let Anna look at your little masterpiece here?" he said.

"When I'm ready."

"I don't see what the hell you need her for."

"Oh, she's necessary."

The girl shifted her weight uneasily, and Villanova glanced at her. Her face was plain, and its expression had a false, artificially precocious sullenness. She was skinny and badly put together, too; her head was too large, her hips high and bony. He looked away. "How long's Anna been posing for you?"

"A few weeks. Since Liz quit. She's no Liz, but she's got a soul. Liz, she was one in a lifetime."

"Anna was here when Liz came to the door Tuesday, wasn't she. That's why you wouldn't leave. That's why you stood outside the door to argue with Liz."

"You're off target. It was 12:30. Anna was in school."

Villanova turned to the girl. "That true? You a high school student?"

She nodded.

"You were in school Tuesday? What school do you go to?"

The girl said, "Look, if you're gonna talk to me, I'm gonna put clothes on."

"Leave her alone, she's working," LeClerc said.

"Why don't *you* leave her alone? How old is she, for Christ sake?" An image of the bodega owner with his daughters and his big, stupid dog popped into his mind.

"Fuck you. Why don't you get lost and let me paint."

"What other kind of work does she have to do around here?"

Sneering, LeClerc reached over and punched up the volume on the Sanyo. "...Welcome to the jungle/ watch it bring you to your knees..."

Villanova snatched the box and flung it against the wall. He stood glaring into LeClerc's ugly, insolent face... then turned and stalked out.

"You know what?" LeClerc's voice followed him into the alley. "You're in the wrong fucking profession! You belong leading the rosary in some fucking church!"

The tinny racket of the Sanyo started up again before Villanova hit the street.

* * *

He was in a rotten mood by the time he got to the hospital. He felt as if he'd lost charge of his day, been buffeted and blind-sided at every step. His impulse, as he got near the sick woman's room, was to channel some of that frustration at her; but that strategy was thwarted too as soon as he put eyes on her.

Julia looked dramatically more ill than she had earlier in the day. That delicate face of hers was distorted with swelling, and her eyes seemed full of pain. The buzzer-cable to the nurses' station lay draped in easy reach over the bedrail, as if she were poised for a crisis at any moment. Even so, she smiled when he came in, and looked glad to see him. "I was just thinking of you," she said, raising herself up. "I wanted to see you again. I have things to tell you."

"Good. Let's talk." He made an effort to speak crisply, but it didn't even fool himself. "I see you've got a roommate now." In the other bed, a very old woman lay asleep on her back, toothless mouth open, wisps of white hair matted on the pillow.

"They brought her in here to die, poor thing," Julia said. "She's the second one. So many of them here, these poor bags-of-bones. Such a long, hard life, such a sad finish for them, all alone. And tomorrow, the next day, it's my turn."

"Don't say that."

"Look at me. Don't you see how much worse I am?"

He adjusted the pillow behind her head. "Can't they do anything about the pain?"

"The pain isn't only mine. It's my son's too."

"What do you mean?"

"My son is suffering, I feel it. If I could take his pain, I would."

"For Christ sake, don't you have enough trouble of your own?"

"But it's true that Manny's suffering, isn't it? You know where he is. You know what he feels right now."

She was going to do it again, he realized. She was going to tie his tongue with that uncanny sensitivity of hers, that compelling, intuitive gentleness.   "Yes, I know where he is," he said. "We have him."

"Must you hurt him?"

"I'm not hurting him, Julia."

"But your partner is less kind than you are."

"I'm not such a kind man as you think.   I actually came here to bully you a little, to get you to tell the truth."

"And yet already you've changed your mind.   Deep down you know I'll tell you all the truth I can remember. And besides, you're not the one to hurt anyone. You know what it is to *be* hurt.   Something already has hurt you today, disheartened you, I could sense it when you came in. You want to be angry, but you can't."

He made a face, and groped, pointlessly, for his cigarettes.

"You don't like this talk, do you?   Knowing more about people than they reveal is your vanity. You don't like to meet another person like yourself."

"Oh, come," he said, "what do you really know about me?"

"Not so much. But something."

"Tell me, then. I'll listen, I'm as vain as the next man."

His glib tone got no reaction in kind from her.   "Now you want to test me," she said, and she looked away.   "Yet I don't mind being tested. I don't blame you for not trusting me."

"I do trust you," he said. "Talk if you want to."

She was silent for a moment.   Then her eyes returned to his. "I know you have a struggle in your heart," she said.   "I know you're a sad man who believes in happiness."

"Really? Anyone who knows me would be surprised to hear I was a sad man."

"And yet you are. But sad is not the right word. You laugh, you have your appetite for life, your pleasures. But your eyes are always open to the presence of evil. *Tragic*, that's the word I mean. Here, give me your hands, I'll show you."

He did as she asked. She turned his palms up and studied them closely, tracing the lines with her thumbs. Her own hands were very warm and incredibly gentle as they took the measure of his.

"You have a long life, a full life," she said. "A very rich life, not in money, but in people, in work, in creativity. And you have desire, too, very strong. You're a romantic man. But look here, you see this break? Didn't I say it? You have a great sadness also, a loss."

"Everybody has a loss, Julia."

"Not like this, not the kind that nearly kills the soul. Ah...but this sadness I see is not recent, but from long ago. Is this true?" She looked up into his eyes.

"You tell me, Julia," he said, and then he knew that that was cheap and pointless. "Yes, it's true," he said.

She was still watching his face. "You're not a man that lives much in the present, I think. The past holds more meaning for you. And the future, too. You live full of hope, you save the best of yourself. You believe that the future will bring you the happiness the past took away." She shook her head slowly. "But don't you know that the future and the past don't exist? Only the present exists."

Her words, so softly spoken, didn't sound reproachful. They lapped over him like a gentle wash of sympathy. He allowed them, and said nothing.

She turned her eyes to his hands again. "The line of love is very deep. You are a passionate man, you have much to give a woman, a child, whoever is close to you. Tell me, is there someone close?"

"Yes," he said.

"A woman?"

"Yes."

"And do you love this woman?"

His ordinary reticence seemed to vanish, and his uncertainty too. "Yes," he said.

"Why is it you don't tell her?"

He hesitated. "I don't know."

"You're afraid of something. Not in the present, but in the future. You're afraid to trust this love. But why?" She ran her thumb again and again over a certain crease in his palm. "Yes, part of it, I see. This woman is of a different religion than you. That's it, yes?"

"No," he said.

"It must be. I see it."

"I'm sorry, you're way off."

She looked to his face again. "Your religion matters to you a great deal, I think."

"No."

"I believe it does. You're a proud man, very proud. From your pride comes all your strength." Again she shook her head slowly side to side. "But this woman--what is her name?"

"Helen."

"This Helen, her religion is not so different from yours as you think. And to her it matters not so much, not like with you. In that way she's like any woman, she will change her religion to yours, because she loves you."

It suddenly struck him that she wasn't talking about sects and creeds at all. She was talking about values, character, the ethos of masculinity and femininity. And she had hit a big, murky truth so precisely that, with a strange excitement, he rushed to play it through.

Julia looked away and gave him time. A minute passed before she said softly, "Helen does love you, doesn't she?"

"Yes."

"I know this, I see Helen in *you*. She loves you very much. She is ready to give herself to you, not just her body, not just her heart, but her whole self. She is waiting for you, and you are holding back. Why, when there is such a power of love in you? What does it matter what she's done in the past? Here, do you see this line, how deep and strong it is, even after it splits...?"

She stopped. She ran her thumb along the line, then looked up at him; those eyes with their strange, deep focus held his. "I see it now. You love not just one woman, but two. Two at once."

He shook his head.

"It's true. Two women. One is dead, the other living. Now I understand where the sadness comes from."

He removed his hands from hers.

"But listen. Don't you see, the past has gone from us, and the future never comes? You must let what is dead lie in peace. Its beauty is frozen like marble, it has nothing more to give you. I know this better than anyone." He didn't answer. Instead he looked out the window, at the endless trains of cars looping around the interchange, at the massive lobes of cloud, purple and pregnant with rain, that were piling up from the north. His heart was pounding. Something was about to tear apart inside him, and he fought with the desperate stubbornness of habit to hold it in one piece.

"Shall I be quiet now?" Julia said.

"Yes." He had a very bad time coming, now, he knew; there was plenty of dark turbulence in store for him.

Julia sighed and settled lower into the bed. There was a long silence. For the first time, Villanova heard the faint rasp of breathing from the old woman in the other bed.

"Maybe you should leave me now," Julia said. "I feel very tired."

"In a moment." He turned slowly from the window. "You said you had things to tell me. About Manny."

"I will tell you, if you want. But will you do something for me first? Will you make me a promise? Will you bring Helen here to me? Let me see her, just once?"

"Why?"

"Because I care about you, and her. Because you're a good man."

"I'm a private man as well. What do you intend to ask her?"

"I only want to see her. Please, make me this one promise."

He thought it over.

"Yes?"

He shrugged. "All right. Now tell me about Manny. Did you remember more about Tuesday morning?"

"Yes, a few things."

"Go on."

"I remembered that when I came home, after I saw Maria Iglesias, I went upstairs to open the door. But the key wouldn't go in the lock."

"The lock was jammed, we know that."

"So I knocked on the door and called to Manny, but there was no answer. I knocked very loud, two or three times...and then finally Manny pulled the door open. 'Why didn't you answer?' I asked him, and he said he was in the bathroom."

"Did you ask him what he was doing home?"

"I tried to. He went into his room and shut the door. But one other thing I remember. There was a strong smell in the apartment. I was sure Mirabel wet the floor. But I couldn't find any wet, even in her box. I couldn't even find Mirabel. Then finally I found her, on top of the refrigerator. And that was the other strange thing."

"What's that?"

"She was very upset, she was hiding. She wouldn't come down to me, no matter what. And when I tried to reach her, she backed away and made this noise, like a child's cry, a moan. I never heard her make such a sound before. It frightened me. I thought she could sense how sick I was."

He nodded. "What else?"

"No more."

"No more? Come on, Julia."

"What I remembered, I told you. Please, now I'm tired."

"Why didn't you tell me these things before, Julia?"

"I tell you what my memory lets me."

"Is your memory as full of tricks as that, Julia? All because of your illness?"

"My way of knowing is not like yours. You must trust it, as I do. If you want to know more, ask Manny."

"And can we trust what Manny says, Julia? He told us something about his little sister dying when he was a kid. Is that true?"

Julia's eyes turned to liquid discs of sorrow. "Ah, my little Vidalina. He told you about her?"

"He said she died in her crib."

Julia nodded sadly. "It's true, the little angel. She's been gone for many years now. And every night she comes to me in my dreams, and every night I ask her to forgive me."

"For what?"

"For leaving her alone. It was only for a little while. It was to get medicine for her fever."

"Manny says she wasn't alone. He says you left him with her."

"Yes," she said quietly, "Manny was with her."

Villanova searched her eyes. Whatever was there was hidden. "How old would she be if she were alive?"

"Twenty-two, twenty-three years."

He fell silent; the rasping breath from the other bed was faint as a whisper. "And your husband left you after she died?"

"A year later."

"And he's in jail now? For doing what?"

"For killing a man. He's a brute, Manuelo. Always was."

"How did you come to marry him?"

"He raped me."

"He made you pregnant?"

She nodded.

"I'm sorry."

"You didn't do it."

He was dammed up good now, and in a crazy, dispiritng way, he had a glimmer of sympathy for Manny. "You love your son, don't you, Julia. No matter what he's done, you won't betray him, you'll do anything to protect him."

"Not anything. But it's true, I'm his mother, and he's my son."

"The girl who was murdered also had a mother."

Julia winced.

"I know you feel just as bad as I do about what happened to that girl, Julia."

"Yes, you do know it," she said with a touch of rancor, "or else you wouldn't come here. A dying woman doesn't have to tell you anything. She can speak to her own conscience, alone, in silence. She doesn't need your hand pressing on her heart. And yet I've told you what I can."

"Why not tell me the rest?"

Her mouth was drawn; a conflict seemed to rage behind her troubled eyes. "Believe me when I say I've told you everything I can remember.   Leave me be, now, I ask you..."

"Tell me the rest, Julia. Just tell me the rest."

She looked at him with a somber intensity; her suffering eyes pleaded with his, but he gave her no quarter. At last she looked away. She nodded, and her voice came out soft and resigned: "There's only one other way, if you must have my help."

"How, Julia?"

She hesitated. "Do you know what a seance is?"

"Yes."

"Well, that's where the final truth will come out. There's no other way, this I can swear."

He stood there looking at her unhappily.   "You want to hold a seance?" he said.

"Yes."

Those gathering clouds of frustration inside him darkened, and with them came the first rumblings of a volatile anger, but he warned himself to stifle it; he needed to know what she knew--nothing else mattered. "When? Now?"

"Soon. Tomorrow."

"Why not now?"

She shook her head. "You must come back tomorrow, after dark. There are preparations to make." She glanced at him, and her voice grew more resolute. "You must trust me if you want my help. There are three things you must bring with you. First, a trunk. Second, something worn by the dead girl, something worn not long ago. At the time she died, if possible."

He gritted his teeth. That request meant scavenging in the morgue, or else going back to the Albano household.

"And last, a friend you can trust. We must be three, at least."

Rizzo's was the first face to pass through his mind, but Julia was already shaking her head.

"It must be a woman, a young woman," she said. "One who believes in the spirit." She glanced at him solemnly. "You must bring Helen." She let out her breath and sank down into the bed.

He stood staring at her with a half dozen feelings warring inside him. A minute passed, then another.

"Go now," Julia said. "Come back tomorrow." She closed her eyes.

His face grew hot. "Why not just tell me what you know?" he snapped. "Why not tell me the real reason you were hurrying back home on Tuesday?"

"Please, go, I'm not well," she said. Her face tightened, and new tributaries of wrinkles appeared among the old.

"Come on, Julia. Why not just tell me you had an appointment with that girl who was killed!"

"Oh!" she whimpered. Her eyelids fluttered open, and an afflicted expression formed on her face. Her eyes filled with sudden grief, a grief that swelled in an instant to encompass the whole race of her fellow creatures. "Oh, the poor thing! Oh, she's dead! She's dead!"

"You're damn right she's dead!" he cried. "She's worse than dead...."

And then he stopped, because the horror in Julia's eyes was all the wrong kind, and the strange, fateful way she looked beyond him took all the force out of his words. A chill passed through him, and the skin on his neck and arms went all goose-bumps. He turned and followed her gaze across the room.

The white-haired old woman in the other bed had stopped making that rasping sound. She was as still and grey and absolute as stone.

- NINE -

Helen sat waiting for Mike Villanova on a barstool in the Shamrock, her legs crossed at the knee and a copy of *Washington Square* open on her thigh.   She wore a buff raincoat over her uniform, and nothing but hose underneath: her panties, for purely superstitious reasons, had spent most of the day in her handbag.   A fresh Campari and orange juice stood in front of her, and in the big mirror she could see nearly all of the bar as well as a few of the booths and the upper half of the action at the pool table. On the TV, the Mets were playing the Reds in a twi-night double-header, and most of the men elbowed up to the bar were vocally partisan, though not so noisily that she couldn't read.

Reading was a good way to sit and keep watch for Mike without having some mug try to strike up a conversation; but she read chiefly because she liked to. *Washington Square* was a book she'd started in high school, back in Anaheim, and never finished.   The story of it had pulled at her, too, with an odd, personal power: the sinister, destructive father whom all the world looked up to, the daughter helpless in that incestuous undertow. She'd lost the book in the rain on the night of her sixteenth birthday, in the course of a bizarre, booze-fueled exorcism. She'd peeked at the ending back then, and still remembered it, but now she wanted to know about the middle, and the left-out middles of all the other stories. She wanted to know how girls who started out holding their fathers' hands to cross the street wound up stuffed in a trunk on the sidewalk like yesterday's garbage. She wanted to know just where between her own beginning and end that drunken rite in the rain twenty years ago belonged.

The guy beside her at the bar was pretty drunk himself. Handsome guy, knew it, too, tall, nice shoulders, herring-bone sport coat over white button-down and jeans, silver-black hair curling over his collar. Started out watching her from the other end of the bar, just drifted over. Trying to catch her eye in the mirror. Ordering one refill after another and taking casual glances. She ignored him, though now she was reading the same paragraph for the third time.

"That's a wonderful color, that drink," he said suddenly. "Like a popsickle." He had a smile that was supposed to be winning.

She nodded.

"Does it taste as good as it looks?"

"No," she said, and kept reading. It *was* a beautiful color, pinkish-orange, full of sweet promise, a color for a baby bonnet, a child's picture book. It was the wrong color for sex. Her first time, the color was a murky henna, the hue of fever-piss. The potion was of her own mixing, a half-inch drawn from every bottle in her father's liquor cabinet, enough to fill a Seagram's quart. That was for Richie, her Adonis, the varsity hoopster who first asked her out, little Miss Nobody, after she accidentally bent over in front of him at a school picnic with nothing on but a shift. Not that she had that much to flash in the way of tits, but enough to please, high and firm too, not droopy like now. She'd always known what her good points were, and her bad. Sexy little body, she'd always had that, still did. Good legs, good ass, good back. Bony knees and wrists. She knew how to dress, how to bring out the shapely legs and the round little ass, and make the most of the chest.   Always sexy, yes, but she never saw herself as particularly lovely, never a heart-stopper like her cousins with the black hair and the high cheekbones and the wide-set dark eyes.   Just a home-grown sort of prettiness, little nose, round chin, smattering of freckles, her honest blue eyes her best feature.   If she was interesting to look at, it was because she made herself so, because she knew herself and let her face tell the truth about what was going on inside her.   No bullshit.

She took a swallow of the Campari: pleasant, halfway between sweet and bitter.   Not like that first concoction, which Richie wouldn't drink, which she'd had to swig down on her own.   Her first time really drunk, that night, Sweet Sixteen. Her first time with a guy, too, because he'd been trying to fill her up from the very first night, and she was going to lose him if she didn't get down and do it.   So on her birthday she did it, the rain pouring down, beating on the roof of his old Chevy Malibu.   She was adamant, eager, once her mind was made up. Drunk at last, she just told him to stop the car and fuck her. And he didn't want to, he was scared because she was so drunk.   But she made him do it, there, in the car.   And then naked, she got out into the rain with her book and started walking; it was a declaration he couldn't possibly understand. He begged her to get back in the car because people could see her, and she ignored him until he tried to drive across the mud after her, and got the wheels stuck.   And they had to get a tow, and she sat there drinking from the Seagram's bottle for two hours, the book lost somewhere in the dark.   Got home way past her curfew, stinking drunk, ready for the hell that had to come, ready, for the first time, to give it back.   Childhood done, the misery finally penetrated, confrontation at last.   In through the front door she went... and everyone was asleep. Just Packy, her dog, got up to sniff her crotch, and he was the only one that knew.   Not even her stupid mother knew.

Packy, half Lab, half mutt, killed by a car in front of the house two weeks later. How she cried.

Packy was the only one that knew the other secret, too. Those black, odious nights, the two year nightmare: the sound of the clock ticking, the creak of weight on hallway floorboards, the slow turning of the doorknob.   The torture. Herself, the lone child at the mercy of one merciless pair of hands. An incomprehensible evil. Not every night, no, the greater horror of the random element, twice a week, maybe more, maybe less. Until Packy one night. Packy, growling, snarling at that shadow-man in the corridor. Packy, banishing the demon-master to his own roost. And sleeping after that outside her door.

Loyal Packy, burst and broken by a car that never stopped, speeding in the chain of happy families on their way to Disneyland.   All those children's faces smiling in the windows. She cried, and she dug a hole for him in the back yard. Dazed, she just kept digging and crying, until her father came out and stopped her. She'd dug a pit six feet long and three deep, a fucking grave. Her father snatched the shovel from her with a curse, as if he understood who the grave was for. And after that she fucked Richie everywhere and every chance she could, until he graduated school and went off to college.

"That Henry James you're reading there? Good for you."

The voice was resonant, full of male assurance. She glanced over; the guy was new in the place, slumming, probably.   There were times when flirting made a nice diversion, others when it was just a nuisance. Once in a while the raw, animal attraction was palpable, compelling. Not lately.

"Ever see the old movie version?" the man said, again with the smile.   "Olivia de Haviland.   And whatsisname... Montgomery Clift. Very nice work."

She nodded and went back to reading.   He was handsome, but Richie had been handsomer, and there'd been lots of handsome men after him.   And less-than-handsome men too, and users, and jerks, and lots of self-hatred to go around. Lots of soothing and excitement to hunt for, lots of comfort, caring, lust; but not love, never the whole thing with no piece missing. The best of the lot, a Jewish man ten years older, the only child of a pair of Buchenwald survivors, a homely man with a sad, big-boned face. She'd been drawn to the deformity written in that countenance that carried so much death inside: barbed wire, armies of murdered children, experiments, all that inherited anguish, a whole people who, like her, were forced to look right into the Devil's eyes and not shrink back. It was good for the short while it lasted.

But too many years of that, giving herself away cheap, getting fucked by a father she hadn't seen since seventeen. Then that asshole who spilled the hot coffee on her in the middle of an argument, claimed it was an accident. Scars on her legs, still.   She'd pulled herself together after that. Therapy, and lots of books, "deep," serious, wonderful stuff. Then coming east, nursing school, and, damn, she looked good in nurse's whites, with the round ass and the sexy walk. She liked to wear her whites still, chose to, even though it was no longer the thing; the uniform declared her, protected her.

Then Ralphie. Why? Because he was safe and so much older, and had a great big family in a great big house, a real family of parents and brothers and cousins and kids and fighting and making up and sitting down at a table to eat and cursing and threatening and sticking together against all the world outside. Because Ralphie had money and wanted to *marry* her, the girl with the past.

So she took vengeance on her father and married him. No viciousness right away, not until he got possessive and nasty-jealous, not until he hit her the first time. Then she gave him his turn on the rack, showed him what it felt like to deal with the sexuality of a grown woman. Never cheated on him, didn't have to--in fact, gave up sex altogether for quite some time, just to prove it wasn't the whole center of her. And meanwhile she let Ralphie drive himself crazy thinking of the men she was fucking on the quiet. No special cunning needed, he was sick about sex anyway, only dreamed himself a stud, was shy and squeamish as a boy inside. Got him so desperate he started cruising for chippies for real, found one who would sleep with him, and moved out. Good riddance, all accounts settled. She stayed put, with all those people around her, the noise, the cats and dogs, the kids that no one but her had time to take care of.

She stayed put, and she stayed quiet, and it was just as well, because a couple of months later, doing the laundry down in that dark basement, she met Mike. Scared, she was, going down those steep wooden steps into the gloom with the one meager light and all those dark niches for some creep to hide in. Scared every single laundry day, just like she was scared in her bed as a kid, and that was half the reason she went down, to face that demon twice a week and keep it backed into its corner, to stare down the evil she'd worked so hard to understand. She went to it like a lion-tamer, throwing the basement door open with a crash, trying to jar her fear and her stalker off balance. Pounded her way down those steps and flung things around. Then jumped like a rabbit that time, all the courage gone to flight, when he, a stranger, came down the steps after her so steadily and purposefully...how was she supposed to know he had a pillowcase full of soiled clothes over his shoulder? But that was just the right beginning, she realized long afterward, so accurately portentous: to be frightened by the sudden appearance of this man, as if she sensed from the start that she was going to lose herself to him, and might still save herself by running and hiding.

She tried to envision Mike as a stranger again, and couldn't, could only see him as she'd learned him bit by bit, a lean man with deep Italian skin, thick brows, high cheekbones, beautiful, large, deep brown eyes with a surprising expressiveness, lips full and pink and fleshy, not like hers, so pale as to be hardly there. She could see the wide chest, wing-like and strong; the muscled shoulders, the delicate wrists, the slender, sensitive fingers. The long stretches of hard-packed muscle in the thighs, narrowing suddenly to the sweet indentation behind the knees, the rounded calves and slender ankles.

She tried to remember him the first time he'd made love to her, so confident, so insistent, but in such a sweet way. Not shy at all like she'd expected, but knowing exactly what he wanted, freeing her to take what she wanted too. Gentle and loving, and after she'd come, he'd got up on his knees and turned her over, just put her bottom where he wanted it like he owned it, and she liked that too, the self-assurance, the strength of that need and all the tenderness underneath. And afterward, she'd told him everything right away, she'd blurted out her glib yarn about all those men and all that fucking, partly to discourage him and give him his chance to stay aloof, partly to remind him that disposable women like herself were real people with intellects and vulnerabilities like everyone else. And to her surprise, though her spiel fazed him a bit, it didn't stop him.

So resilience was on top of the list of things she liked about him, but she really liked all of him, his seriousness, his sentimentality, his directness, his range of knowledge, his love of movies and books and music, his genuineness with people, his smile, his voice, deep and resonant but somehow full of youth, caught somewhere before the hardness of manhood. And the fact that he liked her too, listened to all her stories and loved the details just as enthusiastically as she did, laughed when she was funny, told her she was *pretty* and touched and admired her body, even swore that little freckled nose of hers was pretty, and made her believe it too, so that she started glancing at herself half-sideways in mirrors. She liked the intelligence dancing behind his eyes, and the way he saw the world with all its evil too, and had his share, like her, of dark memories and gruesome sights that he struggled to keep from dimming the sunshine. She liked the way other people looked up to him, and wanted him to listen to them and smile at them and like them, just as she did. She liked his deep reservoir of kindness, and the way he could be open and undefended, too, as she had to learn to be from him. From the inside out, he'd opened her up, reminding her of the parts of herself she'd once admired: her loyalty, her honesty, her ability to love completely. Most of all she liked his masculine courage: not that macho tough-guy stuff, but the courage to face the world alone, to be an outsider, to live by his own thoughts and spurn all that collective, female safety. Not one of her friends wouldn't have fallen for him, and she was jealous, jealous of his partner Rizzo and their rich, male closeness, jealous of the ease and trust between them and all they knew about each other, the guns and violence and dreads and lusts and conquests and wives and jump shots and pool cues and every other item in the male catalogue, jealous of the way even their looks complemented each other--Rizzo with the squatter build, and lighter hair and deeper-etched, heavier-boned face--and jealous of all the time they got to spend together, too.

Yet she'd had moments Rizzo could never have, beautiful moments that lived forever fresh in her memory. The time she'd put on that dress for him, a pretty, girlish frock that he'd seen in her closet; and she'd put on the red pumps

too and the big sun hat, and he'd stood there memorizing the
sight, so full of delight that he made her *feel* the innocence
she'd spun around herself, not from outside but from some
undiscovered inner source. And the time they went swimming
out on Long Island, driving through that pretty harbor town
down to the pebbly beach, the tiny black bikini she wore, the
way the men stared and he didn't mind, the way the little girls
put their shy eyes on that dark, muscular man with the
shameless woman clinging to him and carressing him
everywhere; the way he just dove into that cold, cold water and
then stood up, dark and gleaming, and held out his hand:
"Come to me, babe. Just do it." Do it, yes, that was the day
she'd let go and fallen all the way. Out in the deep water, way
over her head, holding onto the slippery raft beside him, his
face so close to hers in the thick air with the droplets of brine
tracing every contour and line, his hair dripping, his brown
eyes clear and shining in the sun, his quiet voice telling her
how the boats used to race these waters, the Lightnings and
Blue Jays and Comets, describing how the ice formed one
bitter cold winter and invaded the beach in monstrous,
grinding plates, how an oyster boat went down and two men
froze to death in a dinghy in sight of the beach, his tone full
of the world's helplessness in the face of beauty and death, his
face all naked, wet and tender, so that even though she knew
he had swum in this same place and basked and talked and
laughed with that child-wife of his that he could never forget,
even though she knew there was a sorrow all mixed in with the
ease and pleasure and sensuality of his feeling for her, she
loved him for the first time wholly, exactly the same way she
loved herself, just as he was, with every dent and bruise and
scar the years had put on him. That was the day she knew she
could put her arms around this man and hold him forever, the
day she fell all the way in love, so that afterward, any time he
laughed that soft laugh of his, she could hear the water of

Long Island Sound slapping at that raft. That was the day all the other men in the world, in theaters and restaurants, in friends' living rooms, in business suits, in surgical greens, in friendly pubs and cabarets, became small and inconsequential in her eyes, their lusts all foolish and juvenile and as far away from her as her own miserable adolescence. That was the day she'd re-dreamed her childhood and begun her rearward pilgrimage toward her trapped and ravished innocence, the innocence she knew Mike yearned for, and every time he made love to her after that day, he took her another notch back. She wanted him soon...*now*. She could see him, almost feel him slipping into her so generously and irresistibly, his face set in such fine concentration, eyes aglow, lips so full and dark they seem swollen, giving her her pleasure before he takes his. Then, turning her over, that look of conviction in his eyes, so sure of her consent, her need to give everything...that benign sense of his power, taking what already belongs to him. And she, rolling her hips with him, feeling him touch the soft core of her and pull away, squeezing down hard to hold him in and thwart those feigned retreats, bringing him back into her again and again, wanting to feel him give back what he's taken, reaching her hand back between her legs to hold him there just as everything tightens and he's about to come, feeling all that tension and pulling in before he lets go, and then the crack of his voice through the room, and her own voice joining in the long moan that releases everything, everything... and then falling forward onto the sheets, face nuzzled to face, and the lamplight all haloed as their hot breath mingles in one golden fog...

"Jesus," the man said.

She flushed, and recovered herself. He was watching her face. He'd been watching in the mirror all the while.

"Jesus, what chapter's that you're reading? I don't remember ever getting a flutter from *Washington Square*."

She snatched her drink and took a swallow. She didn't care to see her face or anything else in the mirror. On the TV screen, those athletes in the blue and white uniforms had suddenly vanished, and ranks of groundskeepers were unrolling a huge, glistening, blue tarpaulin. It was raining like fury.

"Were you doing what I think you were doing?" A bold tone had come into the man's voice.

"Listen, do I know you?"

"Not yet, beautiful."

"Save it. I'm waiting for someone."

He laughed, warmly, familiarly. "Lucky him." When she didn't smile, he just shrugged. "I'll wait with you. You'll be glad I did, I'll bet you a drink on it."

"Why don't you just go home to your wife?" The untanned stripe where his wedding band had been was as plain as his ruddy nose.

"Wife? Which one, my dear?" He downed his drink in a gulp. "The last two, I've misplaced."

But for the first time something false had come into his voice. She glanced up and glimpsed that look she despised above all others, that shadow behind the eyes, that look of secrets, the look she had taught herself never to hide from; she stared...and it was gone.

His smile broadened and he leaned closer. He was unshakeable: cocksure, smooth, desperate, and half-drunk all at once. "Bartender," he called, and with a nod, he signaled for a fresh drink.

* * *

For the hell of it, Mike Villanova timed the bus ride from Jacobi down Pelham Parkway, past the posh brick homes and the well-kept apartment houses flanking the old bridle path, past the Zoo and the Botanical Gardens, past JFK High

School and Fordham University into the gritty bustle of Fordham Road; the ride took thirteen minutes.

He got off at Webster and started the seven block walk up to the Shamrock. The evening had closed down damp, cool, and overcast. After only a block or so, thunder rumbled up behind him in uncanny replication of the sound the El trains used to make twenty years ago, when he was an undergraduate heading off campus for beers at the Web. Moments later, the sky split under its weight, and the first drops hit the pavement.

He was seething himself, he'd been seething since leaving Julia's room. The world was turning surreal, and it was all her fault. A seance! And Helen would be the one to jump at the idea, too--and yet who in his universe was more real than Helen? She was as real as the landscape, and if any landscape had the power to mock him with its solidity it was the Webster Avenue strip, where his old haunts now slid past him one after another in the gloom: Joe D's, the old Webster Avenue Bar, Sonny's...

A flash of lightning and a terrific clap of thunder propelled him into a trot. He had five blocks to go and he wasn't going to make it. He loped past the Sundance and the Flim Flam Club; the bold ugliness of those flamingo-pink doors was as real as anything could be, and so were all the paychecks he'd earned on the inside as a private dick starting out, and so were all the women he'd picked up there and fucked in the not-so-distant past, the young and not-young, the clever and vain, the hopeful and forlorn, grist to the mill of some desperate anti-quest of his, a search for the eternal grail through a perverse march toward its opposite. The sight of those pink doors brought all of it back, the blast of music, the throb of the bass in his ribcage, the watered liquor, the predatory eyes, the Neanderthal conversation, the reckless amatory strikes, the couplings in cars, vans, rented rooms:

confidence the passport, male insistence the talisman, invisible pheromones leaching out from a strong, red, wholesome heart. So many wives, such epidemic disaffection, so many arabesque betrayals, shameless juxtapositions, sacrileged icons, sleeping children, close calls. Such a vigorous charge at life's confusion, all done with Rizzo's hearty encouragement, until....

Until he found too easy a mark one night, and left the Flim-Flam with a woman far too poised, intelligent, sensitive, and genuine for that place, a woman vulnerable in her candor and with good instincts, who had watched him for a while and then latched onto him almost with relief, put down a few drinks very quickly, and then asked him to take her somewhere and have sex with her. Outside, walking up Bedford Park Boulevard, she'd told him it would be just this one time, that she'd never been with any other man than her husband, that he ran around on her and maybe she deserved it, that she'd yielded him her virginity and obligated him into marriage, which was the way it was for shy, old-fashioned girls twenty years back, but still too high a price, maybe, for a man to pay for sex, a lopsided contract that called for perpetual redress. She'd told him she was drunk and a little confused and acting on principle--no offense intended, he was a very attractive man--and that her husband had never been directly malicious toward her, and maybe loved her; and that, not to be evasive, he was a cop and carried a gun, was one of those proud Italians, a detective and a good one, a higher-up in the Homicide Squad, but not a very suspicious man, not vindictive, a bit inclined to denial, certainly not the crazy-jealous type-- better for her if he were, maybe, something to steady her through the long arc of less-than-happy marriage while her husband hid himself for weeks at a time in his work...

But he'd stopped in his tracks, and shut her up before she could utter the name he didn't want to hear; with his heart laboring dolefully, he'd turned her around and hurried her back to the Flim-Flam and left her at those pink doors staring after him perplexed, and he'd only hoped she was drunk enough to forget his face forever, and he'd made a vow right then and there never to go back to the Flim-Flam again, and he kept it. And after a while he stopped going to all those places, and he didn't miss them, and now, hopelessly drenched in a thundershower that seemed almost as full of rumbling self-rage as he was, he only wanted to see all those brick and concrete tombs melt away as absolutely as ice, and get himself inside the Shamrock where there were plain people and honest talk and a familiar bartender and no spite and no serpentine ugliness, and cold beer, steak fries, corned beef sandwiches, decent coffee, and the warm touch and genuine voice of Helen.

Shivering and miserable, he pushed through the heavy swinging door, shook the rain off, slicked back his dripping hair, and wove through the crowd. He spotted Helen at the far end of the bar. There was a guy talking to her, and Villanova did a quick take, because something in their postures told him the guy was hitting on her and she wasn't liking it; you had to know Helen's *body* to tell when she was pissed off. He caught a look at the guy in the mirror then, and did another take, because he recognized him. He headed over.

The man turned around as he came up. His eyes widened in recognition. It was that sonofabitch McVicar.

"What gives here?" Villanova said.

"You looking for *me*?" McVicar looked nervous.

"Should I be?"

McVicar frowned. He took a glance over to Helen, then back to Villanova.

"You know this guy?" Villanova said in Helen's direction.

The light of understanding came to McVicar's eyes. "Oh, I get it." He relaxed, and gave Helen another appraising look. "This is yours." A smirk formed on his face.

Villanova hit him. He didn't know he was going to do it until McVicar was sitting on the floor and his own hand was throbbing in pain. It was the hardest he'd ever hit anyone in his life. McVicar wasn't smirking any more. He was holding his jaw, which had to be busted, and people were moving out of the way, making that ugly little arena, and the place was suddenly almost quiet, and Donny, the bartender, was hurrying down the bar. Helen looked stunned; her mouth was open. Villanova pulled her off the stool. She stood behind him and held his arm as if she was afraid it might suddenly swing at someone else. He was flushed and angry as hell, and the worst part of it was that he was mad in three or four different parts of himself at once, and couldn't tell one from the other. He said to Donny, "If this guy wants the cops, you know where I live."

"Sure, I know where you live."

"I'm in the wrong," Villanova said. "I sucker-punched him." McVicar was lost now in the knot of men helping him to his feet.

"That was no sucker-punch," Donny said. "He provoked you." Donny was an old-line barman, loyal to his regulars.

Villanova pulled Helen through the crowd and out of the bar into the rain. It was raining harder now, and the pavement shimmered with headlights and streetlights and neon from the storefronts.

"Where are we going?" she said.

"Home."

"We'll get drenched."

"Right."

"What about food?"

"Fuck food."

She gave him a look. "You gonna tell me what that was about?"

"Afterward."

She kept watching him. Her face was wet, fresh, brand new and fearless like a teenage girl's. "You want me, sweetheart?"

"You're damn right I want you."

"How? How do you want me?"

He didn't answer.

She looked happy. She looked more than happy. She said, "Don't worry, sweetie. Don't worry about anything, ever."

* * *

It was a turn-on, she said, to watch him work, and she had some quirky thing against beds, too, and most of all she wanted a mirror, so all in all it was lucky he had the room with the lock and the window. The black vinyl office chair seemed to turn her on too, and the cold feel of it against her skin made her nipples erect before he even got his mouth to them, but he knew what she liked and knew she was going to enjoy herself, and he went about it deliberately, squatting between her legs and working his way down her front, tongueing the underside of her breasts, her navel, the crease of her groin, tugging her hips until she slid her cheeks right to the edge of the seat and lifted her legs and opened herself to him, all groomed and perfumed--she was class, all right. And that's why Tony Rizzo didn't mind squatting in the semi-dark on his own office floor with Gilman and the others right down the hall and that shaggy bastard Manny in a holding cell two floors down, and the night traffic on the Cross-Bronx Expressway roaring by a half dozen feet below his window.

He spread Daphne out and and went to work until she began to moan, and then he got up on one knee and slid into her while their mouths found each other and he gave her back her own taste with his tongue.   He pumped her a few times, too, nice and slow, but that was just a tease, and next he was squatting down again and getting ready to finish her off.   And when she got close, she began rocking her hips and mashing herself against his mouth, and then she shivered and let go a quick, soft series of moans, and she was done.

He let her stay there flung back in the chair for a minute with her eyes closed and her chest wet with sweat and her legs slowly collapsing.   But then it was his turn, and they traded places, and she got him hard again with her mouth and then climbed on his lap and rode him.   She had that look on her face like she wanted to come again, and he saw her glancing sideways at the window, and he took a look and saw in the glass a pale image of them against the rooftops and the night sky, leaning back in the chair at a crazy angle, and the image flickered as a hundred headlights sped past below, and he saw her breasts bobbing as she rocked, and he thought of his wife and the way those heavy breasts of hers swung when he took her from behind, a lovely sight with the nipples dark as grapes, and he had the urge to fuck *her* too tonight, and he would, he'd make the time to get home, and now he was almost ready to come, and some kind of monster truck went hurtling by with a foghorn blast and a plume of ember-studded smoke, and he remembered that his wife had cheated on him, or *almost*, she'd told him so, she'd told him how close she'd come, and why had she done that? why had she *told* him? and now he was losing it, and the phone was ringing over in the Squadroom, and he stared at the window and thought of his wife's big, swinging breasts, and why wouldn't she ever take him in her mouth? why not? and now the fucking phone on his desk was ringing too, and Gilman was calling his name down the hall, and he wanted to come, he was about to come, and maybe tonight, yes, when he got home, in her mouth, yes, and Gilman was shouting his name now, and he was painfully pent, and with a groan and a great throb of pleasure he flooded into Daphne like a Samson, and by God he filled her up!

And he was still in her when he picked up the phone. It was his partner. "Buddy!" he managed to get out.

And after a minute, he said, "You what?"

And then, "You hit him? Are you crazy?"

And then, "Look, Buddy, no joke. You stay the fuck away from that guy! If the D.A. pulls me off this investigation on account of some bullshit thing you've got going with this professor...! Damn right! Go to sleep!"

He hung up. Daphne slid off him. She stood in front of him for a while and he could feel her looking at him. He lifted his eyes finally and saw, even in the semi-dark, how full her expression was, how she was struggling between hope and sadness and a feeling of foolishness. He ran his hand gently along her hip; it was the most genuine gesture he could make. "It was good," he said. "It was great." She nodded and put her hand over his. He could read her watch: 11:15.

He sat, brooding, as she gathered her clothes and dressed.

When she was almost done, he pulled on his socks, then his drawers. He swiveled the chair toward his desk. He was angry, but not at anybody in particular, just at everything. He didn't want to go to sleep, and he didn't want to fuck anyone now, and he wasn't sure what the hell to do with Daphne, and he didn't know whether to say nothing to her at all or to start talking and never stop. He picked up the phone and punched the Squadroom line. "Gilman? Get Manny Cruz up into an interrogation room. I wanna work the creep." He hung up.

"You're awful sure about Manny, aren't you," Daphne said.

"Yeah. Aren't you?"

"Not as sure as you."

He could feel thimself closing up and couldn't hide it. "No? He's innocent? We should let him go?"

"If you let him go, he's going to hurt somebody. I can guarantee it, I sat in a room with him. He's already been blamed, he doesn't care now. He's a hell of a lot more dangerous now than he was before."

"I get it. *He's* the victim." He didn't mean that but couldn't help saying it.

She shook her head slowly. "You know, what I like about you is the same thing I don't like about you. You really don't think you can make a mistake."

"Sure I can. I make mistakes all the time."

She nodded.

"But I'm not making a mistake this time."

She stood there smoothing down her hair. Then she dropped her arms and just stood where she was. She said softly, "I don't do this sort of thing for fun, you know." The flickering headlights outlined her form against the window. "When I do it, I mean it. Even if it doesn't look that way."

He tried to think of what he really wanted to say to her. Finally he said, "I know you mean it."

"I know you know. Otherwise it wouldn't be fun for *you.*"

A minute passed. The roar of traffic rose and fell behind her. She picked up her handbag and went toward the door. One of her earrings caught the light from the window, an eerie gold ring floating in the dark. She paused with her hand on the knob. "Can I get you anything?"

"Yeah," he said quietly. He switched on the desk light and threw open the file on the Albano murder. "Coffee."

- TEN -

Friday morning broke gloomy and cool, and Villanova slept late, lulled by the sound of rain on the eaves. He woke up a few times and checked the clock and figured Rizzo must be pretty sore to have waited this long to phone; and then he rolled over and fit himself snug around the curve of Helen's backside and went back to sleep, like he wished he'd done two days earlier.

When the phone rang at 10:05, it wasn't Rizzo but Sally Houk, his editor at the *Spectrum*. "Got your column?" she snapped by way of greeting.

"Yeah, sure," he croaked. "What's today?"

"Friday. Tomorrow's deadline day, remember?"

"Sure, I remember. It'll be there, just watch your fax."

"By 2 p.m. Don't forget." She hung up.

He sat up in bed, lit a cigarette, drew on it deeply, and looked around the room. The half-empty Coors bottles stood on the counter, the chili sat untouched in the dishes on the table, clothes lay scattered where they'd fallen, Helen's stockings draped the TV; it had been an impulsive night all around. Helen went on sleeping, her face peaceful, her mouth fixed in a half-smile. The cat, Mirabel, lay on the coverlet at her feet.

At 10:15 the phone rang again. It was Gilman from Homicide Squad. "You're a bad boy," he said.

"Where's Rizzo."

"At the D.A."

"Yeah? Did our friend Manny crack?"

"Not a chance.   And Rizzo's in one helluva bad mood."

"Shit. What about those trunks?   You hear from the Lab boys yet?"

"They're finishing 'em up now.   Meanwhile we could use those ESL rosters from JFK."

"Tell Rizzo I'll pick 'em up. Anything else?"

"The Albano wake's this afternoon. Rizzo says to meet him there.   And listen..."   Gilman's grating laugh came through the receiver. "Don't hit anybody in the meantime." He hung up.

Villanova put a call in to JFK.   The principal, Newmark, wasn't in yet, but was expected soon, or at least had trained his secretaries to say that. Villanova left word that he was on his way.

He shaved and dressed on the quiet and left Helen sleeping--it was her day off. The drizzle had turned to a mist, and he nursed a deli coffee down Webster and most of the way through his short-cut across the Fordham campus. The cup ran dry just outside Dealy Hall, and on a whim, he turned into the building and headed up to the Administration offices on the third floor.

The dean was in.

Dean Roger F. X. Hennessy was an old-line priest, a tall, fit, pink-complexioned man of about sixty, whose full head of white hair made a striking complement to his black suit. He had the affability and the directness of speech of a harried administrator glad to come up for air, and that Jesuit manliness that Villanova had spent his younger years learning to appreciate.   They hit it off, especially when Villanova, sitting opposite the man at his big, cluttered desk, reminisced a little about his varsity track days on Rose Hill. Dean Hennessy grew warmer yet when Villanova requested Archive privileges to inspect the Robinson material: the athlete/scholar held an almost mystical status among the campus old-timers. Hennessy immediately searched out a pass from his desk drawer. "I'm the one who got that material for the University," he boasted as he put his signature to the form. "It might have gone to Columbia otherwise."

"That would have been a shame, I guess, when you've got a major Hawthorne scholar here at Fordham."

A look of contempt filled Hennessy's eyes. "You mean Brian McVicar? That's a name I don't want to hear just now."

Villanova tried not to appear too curious. He should have acknowledged his role in the Albano investigation right off, but the truth was he was acting on wildly personal impulse as well as the instincts of years as a private investigator, and Hennessy looked as pent as a shaken bottle of beer. "I guess it's common knowledge, his involvement with that dead girl," he said.

Hennessy gave a disgusted wave of his hand. "The man's recreations are only the half of it...and the more excusable half." He groped around his desk, found his pipe in the ashtray, shoved it in his mouth, and struck a match to the bowl; a rich, chestnut aroma filled the air. Villanova pulled out his Chesterfields and lit up.

"I'm the guy that hired McVicar, and he's made me look bad ever since," Hennessy said. "He came up through the program at Columbia, studied under Eliot Robinson--*there* was an unrecognized genius. Robinson was *my* hero as a student, *lived* for books...died of a heart attack right in the Low Library, not long after I got my degree. That's where I first met McVicar, at Robinson's wake, the *protege*. So a year later I'm a department head here at Fordham--that's shortly after your time, I imagine--and along comes McVicar applying for a job, and my eyes light up, and I make a fuss to get him. He had this arrogant, showy manner and all, but he'd written this book, this brilliant dissertation that Oxford University Press was putting out in hard and soft cover. Here, you know the book, I'm sure..." He reached to the shelves behind him and flipped a copy of *The Dimmesdale Complex* across the desk. "It *is* brilliant. It was some kind of blockbuster, as academic books go. I mean, the guy had such *promise...*"

"So?"

"So that was fifteen years ago." Hennessy's face puckered, and he leaned back in his chair, casting a hard look out the window where the Keating Hall tower rose up dark against the overcast. "Look, there's only two ways you earn your keep in this university. You're either some walk-on-water teacher, or you make a reputation as a scholar. McVicar, the first few years, he published an article here and there...he was still mining the old material, I could see that, but we were all happy to wait for that next book that was supposedly in the works. We gave him his rank promotions, we gave him tenure...and what happened?" A look of perplexity mixed with hurt came into the priest's eyes. "The minute he got tenure, the articles stopped. I mean altogether."

Villanova nodded. "The guy took you."

"No, no, worse than that. We've been taken before, but McVicar took *himself.* He traded a magnificent talent for a nice, comfortable associate professorship. The man cheated his own gifts! That's why he's so despised around here."

"Is he? I hadn't realized that."

"Sure he is. The students don't know it, of course, not till it's too late. Every semester he gets one or two of the women in bed." He colored, and his gaze shifted toward the window, where the muffled shouts of athletes down on

Edwards Parade washed up against the panes.   "It's all compensatory, that's my theory.   In the beginning, when he was the *enfant terrible*, the star of the department, he was clean, or at least discreet.   Something awful happened to that man when he couldn't produce that second book.   He started drinking and, once he was tenured, began *flaunting* his affairs. He got greedy about it, you know?   I mean, he had to be sleeping with two, three women in the same seminar.   At a department party, there had to be at least one catfight, one seething husband, one or two broken hearts drowning their grief in sherry.   You should have seen him at the last party, having a lover's quarrel with that Albano girl in one corner, making her some desperate pitch while the latest girlfriend sat sulking across the room.   And him glancing over at *me* every minute, mocking me, as if he knew he'd cut the girl off from me... "

"Which girl?   The Albano girl?"

Hennessy nodded.   "I knew she was in trouble.   She'd come in here to talk to me about a week before, wanted to take an indefinite leave from the program.   Can you imagine, one of our best students?   I wouldn't hear of it, I insisted that she stick it out.   She kept saying how exhausted she was, unhappy...   I wouldn't accept it.   I wanted the *real* reason, you see, and I couldn't get her to say it.   If only she'd confided in me, *then* I could have helped her, with pleasure.   Fact is, I sit on the Sexual Harassment Committee here, I was one of the authors of the university's Guidelines.   We don't have to tolerate McVicar's kind of behavior any more.   With Liz's cooperation, I could've got rid of the man for good... vindicated myself doubly."

"Doubly?"

"Sure.   *I* was the one who encouraged Liz to start the doctoral program in the first place.   I could see, even as an undergraduate, what a wonderful potential she had, as a person and a student both. And I was right. Why, *she* was as excited as I was when the Robinson material arrived." He frowned, studying the stem of his pipe. "Deep down that man McVicar *wants* to be despised. He's so ashamed of himself as a scholar that he can't let anyone forget it. Especially me. He knows I still hit that library, I still produce. I'm busy as hell, but I still follow my field. *I* was the one who paid heed when Robinson's widow passed away this June, *I* acquired his personal papers from the estate. I was up to my ears with the new MFA program this summer, but I still stole the march on those Columbia boys, not His Holiness." He leaned back in his chair and put the pipe to his lips, sending up a chestnut-scented cloud. "Now that the semester's under way, I can finally savor my prize. On a Saturday, in this weather, the Archive is the only place I want to be. You know, watch the Rams play out on Coffey field, enjoy a warm brandy in the refectory, then settle in with the documents. Make *use* of my God-given talents, like *he* ought to be doing."

Villanova nodded; the priest's petulance was full of odd depths and nuances. "It's guilt, then, all that Casanova strutting," he said.

"Guilt, sure, but nicely displaced. The man wants to be punished for the wrong sin, a sin that suits his *vanity*. You know, like in his book." He smiled ironically and gave a quick shrug. "Now who would be an expert on the 'Dimmesdale complex' if not McVicar?"

Villanova waited for more, but Hennessy seemed satisfied he'd been understood. Underneath that ironic resignation was something that wasn't supposed to show, something personal and unforgiving. "I guess I ought to read the book," Villanova said. "I keep hearing about it."

"You haven't read it?" Hennessy looked surprised, then confused; it was clear he'd taken Villanova for a serious Hawthorne scholar. "You're joking, right? You really haven't read it? Here, take this copy." His brow furrowed, and he cleared his throat; he seemed to realize for the first time how much he'd said. Clouds of pipe smoke blossomed around his blushing face.

Villanova was embarrassed for him too; though academic gossip was a fact of life, the priest had revealed an ego of unexpected dimensions. Villanova took him off the hook by glancing at his watch and gathering himself to rise.

"Take the book, seriously," Hennessy insisted, thrusting it forward along with the Archive pass. "It's a wonderful piece of work, in spite of all."

Villanova accepted it; it was Hennessy's gesture of redress to McVicar's reputation. He stubbed out his cigarette, thanked the priest, shook his hand warmly, and left him him sitting there shuffling papers and puffing away.

From the first floor lobby he put in another phone call to JFK; Newmark was still not in the building.

He stood for a few minutes on the edge of Edwards Parade with a foot propped on the old iron rail fence, watching the rugby players. A fine drizzle was slanting through the mist now, deepening the greystone of the flanking buildings, coating the ivy on their walls and the dying leaves of the big shade trees. The grunts and shouts of the ruggers, the flyer-festooned fence posts, the wide stone steps of the gym, the blinking red light atop the Keating Hall tower, everything here was just as it had been twenty years ago. But it was the rich smell of wet earth more than anything else that swept him back in a cruel rush to that September day when he, scrimmaging with the college's pioneer rugby squad, had noticed the pretty girl watching from beyond the fence, those dark eyes and the open smile and the long black hair, the canvas guitar case slung over her shoulder, the sandal shod foot propped on the rail and the slender white fingers wrapped around the fence post...

This wasn't good. This was very bad. He pulled himself away and headed for the back gate off the campus.

He avoided Webster Avenue this time and walked homeward up Bainbridge, even though the gusts showered him with big, cold drops from the trees. As he approached the Topless Towers, he felt with sudden keenness how opposite this chaotic place was to the grace of his long ago life with Ginny at Fordham and at Belle Haven, how brashly it proclaimed its sabotage of any human design, growing hardy and riotous like kudzu, ingesting into its grotesque sculpture any human life that came close, including his own. How had this place become his real home? This place with all the half-disassembled cars in the garages, his own T-Bird with the hood up and the heads off and the pistons and rods on a sheet in the trunk and the camshaft in the back seat and the tools scattered and the torque wrench and most of the sockets somehow disappeared. This place with all the cast-off projects of the cast-off children cluttering his rooms and every stairway and passage: the broken toys, the hockey sticks, the hand loom, the fishtank, the build-your-own-cuckoo-clock, the rock polishing machine, the cactus garden, the tarantula enclosed in the terrarium with its cricket-victims like the Minotaur in the labyrinth. This place with all the wild kids themselves, rough and loud and larcenous, the ones with the most trouble turning out to be the ones he liked the best: Celeste, an uncelestial girl of fifteen, a drinker, a smoker, a hot-tempered, voluptuous tease with a dozen unhappy habits and compulsions: shoplifiting, hitchhiking, crash dieting, streetfighting; a girl given to fanaticisms like body-building, diary-writing, and intense romanticizing of street gangs and movie desperadoes; a self-conscious, sensitive girl, always ready to take a comment the wrong way and claw at someone's eyes...and also a girl who read books and daydreamed so deeply she couldn't hear her name spoken, who loved animals and misfits, who had a poet's anger at the world's indifference to everything important, and a beautifully tuned internal bullshit detector; she was a pressure-cooker of warring forces, and he'd been to her school a half-dozen times bailing her out of trouble, and had taken memorable lashings in her behalf from an assortment of functionaries, including a fascist attendance officer and a harpy of a math teacher.

And her kid brother Joey, he was almost as irresistible, a good-looking, good-natured, hapless thirteen-year-old, a kid who was always losing things, always forgetting where he was supposed to be and what he was supposed to have with him, always getting hurt. Joey and he had been so many times to the emergency room at Montefiore that the doctors had finally called in the child abuse team, one of the great indignities of his life. The kid loved cars, bikes, motorcycles, skateboards, anything with wheels that he could fall off of or get hurt on. He was nuts about trains, and together they'd ridden the whole New York subway system with their faces pressed against the glass of the first car. Joey was good company, sweet, funny, willing to learn, though putting a tool in his hand was like dropping it in the mailbox. Still, they'd built that model train layout in the basement together, and he'd let the kid make up most of the design for it, and he'd let him build the mountain all by himself, even though he did it wrong about eight different ways and dyed everything in sight black and wasted some of his mother's best bedsheets in the process; he'd let him build all the crooked little houses and stores and hotels and water towers he wanted. Every week when the *Spectrum* paycheck came, he would take the kid up to the hobby store on Fordham Road and stand admiring the serious layout they had there, and ask questions, and buy some H.O. track, a couple of switches, a building kit, an engine, some lights and wire, a couple more cars for their Santa Fe line or their old-time B & O, a steel truss bridge, some miniature autos and trucks and people; it was a wonderful ritual, capped by a few slices of Sicilian pizza and a handful of garlic knots, or maybe a calzone or two. For months they were engrossed together in the dark basement night after night, listening to each other's music on the tape deck, planning, building, revising, expanding, testing, playing, and forgetting everything else in the world, and when they were done they had the one thing in the Topless Towers that worked by design, a model town with a freightyard and a business district and a schoolhouse and a movie theater and streets and traffic signals and a harborfront and houses set on hills and a pond with rowboats and a park with a bandshell, a town that seemed made for people and that had, unwittingly, come to be a near perfect replica of a pretty Long Island village known as Belle Haven...

And there it was again, no matter how much junk was piled against it. And he didn't like to think he was a soft-headed man, and what was he supposed to do about it anyway?

"Yo!" someone called to him as he climbed the Topless Towers' front steps: it was Celeste Marinelli on the other side of the street, lounging against a car along with two leather-jacketed punks. She gave him a wave and the closest thing to a smile she could manage with a cigarette dangling from her heavily-rouged lips. He waved back, ducked into the house, and headed straight downstairs to the basement. Here, sealed away from the sight and sound and even the atmosphere of the outside world, he liked to do his reading, and thinking.

First, by ritual, he took a long look at the miniature village in the artificial dusk made by the lone 40-watt bulb at the foot of the stairs. The layout's tiny streetlamps, which were always left shining hopefully, the glow from inside the little houses and stores met and melted into the false twilight and gave the model hamlet a soft and convincing realism, like

Belle Haven seen from High Point at night. He started the trains in motion, ran through all the switches, found one that wasn't working, and spent a quarter hour crawling around under the plywood table tracking down the broken splice. But then he had everything running smoothly, and, soothed by the tick of tiny wheels on tiny rails, by the movement of the little cars in their eternal ellipse, he settled down into a cast-off Marinelli armchair, turned the bulb in a fifty-year-old floor lamp, opened up *The Dimmesdale Complex,* and commenced reading.

The first sentence began: "One of the most subtle and therefore most pernicious errors made thus far by all Hawthorne scholars is the failure to appreciate that Roger Chillingworth and Arthur Dimmesdale are but two personae of the same man, whose interactions thus constitute a paradoxic reification of the author's own self-love."

It was going to be a day for unpleasant chores.

* * *

The long row of double-parked cars along Morris Park Avenue meant a large wake at Grippi and Sons.

Villanova found the foyer of the funeral home crowded with mourners. The dead girl was laid out in the largest of the rooms, and besides the usual contingents--dark-suited men standing in groups with their hands in their pockets, women in dark dresses and dark pumps sitting on the couches or in huddles of folding chairs--there were numbers of very young people in large groups, mostly girls, looking awkward and distressed: Elizabeth's students. Babbling conversation and the heavy perfume of flowers filled the air, but without the occasional runnel of laughter or heartiness. It wasn't one of those expansive wakes full of the energy of relief; it was sober, and its energy came from youth and a subsurface tone of outrage. Villanova, standing in the rear of the room, could see Mrs. Albano seated near the casket, flanked by those big, handsome sons; her pale, immobile face looked almost stupefied.   In the seats behind her were a number of young couples with deep, attractive coloring and lustrous dark hair; the clan in its natural state seemed endowed with health and beauty.   Tom Albano, ever alert, detached himself from a circle of men near his wife, and, sober and handsome in his dark blue suit, came rearward to greet Villanova; among the men he left behind, easily recognized by his small stature and white hair, was Dr. Parisi.

Albano was sincerely appreciative that Villanova, like so many others who were unexpected, had come, but the first thing he wanted to know was when his daughter's killer was going to be found.   Villanova didn't lie to him, but he didn't tell him about Manny Cruz.   That seemed too cruel for a man with Albano's beliefs and hopes.   Instead he filled him in about the cab driver, the canvassing squad, JFK, the ESL roster, and whatever else was safe to mention.   He made it sound like a lot.

"What about that English professor?   You talk to him?"

"Sure."

"And that Jack character with the long hair?"

"Him too."

"I hope they turn up clean," Albano said with quiet conviction.   "I wouldn't want to think it was someone who sat in my living room.   I wouldn't want it to be someone who might come walking into this room."

"I don't think you need to worry about that," Villanova said.   He caught Parisi's eye and exchanged a nod.   Had the doctor told Albano about Elizabeth's office visit, or about his own?   He guessed he hadn't.

Albano looked in the direction of the casket, mostly hidden by the knots of mourners.   "It's hard," he said.   "It's harder than I thought, seeing your own kid there.   Look at her, a child, a little girl.   Never even got the chance to finish growing up." He shook his head. His face, long and thin, looked haggard. "Till now, life hasn't been bad to me. But I tell you, this is the worst. If I could take her place in that coffin, so help me God, I would." His eyes were brimming.

"Take it easy," Villanova said. "You've had a tough few days. You're worn out."

"What did she ever do to anybody? What?"

"Easy, it's almost over. Another day of this, and then you just get through the burial."

"The burial's tomorrow, Saint Raymond's," Albano said. But he seemed to appreciate Villanova's support.

"How's your wife?"

"Not good. Bad. Doc Parisi's got her medicated." He cast a grim glance in her direction. "The women go all to pieces in this kind of thing. She'll never be the same."

"Sure she will. Come on, come into the hallway and let's have a smoke. Calm your nerves."

"Not me, no, I gave it up. You go ahead. We'll talk more." Albano gave his arm a touch and turned back to his group.

Villanova went into the foyer just outside the doorway and lit a cigarette. He was damned if he was going to ask that man for an article of his daughter's clothing to bring to some seance. He was damned if he was going to walk too near that casket, either, not in the mood he was in. He'd been to plenty of wakes, for the young and the old, but this one reminded him too much of the only other wake that still gave him nightmares. This one made him angry all over again for the tenacity and resilience of injustice. If he thought too hard about it, he'd have to admit that he wanted to do something black and savage to Elizabeth Albano's killer. He wanted that man dead, and he wanted the person who had extinguished the life of Ginny Romano Villanova to be worse than dead, to have never existed.

He drew deeply on his cigarette, desperate to smother the anger in his chest. A tall, well-dressed man with grey hair and a formal bearing entered the foyer From the back he looked and moved a good deal like Brian McVicar, but a clear look at his face dispelled that illusion. McVicar would be teaching a class till 4:10, anyway. After that, any grieving he had to do he'd be doing in private, in absolute secrecy, if his book reflected his own psyche in any way. As for guilt, he'd probably be back at the Shamrock tonight picking up a woman, or pumping away at Dolores Loughlin: "Sublime Sublimation," that was one of the chapter titles in *The Dimmesdale Complex.*

Villanova shook his head.   It was funny how McVicar's presence remained stamped in the mind, as if the man wanted the people who knew him to think about him when he wasn't around. And more than that, something about the guy just didn't add up, and that enigmatic quality was, in one way or another, irresistible.   Villanova stood there enveloped in cigarette smoke, letting all the odd-shaped pieces of Brian McVicar form and re-form themselves: the brilliant book, the attractive wife, the young conquests, the bar pick-ups, the bitter dean and his cartons of documents, the trysts in the Archive, the pregnant girlfriend with the half-written dissertation...

"You Villanova?" a man's voice broke in.

He turned. It was the tall, grey-haired newcomer.

"I'm Gary Newmark," the man said. He had a smooth, soft voice and a solid look, with a high forehead, wide-set grey eyes, a sharp, clefted chin. He wore a vested charcoal suit, quality stuff, and looked to be nearing fifty.

"Principal at JFK?" Villanova said.

"That's me. I hear you've been looking for me."

"I sure have." He shook the man's extended hand. The scent of good cologne reached his nose. "You're one difficult guy to get hold of."

Newmark smiled. "I have what you want. I've been carrying it." He reached inside his jacket and withdrew a folded printout. "The roster from Elizabeth's ESL class. I hope it's a help."

"Sure, sure, everything's a help." Villanova opened the sheet and gave a quick glance to the list of twenty or so names.

"I apologize for the delay. No excuses. Maybe I can help you with something else."

He seemed to mean it. "Some information, maybe," Villanova said. He folded the sheet into his hip pocket. "One of our suspects is a guy who works in your building, a custodian by the name of Manny Cruz. You know anything about him?"

Newmark shook his head. "Not much. Used to see him in the halls now and then. He never said hello, never even looked me in the face. Sullen sort of guy."

"Ever get complaints about him?"

"A couple reached me. You know, like he looked funny at a girl, or she thought he was following her when no one was around. Once one of our female custodians caught him in the girls' locker room. We weren't sure, but it looked like he spent half his shift crammed in a locker peeping through the vents. He gave us some crazy excuse. After that we got him to switch to nights."

Villanova nodded. "Was there ever any trouble between Manny Cruz and Elizabeth Albano?"

"None that ever reached my office. Sorry." And he really did look sorry. Those small eyes of his, hard to read, were rather sensitive. He was a more complex man than he first appeared, a man with an inside far less undamaged than his smooth, complacent outside; in fact, for all his solidity, he projected something hollow and fragile.   Villanova said, "To your knowledge, was there any contact between those two at all?"

"No. They were in the building at entirely different times."

"Until this term, right?"

"Yes, until this term."   Newmark leaned pensively against the wall beside the doorjamb.   Beyond his shoulder, the shifting groups of mourners afforded transient glimpses of the beautiful girl in the open casket.   He said, "Night classes never meet the first week of school, and the second week we were shut down Wednesday at 3:00 for Rosh Hashanah.   That means Cruz was only in the building with the Albano girl last week Wednesday, her first night on the job."

"And Cruz's last."

"I see what you're getting at.   You're asking me, did something happen between them last Wednesday?"   He shrugged. "I can't say. Funny thing, though, just yesterday I got Manny's last time card back from Central Payroll. If there's a glitch, see, they circle it in red and send the card back to the supervisor. It turns out Manny punched out early that Wednesday night.   7:46.   I assume he left the building. There'd be no other reason for him to punch his card."

"And where would Elizabeth have been at 7:46?"

"Well, *ordinarily* in her classroom.   Night classes run from six to nine, with a ten minute break at 7:30. The thing is, some teachers, on the first night, just dismiss the class at the midpoint.   That's what Elizabeth did last Wednesday.   It's technically against the rules, but we wink at the practice in the Office."

Villanova raised his brows.   The tantalizing surmise was that Manny had had an encounter with Elizabeth and

followed her out of the building.   "How do you know
Elizabeth left early? Did she sign out?"
        Newmark shook his head.   "Teachers don't sign out."
        "Well then?"
        Newmark cleared his throat.   "I was there that night.   I
went by her room at around eight o'clock.   To tell the truth, I
was surprised to find it dark.   Disappointed is the word.   First
night or not, she wasn't the type for early dismissal unless she
was physically ill."
        "We have reason to believe that she *was* physically ill."
        "I know that."
        "Is that why you were checking up on her?"
        "I wasn't checking up on her."
        Villanova was perplexed.   All else aside, he hadn't
pegged Newmark as the kind of administrator to be on the job
at eight p.m.   Newmark seemed to be thinking the same thing.
Nothing in his expression changed, but it was obvious now
that he had more to say, that that smooth, pleasant face hid a
troubled spirit.   He shrugged and said quietly, "I'd left a note
in Liz's mailbox asking her to see me at the end of the night.
It had nothing to do with anything.   It was just personal."
        Villanova studied him.   "Were you   a   friend   of
Elizabeth's?"
        "Not really." Newmark rocked gently against the wall.
In the big, crowded room behind him, the lights went out, and
the babble of talk tapered off.   "The truth is, in the past I
stayed away from the girl as much as I could." He rocked
again, and the lights went back on.
        "Really? You going to tell me why?"
        Newmark let out his breath.   "I will if you think it'll
help. But I won't be surprised if you don't understand." He
took a long look into Villanova's eyes, a tentative, exploratory
look; his face opened a little, his shoulders relaxed.   "I've been
principal of that school twenty-two years.   I rode in there on a

wave of Peace Movement, Civil Rights idealism, and I watched it all turn to ashes. In a nutshell, I'm your basic burnout." He said this in a quiet monotone, eyes level. He rocked some more, and the lights in the big room behind him went off again, and on; the conversations faltered and picked up in phase. "I'm not going to bore you, but my career is a testament to disillusion: Civil Service is my name, Early Retirement is my game. When the students torched my office a few years back, they didn't do anything to me that wasn't already done. In fact, I admired their instincts."

Villanova drew closer, trying to penetrate that sweet cologne; sure enough, he picked up the scent of liquor. Newmark rocked again, and then, brow furrowed, reached behind him and discovered an old-fashioned push-button switchplate. He pressed the buttons a few times, looking up puzzled at the foyer chandelier. Behind him, the lights blinked off and on, off and on.

"What's all that got to do with Elizabeth?" Villanova asked.

"Liz Albano was the first live human being I saw in a decade. She was the only *good* thing we had in the building. She reminded me of the way I *used* to feel, that gentleness, that hope we all had twenty years ago. She made me realize how the guts had all trickled out of me like sand...how nothing was left inside but lies." He drew a deep breath and let it out. "Liz Albano broke what was left of my goddam heart. That's why I made myself stay away from her, that's why I still haven't walked over to that casket." Newmark fixed Villanova with those little, grey eyes of his, and now, suddenly, a spark of feeling appeared in them. "See what I mean? Even now I can't stop lying. The real truth is, I didn't stay far enough away from Elizabeth. I finally made a fool of myself with her...but I don't regret it. At least I showed I was alive."

It wasn't what Villanova had expected, but he went with it. "Tell me about it," he said.   He held Newmark's eyes, admiring his candor, careful not to show any other emotion.

"A week ago Tuesday she came into my office to sign her contract and pick up her rosters. She looked different... anxious, harried. I asked her if she was feeling ill. I think she was surprised that I knew her well enough to notice. We talked for a minute, nice and easy. I was on my way to an early dinner. I took a flyer and suggested she come with me to the Blue Spruce and have a drink, unburden herself."

"She accepted?"

Newmark nodded. "That perked me up pretty good, but I just eased into the safe, avuncular role. I was afraid of my own goddam feelings, see? So I sat with her in a back booth in the Polo Room, low-key as a priest, putting down three drinks to her one.   Inside, my heart was pounding.   I wanted something miraculous to happen between us."

Villanova felt a pang on Newmark's behalf.   "You make it sound as if you were half in love with the girl."

Newmark shook his head.   A confessional blush tinged his cheek. "I could have been *all* in love with her, from the beginning, but I hadn't let myself. She was the one who could rescue me, and I knew it. So beautiful, so full of health! I was desperate. If she could have felt something for me, I would have risen from the dead like Lazarus. But all that was preposterous, I knew, a pathetic fantasy. So I sat there, Mr. Principal, Mr. Burned-out Marriage and Burned-out Career, buying drinks for a girl my *daughter's* age."

"You didn't come on to her at all?"

"I didn't have to. That was the surprising thing. She knew. All the tension was there, the man-woman stuff, and I realized she'd copped to it from the start. We were already on a date, sort of, and the main revelation was how sophisticated she was, how brave she was out in the world. That's when I started to get hopeful."

"What'd you talk about?"

"Her. We started safe, her graduate work, her dissertation. I could be helpful there, I'd done my own suffering in an Ed.D. program. 'I'm stuck,' she told me, 'What I've written is good, and I can't finish it.' I laughed. 'Everyone says that,' I said. 'You're looking for that last piece of research, that missing link. You'll find it. Everyone does.' She shook her head. 'I already found it, that's the trouble.'"

"What'd she mean by that?"

"Damned if I know. It was so hopeless the way she said it, I didn't know how to respond. And then she changed the subject: her father, her brothers, the two guys she'd fallen for over the last year. Mostly her father, what a terrific guy he was, how he worshipped her, what a narrow pedestal he'd given her to live on, how it would rip him up to know the parts of her he'd never seen. The way she talked, it was as if he hadn't noticed her change since she was fourteen. To be honest, it shocked me to think that a girl as pretty as that should have to struggle that way. It was almost as if she was leading a double life, but without the cynicism, genuine on both ends. I let her talk away, trying to guess what she was working up to. I mean, clearly she was desperate for someone's help, some *adult*. But why *me*? Was there a chance I was going to be Guy Number Three?"

"Maybe it was because you asked."

Newmark gave him a glance, and shrugged.

But Villanova didn't mean to be cute. He understood Newmark precisely and felt a real empathy for him, and at the same time he was turning the new information this way and that and waiting for a click. "What'd she say about Guy Number One and Two?"

"That they were both rats, and she knew it...a little too late the first time. *That* guy was the king of the rats, and he still had her cornered. The second time she'd gone in with her eyes more open. All any of those guys wanted was a piece of her, anyway. And now everything was going wrong for her at once. She felt as if there was a wall in every direction, that's what she said. She looked as if she was in real pain. I mean, I could see her trying to hold back tears a couple of times...but she also looked determined to get over that wall, one way or another, and in one piece, too. For a while I thought it was guilt that was eating her up, you know, the good-girl/bad-girl thing. I could've given her some answers there. But it wasn't as simple as that." Newmark peered into Villanova's eyes and lowered his voice. "You know what she told me? That she knew exactly who she was when she made love to a man: she was herself, even if the man and all the people who knew her best couldn't see it. She said she felt she was being split apart from the *outside*, not the inside, split by other people's cock-eyed vision, and then boxed into a place too small for a whole person. That was the phrase she used, 'boxed in.' I knew exactly what she meant. I had to go home soon and play man-of-the-house to people who never knew me."

"But you didn't go home right away, did you," Villanova said.

"No, I made a fool of myself first, like I said. I told Liz maybe it would be different with the next guy she fell for. Maybe he would see her whole and love her that way. She looked at me. Everything was there in her face, the sweetness, the kindness, the curiosity, the hunger. I turned red, I couldn't help it. She told me she really liked me, that that's why she'd confided in me. That something about me made her think of her father, that *he* was really the one she needed to say these things to."

Newmark hesitated. His face was miserable, and his voice had dropped to a murmur. "My heart hit the floor when she said that. But it wasn't a total brush. I was still hanging by a thread, barely alive." His eyes filled with the same anguished hopefulness that Elizabeth Albano must have seen that night. "I told her that Guy Number Three might be her way out of the box. A guy who could admire her through her father's eyes and still see her as a woman of flesh and bone."

"What'd she say?

"'It's too late.' She said it real quiet. And then she shook her head, and she lifted her drink and took the last swallow. And the waiter came charging over to see about a refill. He was a young fellow, nice looking, all eyes for Liz. I mean, the guy was smitten, and she was just real sweet to him, real human, without leading him on. You think I didn't envy that man, apron and all? Soon's he was gone, I looked her square in the eyes and said, 'It's *not* too late. Guy Number Three...a guy who could *save* you, and you could save him.' It was the wrong word to use, but I don't regret using it because my end of it was so true. That girl could have saved my life." The hopefulness washed out of Newmark's eyes, and only the pain was left. "She looked right back at me, and after a minute she shook her head. She said, 'I don't think that's the way out of the box.' She said it very kindly. 'That's the way into a smaller box.'"

Villanova nodded; she was right. "Did you push it?"

"I said, 'You're a girl who can have anything she wants.' I meant it to embolden her. She said, 'All I want is for the noise to stop. I want to walk without dead things stuck to me, other people's needs.'"

"What then? You keep trying?"

"No. I was stung. I knew I was one of those dead things, even though she didn't mean it that way...me, with the 'saving vision'! I clammed up, and that was the end of the conversation." He sighed. "I'm not much when it comes to guts, I guess. Liz tried to put money on the table before she left, but I wouldn't let her."

Villanova mulled it over. "That was Tuesday night. I understand now...the next night you stayed around JFK hoping to see her after class, is that it?"

Newmark nodded. "It was a little silly, leaving a note for her that way."

"Could it be that she left work early that night to avoid you?"

"I suppose. I'd rather not think that."

"What'd you do when you found she'd left the building?"

"I went outside looking for her. I walked up Fordham Road all the way to White Plains Road. I was in a crazy state, humiliated, desperate, confused, like some teenager. I *felt* more in a half hour than I have in the last ten years. You should have seen me. It was windy and I was wearing just a blazer. I was like some guy in an opera, wild. I didn't want to go home ever again." The color came to his face just recalling it.

"What would you have done if you'd spotted her?"

"I don't know. Nothing probably. Followed her."

"Followed her? Why?"

Newmark shook his head. "I wanted to see where she lived. I wanted to know things about her...what her house looked like, where her room was. I wanted to see the people she came from."

Villanova drew on his cigarette. "Look around, then." The foyer was filling with people leaving the big room.

Newmark did look around. The color had collected in two crimson dots high on his cheeks; he seemed younger, handsomer. "That the father there, the one in the blue suit? I

should go introduce myself. He should know who I am.
Really, I should talk to the man."

"Take it easy, now. What do you want to tell him?"

"What I told you. All of it."

"Are you kidding? What the hell for?"

Newmark turned to face him. His eyes had a peculiar,
earnest glow in them. "Because I'm a selfish man. Because I
know confessing will make me feel better."

Villanova gave a dry nod. "But how'll it make *him*
feel?"

Newmark didn't answer for a minute. "It would be one
thing I could give her, her father's understanding," he said
quietly. The glow in his eyes began to fade. "Don't worry,
I'm not going to do it. Like I said before, I'm short on guts."

"You've got guts enough, as far as I'm concerned."
But Villanova understood now how deeply the sickness had
corroded those insides.

Newmark just shook his head. The crimson dots had
faded away. He pushed his hands into his pockets.

Villanova flicked his cigarette ash to the floor. His
head was heavy now with new details to ponder, and, much as
he was fascinated by Newmark's candor, he longed for a few
wordless minutes. "You going inside to the casket now? I'll
go stand there with you."

"I'm going home for a drink," Newmark said. "I'm
through." He drew himself up and adjusted his tie into his
collar. The last of the brightness left his eyes, and a sad,
hollow look emerged in its place; then the smooth cover
closed over his face. Villanova stood there helpless to stop it.
Newmark put out his hand for a shake and excused himself.

As the tall, grey-clad man crossed the foyer, Villanova
watched without seeing, his mind whirring on playback and
his hand absently raising the cigarette to his lips, one drag,
another, another. 'It's too late,' the girl had said. 'I already

found it.' Too late for what? Found what? He sucked the
cigarette down to the filter as Newmark worked his way
through the group clustered near the street door, bumped
shoulders with a late arrival, and headed out to the street. 'I
already found it, that's the trouble.' What trouble?

And then it clicked.

'That's the way into a smaller box.'

Exactly! And he burned the inside of his fingers on
the cigarette and cursed and flung it almost at the feet of the
late arrival.

"What the hell?" the man growled at him, and it was
Rizzo. His clothes were dripping.

"It's raining?" Villanova asked stupidly, a smile on his
face; his mind was racing, his body pulling against itself.

"What's funny about rain?"

"Listen!" he said, making a grab for Rizzo's arm.
"Listen! The girl was writing her dissertation, right?
Everything was dandy, then all of a sudden she's stuck. A girl
as bright as that. Remember her manuscript in her room? For
ten chapters, every third citation was *The Dimmesdale
Complex,* then all of a sudden, not a single reference. That
was months back, mid-summer. What happened in mid-
summer? Not the big blow-out with her boyfriend, *before*
that. The Robinson material! That's where she was every day,
in the Archive, signing out one box after the next. Don't you
get it? There's something in one of those *boxes!* She found
something! And now *his* signature shows up there too!"

Rizzo glared at him. "Whose signature?" He withdrew
his arm and shook the wet off his sleeves.

"McVicar's! The big-shot scholar goes years without
visiting the Archive, and suddenly Tuesday this week, while his
girlfriend's getting killed, there he is looking in a box. He
even goes back twice! What's he looking for?"

Rizzo didn't seem anywhere near answering or caring. His eyes hardened and his face darkened. "Do me a favor, don't talk to me about McVicar any more. Don't tell me you hate his book, and don't tell me he's looking in a box. Okay, Buddy?"

"What the hell's with you? What's your problem?"

"My problem is, on account of you've got a thing with this horseshit professor, on account of you've got a hang-up with Fordham and this dead girl, on account of you have to go and assault a suspect during an investigation and crack his very expensive bridgework, *I'm* fucked! That's my problem!"

Villanova's elation dimmed. "What happened?"

"Your friend McVicar phoned the D.A.'s office and lodged a complaint. That limp-assed bitch Bev Cohn called Homicide Squad in a snit, found out we still hadn't arraigned Manny or gotten him counsel, and blew out the rest of her gaskets. You want the long and the short of it, Buddy? Manny's out. My killer's on the street, thanks to you and your pal McVicar."

"Out? Hold on...with the case we've got against him?"

"What case? The guy didn't talk, and we never got the chance to finish squeezing him. Look, without a witness to place the Albano girl anywhere near Manny at the time of death, there's no way in hell Cohn's going to risk pressing the case at arraignment. Remember when she jumped the gun on that Claremont Park case last month, and the Grand Jury wouldn't indict? The *News* mauled her office good over that one, and she's not going through that again. She insisted on a not-on-the-merits release until we pull our case together. I went over there and argued myself hoarse, for nothing. We had to put Manny on the outside."

"Christ! With a tail, I hope."

"What do *you* think?" Rizzo took a look toward the big room, which was now nearly empty. His face, when he was angry, grew more angular, and his mouth turned almost sad; his eyes were the size of raisins. "Cohn wants me to dump you," he said. "Christ, you're not even a cop. She wants you out of the picture, like *now*."

"What'd you tell her?"

Rizzo took a hard look at him. "I told her I need you. I told her you're my main link to the only witness I've got. I told her you wouldn't go within a mile of that McVicar creep or even say his name. I gave her my word."

"You shouldn't've done that."

"Fuck you, I know that."

"You're sore at me."

"You bet," Rizzo said flatly.

There was a pause. Villanova studied the pattern of cigarette ash at his feet. "None of this was my idea, remember?"

"Don't play with me, Buddy. I got too much on my mind." There was another long pause. Rizzo pushed a hand through his hair and shook out some of the wet. His voice was a little closer to normal when he said, "Did you get over to JFK, at least? Did you get that roster for me?"

Villanova dug it out of his pocket and handed it over. "How about the trunks?" he asked hopefully as Rizzo studied the list. "What did the Lab boys have to say about them?"

Rizzo scowled and shook his head. "Similar vintage to the trunk we found on Mosholu Parkway, similar condition. They *could* have all come from the same place. If there was anything in that first trunk besides the body, a piece of insulation, maybe, or a bit of tape, the Lab might be able to prove it. But there wasn't." His eyes worked down the column of names.

"What about Manny's goods? The Lab come up with anything there?"

"Not enough.   A few fingerprints, none matching Elizabeth Albano's.   And remember that snapshot his mother was carrying around in her handbag?   Well Manny's got the same photo, all worn out like a tissue.   They found it wrapped inside a woman's shawl."

"What kind of shawl?"

"The same shawl his mother's wearing in the photo. Sick."

"How about that Tom Reilly guy upstate?   Any word?"

"Those Sullivan County hicks haven't found him yet. He's sleeping in the woods somewhere."   Rizzo looked up, glanced around the room with a frown, checked his watch. "Where the hell's everyone going?   It's only three o'clock."

Villanova turned around; the last of the crowd was in the foyer, saying goodbyes, pulling on raincoats and limbering up umbrellas.   "Christ, that guy Newmark put the kabosh on the whole wake!   All he did was flick the lights off a few times.   What a stupid goddam world we live in."

"Newmark was here?   From JFK?"

"Sure.   We talked."   Villanova gave the quick version of Newmark's spiel while Rizzo pored over the printout.

"Him too, huh?"   Rizzo said when he heard the part about the pining heart.

"Him too."

"Say, Sherlock, did you bother to look at this list?" Rizzo's brow was furrowed.

"Something there?"

"Does the name Iglesias ring a bell?"

"Iglesias?   That's the woman Julia waved to on her way home from the bus stop.   Maria Iglesias."

"Right.   There's an M. Iglesias on the roster here."

"Yeah?   That's a kind of common name, I think. What's the address?"

"3920 Washington Avenue."   Rizzo looked up. "Washington's two blocks over from Bathgate."

"Washington runs the length of the Wedge. It *could* be the same person."

"I'm gonna check it out. One crossover's all I need." Rizzo's mouth looked a little less sad, his color a little brighter as he took another look around the deserted room. "Want to come?"

Villanova drew a breath. "I'll catch you up. I've gotta make a stop."

"What's the problem?"

"You don't need me.   Let me take care of some business."

"What if Iglesias doesn't speak English?"

"Take Arcario. I'll catch the two of you up later, I promise."

Rizzo's face darkened with vexation. "Tell me you're gonna be with a sick woman at the hospital who's our best chance to nail a sick creep. Tell me you've got a date with Julia Cruz."

"Well, I do, as a matter of fact. In fact, there's a few things I've got to get ready..." He stopped himself; he'd resolved earlier not to mention the seance to Rizzo.

"But first you're gonna go looking in a box in a library, aren't you, Buddy?"

Villanova pursed his lips. "I have to. I've got an hour to get there before he does."

Rizzo studied him. "Say it straight out, Buddy. Is this professor a murderer. Is that what you really think?"

He didn't hurry his answer. "There's more to murder than choking the life out of someone," he said. "That girl lying in the coffin there...she was murdered twice. Her spirit was suffocated just as much as her body." He held Rizzo's eye to make sure he was understood.

"Yeah? Well, I'm a cop.   They pay me to solve the second crime, not the first."

"There's two crimes, and two of *us*," Villanova said. "We don't have to go hand in hand.   That's why we're good together."

It was said frankly, and it registered as such in Rizzo's eyes.   But his mouth was as droopy as ever.   He didn't speak for a few long moments.   Finally he muttered, "Have a ball," and turned and walked out.

Villanova watched him go.   He felt shitty.   Was he letting things get bent?

And there was still one more gloomy chore to face before he could leave.

He waited until the street door had shut behind Rizzo and the foyer was completely silent.   And then he waited a little longer, steeling himself, and then he turned the corner into the big, vacant room.   The couches ringed the perimeter, the folding chairs formed ragged clusters in the center, the banks of cut flowers converged on the open white metal box. The dead quiet of the room was laced with irony; not only the girl's life, but even her funeral had been cut short.

And that's when he noticed the man standing motionless at the foot of the coffin, a black suited man, tall, white-haired, poised forward, lost in some brooding meditation, some deeply troubled reverie...

And just as Villanova recognized him as Dean Hennessy, the man gave a start and swiveled his head around, and for a moment there was something so furtive in his eyes that Villanova thought he'd mis-identified him.   But then the normal composure returned, and the priest straightened and colored; he quickly gathered his black umbrella and raincoat from the folding chairs and withdrew, giving a cursory nod at Villanova as he passed.

Villanova stood where he was until he was sure the priest was gone. He felt uneasy at having interrupted such a personal act of grieving, but that glimpse of strangely familiar stealthiness troubled him almost as much.

He walked forward to the casket. Elizabeth lay plainly adorned, in a pearl-colored satin dress with blue trimming, and white shoes, with her long dark hair arranged neatly on the pillow, her long-lashed eyes closed, a rosary held in her folded hands. Someone, her mother, maybe, had done even this last grim duty with care, had chosen this last wardrobe with hopefulness and taste.

He felt a piercing sorrow for her, a sorrow much keener than the one he'd felt gazing into the trunk on Mosholu Parkway. She was dead not because her luck ran out, not because she was beautiful and good, but because of what her beauty and goodness *stood for* to half a dozen different people.

He put one hand on the cool metal of the coffin. With an effort, he could pretend she was sleeping, and do what he had to do. He could forget what had been done to her in Manny's bedroom, and in the morgue at Jacobi, and in the basement at Grippi and Sons. He could step into the necromantic text of his culture like all the other men in Elizabeth Albano's life and pretend she was a maiden from a fairy tale, and that, so long as he didn't kiss her awake, neither she nor anyone in the world could stir.

He had tried the kissing magic with Ginny, and it hadn't worked anyway. Ginny had remained dead, and his grief had remained impenetrable.

His heart was racing now, his skin was queerly sensitive under his clothes. He took a careful look. She wore rings on two fingers. One was her Fordham college ring. She had a tiny pearl earring in each ear, an onyx strand around her neck. There was nothing easy like a scarf.

He reached out and touched her hands. They were cool and clammy. The rosary practically fell out of them.

He took it. It was enough. Everything inside him felt like lead.

And that's when he realized he was being watched. The priest had come back. And now, suddenly, he recalled where he'd seen that furtive glance before. It was in LeClerc's mural.

He whirled round.

It wasn't the priest. It was a squat, swarthy man in a dripping leather jacket, with a face so sad that even its puzzlement looked mournful.

It was the cabby, Hector Rodriguez.

- ELEVEN -

Rodriguez was off duty, but with sheets of cold rain lashing the streets of Morris Park, Villanova had no scruple about pressing him for a lift to the campus.   Rodriguez obliged with that same gloomy demeanour.

"I shouldn't be doing this.   I shouldn't be anywhere near you guys."   The voice traveled thin and flat through the opening in the Plexiglas divider.   "I haven't had a wink of sleep since that killer saw my face."

"What made you show up at the funeral home?"

"I don't know.   It was something I thought I oughta do, see the dead girl, you know?   Show my respect."   He was smoking, taking one quick drag after another on his cigarette. His hack was running with the meter off.

"You've got good instincts, you're a human being. Don't lose your nerve now."

"What nerve?   I sat double-parked outside there fifteen, twenty minutes, couldn't get myself to go in.   I'm afraid of what I see, that's my problem.   Can't get things outta my mind.   That's why I don't sleep."   His face in the rear-view mirror was drawn and anxious.

"At least you've got a clear conscience.   You'll sleep eventually."

The windshield wipers beat noisily across the glass. Rodriguez shook out a fresh Marlboro from his pack and lit it off the glowing stub in his mouth. "Now I'm afraid to pick up fares in my own neighborhood. I'm afraid of who's gonna be sitting in the back seat there, looking at the back of my head." His gaze darted across the mirror. He jumped the light at Pelham Parkway and made a wild left into the westbound lanes. A horn blared after him.

"You hear any talk from back here about the murder?"

Rodriguez shook his head. "Just that people are worked up about it, sore. The macho guys, you know. I don't listen, I change the subject." His eyes passed over the mirror again.

"For Christ sake, why do you keep looking at me? You expect me to change into somebody?"

"Sorry, I can't help myself. I keep seeing that guy with the long hair. I keep thinking I'm gonna look in the mirror, and there he'll be to finish me off. It'll serve me right." He hit the S-curve at the old Bronx Zoo entrance and veered badly over the lane stripes. Angry bleats rose up from the cars on both sides.

"Jesus, you keep driving like this and you'll finish *yourself* off."

"What's it matter? That guy's gonna get me, I know it."

"It matters to me. Listen, you're spooking yourself. You need to take a few days off. I'm serious." He wanted Rodriguez in one piece to give his testimony. It struck him that the man had more than a case of bad nerves; his life had its own neurotically superstitious spin.

"I can't afford any days off. I got kids to feed." The cab fishtailed on the slick asphalt of the Arthur Avenue bend. "While you got that animal in a cage, I'll work. At least I know where he is." He cut hard round the corner of Bathgate Avenue and pulled up to the south entrance to the Fordham campus. Cars were not permitted beyond the gate; the library was a short sprint away.

Villanova cleared his throat uncomfortably. "Listen, I got to tell you this. The guy with the long hair's not in a cage anymore. He's on the street."

Rodriguez's broad, sorrowful face turned toward him. A lot of bloodshot white showed around those dark irises. "On the street? How come?"

"He's being shadowed round the clock. It's technicalities." Villanova could actually feel the cabby's pang of betrayal, right through the thin plastic sheet. "Hey, nothing's going to happen to you, don't worry."

"Yeah? You weren't alone with that guy. I was."

"Look, ease up on yourself. Take some time off, take your kids on a picnic or something." He dug in his wallet, drew out a twenty and dropped it through the opening in the Plexiglas.

"I don't want money from you," Rodriguez said. Those eyes were full of fatalistic despair now.

"Go home, get some rest." Villanova turned up his collar and charged out into the cold drizzle.

* * *

There were six cartons crammed with the papers of an eccentric, untidy scholar, and Villanova had an hour before closing time to go through them all.

While Dolores Loughlin fetched out the first carton, he took a careful look at the registry. McVicar was on the hunt too: he'd been there yesterday during the twenty minutes between class dismissal and the 4:30 closing time. Today afforded him another twenty minutes if he chose to show up. But tomorrow was Saturday and the Archive would be open all day. Villanova had to work fast.

What he saw on the index card taped inside the lid of the first carton prompted a quick new tack. Elizabeth Albano had signed the card a half dozen times. An "R. F. X.

Hennessy" had signed below her.   And below Hennessy's signature was McVicar's.

Villanova didn't even bother to search the carton; on a hunch, he asked Dolores to exchange it for carton number six. She complied with a scowl; she seemed generally more sullen and less combative than the day before.   He wondered if something had happened between McVicar and her.

While she was in the vault, he checked the registry again.   Dean Hennessy had been in the Archive the previous Saturday afternoon for a solid three hours.

When the sixth carton arrived, he found no signatures on the filecard besides Elizabeth Albano's.   That suited his hunting instincts better.

The rain rattled on the roof of the greystone tower, the gloom sat like night around the leaded-glass windows, and against it the poor yellow light of the old incandescent fixtures could only draw dim angles inside the niches and the eaves. Dolores sat at her desk with her book and her eyeglasses and her tight jeans and her little lipsticked mouth, and Villanova sat opposite her with his carton in the remotest carrel, and in between sat the same elderly man who'd been there last time, in the same worn brown suit.   And for almost an hour there was nothing closer to a human sound in that dim, vaulted space than the sighing of the wind through the old casements.

And Villanova paged through folder after folder of memos, letters, and typescripts, through notebooks crammed with jottings, through photocopied excerpts dense with marginalia, through personal correspondence from scholars, editors, students.   Because he didn't know what he was looking for, he had to look with equal care at everything, and after a while his head grew heavy, and he felt the hypnotic pull of scholarship with its cloistered breath and pale voices of people long dead, its quaint codes and monastic protocols and morbid civility, its much-steeped, much-aged elixirs of insight and apostasy. And he saw how completely Eliot Robinson had lived in his mind, and what a lonely and undervalued and uncertain and brilliant mind that actually was.

And when he found what he was looking for, he was so entranced that he didn't realize it at first, and he kept on going into the next folder of documents, and then he went back and looked at it again, and then his heart began to race, and he began to read very carefully, and he glanced up at the wall clock above Dolores' head, and made himself read faster.

The folder had the words, "Work in Progress" scribbled in pencil on the front; inside, among other things, was a stapled, onionskin carbon copy of a typescript draught for a journal article, very rough, very littered with typos and deletions, and very faded. It was a long piece, thirty-four pages, with a slugline in the upper left on each page: "freud & dimmesdale." It began with the sentence: "The most subtle and dangerous error made by Hawthorne scholars to date is the failure to apprehend that Roger Chillingworth is actually engaged in an act of love for Arthur Dimmesdale, which, because the two are personae of the same man, must be understood as an exquisite and rarefied expression of Hawthorne's own narcissistic shame."

The article went on to make a wholly original argument, thinly documented but surprisingly vigorous, for a psychobiographical reading of the Dimmesdale character in *The Scarlet Letter* as a manifestation of--a confession of--Hawthorne's putatively incestuous and auto-erotic childhood. The piece was stunningly creative: full of energy, risk, personality, and wisdom as well. It was the heart, bone, and flesh of McVicar's "brilliant" critical volume, and, beginning with the first sentence, it was the very voice of it as well.

Villanova leaned back in his seat. McVicar was a fraud. He'd launched his career by stealing his dead mentor's work wholesale. No wonder he'd never been able to produce another book.

He took a look up at the wall clock. It read 4:08. Dolores was looking up too; she had her eye on the mirror behind him.

He had a lot of thinking to do very fast. For sure Elizabeth had seen this document, and for sure it compromised the hell out of McVicar professionally; it made him a plagiarist. Was this the cause of their 'blowout' back in July? It would certainly explain why she'd stopped citing *The Dimmesdale Complex* in her dissertation...and why she'd told Newmark she was "stuck." It explained a lot of Elizabeth's behavior in the last two months, and McVicar's too, including his visit to her house. He must have bent himself into a corkscrew trying to think of a way to keep her quiet and on the string.

No wonder the girl was sick. No wonder McVicar drank like a camel.

The clock read 4:12. Villanova got up suddenly and strode to Dolores' desk. "I'd like to photocopy something," he said.

"You can't."

"Why not?"

She gave him a patronizing look. "It's illegal to copy original documents. The university is in the middle of a huge lawsuit." She made a sweeping gesture toward an empty alcove near the Archive door. Evidently a photocopy machine had once stood there.

That explained a hell of a lot. If this onionskin carbon was the only copy, and if this one document were to vanish before anyone else who understood its significance should come upon it, like Dean Hennessy, for instance... *That's* what had brought McVicar here with such sudden zeal.

He went back to his carrel. He'd have to wait Dolores out. And if McVicar showed up now, fuck him, he'd do it anyway. What was the guy going to say, me first?

He found himself sweating and checking the time twice a minute. No one climbed the metal stairway, and the heavy wooden door remained shut. At 4:28 Dolores stood and announced "Time." The man in the brown suit rose up and shuffled forward with his carton. Dolores went through the ritual of checking in his box and returning his attache case.

And after the door had closed on his clanging footfalls and Dolores had gone inside the Archive to re-deposit his box, Villanova removed the staple and separated the Robinson document into two halves, folded the second half into his inside jacket pocket, and packed up his carton. It was easy. It even seemed fair.

He had the carton ready on Dolores' desk when she came out.

"Bring a notepad next time," she said drily, checking the folders; she was counting them.

"I'll do that." She was inspecting inside each folder. "I read that book, by the way," he blurted out. "*The Dimmesdale Complex.*"

"Good for you."

"Still think McVicar's Mr. Wonderful, huh?"

"You bet."

"Where is he today?"

"Oh, he'll be back."

"Yeah, he'll be back, but not to see *you*. He'll be back to look in these boxes." He saw that hit home. His hunch about her sullen mood must have been correct.

"Sign the card," Dolores said coldly.

He put his signature below Elizabeth Albano's. "Don't you think it's funny," he said, "the only file he wants to see is the one *she* was interested in?"

For the first time she had no comeback. Her eyes, behind those round lenses, looked stung. She was only a woman in love after all, a very young woman. She fitted the lid to the carton.

"He *will* be back. He's not done with her yet. Want to do yourself a favor, Dolores? Want to do the smartest thing you ever did for yourself? Next time he's here, give me a phone call."

She didn't answer.

"It may be tomorrow, it may be next week. Call me. Mike Villanova, at the Homicide Squad."

She hefted the carton and carried it into the vault.

He headed down the stairway.

He'd just reached the bottom and was turning through the doorway toward the main collection when he heard a book drop somewhere behind him in the stacks. That wasn't so odd. The odd thing was the silence that followed.

He turned back into the stacks. The unnatural silence persisted. He walked slowly down the center aisle, scanning to the left and right. A quick, muffled sound came from deeper in the stacks, and he thought he glimpsed a dark blot passing across the chink. His senses were very alert now, the skin down the back of his neck alive with sensation. He had always been quick to the game of stalk and pounce. He knew these stacks, too; he'd spent a year of his life shelving in the Philosophy section. It was a predictably under-used, if not deserted part of the library.

Four rows in, he found the fallen volume, a musty commentary on Sartre's *Troubled Sleep*. He flipped through the book and replaced it on the shelf, then kept moving, taking care not to let anyone slip around the stack ends and escape. Whoever had been lurking near the iron stairway was being cornered, because there was no egress at the west end of the Philosophy wing. He gave a thought to Dolores, alone in that vault so much of the time. He wondered how she felt when she heard foot-treads rising on those metal steps.

He closed in. There were only two rows left, then one.

He readied himself. He snapped round the last turn.

No one.

A gaping, oak-jambed doorway stood where he had remembered a plaster wall. It looked as old as the building.

With a silent curse, he passed through it. It gave passage to the vast center stacks, the main stairway, the central lobby, the reference rooms, the periodicals desk, the reading rooms, the basement stacks. He muttered a curse aloud this time, then shook his head as a second, more subtle disappointment blossomed in him. The "mother of sciences" was not as cloistered and exalted as he had recalled.

It was not good to be greedy for luck. He left the building with his stolen papers, unchallenged.

* * *

To be greedy for luck was not good, and yet the afternoon was lucky in more ways than one. It was lucky that Helen hadn't taken an overtime shift as she sometimes did on a rainy day off, and it was lucky that she was in a fairly normal state of mind and saw the prospect of a seance as a piece of serious and important business; and it was lucky that they managed to dig up an old dormitory trunk in the basement of the Topless Towers, and that they managed to get a taxi in the rain and get themselves and the trunk inside it and reach the hospital not long after the start of evening visiting hours. And it was lucky that Helen had decided to wear her whites, because once inside the hospital, that made it easy for her to get the trunk, veiled on the undershelf of a gurney, past the nursing station of the surgery ward while Villanova stood distracting the staff with a series of businesslike questions about Julia's condition.

The unlucky part was that Julia's illness had continued to worsen, and that her priority in the surgery line-up had been upgraded.

When Villanova entered Julia's room, he found Helen standing at the bedside, and the two women engrossed in conversation. The second bed had been removed. Julia, propped up on the pillows, one eye nearly shut by the swelling in her skull, was cradling Helen's hands and looking deeply into her eyes as she spoke. Her expression was kindly but intense, so much so that Helen looked almost dazed by contrast. It seemed as if something precious and healing was passing between the two women, from the sick woman to the well. But above all there was an aura of intimacy around them, a confidential air that made Villanova uneasy and strangely envious.

Julia turned to him and said quietly, "I knew I would like your Helen. She has a beautiful spirit. She's lovely and strong, inside and out. I thank you for bringing her to me."

Villanova glanced at Helen. She seemed flattered.

"And do you know, she has natural powers?"

"Natural powers?"

"Like mine."

Helen said, a little proudly, "Julia thinks I'm psychic."

"It's true," Julia said. "More than anyone I've ever met. And with these powers comes compassion and the strength to change completely. And to love deeply. You would be a fool not to love this woman the way she loves you."

Villanova nodded dumbly. Nothing he could think of saying seemed right.

"But come, let's begin. Is the door closed? Are you ready to do as I tell you?"

Villanova nodded again. He'd resolved to dampen his skepticism and carry out his part of this business without complaint.

Julia, in obvious pain, gave her instructions crisply: the privacy curtains were to be drawn around the bed, the trunk to be placed on the floor at the foot of it, and all the lights to be shut except for one small lamp. "Now," she said to Helen, "please open the window, just a few inches." Helen did so; the sound of rainfall entered the room.

Julia turned back to Villanova. "What have you brought me that belongs to the dead girl?"

"This," he said, holding out the rosary beads. "It was in her hands only a few hours ago. It's all I could get."

Julia took the beads from him and examined them. "It will do," she said. She motioned Helen to come close. "Are you willing to help us do this thing?"

"Yes," Helen said.

"Will you do what I ask you?"

Helen nodded.

"Put this rosary over your head. Slip it around your neck like a necklace."

Helen complied. The beads circled her neck, and the crucifix lay flat against her breastbone. Villanova's brows went up, though he said nothing.

"Now, join hands with me, all three of us in a circle," Julia said.

They obeyed. Julia closed her eyes and turned her face in the direction of the open window. Her hand, in contrast to Helen's, was tiny, frail, and hot. Villanova kept his eyes on her face. In spite of the pain she was in, she was concentrating deeply. "It's good, I think," she said softly. "It will come." She opened her eyes, nodded, and looked at Helen. "The girl is dead, and her spirit is no longer with her body. It has joined the spirit of everything, and so it is here as well as everywhere. Whether it is in peace or no, what we are doing can no longer hurt it. The justice we seek is for her poor body only, which is soon to be in the ground."

She crossed herself and turned her gaze to Villanova. "There are many holy saints who died young, many beautiful girls who were murdered for their purity. But, because you are not a believer, I do not do this in their name, or even in God's name. I do it in the name of justice, a smaller god, but one that you believe in, yes?"

"Yes," he said.

She turned back to Helen. "The dead girl was good and innocent, just like you, and so her spirit will be drawn to yours. I ask that you be brave, now. I want you to climb into the trunk."

"Hold on, now..." Villanova started, but Helen quieted him with a hand on his arm. "It's all right," she said. She'd obviously been expecting this request, but still gazed doubtfully at the trunk. "I don't think I'll fit."

"Try to make yourself fit," Julia said. "Even if the lid doesn't close."

Helen did as she was asked. Villanova held the lid open and tried to guide her. She lay on her back first and doubled up, then swiveled half sideways until her knees were up against her chest. "I won't be able to get out again."

"I'll help you," he said. His heart beat uneasily at the sight of her crammed into exactly the same position as that beautiful dead girl on the sidewalk on Mosholu Parkway.

"Close the lid, if you can," Julia directed.

He did.

"Now don't anyone speak." Julia lowered her head, shut her eyes, and placed both hands over her face. Her breathing became regular and deep. A minute of silence went by, then another. Gusts of rain rattled against the window. Another minute passed. Suddenly Julia stiffened. "I can see..." she began in a hoarse whisper, "...the door to my apartment. My son is waiting behind it. He's opening it." Her breathy, sibilant voice drew out the final syllable of each phrase. "I see...a beautiful, dark-haired girl coming in. Now, Manny closes the door and puts his back to it..." Julia began rocking her head from side to side; her voice, devoid of all human coloration, hissed through her lips flat and inexorable. "I see the girl now in my room...she's frightened, she's looking for a way out. Manny is behind her, he puts his hand over her face. She struggles. He drags her to his room, forces her down on the bed...his hand is still over her face.... She faints.... Now his hands are under her dress...."

Another silence. Villanova looked anxiously at the trunk. There wasn't a sound or a stirring from inside.

"Now the girl is alone on the bed," Julia whispered. "And Death has come to stand over her."

There was no sound but the whistling sigh of wind beneath the open sash; a cool draught crept along the floor.

"Now I see Manny again, carrying a trunk through the door. I see him lift her up and put her in. I see him put her shoes on her feet. He puts her pocketbook in the corner by her head. Now he's looking for something on the floor. He's looking everywhere...but he can't find it. But I see it, in the other room, by the leg of the table...a streak of gold, glistening.... Now Manny is closing the lid. Now he is dragging the trunk to the stairway. He's bumping it down the steps...."

She stopped suddenly. Her breathing was rasping audibly, in and out. There was another angry flurry of rain against the window glass. Her eyes fluttered and opened. "What happened?" she murmured. She was trembling, though the room was warm.

"Don't stop," Villanova said. "Keep talking. What was Manny searching for on the floor?"

"Something's different. Something's wrong." Julia looked around, frightened.

"What was on the floor by the table, Julia?"

There was a whimper from inside the trunk. Villanova leapt down beside it and threw back the lid. Helen was struggling to get up, and he put his hands under her and helped her sit upright. Her face was almost as pale as her uniform. "Jesus Christ," she gasped.

"You all right?"

"I couldn't breathe!" Her hand went to her throat, and she sucked in air as fast as she could. The dread in her eyes went far beyond claustrophobic panic. She was staring in terror somewhere beyond his shoulder...

He turned, and Julia did too.

The curtains had been silently parted. Manny Cruz stood in the opening. There was no way to know how long he'd been there. His eyes were on his mother, and that scowling expression of his had collapsed into abject, infantile need. He looked as if he might rush across that small space into his mother's arms...as if he expected his mother, sick as she was, to rise from the bed to meet him.

But then his focus widened, and his brow furrowed and his face darkened as he took in Helen and Villanova. A whole procession of feelings marched through his eyes: terror, outrage, and finally, as what he'd heard and seen caught up with him, the black sting of betrayal. Villanova tensed as he felt Manny's gaze slowly drawn to his own just as it had been the day before in the interrogation room; he could only hope the plainclothesman tailing him was close at hand. His heart pumped as Manny's wolf eyes glared into his. Through that animal hate, he saw the light of comprehension come to Manny's mind. He saw that sense of betrayal intensify and blossom into a vindictive rage. He saw Manny's black gaze shift over a few degrees and lock cruelly onto Helen's face. A soft cry escaped her throat, and from Julia came an involuntary "No!" Manny looked tensed to pounce...and then he wheeled around and vanished. The corridor door thumped shut behind him.

Villanova pulled Helen to her feet, drew her to him and folded her in his arms, stroking her damp hair. "My God," she moaned. "My God. Who was that?" She was trembling.

"Get the beads off her," Julia croaked.

He pulled them over her head and flung them onto the bed. It was hard to tell who looked more shaken, Julia or Helen. Julia seemed to be struggling for breath. At last she said, "Why wouldn't my son come near?" She stared at Villanova through one angry eye. "Three days he hasn't seen me!"

"A lot has happened to him in three days, Julia."

"So! I knew bad things were being done to him!"

"No one mistreated him. No one hit him or humiliated him. He was handcuffed and questioned."

"And you let him go? Then he didn't do what you thought he did."

"He lied, Julia. Whenever he opened his mouth, a lie came out." Some of the hatred he felt for Manny seeped into his voice. "But *you* know the truth, don't you. I heard it. Helen heard it too."

"I heard whispering," Helen said weakly. "No words... I couldn't make them out."

"Whispering?" Julia said. "Then I spoke?" She looked to Villanova with some alarm. "I went into a trance?"

"You don't know?"

"I never know about that." Her anger gave way to a visible dread. "How much did I say?"

Villanova studied her perspiring face. Her worried gaze met his directly; she was completely sincere. "You said plenty," he said. "You saw something gold glistening on the floor in your apartment. I want to know what it was."

"No! Don't tell me anything I spoke about! It's not good for me to know!"

"Oh, come."

"You don't understand. It's not me who speaks when I'm in a trance." Her expression seemed truly afflicted.

Villanova eyed her cooly. "What was it you saw glistening on the floor, Julia? It was a gold chain, wasn't it?"

A look of horror filled her eyes. "I beg of you, don't say any more! It's finished now! Leave me be!" She sank back onto her elbows. She looked exhausted and, if that were possible, even more swollen and deformed than before. "As for my son..." a grimace of pain shot across her face, "...what I've done, it's too late to undo. More than that, you can't ask me. Please go now. I'm feeling very bad right now."

"What's wrong, Julia?" Helen spoke up before Villanova could retort. "Is the pain worse? We can get the doctor for you."

"No, no doctor. Just go, let me be in peace. Leave the rosary here, I'll make use of it." She took up the beads and withdrew them under the blanket.

But Villanova wasn't done. "Don't you understand what we're talking about here, Julia?" he growled at her.

She closed her eyes stubbornly and turned away from him.

"We're talking about murder!"

"Leave me! Leave me!" she cried, clamping her hands over her ears.

"It's not enough!" he shouted, and he could feel Helen's hands on him trying to quiet him, and he shouted again, "It's not enough, you hear?"

A cry broke from Julia's lips, a cry so full of pain and despair that even Villanova stiffened. Helen rushed to the bedside as Julia's wail dissolved into a moan of anguish.

There were footfalls in the corridor then. A moment later, the door flew open, and the white-clad angels of mercy came flocking in.

* * *

From within the tiny steel closet where he had hidden himself, sounds reached Manny's ears full of distortion and echo, so that all the world seemed to be howling distantly in unison. The metal walls, warm against his skin, amplified his labored breathing, making it hard to hear footfalls approaching and receding in the overheated basement corridor. Through the vent louvers, he could spy the occasional nurse or orderly passing by--pieces of them, actually, white-stockinged legs and rubber-soled shoes, white pants, hems of green smocks. He waited. Once he even saw the brown pants and big, worn shoes of that clumsy plainclothes dick who was following him. He held his breath, and, afterward, laughed to himself. Motherfucker. Clumsy piece of shit. He waited. His hiding place was so small that he could barely move, but that didn't bother him...he liked it. It calmed him somewhere deep inside. Besides, he liked being in places where he could see people but they couldn't see him, and the smaller the better. He could stay crammed in this little niche forever. It was made for him, like a shell.

He stayed put a long time, till he felt the world had forgotten about him, and he couldn't hear anything but the rise and fall of the wailing through the tiny vents. For a while he slid into a peaceful daze, then shook himself awake. He cracked the locker door, scanned the corridor, and slipped out toward the darkened end of the passage.

Passing through the dry-chilled, dim-lit rooms at the far end, he spied a sheet-covered corpse on a gurney. A feeling of cold dread snapped round him like a shroud. His mother...? But it would serve her right, serve her right! Her own son! To those strangers! Bitch! How he hated! ...his only ...his *mother*... God, no! No, let her not be dead!

Shaking, he pulled back the sheet before his thoughts could paralyze him. A dead man, young, his own age, dark like himself, stared up into nothing, mouth open, expression frozen in bitter accusation. He flung the sheet back over that outraged face and ran for the outside.

Cold rain met him, slick black asphalt, trees shivering in the wind; people stood waiting at the bus stop, hunched like pigeons, collars turned up, umbrellas dripping. Staying out of sight under the trees, he saw the bus lumbering up from Co-op City, one headlight out. He saw two people running for it up from the hospital, man and woman, her arm through his, white stockings, nurses' whites, the man tall, dark, thick brows--*them!* That woman, the one who put herself in the trunk, all folded up like a doll--*them.* He shrunk back, watched them get aboard.

Then as the bus, bellowing, dragged itself away from the curb, he charged and sprang for its back end. Fingers clutching the hot vents, knees squeezing the wet curve of the blind flank, he rode as he had ridden many times, and his anger flamed up as the bus gathered speed. *Them.* Pushing in, trying to get inside, working his mother over! Bastards! Humpers! And lovebirds, too! Her in the white skirt. A bride, white skirt up around her belly, white legs kicking the air. Fuckers!

He clung to the bus's wet metal rump and breathed its stinking, gut-poisoned blast all up Pelham Parkway, eyes squinting against the cold downpour, past the brick homes and the fancy apartment buildings, past the school for the blind, the el, the zoo, the high school, the university, past everything big and complicated and beyond comprehending, past the whole array of structures and images that eluded and excluded him, from the spires and stained glass windows of the university to the open-mouthed, big-titted, white-skinned blonde on the billboard overlooking Fordham Road.   He breathed the hot fumes and rocked himself into a predatory daze in which, in brutish comfort, he could see and feel one thing only, his rage.

And when *they* got off two blocks past Webster, he got off too, and when they stopped in the Video Club on the corner, he lurked beneath an overhang across the street, hating them for the pleasure they intended to share.   And when they hurried down Bainbridge, he hurried after them, his dick alive and rubbing against his soaked jeans, his whole being giddy with the thrill of *inside-out*: stalking the assholes who dared stalk him.   And when they disappeared inside # 4951, he slipped into the mouth of the unlit alley across the street and crouched against the wet bricks watching until the dull yellow lights of the highest storey snapped on.   And, eyes fixed on the flickering shadows in that high window, heart pounding away, he dreamed their lives for them, lives robotically connected to all the movement, purpose, pleasure, and comfort of the vast, faceless machine-world which chewed him in one set of gears after another but never let him in to trip a ratchet or push a cam.   He dreamed the incessant mystery of human life: laboring, resting, sleeping, bathing, robing and disrobing, sitting near, eating off plates, touching, speaking, teasing, courting, watching in silence, and most of all, laughing, making noises of enjoyment at words, looks, images.   And after a while he himself entered his dream of the collective life into which he could never find any door, and, half-dazed, he skulked across the street and into the dim entry of # 4951, and he let the shadows of his dream pull him downward and absorb him, and he hid himself where, like Satan spying from a mountaintop, he could see the whole of the world tiny and slumbering, alien, self-occupied, and defenseless.   And he unzipped his pants and took a long, hot, delicious pee on the floor, on the junk around him, on himself.

And then he did something he'd tried to do for many years but had only just learned to make work. He kept his hand on his dick and dreamed that woman in white coming to him. He dreamed her pulling off those white garments one by one, and coming down those steps naked to him, her skin pale, her eyes glazed and helpless, her limbs moving in that sluggish, robotic way.

And he began to smile, and a pleasure began to throb in his cold, wet body. Because now he knew that he *could* make her come, and she *would* come. And no matter how far away she was, she would have to come, she would have no choice...but she wasn't far away at all, she was very near...and she *was* coming, and it was in his hands and nothing could help it now...

* * *

As soon as they'd reached the garret, even before shucking his wet clothes, Villanova had tried, without success, to reach Rizzo at Homicide Squad. He wanted the news about the gold chain to be relayed to Bev Cohn, and he wanted Manny Cruz hauled back into custody, and more than anything he wanted to vent his anger at the way Manny had surprised him in Julia's room. And even after he remembered that Rizzo was going to tell him it was his own fault that Manny was free, he still kept trying to reach him, and all he got was Gilman, who didn't know where Rizzo was. He told Gilman to be sure to give a callback when Rizzo checked in.

Helen was unusually quiet. With no real gusto, she hunted out leftover Chinese food from the refrigerator--roast pork egg foo young and chicken lo mein--and thrust it in the microwave. She got out of her clothes and into a bathrobe.

"You still upset?" he said to her.

She nodded.

"You look angry.

"I am. How could you guys let an animal like Manny go? God, you'd have to be a woman to know what that look of his feels like."

"We had no say about that, and we're going to get him back. But I'm sorry about everything. It was stupid of me to bring *you* into this."

"No it wasn't."

It was stupid to ask you to do what I did. I apologize."

"Stop apologizing, damn it! *That's* what I'm angry about." She turned those blue eyes on him, and they were steely with vexation. "Don't you get it? Look, why do you think I went along with it all, why do you think I crammed myself inside a moldy old trunk? Do you take me for some superstitious ninny?"

"What do you mean"

"Don't you think I haven't seen what's going on with you? Don't you think I can't see you struggling with yourself, or that I don't know what this Elizabeth Albano case is all about?" Her eyes were brimming now and she was clutching the bathrobe closed around her throat. "I know more than you think. I know *you*." She took a breath and cast a doleful look toward the cat, who sat daintily beside the couch, studying her. "I can't be that girl for you, Mike, no matter how bad you want it. I can't be twenty-three and I can't wear a cross around my neck, and I can't play a guitar and sing." Her eyes spilled over, but she brushed the tears away impatiently, and now she no longer looked angry, or even hurt, she just looked adamant. "I'd do all the penance in the world if it counted, but it doesn't, because I don't believe in it. And if I did, then Ralphie would have been my penance, and Ralphie's got to be erased anyway, doesn't he. You know he does. So all I can do is love *you*. Not the way anyone else does, but the way *I* do, *me*."

Miserable as he felt before, he felt even worse. "Listen, he said. "Listen..." and he tried to wrap her in his arms.

But she twisted free. She stood there, alone in her own space, small, slight, immensely strong, a woman solidified by the daily horrors of very real pain on a very real pediatric ward. "Don't you know that that you're my *universe*? Before and after you, there's nothing."

A pang of fear shot through him, for her and for him as well. He'd hurt her, and he did love her, and she had no idea how deeply, because he'd never let himself say it. And he wanted to. "Listen," he began again, but she interrupted him with a shake of her head.

"Don't. If you said it now, it would just be because I was mad. Let's stop talking, let's just put the movie in the VCR and watch it."

"The hell with the movie. Listen to me."

"No, I'm all right now. Let's watch the movie. It'll be good for me to see it. *The Best Years of Our Lives* is just what I need. It'll cauterize me good." She turned and got the videotape out of its box and stooped to the TV to set it up.

She was still upset, he could tell, but anything he did now would only make it worse, and he made himself be still. He shucked his clothes and got into a flannel shirt and jeans while she gathered the wet garments into the laundry basket. Then they started the tape and slouched down on the couch to watch, with their legs on the coffee table, and the telephone and the Chinese food in easy reach. Helen sank against his chest and he put his arm around her and let what he felt for her beat through the contact of body to body. Mirabel leapt onto the cushions and settled herself in with them, half on one lap, half on the other.

The Best Years of Our Lives was a compromise selection, made in haste. She had wanted *The Heiress*, the old Hollywood version of the book she was reading, complete with Hollywood ending. He had wanted *Odd Man Out*, with its beautiful lovers' martyrdom at the finish. It was Olivia DeHaviland, Ralph Richardson, and Montgomery Clift versus poor old James Mason and Kathleen Ryan. After the seance, neither of them had enough focus to be insistent, so Teresa Wright and Dana Andrews won out.

They watched the screen without speaking. What talking they'd had to do about the seance, they'd done on the bus. *She* was a believer in magic, spirits, and the oversoul; *he* was a believer in repression, psychogenic amnesia, and the uncanny dynamics of a mind under stress. He'd told her what Julia had said in her trance, she'd described the nightmarish suspension of time and the flood of lurid images she'd experienced in the trunk, images that had blended Elizabeth's terror with her own ordeal in the dark as a child. Both of them were shaken by Julia's revelation of things she apparently couldn't know: the situation of the girl's body on the bed, the placement of the handbag in the trunk, the bumping of the trunk down the steps.

What deeper thoughts they had on Julia's betrayal of her son, they mulled in silence as the movie played. The faint grid of interference on the screen told them that Tina's dishwasher was at work downstairs; the house's wiring was a nightmare of piggybacked, pirated, labyrinthine circuits that were always blowing fuses. But not even that distraction kept them from drifting into the intense, painstaking realism of black-and-white post-war America. They stayed absorbed there for over three hours, until he, tired of waiting for the phone to ring, fell into a doze; at which point she, too full of old wounds to bear watching that wedding-gowned child-next-door descend the stairway of her wholesome American home to make her brave, sweet vows to the sailor-with-no-hands, slipped away with the laundry basket down her own dingy stairway to see to her own white costume.

Down, down she went, landing by landing, into the gloomy chamber beneath the house. The basement could have been an extension of the stark world on the TV screen, ghostlit and colorless, so insulated that the angry rainfall outside and the crazy life in the rooms above were silenced, so remote from all the banal activity of the spinning planet that the tiny railway village with its moviehouse and diner and barber shop and its streetlit highway and tree-dotted countryside seemed as real as the town she'd grown up in.

She slipped through the maze of clutter and stood for a minute alongside the layout. There was a time, after she'd first recognized the village for what it was, when she'd wanted to smash those little houses to bits. Her own childhood home had stood--red-shuttered and prim, a pretty, ulcerating lie--in easy sight of the railroad, and it used to fill her with rage to see this model Belle Haven and be reminded of what she'd been cheated of.

But that rage had passed, finally. It did her no good. She was a practical woman, and if dreams were the practical route, then let there be dreams. And so, lately, she'd gotten into the habit of suspending all disbelief, studying the slumbering town and guessing at the lives in each of the little buildings. Which house would be hers? The small one there, with the front porch and the VW bug in the driveway? Could she have passed a sweet, safe childhood there, sheltering her sexuality, budding and blossoming into a guileless, soft-eyed bride?

Why not? And if this was a form of self-mockery, then yes, she would mock herself. She would bear it for the look in her sweetheart's eyes when he saw those pure images conjured on the glowing screen, those ageless ghosts of

Hollywood ingenues and innocents. She would bear it for the passion with which he had built this pseudo Long Island Eden, so faithful to the smallest detail. For his faith, yes, she would bear it, and for the vulnerable core he had uncovered in herself. And if he could do that, then maybe there was no mockery in it at all, and she could drop that shield and go forward with the frank fervor of a convert. Why not?

She turned away, went to the washing machine, and opened the lid. She set down her basket and checked to make sure the dryer was empty. Thanks to the ancient wiring, only one could be used at a time.

And then she heard a noise that stopped all her daydreams. It was the creak of a step from the shadows behind her, a creak made by the full weight of a human being, followed by a long, shrewd silence.

And she knew. She knew with a clairvoyant certainty what it meant. She was an expert at this, her whole body had learned to read its fate from the sound of a creak in the dark.

Her heart was pounding, but she stood frozen, knowing that she mustn't turn around or move carelessly, knowing that until she signaled awareness she had a few seconds for deception. Should she scream? Not yet, she wouldn't be heard. Not till there was no other chance. Run? Never make it to the stairway. Hide, then? Quick, choose a place. Behind the old freezerchest. No, too late, in plain sight. Think! But why was this happening? What did it mean? Her mind was so sluggish, so full of dreamy images. Since climbing into that trunk. The hands around her throat. Pawing at her body, touching her. Just the way her father...

Another noise behind her, nearer. The odor of urine reached her nose, an animal stink. Think! Signal Mike! Garret and basement linked. The washing machine, more TV interference. No, blow the fuse! Shut everything off upstairs, wake him up. In a minute he'd be down the steps fuse in hand. Twice a week, it happened, a ritual. Twice a week, at the least. His hands on her. A hand over her mouth, no noise. The hideous dream. No--reality. The waking life a dream. False talk, false smiles, false postures...

Think! He was nearer yet, she could hear him coming! Blow the fuse, put the basement in darkness! Hide in the dark! Quick! Now!

She closed the lid of the washing machine, set the dial to Spin, and pushed it in. The motor engaged and the light behind her dimmed. In one quick movement, she spun the dial of the dryer, pushed the Start button, and blew the fuse. A second later she was squatting in the darkness behind the freezer-chest, and he was coming for her, groping for her, muttering curses and knocking things over. Closer! Closer! The urine-stink stronger. The crash of metal on the cement floor. She could see movement, a silhouette, a hulking shape. How a silhouette? The layout lights, *still on!* Miscalculation! Treachery!

No crying out! Silence! Quiet the breathing, the little sobs! Muffle the pounding heart! Not a sound! He wouldn't hurt her, no, if she were still. If she lay quiet. The demon, waiting all these years. Stalking her. Not fair. No finish, ever.

Closer! Something brushed her. She yelped, and before she could scream, a hand closed over her face, big and hard. Dragged her up, arms locked to her sides, so full of brute rage, so powerful! Hot breath on her neck. She struggled, the vise tightened. No air! Eyes wide, the glow of that beautiful village, lovely, false. Betrayed, served her right. Peeling off her armor after so long, opening herself. Going home to innocence, a laugh. Dizzy now. Sucking for breath, a pain in her chest. Fainting. Those little lights winking at her, mocking. Dimming. Her justice. Yes. Finished.

* * *

Villanova was wakened by an eerie wail of anguish, a rising feline cry that broke into a barely human scream before subsiding. He opened his eyes to darkness and the glowing green eyes of Mirabel. "Helen?" he called.

The cat moaned as if in pain. Till now it had never made a sound.

"Helen?"

No answer.

He moved fast. He didn't know how he knew he should do that. He stumbled out to the landing, where there was light and the murmur of TV noise from Sal and Roseann's apartment below. "Helen?" he shouted down the stairs.

Then, barefoot, he hurried down.

The basement was dark, he could see that from the top of the wooden steps as soon as he flung back the door. There was a noise from below, a clatter, and he charged down and nearly took a header. "Helen?" He was disoriented, knocking into one thing after another. His eyes started to adjust at last; the layout lights threw an eerie starlight into the gloom. He crouched, afraid that if she'd fallen he might step on her. Groping, he worked his way toward the washing machine. He bumped something, and a rain of little cartons fell on him: Tina's Christmas decorations. Another bump and camping equipment hit the floor with a crash. From a few feet away, there came a moan.

He scrambled over. She was on the floor behind the freezer, and she was moving. When he touched her, she whimpered and recoiled, and when he tried to get hold of her she cried aloud and jerked away from him. "It's me, babe, it's me!" he told her. "It's okay!"

She whimpered again, and he put his hands on her. "You're okay now, babe." He wrapped her up. She was trembling violently. "Are you hurt? What happened? The lights go out on you?"

"*He's here!*" she cried. "*He's here!*"

"Who?"

"*Him!* He was choking me!"

Viannova got up. Understanding flooded into him, and with it, rage. He looked around. In front of him were a score of murky forms, a hundred inky shadows. He started to hunt, to thread the maze from one end to the other, but his heart was filling so fast with hate that he couldn't be methodical. He began knocking things over and kicking viciously into the shadows. And then, as if something had burst inside of him, he went completely mad. Murder gushed through his spirit...he ran amok, trashing everything in front of him, kicking and swinging, trying to beat the hidden demon into flesh so he could rip into its guts. Fifteen years of contained violence exploded out of him. Cartons, garment bags, furniture, things he could hardly lift went flying through the air. An angry thumping started from the ceiling above-- Tina's apartment--and he kept going, racing against his exhaustion, wanting to get his hands on his victim while the murder-lust was hot and red, while all distractions and promises and duties and strategies were muted.

And then the light at the foot of the stairs went on. The washing machine started up with a hum. He turned. Helen stood at the fusebox, her face frozen like a mask, lines of fear scribed all around her eyes. She held something in her hand: a fuse. She'd done a switch in the dark.

A moment later there was movement in the apartment above, and then the sound of Tina's door opening on the landing. "Hey!" a man's voice called down. "Who the hell is playing around with the lights!" It was Phil, Tina's husband.

"Get down here, Phil! It's me and Helen! Hurry up!"

"I'm in my goddam pajamas."

"Just get down here, goddamit!"

* * *

It was nearly two hours past midnight when Rizzo finally called. "Want the good news first?" were his opening words. The sullenness was gone, his voice was full of self-vindication. "The Iglesias on the ESL roster turned out to be the niece of Maria Iglesias, the woman Julia saw on the street on Tuesday."

"Yeah?"

"Yeah." Rizzo was almost gloating now. "The girl was in Elizabeth's class. Want to know her name?"

"Why not?"

"Margarita. That ring a bell?"

"Margarita? Sure. The glass heart."

"*Good,* Buddy. This Margarita came here from Puerto Rico four months ago, moved in with a girlfriend on Washington Avenue, signed up for the class a few weeks back. And listen: last Saturday she got married. She's off on her honeymoon in Puerto Rico. Is another bell ringing?"

"Sure. She's the cousin the Super fixed up the apartment for."

"Bingo. They're *all* related, these people, the whole damn Wedge. Listen, Buddy, this Margarita's our pivot person. She knew Manny, she knew Elizabeth, and *all three* were in the JFK building at the same time. *She's* the one we want to talk to."

"How do you know she knew Manny? You talk with her aunt?"

"Uh-uh. The Super. The aunt's in Puerto Rico too, but they'll all be back tomorrow morning. *This* morning, I guess. What the hell time is it, anyway?"

"It's almost two a.m. Where the hell've you been? You were with the Super all this time?"

"I was at the Albano place, Buddy. A little trouble. Seems your friend from JFK got himself roughed up."

"What friend?"

"Newmark. Albano caught him trying to break in. Caught him in the bushes under his daughter's window. The father and the sons beat the crap out of him, broke the guy's arm. Now he's in Jacobi with maybe a skull fracture."

"Are you serious? Why didn't you call me?"

"I just did. Hey, I'm a busy guy, I got a murder to solve." He paused a moment to let that sink in. "What about you? Find anything in that box you were looking in?"

"Fuck you. Is that all the news you got? When do we get to the bad news?"

"Hey, Buddy, don't take it personal."

"Let me guess. Manny shook his tail, and you don't know where he is."

"How'd you know? Gilman tell you?"

"Gilman told me shit."

"Don't blame *him*. Reinhart didn't phone it in right away. He lost Manny at Jacobi. The creep never came down from the surgery ward. Reinhart spent some time trying to pick him up again, checking all the stairways, the outside, and all. Found the slimeball's traces later, down on the sub-floor. The punk squeezed himself into a locker, slipped out through the morgue when the coast was clear. He was long gone when Reinhart phoned in."

"Yeah? Wish someone had phoned *me*."

"Why, what happened?"

"That creep bastard saw me and Helen in the hospital tonight. He must've followed us home. He grabbed Helen down in the basement. How's that for taking it personal?"

"What?"

"We just finished turning the place upside down looking for him. He must've scrammed before we got the lights back on. Running for his life, probably, while I was busy going ape-shit and throwing things around."

"The two-bit bastard! She okay?"

"Yeah, no thanks to you or me. Shit, man, that's not the kind of thing she needs."

"Jesus, I'm really sorry, Buddy, really. You sure Helen's okay?"

"She passed out. The creep had a hand over her face."

"The lousy sonofabitch! Stupid, hopeless bastard! But hold on! This gives us the card game! Helen saw his face, right? She can ID him?"

"No."

"No?"

"That's what I said. He got her in the dark."

"Oh, shit. Too bad. But it doesn't matter, long as we can get prints, or something from Hair and Fiber. I'll send a team over from the Lab. Did you call in a sector car? Don't let anyone touch anything."

"I didn't call anyone yet. We just got back upstairs this minute, just got Helen settled down. I sent Phil back down to watch."

There was a pause. "You're sure it was Manny, Buddy?"

"Sure I'm sure! What do *you* think? He was staring at her in the hospital as if he was going to eat her. And he used the same M.O. as with Elizabeth, the hand over the mouth and all."

"How do *you* know what he did with Elizabeth? The Lab figured a pillow, something soft."

Villanova hesitated. He was surprised at himself, and a little confused. He went ahead and told Rizzo about the seance and what Julia had said.

Rizzo was silent for a moment. "You're a busy guy yourself," he muttered. There was another silence, and then he said dryly, "The woman's jerking us around. She's one cagey dame. Nearly everything she told you is inadmissable.

Psychic or not, Julia doesn't know what happened in that apartment when she wasn't there."

"Maybe not, but the gold chain is a different story. She practically admitted seeing it on the floor."

"Yeah, and then she took it back. If she won't testify to it, we've got nothing but your own hearsay."

"Testifying's not what it's about. She's letting her son go, telling us he's a killer. We've already got enough to take him in again, right? I mean, you're going to stake out the hospital, right?"

"Sure I am. But we're missing one thing, and without it we're never gonna get a Grand Jury to indict. And that one thing is a solid piece of direct evidence connecting Manny and Elizabeth around the time of the crime. Good physical evidence, a hair, a handprint, anything. Julia can't give us that. All she can give us is words."

"Let her give us what she can. I say with one more push, she'll let Manny drop. She'll tell us something we can use to finish him. Let her have a day or so to get over being sore at me..."

Rizzo cleared his throat. "Yeah, well, that's the rest of the bad news, Buddy. Time's up. The squadroom got a call from the hospital about an hour ago. That Doctor What's-his-name...Capogrosso?"

"Yeah?"

"Julia's back up in Intensive Care. Took a turn for the worse."

"Fuck."

"Capogrosso wanted you to know, he's cutting her tomorrow morning. Emergency operation, ten o'clock. Shaky proposition all around."

"I know it's shaky. Shit."

"He said she asked to see you again before she goes under."

"She did? Christ, maybe this is it! Let me just throw some clothes on and..."

"Not now, Buddy, she's knocked out for the night. We'll hit the ward soon's I get the word in the morning. I'm gonna be right there too. And Buddy?"

"Yeah?"

"She asked you to be sure to take good care of her cat."

Guilt settled like a cold weight in Villanova's stomach. He turned around and scanned the room. The door was still open. Mirabel was nowhere to be seen.

- TWELVE -

A precinct cop spent the night on the front porch of the Topless Towers waiting for the Lab team, but Villanova didn't sleep with anything resembling peace. He heard the rain beating down in periodic surges, the wind at the drafty old windows, the intermittent rumble of thunder. He woke up half a dozen times, and finally, somewhere in the middle of the night, he gave up and just opened his eyes.

Helen wasn't in the bed with him.

He lay waiting uneasily. He was used to her nighttime restlessness; sometimes she went down to her own apartment to use the bathroom, other times, especially in thunderstorms, she retreated to her own bed. He waited.

He heard her coming in. There was the click of the doorlatch, the rustle of cloth as she slipped off her robe. Her silhouette approached the bed. He stirred and reached toward her, and she came to him, groping gently. Just as her hand brushed his cheek, lightning flickered at the windows.

He sat up. It wasn't Helen.

It was a younger woman, taller, with long dark hair. Her gaze, frightened and helpless, lingered into the darkness. It was Elizabeth Albano. "Wait, this is a mistake," he said.

"Yes, it's *all* a mistake," she said. Her voice was husky and sweet, her breath warm on his neck. Her hands found him, caressed and wrapped him. She was naked, lithe and smooth, warm to the touch everywhere.

"You don't know who I am," he said. Under the weight of her, he sank back onto the bed. She was heavier than he'd expected, broader across the back, solid in the limbs.

"Yes I do. I've been watching you." Her hair, thick and full of the mingled scent of shampoo and her own sweat, fell across his face and neck. "And I know I love you. That's all I know. That's all that matters."

He recognized the forlorn chord that had come into her voice; he'd heard it once before in his life. It was the chord on which youth broke its heart, the chord that contained all of life's sorrow, passion, and beauty. And the instant he heard it, he knew that all his instincts about Liz Albano were true. At the sound of it, the brittle core of him melted and ran like hot lead, that's how fast it all happened, that's how fast he yielded himself to the preposterous reality he found himself in. Tears came to his eyes as he pulled the girl to him. All he knew was that a second chance was miraculously being granted to him.

"I'm not afraid," she said. "Don't you be. We mustn't tell, that's all."

He twined his legs around hers, circled that long, slender neck with his arm, cradled her to him and rocked her, trying to bring every inch of his skin against her. He had no wisdom left to him now except what was in his flesh, and his flesh told him he must hold tight to this pure-hearted creature and never let go.

"My feet are cold," she whispered.

And they *were* cold against his own, and he could feel a vee of callus on the ball of each one, as stiff as the nipples pressing into his chest, and his fingers found the ligature welt around her neck, and a shadow crossed his heart as he realized how fast her skin was cooling. "Don't get cold," he pleaded.

"I can't help it."

And he wrapped her even tighter. "Please God, don't let it happen."

"I don't want it to happen." And the breath on his throat was cool now.

"No," he said. "No."

And she no longer answered. And the lightning flashed at the windows, and he saw those glazed, lifeless eyes. "*No!*" he cried out.

"*What is it?*"

He sat up in the bed.

"What is it? A nightmare, sweetie? Come on, wake up."

His heart was pounding. He felt Helen's hand on his arm.

"I'll put on the light."

"No, no light," he said hoarsely. "Lie down, go back to sleep."

"You okay, sweetie?"

"Yeah...it's just the storm. Go to sleep."

He drew her down and lay next to her.

But he didn't close his eyes again. He listened to the rain on the roof. He listened to the rattle of the torrents in the old wooden gutters along the eaves, and then to the slow retreat of the thunder.

And he listened to Helen breathing beside him, and he knew she was awake.

The last few hours, he held her in his arms. He didn't think about anything, and didn't want to. He only wanted her to know she was safe, and he held her until she finally slept.

At last, when the jays started up in the trees and the dawn tinged the windows, he let himself doze off.

The phone rang at 7:05. It was Rizzo: Julia's surgery had been moved up an hour, to nine o'clock. "I'll come get you, Buddy," Rizzo said.

"Where the hell's that Lab team?"

"Spread too damned thin. Should be there any time."

"You pick up Manny yet?"

"Not yet. We've got the hospital staked out and the precincts on alert. Shake a leg, Buddy."

Villanova took a quick shave, threw on a clean shirt and slacks. He saw Helen watching through half-open eyes. "You all right?" he said.

"You were dreaming about *her*," she said.

"No."

She raised her head from the pillow. "Yes, you were."

"Don't be in a mood, babe. It's a bad morning."

"I'm not in a mood." She sank back down on the pillow. "I had dreams too. I dreamed I was pregnant."

He paused pulling on a cardigan. "You did?" Something happy rose inside him. "Do you want to be pregnant?"

She didn't answer.

"Close your eyes, babe, dream about it some more. I'll leave instructions with the guy in uniform so you don't have to go downstairs with the Lab boys."

"I'm not afraid to go down."

"Phil can take them down."

"I'll take them down myself. I *want* to go down."

"Please, babe, give me one bit of peace today."

"What about *my* peace?"

He looked into her face. She was in more than a mood, and he knew better than to press the point. "Do this much for me. Let me pick you up after work tonight and bring you home. I don't want you walking the streets while that creep is still out there. We'll stop at the Killarney Rose on the way and get us some hot food."

"No, I want to cook for us tonight," she said.   "It'll make me feel better. I want to make us a real dinner."

"Why not take the day off and do it, then? Call in sick and stick near home."

She shook her head.   "There's a ten-year-old girl on the ward with two failing kidneys. *She's* sick."

That was it--he'd been a touch too eager. He gave her a kiss, tucked the blanket around her, and headed out.

He stood on the porch chatting with the precinct cop till Rizzo's Plymouth pulled up. The morning was beautiful, dry and crisp, with a strong northwest wind; after three days of rain and overcast, the sky was a rich blue, with just a puff of cloud here and there scudding along in the breeze. They took the Mosholu Parkway route toward Fordham Road.   Gusts whipped the leaves of the sycamores and sumacs along the boulevard.   The sidewalk outside 658 Mosholu was deserted. Pale yellow leaves danced confused circles around the spot where the girl in the trunk had first been found.

When Rizzo turned down White Plains Road toward Rhinelander Avenue, Villanova braced himself.   They passed the hearse and the black limousine parked outside St. Clare's church without speaking.   Two blocks down they cruised past the deserted Albano house.   The whole street seemed blanketed in sullen silence; though it was a Saturday morning, the houses were shuttered and sealed.   For the private sorrow of the Albano household, the neighboring dwellings offered their mute, shoulder-to-shoulder sympathy...that and a bouquet of garden chrysanthemums laid anonymously on the stoop. Villanova couldn't help wondering what Newmark had been doing around the Albano house the night before.   He resolved to make time to ask him.

He wanted coffee now, but knew they shouldn't stop. They turned down Morris Park Avenue toward the hospital, passed Angelo's market, passed the big plate glass windows of Candella's bakery, full of cheesecakes, cookies, and pastries, but empty of customers.   Across the street, even the fenced park where asphalt softball raged day and night most of the year was ominously quiet.   Cascades of maple leaves swept across the open space and thrashed against the high chain-link fence.

By 8:35 he and Rizzo were in the lobby at Jacobi. Reinhart and McManus were on stakeout, one inside the main doors, one out.   Rizzo went to the house phone, came back with a shrug.   "Capogrosso's in the room checking her over now.   We can have our turn in fifteen minutes."

"The surgery still on for nine?"

Rizzo nodded.   "Grab yourself a smoke.   I'll go phone in to the squadroom."

"I'll look for you by the elevators."   Villanova skipped the smoke and checked with the desk for Newmark's room number.

He found the man in a first-floor single, sitting up in bed and staring out the window.   There was a cast on his left arm from bicep to fingertips, and a half-dozen sutures alongside his right eye.   His face looked like one big bruise. He recognized Villanova immediately and managed a smile of greeting.

"Jesus. How the hell do you feel?"

"Not bad," Newmark said quietly.

"Not bad?"

"Good, actually."

"You kidding me?"

"No, I mean it, I've got no problem with this."

Villanova shook his head.   "You want to tell me what happened?"

"I went to the girl's house," Newmark said with a shrug. "I had to do it. I had to talk to her father."

"Christ, you talked to him after all?"

"Not quite. I never actually spoke. The place was dark, you know. It was after midnight. I thought I heard a TV set on inside. I hung back awhile...I wasn't sure what I should do."

"You should've gone home. Those people have already been through hell."

"I had to see them. I had to tell somebody something. My wife...last night I had a couple of drinks after dinner, I tried to talk to her. If only *she'd* listened to me. The woman won't hear, she won't hear anything." He shook his head and looked toward the window again. "It wasn't fair, you know, that girl dying that way, so fast. She was my last chance to talk the truth about anything important."

"How'd you wind up getting roughed up if you didn't get to talk?"

"I was trying to look under the windowshade. I wanted to see if anyone was awake. It was pitch dark out, but they've got electric eyes or something in the garden there, surveillance gadgets. There I am trying to climb up on some little trellis, and all of a sudden they're coming at me from three sides. They scared the shit out of me, boxing me in that way. I ran."

"You ran? That was a mistake. Those sons are half your age."

"It was the father that caught me. Christ, the first punch was like a sledgehammer. I yelled, 'All I want to do is talk!' and the sons caught up and tackled me into the gutter. That's when I broke my elbow. I tell you, those guys wore out their arms on me. The father was the worst. I couldn't see a thing, but I could feel the heat coming off that man's body. It was like a furnace."

"You didn't fight back?"

"I couldn't. Didn't want to, anyway. I tried to tell them they had the wrong guy. Then I realized they didn't, and I shut up."

"What do you mean, the wrong guy?"

"They thought I was someone else. Some professor. That's what the father shouted to the sons."

Villanova sagged back. "You poor sap, you took McVicar's beating."

"That was the name. What'd the guy do?"

"What'd he do? For openers, he got involved with a nice girl from a nice family when he shouldn't."

Newmark nodded. "Well, there."

Villanova studied him. There wasn't anything pat or superficial in Newmark's face. Whatever construction he'd made of all this went deep into his mind and spirit. "You feel good about this, don't you?"

"Inside I do. I just couldn't go on with any more secrets. You understand me, don't you?"

"I think so." Villanova watched him through narrowed eyes. "You didn't actually *do* anything to that girl?" he said. "Something you haven't told me?"

Newmark looked down at the bedcovers. "I'm through with shame," he said quietly. "I feel white as snow. It's been a long time since I felt this peaceful."

Villanova shook his head slowly. "It's good for me to meet someone who outdoes *me*."

There was a silence. Newmark was gazing out the window again. "You think you could get me pen and paper?" he said.

"You want to write something?"

"A letter of resignation."

Villanova stared out the window with him. There was nothing to see, nothing but leaf-strewn grass and a street jammed with parked cars. "I don't think you should do that."

"No?"

"No. I think you should think it over awhile."

Newmark turned and held his eye for long seconds. "Well, thanks for that."

Villanova gave him a handshake and left him to his thoughts. He beat Rizzo to the elevators by half a minute.

Five minutes after that, the two of them were standing at Julia Cruz's bedside in the Sic-U at Jacobi. There were three other patients in the rank of beds, all very old, and all apparently comatose or semi-conscious. Julia Cruz looked as bad as any of them. One eye was now completely closed, the other so pale its absinthe hue seemed jaundiced. Her skin was pasty. She kept her arms under the sheets and didn't even try to sit up. She seemed relieved at the sight of Villanova, and nodded a greeting to him, but Rizzo's face she studied with a frown as if trying to remember it. Villanova reintroduced him.

The first thing Julia asked Villanova to do was to repeat to her what she had said aloud in her trance the night before.

"*Now* you want to know?" he said.

"Please," she said. Her voice was calm; whatever had been seething in her the evening before had subsided.

Villanova did as she asked. He gave it back to her in summary, painfully aware of Rizzo's skeptical eyes.

Julia nodded. "It's like the dreams I had. For three nights, I dreamed of that poor girl lying alone in the dark, first under the bed, then in a trunk, then in her coffin. But last night, after the seance, I dreamed a different dream. I dreamed that a beautiful angel carrying a gold cross stood watch over three white coffins. Her eyes were the eyes of my own little Vidalina." She looked from Villanova to Rizzo and back. "It means that I can die in peace. The dead girl has forgiven me, you see, because I finally spoke the truth."

Rizzo let his breath out tiredly, and Julia gave him a tolerant glance. "But more than that," she said, "the dream means that now it's all right to tell you the rest."

"The rest?"

She looked to Villanova. "That's why I asked you to come. So you can be a witness to what I say."

Villanova could sense Rizzo's irritation and suspicion, but he kept his gaze on Julia. He wanted desperately for her to keep talking, to say what he'd been waiting to hear. He wanted no balking, no hedging, no interrupting. "Go ahead," he prompted her. "There's not much time."

She nodded. "I'm ashamed to tell you that I held back one thing from you. It was wrong of me, but not to hold it back would also have been wrong."

"What is it?"

"I *did* recognize the girl in the photograph you showed me. I saw her before, only once."

"Yes?"

"She came to my door on Monday this week, about one o'clock. She asked, would I see her, to help her with a headache that wouldn't go away. But I had such great pain of my own that day...I told her she would have to please come back a different day."

Villanova's heart began to race. "Go on."

"And then I took her hands, just for a minute. I felt sorry for her, such a beauty, so unhappy. So young and yet so worn out already by the world. In her eyes I could see a goodness, a kindness toward others. So I took her hands, and as soon as I touched them, I could feel how much she was suffering. The poor thing seemed to be ready to break into pieces. I asked her what her trouble was, and she said she had so many troubles, she felt swollen to bursting. I touched her face. I could feel the heat of all her pain. I tried to soothe her, I told her that everything would soon be all right. She shook her head. 'I'm all alone, I have no one to ask for help,' she said. 'Don't worry, I'll help you,' I said. 'Tomorrow your head will hurt less. In a little while you'll be happy again, this I know.' She looked into my eyes, full of trust, the way a child looks at its mother. 'I believe you,' she said. I pushed the hair back from that pretty face. 'The worst pain comes just before the greatest joy,' I told her. 'You are going to give a gift to the world, something valuable. I'm sure of this.' And it was true, I could feel how her goodness, so deep inside her, was ready to grow without stopping. She nodded, and hope came into her face. Her eyes shone with it. For a minute I saw her whole and beautiful, the way only children are whole."

Julia stopped for a moment. She glanced at Villanova, and the warmth in her own gaze dimmed. "But then a dread took hold of me," she said. "I sensed that Manny was watching us. I turned, and he was standing in the doorway of his room, staring at the girl. In his eyes was something more than desire, something black and cruel...a kind of hatred. I took my hands away from the girl and told her she should leave for now. I told her she should come back the next day, at the same time."

"Tuesday."

"Yes."

"Did she see Manny looking at her?"

"Yes, she noticed him after a moment, and he turned away. I told her, 'That's my son.'"

"And then what?"

"She thanked me and then she left. Her face was still full of hope as she closed the door. And then Manny and I had an argument, like I told you."

"About the girl?"

"No, I never mentioned the girl. About him hanging around the apartment all the time. About his job, the money, everything. We were both very angry."

"What were you angry about, Julia?"

"That look in his eyes, just like the brutes who prowl the streets. My life, that was all turned to sickness and pain. My son, who was a shame to me."

"Did you go to Dr. Capogrosso then, like you said?"

"Yes, because the pain got worse after the girl left. And that night Manny came home with his boxes. And then the next morning we argued again, like I told you, and we went to the bus stop." She looked into Villanova's eyes, her face full of anguish. "I *forgot*, you see? My head hurt so much, I forgot the girl was coming back! I rode the bus to the hospital, and I only felt somehow that there was something wrong. I sensed some kind of trouble, with Manny...and the feeling wouldn't go away. So I turned back. I hurried, but the bus got caught behind every light. And then just as I was almost home, Maria Iglesias called to me...and that's when all of a sudden I *realized*. Because the girl had told me that Maria's niece was the one who told her to come to me..."

"You mean Margarita?" Villanova interrupted. He glanced at Rizzo, whose face was aglow with contained anger.

"That's right. *Then* I remembered, and I ran upstairs as fast as I could. My heart was pounding. I was so afraid!"

She stopped. Her breath was coming with some difficulty. Her anxious gaze went from one to the other of the men standing over her bed. Villanova felt a wave of pity for her, but Rizzo's voice was harsh when he said, "What happened next?"

"When Manny finally opened the door, I asked him if anyone had come. He said no. I asked him about the smell of cat-pee. He didn't answer, he went in his room and closed the door. I lay down, hoping the girl would still come. I closed my eyes, but I saw nothing but death. Even the air was full of death. I thought it was my own death I sensed, you see. I waited for the girl until I knew she wasn't coming, and then I got up. I knocked on Manny's door, but he only opened it a crack. He wouldn't come with me, so I had to leave for the hospital alone." She hesitated and glanced at Villanova. Then she nodded grimly. "But on my way out, I saw something on the floor. It glistened, or else I would never see it. I bent down to look. It was a little gold crucifix, on a chain."

There was a silence. Villanova let out his breath and looked to his partner. Rizzo's face was rigid, the lines of fatigue starkly drawn around his eyes and mouth. He didn't speak. Villanova said to Julia, "Did you know who the gold chain belonged to?"

"Not for sure. Not until last night, when you told me what I said in my trance. Then I had no choice. I kept my eyes closed after you were gone. And I remembered that the girl who came to me on Monday wore a crucifix around her neck."

Rizzo said curtly, "You're lying. You knew about the gold chain two days ago, when we showed you the girl's photo."

Julia shook her head. "The girl in the photo had no chain."

Villanova quickly retrieved the photo of Elizabeth, glanced at it, and passed it to Rizzo. It was true: the chain and cross were not visible in the picture.

Julia said to Rizzo, "I've told you what I didn't have to. Why are you so angry with me?"

"Because all the while we were trying to find out what happened to the girl, you knew, and you kept it from us."

She shook her head. "Only one thing I kept from you. And inside me, I yearned for you to learn the whole truth, whatever it was, even if it meant the loss of my son. For the sake of that poor dead girl, I even put myself into a trance, knowing that what came out of my mouth would betray Manny. I tried to help you every way I could. Should I have put my son in the cage for you with my own hands? What more could I do?"

"You could have told us straight out that the girl had been to see you. How do we know you're not still holding back?"

"But it was I who called you here today," she said with a frown. "You're a decent man, but you don't know what it is to have a child. You don't know what it is to be a woman who believes in goodness and then gives birth to a monster...to spend your life trying to save this monster, to live year after year in dread of the awful thing it will one day do. You don't know what it is to love a child who only wants to destroy himself and you." She stared at Rizzo, and now there was a flash of anger in her own gaze. "Did you think I was free from torment in all this? Didn't I tell you how the face of that dead girl and the face of my son have taken turns haunting me, and already I had a lost child to mourn for? Why bother to torture me, when I torture myself with the thought that I am the one to blame, that if I didn't forget the appointment I made, the girl would not be dead and my son would not be in a prison?"

Villanova said, in an effort to soothe her, "Your son is not in a prison, Julia. Not yet."

"Oh, but he is," she said. "He is in the smallest of all prisons, and now he must strangle there like the girl he killed. The pain he's in, I can feel it, but I can't save him from it now, and neither can you. He and I must both face our suffering alone." She looked at him, nodding solemnly. "You see, this is the meaning of my dream last night. And this is why it's all right for me to tell all the truth now. I might have said more sooner...but it's because of *you* that I held back."

"Because of me?"

"Yes. Because I hoped for mercy for my son, and I knew you were the one to give it. But hidden in you I saw a terrible anger. I knew I had to wait until you rid yourself of it."

"It's still there, Julia."

"Some of it, yes. But I couldn't wait any longer, not after Manny came here yesterday. Not after I saw the way he put his eyes on Helen. I knew what that look meant."

"You knew what that look meant?"

"Yes," she said quietly. "It was the same way he looked at the girl in my apartment on Monday."

Villanova flushed and felt his whole body tense. "You might have warned me. You might have warned *Helen*."

Julia nodded gravely. "*I* am protecting your Helen." She touched her heart. "Here. As long as I live, no harm will come to her."

"Maybe you think so," Villanova snapped. "But now you know why I can't give your son the mercy you want. He's out to hurt Helen, and I'm going to hunt him down like a mad dog!"

She shook her head. "It doesn't matter now. We've done our dance, you and I, and it's finished. In the end, we are more alike than you think. The girl who died, I could have loved her like a daughter. The beauty I saw in her, no one else saw...except *you*." Again she gave that solemn nod. "In you, what happened to her made an anger, in me, a sorrow. But still what we sensed about her was the same. That's why I knew I was right to trust you. That's why now, whatever else you want, I will give you."

There was the sound of voices in the corridor then, and the brief appearance of faces in the doorway. Villanova recognized the Ear-Nose-Throat specialist, Salzman, whom he'd spoken to a few days earlier. Capogrosso loomed behind him.

Villanova turned to the ravaged woman in the bed. Already he felt remorseful for his flash of anger. "Maybe I don't have the right to ask you anything more..."

"Just tell me what you want."

"To do what I've got to do, I need to know what became of the gold chain. Did you leave it where you saw it?"

"I was on my way out," she said softly. "I picked it up. I put it in my purse."

He nodded. "And what happened to it?"

She looked into his eyes, as if to satisfy herself one more time what he was made of. Then she drew her hand from under the sheet and opened it. The gold crucifix with its broken chain lay on her palm.

He took it by the chain and raised it up. The little cross dangled, glittering in the light of the overhead fixtures. The crucified Jesus spun slowly. The figure was delicate and detailed; tiny ruby chips took the place of spikes in the hands and feet.

Rizzo said to Julia, "Did Manny know you had this?"

"I don't know."

"Is that the reason he's been coming here every chance?"

Julia gave him a pitying look. "One day you will have a son," she said softly.

Villanova spoke up quietly: "Julia, do you know where your son is right now? Is he coming back here?"

"No..." she said vaguely, shaking her head. "No."

There was further noise in the corridor then, and a nurse came through the door pulling a gurney, followed by Capogrosso and Salzman. The sight of the entourage brought a sudden heaviness to Villanova's chest. The two doctors nodded greetings to Rizzo and Villanova, and put on confident smiles for Julia. "It's time," Capogrosso told her with a lilt of optimism. "You ready?"

She nodded.

"The O.R. nurses are going to take care of you and get you ready while we scrub. Just like last time, remember?"

She nodded again. She looked to Villanova. "I have to leave you now."

The weight in his chest pressed heavier. "Don't worry, you'll be okay," he said. He took hold of her hand.

"I'm not afraid."

But his own heart had begun to labor. He was full of admiration, affection, and desperate hope, yet all the phrases that suggested themselves were too trite to speak. "It'll be over soon," was all he could manage.

"For me and for Manny, but not for you. A person must be brave to be happy, remember. And for you, I wish only happiness with that beautiful woman of yours." She gave his hand a squeeze and released it.

He stood beside Rizzo watching as she was transferred to the gurney. It was a difficult sight; she looked the size of a child, and already he felt guilty for what he hadn't said.

A minute later the procession departed, with Salzman leading the way and Capogrosso in the rear. Capogrosso gave a look back at them before pulling the door closed. Villanova tried to read his face, but it was locked up tight.

When they were gone, Rizzo pulled a tissue from the dispenser at the bedside and handed it to him.

"What's that for?"

"The evidence, Buddy."

"You were rough on her." Villanova wrapped up the cross and chain.

"Yeah, well, I'm goddam tired."

"I never thought I'd hear you say that."

"Buddy, I could've had this case nailed on Thursday night if it weren't for that woman and her hocus-pocus. I could've spared myself a kick in the pants from the D.A.'s office. I had my killer in custody, and everything else in place."

"Everything but evidence and a witness."

"Yeah. Right." Rizzo didn't smile. "My luck to get a witness who sees things in a trance."

Villanova shrugged.   There wasn't a detective at Homicide Squad who wouldn't have groused at the idea of trances and dreams. "Well, she gave us what we wanted, one way or another. She gave us the missing pieces."

Rizzo nodded, and a little of the bitterness faded from his eyes. "Manny knew Elizabeth Albano was going to be at his door at one o'clock on Tuesday. That's why he was all antsy at the bus stop, looking at his watch every two seconds. He was probably wetting his goddam pants. That's how he broke his key in the lock, he was all worked up. He's lucky he got the door open before the key snapped."

"And he was waiting inside for the girl when she got there," Villanova said, "and he didn't let on to her that his mother wasn't there until after he'd let her in and bolted the door behind her. Maybe he talked to her a minute, maybe not. Maybe he lied and told her Julia was on her way."

"I bet he didn't talk at all, Buddy. I bet the second she got scared, the second she sized things up, he made a grab for her."

"I bet you're right. Got his hand over her face, just like with Helen. She tried to get away, he busted the gold chain. Dragged her to his bed, kept her mouth covered till she passed out. Then he finished the job and suffocated her. Or maybe he just got over-eager and did it by accident. Then he got scared and high-tailed it out of there."

Rizzo nodded.   "Not for long, though.   There was no way to lock the door behind him, remember.   He knew his only chance of getting away with what he'd done was to get the body out of there, and he knew he needed something big to put it in.   He knew where he could get it, too.   But when he got to JFK and Windy offered him his job back, he had to pretend that's what he was after.   It suited him for the time being anyway, because it gave him a place to lie low afterward."

"Right.   Then back he goes to the apartment to wait until his shift starts.   And when Julia surprises him, when he hears her trying to get her key in the lock, he stashes the body under the bed and ditches the girl's handbag or shoes or whatever, and lets his mother in.   That must've been a horror for him, because the one person he most wanted to hide what he'd done from was his mother.   So he holes up in his room with the door closed, fighting panic probably, listening to his mother moan about dying, waiting her out.   And after she leaves, he's finally got the dead girl to himself, and a couple of hours of quiet."

"What does he do for that couple of hours, Buddy?"

Villanova shook his head.   "Whatever it is, he doesn't molest the girl in any way that leaves evidence."

"We know he took her panties off.   Maybe that's all he did.   Maybe he just looked at her."

"Maybe.   He'd been looking at her from his window for about six months."

Rizzo's eyes filled with a grim wonder.   "Jesus, the girl died because one dumb piece of bad luck brought her to the last place in the world she should've ever set foot.   Right into the rat-hole of the creep who'd been having sick dreams about her."

"It isn't just bad luck," Villanova corrected him. "There were *people* behind her bad luck, and dammit, I'm not through with them." He said that as darkly as he felt it, even though he knew Rizzo didn't want to hear it. "And you know what the worst shame is? Elizabeth went to Julia's place full of hope. She thought she'd found her way out of the corner those people had put her in, and Julia knew it. Julia's the one who saw everything."

"So she says."

"It's the truth. *She* saw that look in Manny's eye, she's the one who took the brunt of the whole thing. It must've torn her up, finding out what happened to the girl afterward. On top of the trouble she already had."

Rizzo nodded soberly. "I guess you're right, Buddy. She was square in the middle the whole way through."

"And loaded with guilt on both sides. *Too* much guilt. That's where a lot of the forgetting comes in."

Rizzo nodded again. "I *was* rough on her. I'll make it up."

"I hope you get that chance."

"Thanks, Buddy." Rizzo's expression came as close as it ever did to sheepishness. "Come on, let's wrap things. Let's head downstairs and see if Manny's showed yet. The sap doesn't know we've got a warrant. This time we're going to do the arraigning quick-time. With the gold cross and with Margarita Iglesias, we've got an indictment."

"You haven't got Margarita Iglesias yet."

"We'll have her this morning. We'll pick her up at the airport. I'll do it myself, and let the boys put the cuffs back on Manny."

"You're pretty damn sure this is where he's heading."

"You bet I'm sure," Rizzo said.

Himself, Villanova had a profound uneasiness at the thought of Manny roaming loose. "You know, the bastard has a way of showing up where you don't expect him."

"Don't be nervous, Buddy. I'm not."

"*I* saw the way he looked at Helen. You didn't."

"Relax. He's coming *here*. I'll bet my wife on it."

Villanova shook his head. "Don't bet what you don't want to lose. Do you want me in on the stakeout?"

"Uh-uh.   Your   talents   are   needed   elsewhere. Somebody's got to take that gold cross back to Tom Albano for an ID while I go round up the Iglesiases."

Villanova's   heart   slid   down   a   notch   or   two. "*Somebody?*"

"That's you, Buddy."

* * *

Villanova grabbed a cab on Eastchester Road and headed over to East Tremont Avenue. He ignored his growling stomach and directed the driver straight into Saint Raymond's Cemetery.

The burial ceremony was in progress when he got there; the hearse and limousine stood gleaming in the sun along one of the narrow lanes, with a little string of cars behind. The mourners were gathered in a rough circle among the headstones a short distance away. The priest was reciting a prayer, his vestments whipping in the wind. Villanova sent the cabby on his way.

He was barely in time. The ceremony was ending, and people were laying or tossing their blossoms onto the casket, each in turn, before filing away. The first to approach the funeral caravan were the family. The brothers and sister-in-law led the way, surrounding the dazed and rigid mother. Albano followed a few yards behind. He was wearing the same blue suit. Villanova took a few steps toward him, caught his eye, and motioned him over.

"My   condolences,"   he   said   quietly   when   Albano reached him.

"Thanks. Thanks for coming." Albano looked shaky, but not as shaky as he might have been. He had no color, and his face was drawn enough to show what he would look like as an old man, but he held himself erect and had control over his voice. The knuckles on his right hand were bruised and swollen.

"I know this is pretty rotten timing," Villanova said.

"That's all right. I'm just glad you guys aren't letting up."

"We found something. Do you think you could identify it for me?"

"What is it?"

Villanova pulled out the tissue and unfolded it.

Albano looked. The muscles in his face twitched. "It's hers." He looked as if he might suddenly let go tears, but he fought himself dry and wound up with an expression that was almost hard. "What's the story?" he said. "You found the guy who did it?"

Villanova nodded.

"Well? Who?"

"No one you ever met. Or her either. A stranger."

"Who?" Albano's face was twitching again.

"A guy from JFK High School. A custodian."

Albano stiffened. He looked as if some of his insides had been torn away; it was one thing to want to know, and another to find out. "You've got him?" he said.

"We'll have him today. He's not going anywhere."

Albano's face surprised him with its hardness. "You'd better put him away good. You'd better put the sonofabitch out of his misery, because if he walks the streets, I'm going to finish him off!"

Villanova shook his head. "You don't want to talk like that."

"So help me! So help me God!"

"You already took it out on one guy who didn't deserve it."

"I don't care, damn it!"

"That isn't you. That isn't who you are," Villanova said. "Easy now, your sons are coming over here." He recognized their nervous, solicitous expressions.

Albano glanced over his shoulder. The anguish finally broke on his face; the hardness dissolved into abject pain. "What kind of a world is this?" he said, searching Villanova's eyes for a plain, workingman-to-workingman solace. "What the hell is *wrong* with everybody?"

Villanova couldn't answer. He only knew that the world Albano had come of age in, and meant to pass on to his children, was extinct, and nothing was ever going to bring it back. "Shh, here they are," he said.

"Put that cross away. Don't let them see it." Albano turned away abruptly and intercepted the two big men in their dark suits.

Villanova pocketed the cross and headed in the other direction. He lit a cigarette and roamed among the tombstones until all the passengers had embarked and the little caravan had slid away toward Randall Avenue.

The abandoned casket stood like an obscenity among the orderly ranks of headstones, a flower-strewn white box perched on planks above an open pit, all exposed to the morning sun and that unremitting wind. Only a few hundred yards away, the traffic roared past: the Cross Bronx Expressway on one side, the Hutchinson River Parkway on the other. The sooty arches of the Whitestone Bridge loomed in the near distance.

He walked over and stood at the graveside. The beautiful girl he'd first laid eyes on only three days ago was ready for the long process of obliteration. This flimsy box was the last profile her individual spirit would ever cut in the world of being. At least she'd brought genuine faith to her rendezvous with death, at least her slaughter bore some of the dark dignity of tragedy. Without that, there'd be nothing to feel but the banality of destiny: *If Only*. If only Julia had got back home earlier. If only she hadn't forgotten the appointment, if only the tumor hadn't grown in her head. If only Jack LeClerc had gone with Elizabeth to the psychic, if only he hadn't put her face on a mural. If only she hadn't discovered McVicar's secret theft, if only Robinson's widow hadn't died. If only Dean Hennessy hadn't refused her a leave of absence, if only she'd gone upstate to Tom Reilly. If only McVicar hadn't cut off her assistantship, if only he hadn't goaded her into his brand of worldliness, if only he hadn't made her pregnant. If only her father hadn't been so damned decent, if only Dr. Parisi had discovered her pregnancy. If only Manny hadn't switched to night work, if only he hadn't been home the first time she called, if only he weren't so sick inside. If only Elizabeth Albano hadn't meant so damned much to every confused and angry and desolate soul around her--that was the real tragedy, finally.

He was tired, bone-weary, ready for the letting go. He was even ready to let go of McVicar, that spiritual assassin, that soul-strangler. He picked up a blossom that had fallen to the ground, a wilting yellow rose. Those had been Ginny's favorite blooms; she'd carried a bouquet of them down the aisle on her wedding day. He sniffed the flower's dying fragrance, and tossed it onto the casket with the others. A piece of him, a very old, very entrenched, very exhausted piece, went with it...for good.

He turned to go, and saw Manny Cruz coming toward him, boldly, recklessly. He tensed, his mind racing to absorb the preposterous inevitability of this sight. The murder-lust that he thought was depleted came surging up in his gut.

An instant later, he realized his mistake. It wasn't Cruz, it was Jack LeClerc.

LeClerc recognized him and nodded.

"You're too late," Villanova said, steeling himelf for another rabid go-round.

LeClerc nodded again. His face was expressionless.

"What happened to MacDowell?"

LeClerc shrugged. "This afternoon." There was no more manic sheen to him; he was flat as pavement. The guy had a new personality for every day.

They stood for a considerable time in silence, side by side, gazing at the casket. Finally LeClerc said, "They shouldn't leave it here like this."

Villanova took a look at him. Those big, ruddy features were a shade less ugly without the glasses, he decided. "They'll be along soon," he replied dryly. "The world's a goddam busy place. You know, lots of bullshit to take care of."

There was another long silence. The tractor trailers roared by in trains on the Cross Bronx. Overhead, the 727's and jumbos were circling down for their landings at LaGuardia. Farther up, glinting in the windswept September sky, a lone jetliner began its journey across the Atlantic. Villanova recalled his talk with LeClerc about reality. He wondered how the earth looked to the people up in that metal cylinder on this fall day at this moment. He wondered if the rows of tombstones in the graveyard were distinguishable. He wondered if the green square of Saint Raymond's was detectable within the vast masonry grid. He wondered if the city itself could be discerned on the turf-and-aqua-toned surface of the planet. He knew it couldn't, not from that height. He knew there was nothing to see from those airplane windows but a pastel meld, soft and unintelligible, out of which the lines of transgression and the lines of vengeance could never be explicated, not in fifteen years and not in fifteen thousand. He acknowledged that he was one of those incorrigible fools who have to exhaust themselves drawing forms onto chaos.   He glanced over at LeClerc: another exhausted fool with his own ridiculous forms and metaphors. "Why'd you put the priest in your mural?" he blurted out. "It's been bothering me."

"What priest?"

"Dean Hennessy. Why'd you put his face up there with your Joan of Arc? You know the man?"

"Sure I know him. Everyone does."

"What do you mean everyone?"

"Everyone on campus. Everyone knows his story."

"What story?"

LeClerc cast him a look. "He got himself in trouble, years back. Used to teach in a high school, couldn't keep his hands off the girls. Some parents got upset, he got kicked upstairs, into a desk job at the college."

"What kind of bullshit is that? This is the guy who wrote the sexual harassment code for the university."

LeClerc shrugged. His face was so full of indifference it almost looked sorrowful. "How else you think he got his job? He's no scholar. Spends a lot of time in the library but never publishes anything.   Never writes, except regulations and memos. Hates anyone who's got any talent. How does a pipsqueak like that become a graduate school dean?"

Villanova's heart was somewhere around his lower intestine. He was starting to be angry as hell with himself, too. "Is this on the level? Did Liz know about this?"

"Not at first. Those two were great buddies. First time I put eyes on her, there he was. Every day, I watched them eat lunch together in the Ramskellar. I had plenty of time to see what was in both faces. Till she stopped coming. Then the guy ate alone."

"Yeah? And what'd you see in his face after that?"

LeClerc shrugged again. "You're the man of words. I do my seeing with a paintbrush."

Villanova had that queasy feeling again. The bastards weren't going to leave him anything of the past, he realized.

LeClerc cleared his throat. He brushed back his black mane and said suddenly, "Listen, I lied about one thing."

"What's that?"

"About why I wouldn't go with Liz to see the psychic. It wasn't because I was working on a painting. I was in a funk that day, I couldn't work. That wasn't it at all."

"That right?"

"It was because I wanted to fuck her. I got sore because she wouldn't come inside, and we fought."

"You wanted to fuck her?" Villanova repeated. He heard the sound of an engine, saw a filthy pickup truck approaching with three sweat-shirted, soil-stained young men bouncing along in the back. They had shovels and ropes.

"She had a dress on, and heels. She looked damn good. I knew what she had on underneath. She used to wear that stuff for me. I'm the one that taught her to like it."

"Yeah?"

"I hadn't had a hand on her in three weeks, not since before that party. I wanted her to come inside. I didn't care if she saw that I was packing to leave. I didn't care how she felt about the canvases leaning against the walls, either. I just wanted to fuck her one more time, see?"

Villanova took another look at him. Behind that flatness in LeClerc's eyes, very far behind, there was a confusion, a kind of despair. "Well, you did," he muttered.

LeClerc nodded. The pickup truck pulled up with a squeal of brakes.

Villanova turned and walked back toward East Tremont Avenue. He crossed the street and hailed a cab.

The coffin was lurching into the pit and LeClerc was standing there, rigid and watchful, as the hack pulled away.

- THIRTEEN -

It was almost noon when Villanova got back to Jacobi. The lobby was busier than usual, and Rizzo was nowhere in sight. He saw Reinhart and Dougherty at their posts, and was actually relieved that Manny hadn't been taken yet; he was looking forward to grappling the bastard to the ground with his own hands. The cursing, the flailing, the panting and stink of fear were going to do him a lot of good. Meanwhile, he was content to stand vigil for Julia and constrain his anger.

He was heading toward the desk doing another slow scan for Rizzo when he almost got run down by a man charging out of the elevator without looking. "Heads up," Villanova warned, and then recognized Dr. Salzman.

Salzman stopped and looked at him, his preoccupied eyes taking him in by degrees.

"Done already?" Villanova asked. He remembered that Salzman had only a narrow role in the operation.

Salzman nodded. "It's finished," he said, and turned as if to go.

"Finished? The whole thing?"

Salzman turned back and nodded again, and Villanova's heart, sensing a miracle, had actually begun its rise when the surgeon's flat tone and grim look finally registered.

"Didn't your partner tell you?" Salzman said. "We lost her."

Villanova stood gaping at him.

"Sorry. It wasn't Capogrosso's fault. He'd barely gotten in. Just got the ventricle catheterized, got the cranial pressure on its way down, and the patient's heart gave out. Pulse fell off, and we couldn't bring it up."

"She's dead?"

Salzman's mouth made a tight, impatient line. "I explained it all to one of your people on the phone," he said. "It was a mercy, really. The chances of infection from the drain were high, especially after all the steroids. And the tumor had practically swallowed the basilar artery. Capogrosso had a hell of a lot of guts to even try."

Villanova stared dumbly. He'd been ready for this, and yet in another way he hadn't. "Where is he?"

"You don't want to talk to him now. We're used to losing patients in Sic-U these days, not the O.R. He just got through with the anaesthesiologist. He's upstairs, smoking a cigarette."

"Smoking a cigarette?"

"Right. First one in six years." Salzman shook his head and trudged across the lobby toward the street.

Villanova watched him go. He wanted a cigarette himself, and that was exactly the way he'd started the habit, just like Capogrosso, after one brutal loss. Now he felt that emptiness in the center of his chest that only a warm, toxic inhalation could ease. His eyes drifted across the lobby in front of him, taking in the expressionless people reading their slick magazines, the children fidgeting, the old people staring into space. For a minute, everything seemed so intricately mechanical and lifeless. What was the point of caring about anyone in this world, or anything? What advantage was there in making a peace with evil? What gentler passage, what saner reality did that make? It only gave up more ground to nothingness. A feeling close to panic took hold of him, the same panic he'd felt after Ginny's death fifteen years ago, when the hollow feeling in his chest had first begun. He was tired of good people dying.

He stalked to the pay phone and called Homicide Squad. Rizzo answered.

"We just lost Julia," he told him.

"I know, Buddy. That's our witness."

"That's more than our witness, damn it."

"Sure, Buddy, I know. But right now, it's our witness."

Villanova jammed his hand into his pocket, closed it around the smooth metal of his cigarette lighter. "Are we screwed?"

"No way. What we've got is deathbed testimony now. Plenty of weight there. And we've still got our evidence. --We do have our evidence, don't we, Buddy?"

"Albano ID'd the cross, yeah."

"Great. Evidence, Julia's testimony...it's enough. But guess what? We've got Margarita Iglesias too, and she's all the witness we're going to need. We missed her flight at the airport, but we checked with the limo services and staked out the Washington Avenue address and the aunt's place at 185th Street. The boys picked the both of them up about ten minutes ago, right outside the Cruz building. The Super was waiting on the stoop. It was a regular homecoming."

"The girl's a newlywed. The vacant apartment was supposed to be a surprise."

"Well, I'm not going to ruin it for her. I'm heading there now. Why not get over to the Wedge and meet me, and we'll question her together, okay, Buddy? And listen, sorry about Julia. I mean it."

"Sure."

"By the way, Gilman took a message for you."

"A message. Who from?"

"Some dame. I'll get him for you. See you over on 185th."

A few seconds later, Gilman's flat voice said, "Yeah?"

"What about a message for me?"

"Woman phoned in about a half hour ago. Says, 'Tell Mike Villanova, *he's here.*' Then she hangs up."

His body went rigid, and in its hollow center his heart began to bang like a fist. "That's Helen! That creep Manny is back!"

"No, no, take it easy. It wasn't Helen."

"It had to be! Who else could it be?"

"She left a name. Dolores."

* * *

The Fordham Rams were taking on Georgetown in the season opener, and the distant roaring of the crowd on Coffey Field rose intermittently above the rushing of the wind in the trees. It was an eerie, animal exhalation, somewhere between a hiss and a scream, full of bestial violence. Even as far away as the library steps that ugly noise reached Villanova's ears, and the absence of any other human activity on the campus only made the sound more monstrous The Martyrs Court dorms looked untenanted, the Science buildings were spookily quiet, even the library seemed deserted. But just as Villanova neared the top of the stone steps, one of the big double oak doors swung open and Brian McVicar emerged.

The two men paused for a few seconds eyeing each other. McVicar stood three steps above, his hands in the pockets of his corduroys. He wore a loose-fitting tweed jacket over a black turtleneck, a good choice for thievery, and to his credit his affect was neither nervous nor triumphant.

"You and I need to have a word," Villanova said to him.

"You stay the hell away from me."

"Did you find what you were looking for?"

"I've got nothing to say to you."

"I guess you did find it. I guess you've been real busy up there. Poor, negelected Dolores."

McVicar eyed him, working that remark through. "I know just what to do about you," he said. "I know who to talk to."

"Who? Dean Hennessy? He'll be along, soon's the football game's over."

McVicar stiffened and his face colored. He was a handsome man when the blush came to his cheeks, accentuating his blue eyes. That animal hiss rose up above the treetops; it was a cry of relief, the kind that comes when the enemy quarterback is sacked or the fullback thrown for a loss on third down. "Take a walk, chum," McVicar said. He started down the steps.

"Where do you have it?" Villanova said. "Inside your jacket there?"

McVicar stopped and turned. They were on the same step now, eye to eye. The color gathered high on McVicar's forehead. His eyes narrowed and made a quick sweep behind Villanova; there was no one anywhere around. "Fuck you," he muttered, and he turned away again.

"Didn't you notice that half the article was gone? Now where do you suppose that other half went to?"

That stopped McVicar again. The muscles in his jaw were working. He came up a step to face Villanova. There was hate in his eyes. "Where is it?" he rasped.

"See, I told you we needed to talk." Villanova reached inside his own jacket and tugged the corner of the onionskin pages into view.

His hand was still there when McVicar clubbed the side of his head with a vicious short hook. Stunned, he was thrown off his balance by McVicar's lunging bulk...and then the two of them were falling down the stone steps and there was the ripping of fabric as McVicar tried to claw his way to those pages, and in their grapple they rolled over and over each other on those hard angles, and came to rest with McVicar on top. Villanova fought to get out from under, still in disbelief at the brute violence hidden in this stage ham, this phony litterateur. And then he wrenched the man off with a leg hook, and they clutched at each other and went rolling around and around on the grassy hardpan at the foot of the steps, McVicar still clawing for those pages, no more punches thrown but just weight against weight and strength against strength. And McVicar was a big man, and desperate, and Villanova was surprised to realize he might be overpowered, and it struck him that McVicar was a smart man, too. And the damp earth smelled just the way it did when he used to eat it in rugby days with a quarter-ton of human bulk atop him. Another roar rose up from Coffey Field, and this was that chilling, sadistic din that comes when the other team loses the ball in a fumble or has a punt blocked or a pass picked off-- that was it, an intercepted pass--and Villanova was breathing hard now, and McVicar was too, the breath was ripping and groaning out of him, and if he weren't so intent on those pocketed pages he'd have managed to stay on top, but he was grunting like a winded boy now, and Villanova was outlasting him, and he could feel the cold dampness of the ground right through his clothes, the same ground that was now swallowing Elizabeth Albano, and he could feel that unforgiving wind mingled with McVicar's hot breath on his face, and for the second or third time he saw that thick, fresh-shaven neck exposed, and this time he gave it a chop, not the lethal kind, but good enough. And McVicar choked and gagged and clutched his throat, and Villanova rolled on top and straddled him knees to shoulder-joints, and watched his face turn purple, and turned his own hot face to that cold wind and, panting, waited it out. And meanwhile a young woman came walking toward them from out of nowhere, a delicate Chinese student with a knapsack over her shoulder, and she gave them wide berth, and only stared a little, and went up the steps and disappeared into the library with a single backward glance. And as the oak door closed behind her, another roar came over the treetops, and this was a gathering, offensive roar, not a sudden deep strike in the air, but a ground breakout, a pitchout or a draw play that finds the hole in the secondary, and it struck Villanova what a bizarre and useless expertise it was to know these signs, and he realized that what he'd taken for his heartbeat was actually a drumbeat pulsing up from Coffey Field.   And his breathing slowly quieted, and McVicar's too, and then there was nothing but that tireless wind in the trees.   And he let McVicar up.

McVicar straightened his jacket and tugged down the sleeves.   "What're you going to do with it?" he said.

"I don't know."

"You show it to anyone yet?"

"Nope."

"Make a copy of it?"

"Nope."

McVicar took a read of his face.   "What is it you want?"

"The truth.   Aside from that, I don't give a shit whose work you put your name to or who finds out about it.   You and Hennessy and Robinson and the whole crew of you, you're all grave-robbers, as far as I'm concerned."

"You mean that?"

"I mean it.   What I care about is Elizabeth Albano and why on God's earth she loved *you,* and what happened between you two after she found *this* little treasure."   He gave a thump to the papers inside his jacket.

"And if I tell you?"

"If you tell me? If you satisfy me, you can *have* the fucking papers. I don't want them."

It was a rash proposition, but the contempt in his own voice was authentic enough for him. He saw it register with McVicar, too. The man thought it over. "How do I know I can trust you? How do I know you haven't made a copy, or talked to someone?"

"All you have is my word, pal."

McVicar sucked a lip and nodded. He looked unhappy. The knees of his corduroys were soiled, and he bent to brush them. "How much do you want to know?" There was resignation in his tone and the first faint overture of frankness.

"All of it."

"It's a long story."

"Talk fast. Come on, we'll walk. I'm supposed to be somewhere." He checked his watch.

"I've lost a button." McVicar's eyes were sweeping the ground.

"Never mind. Come on." But Villanova was reminded to check his own pockets. The tissue containing the gold chain was still in place.

The two men walked side by side toward the south gate. McVicar was quiet, palpably gathering himself for the piece of business to come.

"You better start," Villanova said.

McVicar nodded. "I never *meant* to plagiarize." He kept his eyes on the path in front of him as he spoke. "It all just fell into my lap. I was Eliot Robinson's T.A. over at Columbia, I was in his office with him every afternoon. He died in the library one day, and I had the job of cleaning out his desk. I found the draft of the Dimmesdale article, and I knew what it was. The guy used to confide in me. He was a real loner in the department, almost an outcast. You see, *that's* why I was in the rotten position I was in." He glanced over to be sure he was understood; he'd donned the white robe of candor and meant to give a first-rate show. "It wasn't *fair*, you understand? I'd gone out on a limb choosing Robinson for my thesis adviser. He was so preoccupied, I couldn't get my own dissertation off the ground. And then he died, and no one else wanted to touch me. I was *nowhere*...and all of a sudden I've got this Dimmesdale article in my hands that no one else knows about, just the one original draft."

"So you put your own name to it, and you published it."

McVicar shrugged. "I figured I'd have plenty of time to square it with my conscience down the line. I meant to settle accounts with my next book." He shook his head ruefully. "As it turned out, I lost sleep for years wondering if I'd get caught. Couldn't concentrate, couldn't write. Wouldn't you know, just when I'd begun to relax, a carbon copy of the article turns up? I didn't realize Robinson kept papers at home. Maybe I should have. He was a pack rat and a slob, both. I found a sandwich in his desk, five, ten years old. Peanut butter. It shattered on the floor like a clay tile." He glanced over grimly. "Bad luck, my whole problem was bad luck. Of all the people to find that carbon, it had to be Elizabeth."

"You should have expected it. She was training to be a scholar, and she was as thorough at it as she was supposed to be."

"No, no, it went beyond that. It was the *timing* that couldn't have been worse. Dean Hennessy had told me there was something in the works with the Robinson estate, but it looked to be months off, and I was sure I'd get first crack at whatever it was. I mean, the man was waving it at me like a carrot. Meanwhile my wife Jeanne arranged a little vacation for us at the end of July, sprung it on me, actually. The timing was *miserable*. I was real happy with Elizabeth then, both of us. I didn't want to go off to fucking Puerto Vallarta with Jeanne." He turned toward Villanova, his eyes full of appeal. "Some vacation. Blistering heat, nothing but stray dogs and peddlers on the beach, and a hotel full of jabbering Mexican families, and a little room with one crummy bed and this goddam needy woman with a suitcase full of lingerie..."

"Tell the truth, you bastard. Who do you think you're kidding?"

McVicar looked at him in surprise. "What do you mean?"

"Your wife was onto you and Elizabeth. Even I can see that. Jeanne isn't any dope, she knew about your affairs. She knew the women came and went. But *this* one was more dangerous than the others."

McVicar's brows went up; he pursed his lips and nodded. "It's true. Jeanne *had* got the scent. Still, what she decided to do about it couldn't work. I just gritted my teeth and sweated it out in Mexico. Ninety-five degrees every morning, a thunderstorm and third-rate mariachi music and Fredericks of Hollywood every afternoon." His voice turned sardonic. "I don't know how I made it through that week."

"And meanwhile the Robinson material arrived sooner than expected, and Liz went through it. She found the carbon copy."

"Exactly. I guess I'm lucky no one else in the department was as eager as she was."

"She confronted you when you got back home?"

McVicar nodded.

"What'd you tell her?"

"I had to tell it straight. She'd copped to it anyway. We had a huge fight over it, 'integrity,' 'trust,' all the bullshit. She stopped seeing me. I'd been missing her like hell for a whole week, and she dropped me, just like that. Said she was confused, needed time to think."

"What'd you do in the meantime?"

"Nothing. Suffered. What *could* I do? Believe me, it's hard to fall off a pedestal that high. Any pedestal." They were passing through the south gate now, and another one of those roars came over the trees from the east end of the campus. It was the biggest roar yet, the roar of real blood-letting, *touchdown*, the enemy speared and fallen, the war drums pounding. And big as it was, the clamor was met and swallowed by the bigger roaring of the busses and trucks on Fordham Road. To the west was the noisy business strip and behind it the graceful old concourse, and to the east was the crowded little Italy of Arthur Avenue and behind it the old boulevards of the Zoo, and dead ahead was the narrow-streeted Wedge teeming with its own predators and scavengers. And as the two men left behind the iron-gated campus and crossed the busy street onto Bathgate Avenue, the Jesuit garden and all its sounds and substance seemed to vanish into air.

"What happened when Elizabeth decided to blow the whistle on you?" Villanova said. "Why didn't the department head act on it?"

"Because Liz wouldn't give a reason why she wanted me off her committee."

"The girl was more loyal than you deserved."

"It wasn't all loyalty. Oh, I appreciate that she wasn't out to ruin me altogether, but the fact is, if she blew my secret and cost me my career, she'd have to start her work all over with a new mentor. And all her research was already tainted by its connection with mine. Not to mention that people knew she'd been my lover." McVicar shrugged, and an ironic smile played on his lips. "She was sort of where I was when Robinson died. In no-man's land."

"The only difference is, *you* put her there."

"That's so. And I was prepared to get her out. But first I had to win her back. I tried telling her how much I loved her. I *did* love her. I wanted her to steal that carbon copy and destroy it. I wanted her to stick with me all the way, let me get her through the program. Take care of each other, you know?" He shook his head. "No go. Liz wouldn't do what you and I did." He gave a touch to his jacket pocket. "That's where she stopped short." He sighed. "We'd've both been off the hook so easily."

"Why didn't you just steal the document yourself?"

"She wouldn't let me. She *knew* me, see? She was in that Archive every day, and every day she checked to make sure the carbon copy was still there. She knew that if it vanished, she'd be back in my power. She was ready to run screaming to Dean Hennessy the minute I signed for one of those Robinson cartons. I didn't even dare walk into the place, much less start hunting for the thing I had to swipe. I had to sweat it out. We *both* had to sweat it out." He sighed again. "That's where the T.A. appointments came in. That's why I got that Archive job for Dolores. I wanted someone on *my* side around those Robinson cartons. I was angry too because Liz had taken up with that artist guy. Jealous, I guess. It was tit for tat. Anyway, the Dolores thing backfired."

"It sure did."

"She turned out to be someone I had to be careful of."

McVicar had no idea how true that was. They were walking down the slope alongside JFK High School now, passing the receiving bay. A big, green-garbed man stood just outside the open doorway, his face tilted up to the wind and his arms slightly fanned as if he were waiting to be launched like a miniature blimp--it was Windy. Villanova nodded at him as he passed, but Windy's eye was on McVicar's back, and he stared and stared as they moved away.

"How did you handle the new boyfriend?   You make any noise?"

"I couldn't.   Liz shunned me completely all through August.   She left me to sit there, sweating out the decision she was cooking up on her own.   I knew just how vulnerable I was.   My academic reputation was like a big balloon ready to pop, and Liz had the pin.   The worst part is, the girl had a righteous streak in her, she was just the type to turn around and do what was 'right' even if it meant ruining herself.   Jesus, all she had to do was give one hint to Dean Hennessy.   In one instant I'd lose her, I'd lose my job, I'd lose the women that came with the job, I'd probably lose my wife too."

"What about this Hennessy guy?   Why's he hate you so much?"

McVicar's face darkened.   "Why?   Because he's a jealous sonofabitch.   Because he wanted Liz for himself."

"You telling me this priest was mixed up with the girl?"

"Not like that, no.   It was a spiritual thing, a friendship.   Hennessy has a thing for talented students.   He likes to play Merlin, he likes to unlock people, he's a real touchy-feely type.   The guy knew Liz before I did, they spent time together.   He was the one who pushed her into the doctoral program."

"And then you came along and seduced her.   That must've warmed his insides."

"It was half his own fault," McVicar protested.   "The guy goaded me.   Soon as I noticed her, he was right in my face.   'Uh-uh,' he says, 'this one isn't for you.   She's got too much class, too much brains.   She's going somewhere in this field.'   Then he pulls the Robinson material out of his hat for her, as if that settled the issue for good.   The sap didn't even realize I'd made her my lover meanwhile."

"When did he find out?"

"I don't know. But by the department party, he knew, I could tell. I could tell by the way he looked at her."

Villanova glanced over. "How's that?"

"As if she'd cut out his heart and stepped on it."

"And how was he looking at you?"

"The same way as always. As if I were walking filth. And that was the irony." An earnestness came into McVicar's voice. "Because the minute I saw Liz coming into that party with her new boyfriend, I knew that *she* was what I cared most about losing. I really *was* in love with her, and everything else was secondary." He met Villanova's eye and held it. "It was a new feeling for me in the history of my life, it kind of swept me off balance. But there it was. And I knew that this party was my chance to talk to her and make her see it. And after that she'd have no choice, she'd have to save me one way or the other, even if she didn't want to save herself."

There was that word again, the same one Newmark had used. Villanova looked at McVicar, and McVicar looked back, lips tight, eyes intense. "Go on," Villanova said.

"I sat in a corner and watched Liz and the artist guy put down a few sherries. I put down a couple more myself, and I watched Hennessy watch her. And just as I was about to go over, *she* came over to *me*. She sat down and asked how I was, and I asked her was she still thinking things over, and she said she was, and I made some lame comment about her orals coming up, and then do you know what she told me?" The brows arced up around those intense blue eyes. "She told me she was pregnant. She said she'd found out a few days ago."

"Ah. Then you lied to me about that. You knew."

"Sure. You knew I knew." His gaze locked with Villanova's for a moment, then moved beyond him up the sidewalk. "Say, where the hell are we going?" His eyes scanned the street uneasily. Eyes were looking back, from this doorway and that second-floor window. A group of young

Hispanics lounged on the corner outside the bodega that sported LeClerc's mural.

"My partner's waiting for me. It's just a few blocks."

"This isn't a good place to be walking."

"Not in a tweed jacket. But you'll be okay. Tell me what you did next. You must've swallowed a bit of air when Liz told you she was pregnant."

"Sure I did. But you know what?" He took a deep breath and let it out. "About a half-minute later, I got happy. I mean I got *happy*. It was the damndest thing, took me by complete surprise. You know, I always thought of a pregnancy as a bad thing. Jeanne couldn't have children, and it was one of the reasons I married her. And here all of a sudden I'm flushed with pleasure. My whole body's lighting up, I'm sitting on a sticky vinyl couch and I can actually feel the heat in my skin. And I'm trying to communicate to Liz. I'm tongue-tied with excitement. To me, suddenly it feels like destiny, like she's the one who's been singled out for me. Like it's the resolution to everything at once...the hand of God."

"What about Hennessy? Is he copping to any of this?"

"He *has* to be picking up something. He's all flushed, and I can see a bitterness in his eyes, a disgust, and in a way I'm glad because I'm feeling so goddamned relieved, so vindicated. I mean, I'm sitting there dizzy with hope, I'm telling Liz, 'I'll stick with you, we'll bring this child into the world....I love you, I'll go on loving you...' And she's got this expression in her eyes which is killing me, because it almost looks joyful, and I can see that she's still in love with me, and this artist guy is just some desperate prop, but underneath I see a black anger, a deep, terrible anger. And she says, 'What about your wife, damn it? What about *her*? Stop saying you love me. You don't love anyone. You love yourself!' And Hennessy's twenty feet away, and Dolores is scowling at me from across the room and looks like she's actually going to come over. And the artist guy is smirking. I tell her, 'I do love you, I don't care what you say,' and I tell her how we've got to stand fast and squelch that Robinson document and get her dissertation approved and have this child together, how it's all one. And she's holding her head as if it's going to split, and she's staring down at the carpet, and you know what she says to me? 'Have your child? I'd sooner have an abortion.'"

McVicar paused and looked over to see if Villanova was as shocked and hurt as he was. He was one hell of a performer. He was good enough to be telling the truth. Villanova kept silent. They were past the mural now and near the alley where LeClerc lived. A couple of half-starved tabbies watched from under the gloomy archway.

"I lost it when she said that," McVicar said quietly. I couldn't help it. 'What's your father going to say when he hears that?' I went back at her. Her eyes teared up. She looked up at me. There was such an expression on her face, a longing mixed with hatred. And she got up and walked away. 'What's your father going to say?' I called after her. Everyone heard me that time, but I didn't care. She gathered up her long-haired lover-boy and left, and I could see Hennessy glaring at her with that bitter expression, and I could see this triumphant look in Dolores' eye as she went past, cruel, a regular lioness, that one." He shook his head. "One brutal day. The hardest day of my life."

"But your brain was still working," Villanova said coolly. "A few days later, you paid a visit to Liz's house. You had a chat with her father when she wasn't around."

McVicar nodded. "I didn't tell him anything."

"You didn't have to. The message was for Elizabeth. The game is called blackmail."

"It was pressure, not blackmail. I didn't want her to have an abortion. I didn't want her to even consider it."

"Then you should've sent her roses, not threats."

"I tried that approach too. We met one more time in the music room to prepare for her orals. I was as sweet as I could be. I was full of promises. Liz was aloof. I could see she meant to make her decision on her own."

"That was a week ago Tuesday?"

"Right."

"You didn't see her after that?"

"No."

"Speak with her?"

"No. That was it." McVicar looked around again. There were men walking behind them; Villanova had sensed their presence since they'd passed the bodega. "I've told it to you straight," McVicar said quietly. "I don't think I ought to walk any further in here."

"Why so nervous?"

"I've got to walk out again, remember?"

"We'll take you out, if that's a problem."

"I'll take myself out. I think you ought to let me have those papers now. I think I've earned them."

"Not so fast. I've got one more good question for you." They were rounding the corner at 185th Street. There was a sector car double-parked halfway down the block, and behind it, Rizzo's battered Plymouth. A knot of people stood on the sidewalk in front of the Cruz tenement, and there were more across the street; two dozen surly faces turned toward the newcomers. Villanova said, "I want to know why you all of a sudden started hunting through the Archive on Tuesday morning. I mean, it was the next day that we knocked on your door and told you Elizabeth was dead. It would make more sense if you'd started your hunt on Wednesday."

McVicar's eyes had widened at the sight of the crowd on the street, but relief came into them with Villanova's question. "The hunt had nothing to do with Elizabeth," he said easily. "It had to do with Dolores. I was with her

Monday night.   And after we got done, she's lying there smoking a cigarette, and she tells me that Dean Hennessy had been in the Archive on Saturday going through the Robinson cartons. *That* finished me. Time was up. I had to find the damn carbon copy before Saturday rolled around again. I mean, it was just dumb luck that Hennessy hadn't already discovered it."

That remark stopped Villanova cold. It was the third time McVicar had used the word "luck." A dark premonition about Dean Hennessy gathered on the threshold of his thoughts...

"So I went to the Archive Tuesday morning, gambling that I could find the thing fast before Elizabeth got wise," McVicar said. He sighed with irony.   "After Wednesday morning, that particular danger was gone. But by Wednesday afternoon I'd been to the Archive three times in two days, and *Dolores* was starting to get curious. That was the last thing I needed, *her* finding the damn carbon. *She's* in the damn Archive four hours a day. I needed a solid block of time to hunt it out, but for me to cancel a class would have been waving a red flag at Dolores and Hennessy both." His voice rose a pitch.   "That's what I mean by the Dolores thing backfiring. She *could've* been a help, she could've let me get at the files without Liz knowing..." He stopped himself, and smoothed back his windswept curls. "There's quite a bit of the bitch in that one," he muttered. "Anyway, what it comes down to is, I had to quit running to the Archive before and after class, and wait for Saturday morning. I knew Hennessy never misses a football game. I did exactly what I had to do. You must have figured it out too. You were there waiting for me to come out."

"I sure was." But that wasn't because he was Einstein.

McVicar was smiling at their mutual cleverness. "Did you know, you can see part of Coffey Field from the Archive window?"

"That so?" Villanova was not amused. Even less charming was the way McVicar played the game of blurting out information he didn't have to give. That was the man's nervous response to pressure, Villanova decided, his weakness. When he was cornered, McVicar either lied or told the truth by impulse. The one thing he wasn't good at was shutting up at the right time. He was a talker, just like Hennessy, full of disarming quirks, sophistries, feints, conceits, petty calumnies....

They'd reached the little crowd on the sidewalk now. There were two uniformed cops standing at the top of the stoop, nestled in the entrance to the Cruz tenement. One recognized Villanova and gave a nod, the other was busy writing notes. The wind was fluttering the narrow pages of his notebook so violently, it looked as if he were trying to write on a captured pigeon.

"Tell you one thing: I'm lucky Dolores didn't catch on," McVicar said. "She's a dirty player. If *she'd* found the article...from the frying pan into the fire, you know?"

"You're not as smart as you think," Villanova told him drily. He called to the cop who'd greeted him, "Rizzo upstairs?"

"Third floor."

"You're not smart, but you *are* lucky. You're going to get to bury your stolen document and your pregnant girlfriend on the same morning."

McVicar glared at him. "You want me to feel guilty? You want to rub my face in it? That wasn't part of our deal. That's between me and me. Just give me my papers and let me out of here."

"Satisfaction was *my* end of the deal.   You're damn right I want to rub your face in it.   You know where we are? See this building? This is where your girlfriend died. This is where her life ended four days ago, up in one of these rooms, while you were busy looking for your goddamned article. See those faces in the windows across the street?   They're angry, and scared. They don't know the whole story, but they know a young girl died somewhere in this neighborhood, and some creep that's still walking around is to blame, and they know we're looking for him. See those guys on the other side of the street, and those guys up the corner? They're husbands and brothers and boyfriends. They want to get their hands on somebody. You better hope they don't smell blood on *you*."

"Fuck you and your games!" McVicar snapped back. "I'm finished. You've *had* your satisfaction. Keep your word, hand the article over."

"You're finished? You lied, you bastard. You told me you didn't speak to Elizabeth after your last conference.   I know you did. She phoned you at home Tuesday morning at 11:27. She canceled her noon appointment with you."

McVicar stared at him. The wind whipped the tails of his jacket and brought tears from the corners of his eyes.

"You think you're finished?" Villanova said. "Go talk your way back to Fordham Road." He turned and climbed the steps, passed between the cops into the building, and started up the dim, sour-scented stairway.

- FOURTEEN -

Except for the drone of game shows from Tina Marinelli's TV, the stairwell was quieter than usual as Helen made her way down toward the street. The cop she expected to see lounging in the vestibule was strangely absent, though the precinct car sat dumbly at the curb. She threw her head outside for a quick look, decided that his vanishing was portent enough, and withdrew toward the basement door.

Bang! She flung it back like some street tough, her ritual, and made herself go down into the gloom like a woman in a hurry, a busy grown-up in nurse's whites. Through the dimness she marched toward the far wall, every step a brisk exorcism. There, the washing machine, there, the full laundry basket, the work she'd left undone. She lifted the cool enameled lid, dug her hands into the damp garments and stuffed them one by one into the opening. Should she start the machine now, or wait...?

Something moved in the back.

So.

She stood and faced that blackness. She was small as women went, she realized, not much larger than some children. And she'd begun to tremble, to her disgust. But she had lungs, a voice. *"Who are you, you shit!"* she called. "There's a cop car right outside!"

Another movement, stealthy, near the freezer.   And then the soft glow of eyes, watching her, small and greenish.

"Mirabel!" Her breath came out in a jagged sigh.

And she groped into the gloom.

* * *

The tenement was darker inside than Villanova remembered. He'd barely begun climbing the stairway when he heard McVicar scuttling in after him.

"What the hell more do you want from me?" the man cried the moment the street door had swung shut behind him. "Liz phoned and canceled, that's right.   But so what? Everything I said is true."

"'*So what?*'"   Villanova mounted the steps with a determined tread. "With Hennessy breathing down your neck, the Tuesday conference was your last chance to win Liz over. There's got to be more to it than so what."

McVicar came clambering up behind him. "All right, sure I was disappointed when she canceled. The thing is, I'd given it a lot of thought, see, I'd come up with a plan. Can't you wait and listen to me a minute, for Christ sake?" He slowed, and kept silent until Villanova slowed too and turned to look back at his face. "I had my ace in the hole. I was ready to tell Liz that I was leaving my wife, that I wanted to be with her, baby or no baby. I meant it." There was a half-convincing glow in the man's eyes. "I was sure that would fix things. I figured Tuesday was going to be the turnaround, the end of my torture."

Villanova turned and kept climbing. Torture was the precise direction of his instinct, and he didn't mean to fight it. "You must've been damned upset, then, when she canceled. What'd you say to her?"

"Not much. My wife was standing right there. I hung up the phone and put my jacket on and went out to try to catch Liz before she left Mount Saint Mary's. It's only a few blocks down Marion Avenue, up on Bedford Park Boulevard. I ran all the way."

"Go on." He took the blind turns in the stairway one after the next, remembering how frightened Elizabeth must have been going up, and Manny coming down, dragging the dead weight of that trunk. The anger was all fresh and whole, and so much for a rose tossed into an open grave.

"When I hit Bedford Park, I spotted her about a block ahead of me already, walking down the hill toward the campus. I was out of breath. I called to her, but there was a truck climbing the hill and she didn't hear." Even now, as they neared the third landing, McVicar was breathing heavily. "I started after her, but I got this pain in my chest. It was frightening. I thought I was having a heart seizure or something. I had to slow up. But I kept her in sight."

"You followed her?"

"Yes. Through the north gate, onto the campus."

Villanova's heart was thumping away too. "And did you catch up to her?" He rounded the last turn and gave a start. There was a man standing in the shadows on the landing, dark-garbed, just two eyes staring. "Who the hell're you?"

"The Super."

Villanova took a close look. It was the same young Hispanic he'd talked to two days before, with the same mop of curly hair. "What the hell are you doing here?" Villanova said.

"Your partner put me out here, man." Muffled voices came from within the Cruz apartment; the intonations were Spanish.

"He put you right outside the door?" Meanwhile McVicar had come up behind him, breathing noisily.

The Super shrugged. "My *cousin* told me wait by the door. She's in a mood, she got her period or something." He gave a disgusted look. "I guy like me can't win. You do people a favor, you make a nice surprise for them--what for? Carpeting, she wants. Where she grew up, they had dirt floors."

Villanova turned the knob and entered the apartment, with McVicar trailing. The voices echoed off the bare walls and floors as they passed the kitchen and bathroom and entered the larger of the two back rooms. There were three people standing in the center of the room, but only one face, as Rizzo came forward blotting out everything behind him with the intensity of his glare. "What the fuck?" he growled at Villanova, making an angry gesture in McVicar's direction.

"Leave it be," Villanova growled back.

"What the hell have you been up to!"

"Nothing."

"Nothing? Why's the side of your face purple?"

"Leave it be!" Villanova repeated, and he caught Rizzo's eye and held it until he was understood.

Rizzo shifted to a frustrated tone. "I told you to get right over here. I've got two people here who barely speak English, and the world's biggest chatterbox in the bathroom." Over Rizzo's shoulder Villanova could see a young Hispanic couple, the girl pretty and wide-eyed, the man tall and mustachioed and very dark. There were suitcases and carry-alls at their feet.

"Where's Arcario?"

"With the Hostage Squad over on Crotona Avenue. Some nut case is holed up with his ex-wife."

"This the niece, here, Margarita?"

"Right. And the bridegroom. Freddie. Doesn't know up from down in English."

"Look," McVicar spoke up, "I don't think I should be here."

"Damn right!" Rizzo said.

"Why not just get done with me, then...?"

"Keep your shirt on, you invited yourself up here," Villanova barked at him.

The newlyweds began talking again, in a nasal, high-pitched, nervously rapid speech that echoed harshly in the small space. McVicar, contempt and frustration in his eyes, drew back a few steps toward the window.

"What the hell're you doing?" Rizzo whispered to Villanova. "Didn't you screw things up enough with this guy?"

"The bastard's getting off too easy. He played his part in this, he's not going to just scoot away from the wreckage."

Rizzo's eyes grew sad. "Buddy, let it go. What happened was a long time ago. It won't work to try to take it out of this sap here."

"What are you talking about?"

"You know what I'm talking about."

Villanova looked at Rizzo. He'd thought he knew all there was in him. Rizzo looked back, his eyes bloodshot. Both men were preposterously tired. The newlyweds rattled away. "What'd you get from the girl's aunt?" Villanova said. "You talk to her yet?"

Rizzo nodded. "She speaks English. She's pretty co-operative."

"Does she know what we're after?"

"Not yet. That's why I kept the Super outside. I don't know how much *he* knows, but I don't like them yakking in Spanish. If Maria catches wise this is a murder inves-tigation..."

"You didn't tell her about Julia, did you?"

Rizzo shook his head. "They think Julia ran out on the rent and they lucked into an apartment. All I asked about was Tuesday morning. Maria says she was sitting on her stoop waiting for the airport van. She saw Julia, called to her, saw her come into the building here. A few minutes later the van pulled up, and off she went to Puerto Rico. And that's it."

"She didn't see Elizabeth?"

"Nope."

"Too bad. What about Manny?"

"She saw him go into the building a little while before the van came. We'll check on the time with the limo company."

"Is she sure she didn't see Elizabeth?"

"She's positive. She's a sharp-eyed gal. A neighborhood busybody, you know? Now she's tickled pink her niece'll be setting up house right across the street."

"Why'd she come back from Puerto Rico after only four days? What'd she go there for?"

"The honeymoon. The niece got married on Sunday over in St. Barnabas, and they all went back to the old village, the aunt too. The niece wanted her there."

"On her honeymoon? The *niece* said that?"

Rizzo shrugged. "That's what *you're* here for, Buddy. Me, I only speak one language."

A toilet flushed a few feet away, with a violent roar and gurgle. The newlyweds fell silent, and there was a moment of queer uncertainty as all eyes turned toward the foyer. Seconds later, a woman came bustling out of the bathroom, plump, dark, middle-aged, with a bulging cloth valise hanging from the crook of one arm. She called over her shoulder toward the hallway door, "What's the matter with you, Jaime? Toilet paper!" As she turned into the living room, Villanova saw a plain, swarthy woman with a broad smile and a nickel-sized mole on one cheek. She paused in the mouth of the hallway, her clear, dark eyes taking in the newcomers.

Rizzo introduced her to Villanova, and she shook his hand, apologizing for her moist palm. Rizzo said, "Will you help us now to ask your niece a few questions?" He'd evidently done a good job winning her trust, because she seemed reasonably open in spite of the uniformed cops down below. She turned to Margarita and rattled something in Spanish about making curtains for the bathroom window.

"Jesus, do I have to listen to this?" McVicar spoke up from across the room. His face had a dark, stricken look. "Can't they speak English?"

"Don't worry, no one's talking about you," Villanova said.

"For Christ sake, why not finish with me and get me out of here?"

"You eager? You can wait awhile, it'll do you good."

"Let him wait in the street," Rizzo said.

"You haven't seen what's in the street."

Rizzo turned to McVicar and grumbled, "Wait in the other room, then, if these people bother you so much."

Villanova noted with pleasure the cornered look that came over McVicar's face when those words were spoken, and McVicar noticed him notice. "Fine," he muttered. He held Villanova's eye defiantly. "We still have a deal, don't we?"

"A deal's a deal. Just keep your end of it."

McVicar withdrew into the back bedroom and pushed the door closed behind him.

Maria had begun to talk in English, but Villanova missed some of what she said because his eyes were on that bedroom door. There was something so uncannily familiar about the way McVicar had swung it behind him...then he remembered the way the bedroom door had shut behind McVicar and his wife in their own apartment three days earlier, and the way Rizzo and he had stood by talking. He shot a glance toward Rizzo, but he was all ears for Maria.

She was yakking about Margarita and Freddie, what a romantic courtship they'd had, how they'd grown up in Puerto Rico as next-door neighbors and friends, how they'd come to

New York separately to make a better life for themselves, how they'd met again by chance at a social club only two months ago; how quickly they'd fallen in love, how eager they were now to make a place for themselves in the world, to have babies, to work, to build...

Maria was a talker, all right, and yet the story suited Villanova; it reminded him of the tale of his own grandparents, who'd been teenagers when they'd voyaged into a new life. He took a good look at the newlyweds while Maria chattered on.   Margarita had a fine, expressive face, not delicate but full of dignity and an unhardened kind of maturity.   Freddie, his brows and moustache a thick black against his golden skin, had a serene sort of quietude and a protective posture.   He'd been holding Margarita's hand undemonstratively the whole while.   The two were obviously in love.

After a polite minute or two, Rizzo interrupted Maria and started with the questions.   He explained to her exactly what he needed to know about Elizabeth Albano and Julia Cruz.

Maria nodded and drew nearer to Margarita.   After a few rounds of discourse with her in Spanish, punctuated by gestures, she turned back, ready to recapitulate: "On the first night of class, the Wednesday of last week, Margarita could see that the teacher was not feeling well.   She could see her putting her hand to her head."   Maria put her hand to her temple the way Margarita had done.   "She felt sorry for her. She was only a girl her own age, and she was so nice, so pretty, too.   So Margarita went to her when the class took a recess. She wanted to tell her she was going to get married and miss a class.   The teacher was very happy for Margarita.   She even promised her a wedding gift, something small but special.   She talked to her like a friend.   So Margarita asked her if her head was hurting her."

Rizzo glanced over to Villanova, and Villanova gave him a nod; the translation jibed with his own rudimentary understanding.   Margarita was nodding also, and she broke in with another string of recollections in Spanish.

"Margarita told the teacher that her aunt knew a woman, a healer, who could cure pains that no one else could cure.   The woman did this without medicine, just with her hands.   She charged only thirty-five dollars, and she lived just a few blocks away.   The teacher seemed interested.   Margarita was surprised.   She thought maybe she would be laughed at.   But the teacher said, 'You've given me a hope,' and her eyes were very warm, very thankful.   She asked Margarita for the telephone number."

"Did Margarita give her the number?" Rizzo said.

"Margarita didn't know it.   But she gave her the name and the address, 185th Street, the third building on the right."

"Good.   Then what?"

After another exchange with her niece, Maria turned to Rizzo and said: "The teacher went to use the telephone in the hall.   Margarita went down the stairs to find the janitor.   Because before the class started, she saw the mop and pail outside the bathroom.   So that's why she went down, to find Julia's son, to tell him the teacher needed to see his mother.   She wanted to do something more to help, you see?"

Rizzo and Villanova exchanged a glance.   "Did she find him?" Rizzo said.

"Yes, mopping the stairs.   She told him the teacher needed him, and he got angry but he came up the stairs with her.   Margarita pointed to the teacher in the phone booth.   It's old-fashioned, a closet with glass in the door.   He went closer and looked.   Then he turned around and walked away, right past her.   He went down the stairs to the basement.   He left the mop and the pail on the stairs."

"He was still angry when he walked past her?"

Maria relayed the question to Margarita. "Not angry. Upset."

"Did he see the teacher's face in the phone booth?"

"Yes."

"What about the teacher? Did she see him?"

"No. She was talking on the phone."

Villanova spoke up: "Did Margarita talk to the teacher afterward? Does she know who the teacher was phoning?"

The answer came back: "She was phoning the operator. To get Julia's telephone number. But the number was not working. But Margarita told the teacher, 'Don't worry, you could go there without calling. The third floor, in the back.'"

Villanova nodded. "Please ask your niece, did she see Julia's son in the building again after he went down to the basement?"

The answer was no. "The teacher let the class out early. After the recess, she gave an assignment and sent them home. Margarita did the assignment, she has it in her bag. Do you want to see it?"

Villanova shook his head. He was out of questions. He and Rizzo took a long look at each other. Maria and Margarita began to speak quietly in Spanish. Freddie's eyes moved from one uneasy face to the other. Rizzo stepped away from the group and, with a motion of his head, led Villanova into the narrow foyer. Villanova heard Margarita ask her aunt whether something bad had happened to the teacher.

"What do you think, Buddy?" Rizzo said once they were out of earshot.

"You were missing something, and now you've got it."

"Motive."

Villanova nodded. "According to your shrink Daphne, all it takes to trigger someone like Manny is a breach between fantasy life and real life. The girl in the mural turned up in the flesh someplace where she wasn't supposed to be, right? Well, that was enough to set him off. That's motive."

Rizzo rubbed his jaw. "I wonder why he didn't attack her as soon as he saw her in the phone booth, or at least stalk her? Why'd he punch the timeclock, quit his job, and run for home instead?"

Villanova shrugged. "It's weird. He must have felt the anger starting and gone into some kind of panic. Just pulled away, didn't want to know she was there. It's as if he was trying to escape what he was going to do...as if he could sense a trap closing, you know?"

"Jesus," Rizzo said. "You're giving me the shivers."

"I'm giving myself the shivers." He could practically feel Manny's fatalistic terror at the sight of that beautiful girl on the other side of the glass pane.

"What about the Iglesiases? Should we tell them what this is about?"

"They're going to find out pretty soon. It would be better coming from us."

"You want to handle it, Buddy?"

"Uh-uh, this one's yours. I've got to finish with McVicar. Give it to them slow. You better tell them about Julia, too. I mean, if those kids think they want to live in this apartment...newlyweds are pretty superstitious. I don't blame them."

"The Super's gonna love us for this."

"That's his problem. And listen. Go easy when you tell Margarita about that crystal heart."

"Christ. Maybe I just won't mention it."

"You should. It's the one thing that might make her feel better."

They went back into the big room. Maria and her niece were still talking. Maria turned toward Rizzo, her expression wary.   Rizzo's face colored and stiffened. Villanova left them to each other and pushed into the back bedroom.

McVicar stood at the window, hands hanging at his sides. He looked round briefly when Villanova came in, his face sullen, then turned back to the window. There were bars across the sash, Villanova recalled. He closed the door behind him and came up alongside. The wind whistled around the casement, three or four different pitches all combined. He peered through the blinds. The midday light threw a whitish glow on LeClerc's mural. Elizabeth Albano's gaze was as deep and disturbing as ever.

McVicar turned to him. "Let's get this done with." His eyes were troubled, but there was recrimination in them too.

Villanova felt bad for him suddenly. His heart was no longer in this game. "Fine," he said with a sham brusqueness. "You followed the girl onto the campus, you said."

"That's what I said."

"Then what?"

"She went past the Campus Center and the music room. She went right toward Dealy Hall."

"Go on."

"I got scared. *You* know what I thought."

"Sure. You thought she was on her way to see Dean Hennessy. You thought *that's* why she canceled her appointment with you."

McVicar nodded drily. He seemed to have lost his appetite for dramatic poses. "I started to run after her again. I knew I had to catch her, tell her what I was willing to do. It was all or nothing. Right there."

"Did you catch her?"

"I didn't have to. She went past Dealy Hall, didn't even slow down. There it was--I was off the hook."

"Just like that?"

"Just like that." The voice was flat. "I stayed behind her a little further. She headed for the Bathgate Avenue gate. I watched her go off campus. I was still upset, I stood there a few minutes watching after her. But then I realized what I had to do. This was my opportunity. I headed over to the Archive. I knew Liz wouldn't be there."

Villanova nodded. "That's it?"

"That's all. You see, you didn't have to shut me in here for that."

"What'd you do in the Archive?"

"Looked through a couple of the Robinson cartons. Then I went to teach a class."

From beyond the door, the sound of voices easily penetrated into the room, but Villanova made an effort not to hear the words. He felt a bit cornered himself. The role of tormentor didn't suit him; a little inquisition went a long way with him. "What class did you teach?" he said.

"The Hawthorne seminar. I gave a lecture on Pearl, the love child."

"Why that?"

"It was the next thing on my syllabus. I'm a professional, after all."

"You're a hack." There was no real edge to the insult. McVicar recognized it as gratuitous too and, with a tilt of his head, allowed it. Villanova reached inside his jacket and pulled out the onionskin pages. "These mean a hell of a lot to you," he said.

McVicar eyed him warily. "It's not hard to understand, not for an academic, anyway. The less you have, the more it means to you." He was trying not to look at the pages.

Villanova had no wish to wave the bait. A revulsion came over him as he realized how little these flimsy sheets were actually worth. "Go ahead, take them," he said. "I'm done."

McVicar took the pages. He flipped through the sheaf, then withdrew his own pages and re-united the article. "It isn't much, is it?" he said. "Maybe you're right, all of us are hacks. All we have is scraps, and so we fight over them. Half my colleagues are frustrated novelists, including Hennessy. They don't have the guts to create out of their *own* lives..." He stopped himself. "Me too. I'm no better."

"Get the hell out of here before you break my heart. Go wait in the hallway with the Super."

There was a knock at the door then, and Rizzo pushed in. Maria stood in the doorway behind him. "There's a problem here," he said, his brow furrowed.

"Did you tell her?"

"Listen. Maria thought this guy here was one of us."

"What?"

"She says she's seen him before. She says she's seen him *here*."

There was a silence, not very long, but in that small space Villanova felt all of reality shift a few centimeters. Rizzo stood aside, and Maria filled up the doorframe. She was staring at McVicar and nodding.

McVicar looked back. His gaze was level, but that dark color had gone out of his face. "She's mistaken," he said.

Maria shook her head. "It's the same man," she said. "He had on the same jacket."

"She's mistaken," McVicar repeated calmly. His face was taut.

"Wait a minute," Villanova said, turning to Maria. "*When* did you see this man?"

"Tuesday. I came down with my suitcase and sat down on the stoop. This man was standing on the sidewalk. It's the same man, I'm sure. The same voice, everything."

"He spoke to you?"

She nodded. "He asked me was there a doctor across the street. He pointed to this building and said was there a doctor? I said yes, a healer."

Villanova and Rizzo exchanged a look. McVicar stood making no response except to shake his head. "Then what?" Villanova said.

"He said, does this healer do away with babies? And I said, she can make babies come and she can make babies go away. She's the best, she can do anything."

"What more?"

"No more. He went across the street. He went into the building."

"He went *in*? You saw him come into this building?"

She nodded.

Villanova glanced at McVicar, who was still shaking his head. Rizzo said to Maria, "Did you see him come out again?"

She nodded again.

"She's out of her mind," McVicar spoke up with some force, and he gave a shrug of his shoulders.

"Quiet," Villanova said. "You saw him come out, Maria? How much later?"

"Five minutes, ten. He came out another building. Two doors over. That's when I thought maybe he was a cop. You know how they go over the roof. I thought maybe I did something stupid, trying to get Julia a customer."

"Did you talk to him again?" Rizzo said.

"He went in the other direction, to Park Avenue. The van was late, I didn't want to miss the airplane. I was looking down the street every minute. Then I saw Julia's son walking on the other side, like I told you. I looked the other way until he went in. He's a bad one, that Manny, I don't talk to him."

"And then you saw Julia?"

"Yes, a few minutes later. I called to her. I wanted to tell her about the man in the jacket. But she waved, she kept going, in a hurry. She went inside. And I saw the van turning at the corner. So I got up and took my suitcase. I got in the van."

There was a silence. The wind moaned and rattled at the window. Villanova looked at Rizzo's pent and rigid face. He felt that cosmic shift again, and this time five or six elements dropped into place. He turned to McVicar. "You followed her," he said. "You followed her here."

"No. I'm telling you, I..."

"It's clear as day. There's no *point* in denying it."

"No," McVicar said simply.

"You followed her. *That's* why you were so damn nervous walking down Bathgate with me. You were afraid somebody would recognize you."

"Somebody did," Rizzo put in gruffly. "You ought to get yourself a new jacket, pal."

Villanova signaled him to stay quiet, but Rizzo returned the signal with a scowl. His face had turned a deep, morbid shade. "This isn't any tea party. A girl got murdered in this room."

Maria let out a gasp. She sagged back out of the doorway. An instant later Margarita and Freddie were on either side of her. A braid of high-pitched Spanish sprung up from the three.

Rizzo looked furious with them, with McVicar, with Villanova, and mostly with himself. He gave the door a push, and it swung closed.

Villanova signaled him again to lay back. "*Why'd* you follow Elizabeth?" he said to McVicar. "What did you have in your mind?"

"There's no law against following someone," McVicar retorted with sudden pique. "I knew something was going on, something strange. The way she was behaving...all my instincts told me to watch what she was up to. I did what anyone would do." He stared peevishly from one face to the other. "I stayed half a block behind her. I saw her turn in some kind of alley. Got close enough to hear her arguing with that artist boyfriend of hers on the doorstep. I figured *that* was it."

"But it wasn't."

"No. It turned out he wouldn't go with her somewhere, and off she went again. I stayed behind her, trying figure it all out. It looked like she was heading for St. Barnabas Hospital. Then something clicked...I knew there was an abortion clinic in the Wedge, somewhere near the hospital. *Now* it all made sense."

"Ah, I get it," Villanova said with grim satisfaction. "It was your nightmare come true."

The conversation in the other room rose in volume. A new voice mixed in with the other three. "Son-of-a-bitch, that's the Super!" Rizzo muttered.

"What happened when Liz turned down 185th?"

"I got round the corner just in time to see her come in this building." McVicar's eyes had settled on Villanova's; there was candor and an undertone of appeal in his voice. "I stood across the street, going crazy. My hands were shaking. I stood there five, ten minutes..."

"You see anyone come out?"

"A couple of kids. And a guy, a creepy-looking guy..."

"With long hair?"

"Yes, long hair."

"Did you see his face?" Rizzo put in. "Could you identify him?"

"Yes, I think so."

"What then?" Villanova said.

"That woman," he motioned toward the other room, "came out of a tenement with a suitcase and sat down on the steps about twenty feet away. I asked her about the doctor, like she said. She told me the third floor, in the back."

"So you went into the building?"

The voices in the other room spread out and rose again. McVicar eyed the door nervously. Rizzo muttered uneasily to Villanova, "Sounds like someone's shouting down the stairs."

"I don't like this," McVicar said; for all his talk, he had yet to disclose a single thing they hadn't already discovered.

"Where are those clowns in uniform?" Rizzo pulled the door open. Maria and Margarita were alone in the center of the big room. Both faces turned wide-eyed and ashen toward Rizzo. Voices rang up and down the stairway.

"Better calm them down," Villanova said. "There's a riot cooking in the street."

"What about this guy?"

"He's not going anywhere, don't worry." For the third time Villanova signaled his partner.

Rizzo looked bitter, anxious, and confused all at once. "Wait on me," he said, and he went out of the room and pulled the door nearly closed behind him. A few seconds later, his voice had joined the shouting in the stairwell.

"You went into the building?" Villanova repeated to McVicar.

McVicar shook his head. He looked frankly frightened now. "I'm not saying more. I think it's time I had a lawyer."

"You want a lawyer?" Villanova snapped. "Go get one."

"Don't be cute."

"I'm not being cute."

There was a sudden brittle *whack!* and the plash of raining glass--something had hit the window. Both men stiffened, and Villanova made a quick move to the side of the casement and peeked through the blinds: a half-dozen grim-eyed youths stood in the alleyway at the foot of the mural, looking up.

"They're shooting?" McVicar said in a voice close to wavering.

"It was a rock. Want to look?"

McVicar came beside him and peeked through the blinds. His face was wholly pale now. "You better get me out of here," he said.

"I'm no cop. If I get anyone out, it's gonna be me."

"Are you serious? What about me?"

"You're gonna keep talking, dammit. You tell the truth, and I'll do what I can to get us both out."

More shouts rose up from the stairwell.

"Let's have it, pal. You came into the building on Tuesday, like Maria said?"

McVicar's eyes darted around the room as if searching for an exit.

"Let's have it, dammit!"

The man nodded weakly.

"Then what?"

"I came up the stairs. Third floor rear. I knocked on the door." His frightened eyes met Villanova's. "Whatever was going on inside, I wanted to stop it. I figured it was some kind of New Age hocus-pocus, you know, something that artist boyfriend put her up to. I gave the door a thumping. No one answered. They were being cagy, I thought. I tried the knob, and the door opened...." He paused.

"You came inside," Villanova said.

McVicar nodded. "The place was deserted. Little statues of saints all over. I called Liz's name. Nothing. My heart was pounding, I had this taste in my mouth, like metal. I looked around. The door to this room was shut. I opened it."

His eyes held Villanova's. He was searching for something, some bizarre form of sympathy. "Go on," Villanova said.

"She was lying on the bed, on her back. She was dead."

Villanova watched him.

"I didn't realize it at first. I stood over her. She looked as if she'd just gone to sleep. I touched her, tried to wake her up. That's when I saw that she wasn't breathing. I realized all of a sudden why the apartment was empty. They'd botched things...given her a drug or something, given her too much, then run off and left her dead. My mind was confused, see, locked onto this abortion thing..."

"You're saying she was dead when you found her?"

McVicar nodded.

Villanova's eyes narrowed. There was an odd, gathering sensation in his chest. The universe made its final shift, and the rest of the tumblers fell into a neat line. "That's great. That solves the whole damn thing. The only problem is, you're lying."

The flatness of the accusation seemed to take McVicar by surprise. He tried for a frown of injury, but that pleading look in his eye washed it all away.

"If she was dead, you'd have run screaming for help. You'd have tried phoning the police, you'd have knocked on a door, you'd have knelt down and cried. You'd have done anything but sneak away over the rooftop and go teach a class on Hawthorne."

McVicar was shaking his head. "I was scared. Think about it: I was in a position to be incriminated..."

"Bullshit. If some quacks killed your girl, *they'd* be in deep shit, not you. You'd be home free. *That* was the only way to think of it at the time."

McVicar's eyes went on protesting, but he fell silent. Maria's voice echoed in the outer room, punctuated by Margarita's softer tones. Voices rose up from the alley too, now, sharp and angry.

"She wasn't dead when you found her."

Exhaustion gathered behind the protest in McVicar's eyes; his face seemed suddenly drawn and aged. "For God's sake, why don't you get some cops up here!" he cried out. "Why don't you call in for more men!"

"She wasn't dead when you found her," Villanova repeated in a voice unyielding as iron.

At last something crumpled in McVicar's face. With a tremor, the resistance let go, and the fear and shame blossomed on his features. The onionskin pages rustled in his trembling hand. "I *thought* she was dead," he said in a hushed voice.

Villanova nodded.

McVicar looked around the little room, as if remembering where the furnishings stood, where things hung on the wall. "I swear she wasn't breathing. I couldn't see any sign of it." His voice was quiet and labored. "She must've been unconscious, comatose. I stood over her...I was scared to pieces." He looked at Villanova, and there was a torment there unlike any Villanova had ever seen. "*That's* when the awful thought came to me."

"What thought is that?"

"The thought that it was *better* that she was dead. That it was a bizarre piece of luck...that in a way I had wished it."

Villanova studied him. This was the suitor who, minutes earlier, had been ready to leave his wife and do battle to save his unborn child.

But there was no room for irony on McVicar's suffering face. "That's when her eyes opened," he said, and finally sorrow and surrender seeped into his voice. "Just a crack." His gaze moved toward the corner of the room where the bed had been. "And she looked at me standing over her... she recognized me." His voice caught. He swallowed. His white-knuckled hand clutched the pages so tightly it seemed deformed. "And there was such a look in her eyes, such an *accusing* look...as if *I* had done this, as if *I* had taken her life...to save myself..." The wind, whistling around the window, buffeted the panes insistently; the voices in the other room had dropped to a low, mournful pitch. "I couldn't bear it. *I couldn't bear it.*"

"You picked up the pillow," Villanova said.

McVicar stared at him. For the first time in his life he didn't seem to know what words would come out of his mouth. His eyes ached for relief. He nodded slowly.

"You put it over her face."

"Yes."

"It was easy."

"No," McVicar said softly. "It was hard. It was the hardest thing I've ever done. She didn't move, at first...but then...at the end...she tried to push it away. Weakly, like a child..."

A sudden scream came from the other room. Villanova started, and McVicar staggered backward a step. "What was that?" he said, his eyes wide.

The hairs had stood up on Villanova's neck. "Someone just broke it to that young girl out there what happened to her teacher."

There were more shouts in the stairwell, and more clamor in the alley. McVicar no longer reacted to them. It was as if he was past being frightened, past any form of terror...as if the scream had pushed him over a boundary into someplace free and desolate. His hands had stopped trembling. The insides were gone out of him.

"You put the pillow back when you were done?" Villanova said.

McVicar nodded.

"Went up to the roof, over, and down?"

"I didn't want that woman to see me again."

"You walked up Park Avenue to the west gate of the campus?"

"Yes."

"What about the Archive? You wouldn't have had time for that if you had a class to teach."

"I went there after class, at 4:10. I signed myself into the ledger from noon to one o'clock. I'd had time to think. I knew it would be smart to cover myself."

"You told Dolores what was up?"

"I just asked her to look the other way. No questions asked."

"Charming."

"I guess I got her in trouble."

"You're in trouble too. You're going to jail."

McVicar stared dumbly.

"Don't feel bad about Dolores. She fucked you pretty good too. You fucked each other."

"I guess we did."

"How'd you manage to teach a class right after what you did?"

A trace of life came back to McVicar's voice. "It was the weirdest thing. It turned out to be the best class I ever gave in my life. I don't know how I did it...it still mystifies me. I mean, the students hung on every word. I was, like, *inspired.*"

"Hysterical is more like it. You know, you could learn a lot from your own book."

"I spotted Dean Hennessy on my way out of class. I actually went out of my way to say hello to the man."

"You did? Tell me something. Is it true, what you told me about him? His interest in the girl, and all?"

McVicar nodded. "All but one thing."

"What thing is that?"

"The part about him goading me. It was what he did *after* I got started with Liz that goaded me. He tried to get her away from me, to 'save' her from me, you know? Save her immortal soul."

"You sure he didn't want to save her for something else? I heard a story about him..."

McVicar shook his head. "It's gossip. I started the story myself, years back, and it stuck."

"*You* did? Why?"

"Like I said. He thought he had to save any girl I took to bed. He thought he had to cancel me, just because he'd hired me. It was an ongoing insult, a mutual one."

"The man knew you were a fraud. He wanted you to know it too."

"He wanted it to *eat* at me. That's his style. He's always giving people chances to 'redeem' themselves, setting up moral tests for them and then watching over their shoulders. It's diabolic...sadistic. There's a reason why the gossip stuck."

Villanova frowned. That earlier premoniton about Hennessy solidified suddenly into suspicion, and the dark, ugly bulk of it pressed away his breath. He struggled to think clearly. "It's a shame you and Hennessy didn't just leave the students out of your games," he muttered.

McVicar accepted the reproach with hollow eyes. He let out a long, low sigh. "It's hard to believe, now, what I did," he said. When I think about it, it doesn't feel like me who stood in this room with that pillow. It doesn't feel like me standing here right now telling you about it."

"It's you, all right. Both times."

"I can't get hold of it," McVicar said. Those hollow eyes of his drifted across the room and settled on the door. "What happens now? You going to get me out of here like you said?"

Villanova went to the door and pulled it open. Rizzo was on the other side of it. "You heard?"

"I heard. It's on the record." Maria and her niece were in the far corner of the room, rocking in each other's arms. The others were gone.

"What's going on?" McVicar said.

"Nothing much. We don't scare as easy as you do, that's all. We got a court case to think about."

McVicar's brow furrowed, and then some of the keenness crept back into his eyes.   "You guys are pretty smart."

"You're not the only smart guy around," Villanova said. Rizzo was trying to hold his eye, to close the truce with him, but Villanova's gaze was on Margarita's tear-streaked face.   Everything horrible, wrong, and irremediable about Elizabeth Albano's death was written on that frank, childlike countenance.

"I'll want that lawyer now," McVicar said plainly.

"Sure," Rizzo replied.   Someone was shouting his name up the stairwell.

"It's not the end of the world. You don't know me. I'll turn it into something."

"You'll make new friends," Rizzo said.

"I'll do some writing. I'll do what I should have done, I'll write that novel."

A wave of loathing swept over Villanova. "Now you've got something to write about!" He could see the bastard sucking his fortune out of Elizabeth Albano's corpse.

"I'm not finished yet. I'll write my book and I'll go right in Hennessy's face with it. I'll have the last say."

Villanova felt the venom flooding up in him. "You don't get it, do you? The man destroyed you, he ran circles around you. He set you up, and you never caught on."

"What do you mean, set me up?"

"Think about it, genius. Hennessy *knew* the carbon copy was in the Robinson file all along. Did you really suppose he was going to give anyone but himself first crack at those cartons? He went through them before he ever turned them over to the Archive. He discovered your little secret and decided to leave it there. He wanted *Elizabeth* to be the one to find you out."

McVicar looked dazed. He shook his head. "No."

"Sure. He wanted you tortured. And he wanted her saved. He was watching both of you from the sidelines the whole time. He had no intention of letting either one of you escape."

McVicar still looked confused, but he no longer shook his head. "Then why would he show up in the Archive on Saturday? Why would he be hunting through those cartons?"

"To stoke up the flames, pal. After that department party, he got a little worried. He saw that you two still had a hold on each other. He needed a way to turn up the heat on both of you. He found it."

Humiliation and anger broke simultaneously on McVicar's face. "He's in trouble too, then," he said after a moment. His eyes burned with chagrin.

"For what? For looking in a box and not seeing something?"

The full weight of his defeat descended on McVicar's exhausted being. He had plenty to think about now, and that was Villanova's only satisfaction. McVicar's stricken eyes looked from face to face, but settled on Villanova's. "It isn't fair," was all he could say.

"Tell that to Liz Albano. Tell that to her family." Villanova was choking with disgust now for these petty men and their petty vanities. He turned toward Rizzo. "Take this sonofabitch in. Let's see if we can get him out of the building in one piece."

"I told the boys to call in for a couple of sector cars. Maybe we better take him over the roof."

McVicar's wretched eyes were still locked on Villanova's. "What about these papers?" he said.

"What about them?" Villanova said.

"*You* know what I mean. They can't see the light of day. They've got to be destroyed."

"It's too late for that, pal," Rizzo put in. "You're under arrest."

Now the ultimate alarm crept over McVicar's features. "Not with *these* in my hands. This is my reputation here. This is all I've got left!" His eyes bored into Villanova's. "Take them from me. You know what to do with them."

Villanova shook his head. A young woman's life had been bartered for these scraps. "A deal's a deal," he said. "You wanted them, you've got 'em."

"I'm begging you."

Villanova turned to Rizzo. "Read this guy his rights." He caught a glimpse of the abject betrayal in McVicar's eyes as he walked out of the room.

Again Rizzo's name was shouted up the stairwell. Villanova stalked out to the landing. "Who wants Rizzo?" he shouted down.

"Gilman wants him on the wire, pronto!" It was one of the uniformed cops.

"What the hell for?

"That guy Manny Cruz turned up. There's trouble."

"Where, for Christ sake?"

"4951 Bainbridge."

Villanova was already in motion. "Go, Buddy, I'm coming!" Rizzo's shout echoed after him. 4951 Bainbridge was the Topless Towers.

- FIFTEEN -

Villanova went plunging down the tenement steps toward the street, turn after turn in the semi-dark. Halfway down, he heard a commotion in the stairwell above, the heavy drum of treads, and then he almost crashed into the uniformed cop coming up from below. "Up!" he pointed, "give Rizzo a hand!" and he kept going. The racket above seemed to be moving upward, not down. When he hit the vestibule, the lone cop there glanced back nervously. Villanova understood why the moment he broke outside. The fifteen or twenty young men crowding the stoop had begun to press forward, all staring grimly, all silent. Freddie and the Super were right up front.

He tried to push through impersonally, like a cop, but lost momentum pretty fast. A guy in a red knit cap, a linebacker-sized guy, blocked his way like a wall.

And then, magically, the whole crowd melted back. Villanova charged to Rizzo's Plymouth, pulled open the door, and was groping under the dash for the extra key when he saw what had happened. The entire mob was peering upward, craning their necks. Something was happening on the roof. Some guy was hanging over the cornice--*more* than one guy; there were arms flailing...and suddenly there was an explosion of beating white wings, and two dozen gulls scattered into the pure blue sky. But it wasn't birds, it was pages. It was the rotted fragments of a dead man's shroud, racing on the wind toward West Farms and Hunts Point and Hell Gate.

Villanova got the car started and wove down the street as the youths on the sidewalk began spilling into the entries of the tenements adjoining the Cruz building.   A patrol car swerved by him as he rounded the corner at Third Avenue. The traffic on the Avenue was backed up behind the light, and another patrol car was beating against the traffic in the wrong lane, lights flashing; he made a quick decision to split off on Bathgate and cut through the campus to Southern Boulevard.

Two minutes later he was through the gate with its "No Vehicles" sign and on the cobblestone drive between the academic buildings, and a half-minute after that he was passing Dealy Hall with the grey fortress of Keating Hall standing opposite it across Edwards Parade, and then he was stopped dead in a sea of jubilant football fans, and drums were pounding, and air horns were blaring, and the Fordham fight song was drifting up from somewhere--"*With a Ram, with a ram, with a ram for victory!*"--and the game was over, and there were a couple of thousand half-drunk kids between him and the Southern Boulevard gate, all swarming in the opposite direction.   And when he tried to bluster his way forward, fists began to thump on the sheet metal, and the big old sedan began to rock, and a pudgy young woman in a maroon skirt and cap climbed up on the hood with a big Fordham pennant and began to dance. By the time he squeezed himself out the door, there were a half dozen people dancing on the car, and the roof was caved in and the crowd was ecstatic, and their roar almost drowned out the refrain of the chorusers: "*...Once more the old Maroon/Waves on high...!*"

He pushed his way on foot. The happy, young faces turned their happy eyes everywhere: at each other, at the heavens, at the immolated automobile, at Villanova.   They searched his face quickly: why was he not happy, why was he outside the fold, how had he lost blessedness and grown old? And he knew he deserved this insult. And he deserved to lose Helen too, he deserved the tragedy that awaited him, because he'd waited too long, and he'd held on too long, and he'd looked backward too long.

And then his progress stalled altogether, and he stood with his arms virtually pinned in a beefy press of beer-breathed youths, and he spotted Dean Hennessy no more than a dozen feet away. The tall man stood trapped in the crush, his white-crowned head topping the young women nearest him, his eyes shrewdly studying the eddies and picking his route...and then his gaze was drawn to Villanova's, and the shrewdness suddenly vanished, and something more composed and quiescent took its place. And Villanova stared hard at him and held the man's eyes; the noise of the throng was like a wall of glass between them, and even through that wall Villanova was determined to penetrate that veil the priest had drawn across his face. The sound of the crowd was shifting now from joy to distress...and now to fright; Villanova felt the breath being forced out of him by that unyielding human press, and he could feel the collective struggle for air and the beginnings of panic around him; a girl's shriek of fear rose up, another echoed it...and still Villanova forced himself through that dusky veil across the priest's eyes. And then for one long moment he saw the sickness and the mortification behind it, the mouldy hue of sin chambered in that delicate and handsome form. And the priest saw that he had seen, and a deep, scarlet flush blossomed on his face. And then the crowd suddenly unlocked itself, and Villanova was released and so were his aching lungs, and the last he saw of Roger F. X. Hennessy was the back of that white-thatched head as the man was carried from view.

A minute later Villanova had pushed through to the edge of the crowd. And as the din subsided, the sound of a siren moving uptown on Webster reached his ears, and he could only hope it was Rizzo and that maybe it wasn't too late. And now there was nothing left to do but run.

He ran. He crossed all the familiar turf from cross-country days, the site of the old outdoor track, the long iron fence, the Conservatory dome of the Botanical Gardens, the dip and the bridge over the Penn Central tracks, the long grey climb up Bedford Park Boulevard. He paced himself up the hill, knowing his legs would go before his wind, and he issued a single abstract prayer monotonously to the empty heavens. And finally he turned, rubber-legged and despairing, down the level stretch of Bainbridge Avenue.

There were two sector cars and an unmarked precinct car double-parked in front of # 4951, and a hell of a lot of activity on the steps and the porch of the Topless Towers. A Crime Lab van was parked in the driveway, and behind it, half in the street, an EMS ambulance.

Breathing hard, trying to ease back his racing heart, he pulled up to the porch. Reinhart, conversing with the uniformed guys on the porch, fell silent as he mounted the steps.

"What's going on?" Villanova panted.

"Cruz. They've got him downstairs."

"Rizzo get here?"

"Five minutes ago."

Villanova hurried down. All the dread that had swelled up inside him burst through his insides in a black flood. Why hadn't he realized the bastard would come back for Helen? Why had he left her alone? Why hadn't he paid attention to the right things? Three coffins Julia had seen in her dream, *three*: one for Elizabeth, one for herself...who was the third one for?

The basement was brilliantly, fantastically illuminated; the Crime Lab boys had set up portable floodlights. He recognized the men's faces: Stefanek and Tommy Layer, the same team who'd handled the trunk on Mosholu Parkway. Rizzo was standing in the back, near the washing machine, talking to a dark-haired woman...but it wasn't Helen. Bev Cohn, maybe? Rizzo's eyes were grim. Everybody's eyes were grim. That was a bad sign. That was just like the eyes of the cops who came to tell him the worst news he ever heard, that day in Belle Haven. A very bad sign. Rizzo gestured to him to come over, but he looked away. He didn't want to talk to Rizzo, or anyone else. He didn't want a single person to say a word. He wanted it all in his own hands, where desperation might still produce a miracle.

Where was she? His heart was banging like a hammer now, and he avoided Rizzo's gaze and turned to scan the rest of the big basement. He wasn't dazed any more; he could see clearly, more clearly than ever. He had no more questions about reality. Those Crime Lab floods drew crisp lines of light and dark, they left no doubt about what was real and what wasn't. What was real was to put your hands on, to touch and to hold, to keep with you and share with and care for. What was real was Helen, and all he wanted to do was see her alive and unhurt.

Where? He started making his way through the sea of junk he'd been throwing around the night before. Two EMS guys, strapping black men in orange vests, were looking over the train table and talking quietly. The layout lights were on, as usual, barely glowing through the glare. The mountain looked stark and synthetic, the town like a cluster of toys. Behind the long table, with her back to the others, a woman was standing in the shadow of a lolly-column. She looked hunched and shaken.

"Helen!" he called.

The woman turned around.

It was her!

"Jesus," he said softly. "Jesus Christ."

Her eyes gladdened at the sight of him. She was holding Mirabel in her arms. "I'm all right," she said.

He went around the table and gathered her up. "Jesus, I thought I was going to find you dead!"

"Not me, sweetheart. No way."

"Babe, I don't ever, *ever* want to go through that again!" He squeezed her hard enough to make the cat squirm and yowl in protest.

"Easy, sweetie."

"What the hell's going on. Who's the ambulance for?"

"Your killer," she said. "Manny Cruz. Over there."

He looked. Stefanek was at the far end taking down a light, and Layer was on his way up the stairs with his camera. The dark-haired woman was busy writing in a notepad. Rizzo had his notepad out too. Again he summoned Villanova over.

"Go on," Helen said. "I'll come too."

They went over, Helen trailing a little behind. "What took so long, Buddy?" Rizzo greeted him.

"I took one hell of a wrong turn."

"Have a peek." His tone was almost offhand. That, plus the open notebook, meant he'd been caught by surprise every which way. The door to the freezer-chest was raised. The reek of stale air spilled out of it. One of the floodlights threw a beam on the inside. Manny Cruz lay curled in the narrow space, his eyes staring coldly up. He was dead.

"What happened?"

"He's been in here since last night, Buddy. Suffocated."

"Since last night? You mean he came back to try again?"

"Uh-uh. He never left. He's been here since Helen passed out on the floor--since you came charging down the stairs. Must've heard you coming and tried to hide. Jumped inside the box here and let the lid come down."

"Christ, he locked himself in?"

"By accident. Shit, I would've jumped in too if I heard a crazed bull on the loose." Rizzo took a quick look around at the shambles of the basement. "What'd you do, throw everything you could get your hands on?"

Villanova couldn't take his eyes off Manny. He was hunched and contorted like a gargoyle, his lips and ears a livid hue, his face congested, his mouth twisted into a grotesque snarl; he looked like a demon from the blackest nightmare. "Who found him? The Lab boys?"

Helen said, "I did."

"You? The Lab boys let you poke around down here while they were working?"

"*Those* guys? They just got here," she said with a lift to her chin.

"You mean you came down here alone?"

"Sure. Why shouldn't I?"

"For God's sake, Helen. Are you crazy?"

"No," she said. "I'm perfectly sane."

He gaped at her.

"All right, it was a dumb thing to do. But look, I found Mirabel." She stroked the cat's head and gave it a rub under the chin. "She was sitting on the freezer, just crying away. Her fur was up, you know, like something was the matter." The dark-haired woman had drawn close behind her, scribbling away in her pad. "So I opened the freezer, and there he was."

"Christ, Helen, what if he wasn't dead!"

"For a minute I thought he wasn't. His eyes were open. I swear to God, he was looking at me! I screamed and slammmed the top shut. I flew up the stairs like a rocket and crashed right into that guy over there with the uniform."

Villanova looked to Rizzo. Rizzo nodded. "Novick said the stiff was still cooling down when he got to him. Dead, though."

"Jesus. Then he was alive last night when your man was out on the porch?"

Rizzo nodded. "Half-alive, is more like it. Probably didn't realize till he was semi-conscious that he couldn't get out. Still, he might have made some noise before that." Behind him, one of the floodlights blinked off; Stefanek was taking them down one by one.

"You mean he was suffocating in this little box all that time, and he never called out?"

"That's how it looks."

"The crazy bastard! The poor, stupid, fucked-up bastard!"

"Right," Rizzo said. "Fucked-up to the end."

"It was the awfullest thing I ever saw in my life!" Helen blurted out. "Those eyes, the hopelessness in them...I'll never forget it. Like someone looking back from the other side of the grave."

The dark-haired woman said to Helen, "That's *good*. I didn't get your name, hon." Her throaty voice was full of easy familiarity.

Rizzo took Villanova aside. "You should've warned me about McVicar. The sonofabitch clocked me the minute I took my eye off him. Made a run for it up to the roof."

"You catch him?"

"I was right behind him, Buddy."

"Good. He's in custody, then?"

"What's left of him. There must've been fifteen punks up there waiting to get a piece of him. The precinct boys took him to the Emergency Room at Jacobi."

"How bad is he?"

"He's a mess. He won't be smiling at any Grand Jury. Funny thing is, all he cared about on that roof was dumping those pages over the edge."

"He murdered somebody for them."

Rizzo was silent for a moment. "I owe you an apology, Buddy. I called it wrong. Dead wrong."

"Forget it. We each got a chunk of it."

"No, I missed it cold."

"You got your piece. I was sending McVicar home when you brought Maria into that bedroom with the crossover."

"Thanks for that." Rizzo glanced over to the freezer; he snapped his notebook shut and shoved it in his hip pocket. "I feel like an asshole. Manny didn't kill anyone after all. He only thought he did."

Villanova nodded. "The girl passed out while he was trying to keep her from screaming, and he took her for dead."

"That's what kept us on the wrong trail. The guy *thought* he was guilty. He never realized someone else had finished the job."

"His *mother* thought he was guilty. That's what really cooked the poor sonofabitch."

"She wasn't that far wrong. He was a killer. He was just a killer who just didn't get the chance. Don't forget, he had his fun with that dead girl once he was alone with her."

"I'm not forgetting. It might've been Helen."

Rizzo nodded gravely. "You know the really weird part of it? Manny and McVicar walked right past each other on the sidewalk while the girl was unconscious on the bed upstairs. Neither one knew about the other."

"And all McVicar ever found out afterward was that someone had cleaned up after him. Put the girl's body out like trash."

"Too bad for him he didn't quit while he was ahead. He should've never come back into the Wedge. That's Rule One if you're gonna be a killer."

"The guy couldn't help himself. He thought his blood was colder than it is. Who knows, maybe in the long run he did himself a mercy."

Rizzo's eyes grew broody. "That girl loved him. He snuffed her out."

"He snuffed out what was growing inside her too."

"He never really wanted that baby, did he, Buddy?"

"No. He only wanted her to be pregnant."

Rizzo shook his head soberly. "There's a man who didn't know what he had."

Villanova nodded. "You want some advice from me? Say that once a day, friend."

"What about this guy Hennessy? How much was he involved?"

"He played his part, behind the scenes. He was obsessed with the girl, like everyone else. He didn't mean for anyone to die."

"Should we take him in?"

"Only if watching people suffer is against the law."

"Don't you want to watch him suffer too?"

"He already is. He's in a dark little place with no way out and nothing for company except a nasty little secret. I don't have to watch."

"What secret, Buddy?"

"He stopped that girl from getting free while she still could. He let her die over some worthless document."

"Not worthless to McVicar."

"Yes it was, only he didn't realize it. That's the nasty part. Hennessy already *had* a copy of that article. He either had the original typescript, or a photocopy he'd made before handing the cartons over. He was playing a game he couldn't lose."

"How do you figure that?"

"If he'd left the only copy in the Archive, he wouldn't have let me or anyone else beat him to those cartons once Elizabeth was dead. He'd've been as eager as McVicar to retrieve it."

Rizzo took a long, careful look at him. "And you want to let him sit and search his soul? You're a nicer guy than I am."

"No," Villanova said. "That's just it. I'm not."

Helen caught his eye. She seemed annoyed with the dark-haired woman's questions. Villanova stepped over. "Who're you?" he interrupted. The woman was young, in her late twenties at the most, and attractive in a hard sort of way, tall and lanky, with a ruddy complexion heavily made over.

"She's from the *News*," Rizzo said.

"The *News*? How'd the *News* get in on this?"

"She's okay, Buddy. We just made friends. Name's Jen Hoffman."

Villanova turned to her. "Who tipped you?"

Her dark eyes held his boldly. "You live here?"

"Yeah, I live here. Who tipped you?"

"One of your neighbors. Saw the commotion, figured one of you macho-men finally killed his wife." She gave him a frank, forward smile.

Villanova frowned at her. "Hey, who the hell invited *you?* Where was your paper three days ago when we found the dead girl on Mosholu Parkway?"

Her eyebrows went up. "What's the problem?" She looked to Rizzo in appeal, using that same forward smile. "We've got a story here, right, guys?"

All the pent emotion in Villanova erupted without warning. "What the hell do you want here now?" he snapped. "There's nothing for your goddam paper in this!"

"Easy, Buddy," Rizzo said. "Give her a break. She's a writer, like you."

"She's a scavenger with a nose for stench!"

The reporter never flinched. "You're wrong," she told Villanova. "I've been around a little, I know an angle when I see one. A prowler who hides himself too good, that's an angle. A creep who puts himself in his own coffin, that's a story. That's what people want to read about. For my paper, it's page three."

"Yeah? But a girl who never hurt anyone and gets dumped on the curb like garbage, that's nothing!"

She shrugged indifferently.

"How about going after what a thing *means*? When do you write about that?"

"That's not my job," she said flatly.

He looked at her, and because she was right, his anger hardened. "Why don't you take your notebook over to the hostage gig on Crotona Avenue," he said with a scowl. "Maybe you'll get a story there." And in that same breath he realized that he wasn't angry at her at all, but at his own stupid earnestness.

The reporter turned to Rizzo. "How many murders have there been in this city in the last three days?"

"City-wide? Figure five a day," he said.

She turned back to Villanova, her face dripping irony. "Every girl that gets iced doesn't make a story. Every sex crime isn't news."

He shook his head. "Get her out of here," he said to Rizzo.

"Now, the way your lady friend with the cat turned the tables on this stiff, *that's* a story."

"Get her the fuck out of here!"

Rizzo sighed, but he did it. He contained her protestations, got a hand on her shoulder finally, and showed her the stairs. She looked back and appealed to the two EMS guys at the train table. They were too absorbed in the layout to pay her much heed. Layer came down to finish packing up, and she even appealed to him. Rizzo told him to see her out to the sidewalk, and he obliged.

Rizzo looked a little puzzled when he rejoined them. "What're you so steamed about, Buddy?" he said. "Be happy, it's all over. Case closed."

"That's good. I'm happy." Another one of the floodlights winked out.

"Come on, we'll pack it in here and hit the Killarney Rose for a few beers before we start the paperwork. Celebrate a little. Treat ourselves to a meal and some brews."

Villanova had been looking forward to raising a mug with Rizzo, but he shook his head. "I've got to stick with Helen awhile...take her upstairs and get us both calmed down. And then I've got a column to write."

Rizzo looked disappointed. "Sure, Buddy. We'll have some fun tonight, then, the three of us. What the hell, Daphne'll come too, and we'll all chew the case over. I'll get us a table at Joe D's. We'll pig out on pasta and then head over to the Flim-Flam."

"Pasta'll be fine," Villanova said. "No Flim-Flam."

"What the hell's the matter, Buddy? Why so glum?"

Villanova blew out his breath and reached for his cigarettes, then changed his mind and put his hand on Helen's shoulders, turning her to him. "I'm sorry, babe, I've got to tell you this. Julia didn't make it."

Helen let out a little gasp. Her blue eyes filled with tears.

"She died in the operating room. About two hours ago."

"Christ, I'm sorry, Buddy, I forgot," Rizzo murmured.

The tears rolled freely down Helen's cheeks and the sorrow throbbed out of her eyes in that open, healing way that Villanova could only admire and envy. He put an arm around her. Another floodlight winked out. The only one left was the one glowing into the freezer-chest. Layer came down the steps with a body bag.

"Jesus, Buddy, think about it. That's around the same time Manny died," Rizzo said. "The two of them at once."

Villanova nodded. "Julia knew it. She told us." He enfolded Helen and felt the warm wetness of her tears through his shirt, along with the cat's soft heat.

Rizzo caught his eye and slowly shook his head. "Shit, no more for me. Enough."

"Not yet. We've still got to get the word to that guy Tom Reilly. Someone's got to tell him why he isn't going to get any more letters."

"The boys upstate'll handle that, Buddy. They'll do it better than we can."

"The poor bastard. I hope there's a lot of wood to cut in Tannersville."

"There's nothing but wood there, Buddy."

Layer and Stefanek headed over. Stefanek said, "We're going to take Cruz outta here now."

Rizzo, shaking his head to himself, waved them a go-ahead.

"Wait'll I take Helen upstairs," Villanova said.

"No," she said, drawing herself out of his arms, swiping her cheeks with the back of her hand. "No, I want to see."

"You'll have bad dreams, babe." He brushed at a vagrant tear.

"No," she insisted, and she was very sure of herself, red-rimmed eyes and all. "I'll watch. I want to see everything. There won't be any more bad dreams, they're finished now." She stepped closer to the freezer-chest and looked inside. He drew behind her and peered over her shoulder. Already the corpse had begun its changes. A leaden hue had settled in, the snarl on those purplish lips had transmuted into a death-grimace. The gargoyle fiendishness had flattened into the throes of the harmless just-dead, like a wild dog run down on the highway, an obscenity to the eye, a thing to look at once and turn away from with pity. Villanova took his look, a long one, and turned away, and Helen stepped away too, with Mirabel wrapped close to her chest. The cat kept its green eyes on Villanova, serenely, as if to soothe him; in the half-light, their rich hue was hauntingly lovely.

Rizzo called to the EMS crew, "Time to clear out, guys."

They nodded, gave the layout a final scrutiny, and headed for the stairs. One man seemed more reluctant to leave than the other. He stopped at the foot of the steps for a last glance back, as if he understood how much better the little village would look from a distance. He was a burly man in his forties, but his eyes were full of dreamy, boyish admiration. "Hell of a thing," he said to Villanova. "Like a real place. A place you could live in, you know? Must've taken years to build that."

"It did," Villanova said. "A lot of years." He flipped open his lighter and lit up the last Chesterfield in the pack.

"So goddam real," the man said. "You want the lights left on like that?"

Villanova looked across the big room. The village did look real again, with the dimness restored in the basement and the little lamps glowing. It looked civilized and whole and safe and perfect for every human aspiration. He heard the

EMS man go up the stairs. He heard the body bag unrolled and unzipped. He heard the Lab boys grunt as the thing that had been Manny Cruz was lifted from its temporary tomb.

He went over to the layout. His hands groped for and found the extension cord leading from the Topless Towers' promiscuous circuits. He pulled the plug.

The quaint and intricate past faded into a forgiving darkness.